Bestselling au
as a journalist, working in the UK, Europe
and Israel. In 1970 he emigrated to Australia
with his Czech-born wife, Eva, and now lives
in Sydney, where he divides his time between
writing his well-researched, action-packed
thrillers and running his award-winning
marketing consultancy.

www.alangold.net

JEZEBEL

ALAN GOLD

HarperCollinsPublishers

HarperCollins*Publishers*

First published in Australia in 2001
This edition published in 2002
by HarperCollins*Publishers* Pty Limited
ABN 36 009 913 517
A member of the HarperCollins*Publishers* (Australia) Pty Limited Group
www.harpercollins.com.au

HarperCollins*Publishers*
25 Ryde Road, Pymble, Sydney, NSW 2073, Australia
31 View Road, Glenfield, Auckland 10, New Zealand
77–85 Fulham Palace Road, London, W6 8JB, United Kingdom
Hazelton Lanes, 55 Avenue Road, Suite 2900, Toronto, Ontario M5R 3L2
and 1995 Markham Road, Scarborough, Ontario M1B 5M8, Canada
10 East 53rd Street, New York NY 10022, USA

National Library of Australia Cataloguing-in-Publication data:

Gold, Alan, 1945–.
Jezebel.
ISBN 0 7322 6695 5.
1. Jezebel, Queen, consort of Ahab, King of Israel –
Fiction. I. Title.
A823.3

Cover design by Darian Causby, HarperCollins Design Studio
Typeset by HarperCollins in 10.5/12.5 Sabon
Printed and bound in Australia by Griffin Press on 50gsm Ensobulky

5 4 3 2 1   02 03 04 05

ACKNOWLEDGMENTS

My sincerest thanks in helping me go to my wife Eva, and my children Georgina, Jonathan and Raffe. Also to Professor David Brooks of the University of Sydney for assistance with plot and structure. Michael Benstock, who enjoys an encyclopaedic knowledge of Ancient Israel, read the manuscript from a Biblical and historical perspective, but the many differences between the Bible's account and this novel lie entirely at the door of the author. My gratitude also the Ephraim ben Matituahu, Consul General for Israel.

In HarperCollins, I am enormously grateful to the best editorial, sales, marketing and management team in the business ... especially Brian Murray, Barrie Hitchon, Shona Martyn, Linda Funnell, Christine Farmer, Jim Demetriou, Darian Causby, Karen-Maree Griffiths, Graeme Jones, and publicity. Thank you, too, to Deonie Fiford and Barbara Pepworth.

But it is to Belinda Lee, my friend, mentor, editor and counsellor to whom greatest thanks must go. Her vision enabled this book to gain far wider horizons than we first observed together.

29 In the thirty-eighth year of King Asa of Judah, Ahab son of Omri began to reign over Israel; Ahab son of Omri reigned over Israel in Samaria twenty-two years.

30 Ahab son of Omri did evil in the sight of the LORD more than all who were before him.

31 And as if it had been a light thing for him to walk in the sins of Jeroboam son of Nebat, he took as his wife Jezebel daughter of King Ethbaal of the Sidonians, and went and served Baal, and worshipped him.

32 He erected an altar for Baal in the house of Baal, which he built in Samaria.

33 Ahab also made a secret pole. Ahab did more to provoke the anger of the LORD, the God of Israel, than had all the kings of Israel who were before him.

1 Kings 16:29–33

PREFACE

The voices of women throughout history – except for a very few – have been muted, silenced, or censured throughout the ages. Those of whom we read in the Old and New Testaments are usually wives, mothers or daughters, and almost never play any sort of leading or pivotal role in the affairs of men.

It is only relatively recently that history and literary criticism have started to read beyond texts and events, and to acknowledge the extent of the true roles of women as equals with men through the ages of society, culture and religion.

The Phoenician Princess, Jezebel, later Queen of Israel, was one such muted voice. Our knowledge of her comes solely from the Book of Kings in the Old Testament, and is almost exclusively from the perspective of the prophet Elijah. She is excoriated in the Bible for introducing idolatry into ancient Israel, for being a harlot and for weakening the strength of the nation. Yet modern archaeology shows that there was a great deal of idol-worship in ancient Israel, and it is evident that poor Jezebel has, for the past three thousand years, taken the blame for the nation's tendency towards polytheism.

In this novel, I have viewed the historical events from an entirely different perspective from that which has come down to us from the Old Testament. Because this is a work of fiction, I know that many who read the Bible as the word of God will find this novel discomforting. I make no apology for this. It does not attempt to be a work of theology, nor to follow any particular theological perspective.

However, after three thousand years of being the 'painted whore', the 'loose and immoral temptress', after three millennia in which wayward women have been dubbed 'Jezebels' as the ultimate insult, it's time to have an alternative reading of this woman's life.

AND SO IT BEGINS

Tonight, she will become a goddess, and all will be well.

The Sovereign Lord of Phoenicia, His Majesty King Abimel, will unite with her, watched by all the priests and priestesses of Ba'al and El and Asherah, and she will know the joy of consecration. He will be exhilarated as she is brought to him, and he will enter her body. At that moment of grace, she will be as one in the glory of a goddess, for she will join the other sacred women who have been so honoured in the service of the gods. And in her glory, she will be raised level with Asherah, the goddess whose smile illuminates the whole of the world.

His Majesty's coupling will change the girl into a woman and make the gods smile. When he reaches his point of ecstasy, he will spill his seed into the sacred cloth placed on the floor of the temple and the priests and priestesses will begin their chanting until the entire hall is filled with the music of their voices.

Wet with his seed and the future of the kingdom, the cloth will be lifted for all the priests and priestesses to see and to attest to its power. There will be a fanfare of trumpets, drums and harps, and the waiting crowd outside will be inspired by the excitement from within the temple. A murmur will spread among the throng. Things have gone well! Relief will sweep over the people, suddenly inspired by the security in their future. Some men and women will go to their homes and recreate the sacred act that the King has just performed with the woman-girl; others will remain and silently pray to the god or goddess who protects their household; others still will go to the river and wash themselves to be clean and pure for the season to come. But most will remain in the forecourt of the temple to witness the coming miracle, for the chief priestess will then emerge from the inner sanctum and stand on the steps, observed by the waiting multitude whose voices will fall into silence until she holds the wet cloth high above her head and begins to chant her prayers to the gods and goddesses to send rain. Then the population of the city of Sidon will see that their King has done his duty, and will roar its relief and gratitude. There will be more music, more cheering, and the cloth will be carried to a field beyond the temple where it will be buried.

Silently, invisibly, the gods who have smiled will take the freshness and wetness of the King's seed and spread it throughout the land, which will then become fertile, like an animal on heat for its mate. And soon afterwards, dark clouds will swell in the sky over Phoenicia and will enlarge and become engorged with water. And then they'll burst and the rains will fall and the crops will grow and the animals will again become fat and everyone will have enough to eat.

And the girl, who has become a woman, will be happy. The people of the land will be happy. And the King will continue his reign with the love and gratitude of his subjects.

The girl's mother, Ramaseda, informed her last night of what her friends in the village had already whispered to her of their experiences when they lost their virginity – that there will be a moment of pain when the King enters her body, but the pain will soon pass, and from then on her young life will be a distant memory. Unlike her friends, this will be a new pain for her, because ever since the visit of the priestess four years earlier, Ramaseda had saved her daughter's virginity to be sacrificed, not to any man, but to the King himself. And when, if the gods smile, she conceives, the child will enjoy privileges which no child in her village could imagine. Her child will never be hungry or thirsty nor know what it is to be cold at night. It will live in a palace with servants to wait upon it, and it will feed on meat every day.

And not only will the girl's issue enjoy these manifold benefits, as will the girl herself being one of the King's concubines, but her family also. Her father Nechuum had spent the past three days telling his daughter what a great honour she was doing for her parents and her brothers and sisters, for the additional land the King will give to them will ensure their prosperity from now and forever.

And all will be well in Phoenicia.

In the torpid heat of the morning, the girl, who tonight will become a woman, slowly walked out of the city of

3

Sidon and up the hill to the sacred grove, the asherah, to commune with her favourite goddess and protector. It always amused her that the grove carried the same name as the goddess herself. Yet the temple of Ba'al wasn't called Ba'al, nor was the Temple of El called El and the temple where her father prayed to Hadad certainly wasn't called Hadad!

She also pondered over the things which would be happening to her once the sun descended into the Eternal Sea and the King entered her. In the moment of his ecstasy, she would become as one with the gods. Would she enjoy the experience, or would she be too frightened? She was looking forward to doing with a man all the things which her friends did, but still was daunted.

As she walked up the hill she could see the grove in the clearing of the trees. Ever since her birth, she had prayed to the Goddess Asherah for whom her mother had a special fondness. She had turned her back on her birth name, Naomi, and for some time had taken the sacerdotal name Isha-Ashtoreth. Yes, she thought, tonight I will be a woman and a priestess and as one with Asherah. Tonight, all will be well.

As she walked towards the sacred grove to spend the last half day of her life alone before she joined the priesthood, in communion with Ba'al and Asherah and El and the other gods who protected Phoenicia, she suddenly realised that she was not alone on the path. As she ascended the hill to the sacred place above the city, Isha-Ashtoreth saw that there was a woman lying prostrate on the ground within the sacred grove. She lay in front of the hallowed pole inside the asherah. Yet even though this woman was lying down, there was something serene, utterly captivating about her. Was it the dark, golden hair which seemed to flow like the waves of an evening sea over her body? Was it the way in which she seemed tall, even though she was lying down, commanding the sacred grove and the attention of the gods? No, it was none of these things, yet all of them.

It was a hot day, a blistering day. There was a heat haze over the surface of the distant Eternal Sea. Isha-Ashtoreth blinked to clear her eyes in case her vision was mistaken, but no … the woman stood up slowly, reverentially, from the floor of the grove and straightened her clothing. She turned, leaving the asherah, and began to walk slowly down the hill towards the Damascus Gate of the city walls of Sidon. Walk? No, this lady didn't walk, she appeared to glide.

As Isha-Ashtoreth looked, the woman with the long golden hair seemed to float towards her, her gown hiding the movement of her legs; she was more gazelle than woman, a fawn in the forest, yet there was a regal strength, a beauty which held Isha-Ashtoreth captive.

And then the woman stopped, for she had suddenly noticed Isha-Ashtoreth walking up the hill towards her. At first, she frowned, wondering who was daring to disturb her privacy. But when she looked at Isha-Ashtoreth's eyes, which were wide as much with trepidation as with admiration, the woman smiled.

Isha-Ashtoreth felt uncomfortable, captured by the stare of this golden-haired woman who looked at her – yet somehow through her – and seemed to understand exactly what she was thinking.

It was a welcoming smile, a smile of recognition, for as she walked nearer, she recognised her. They had seen each other before in the palace when she'd first been introduced to the King, His Majesty Abimel. The woman had stood beside a pillar observing the audience, being there, yet somehow being removed from what was going on, as though the activities of mortals were beneath her. Isha-Ashtoreth had watched the woman as she walked away from the royal presence of His Majesty King Abimel, and the woman had nodded, as though she herself had once been in the same position.

Isha-Ashtoreth had seen a sadness in this beautiful woman's eyes, and wondered why she was staring at her so keenly. She had looked deeply into her eyes, and wondered what thoughts were there, what those eyes had seen in their life. Was this woman of the royal blood? If not, then who could she possibly be? Then it occurred to her that she must be from another country, the wife of an ambassador from a distant land; or maybe she was one of the sisters of the King's wives … it was impossible to know.

And now they met again on the road to the asherah outside of the city. They stopped, just a few paces from each other. The woman seemed to welcome her into her presence. Isha-Ashtoreth uncertainly smiled, suddenly afraid because now she could clearly see the face and body of this regal woman. And as she looked, she saw in her face great pain, the agony of a difficult life. Close up, the woman's face was lined with worry; and now she could clearly see that her hair was more red than gold, that it was the rays of the sun which masked the true red dye rich women used to hide their grey. But there was something disconcerting about the way this woman stood, a confidence, a self-possession which her mother and the other old

6

women of Sidon or Tyre didn't possess. This was a woman of importance, of birth and standing – not a woman to stand beside a pillar in the King's audience hall, out of the sight of the ambassadors and royalty and important people of the city.

'So,' the woman said in a voice which had once commanded people to do her bidding, 'tonight, you're going to give yourself to the King, my brother. You've come here to prepare yourself. Through you, the rains will come, and we will all have plenty.'

There was no malice in the way she said it. Isha-Ashtoreth knew tones in an adult's voice such as vindictiveness and cruelty, but what this woman said was open, lacking in guile and deceit.

She nodded, and said, 'Yes, I am chosen to be the King's vessel.'

The woman smiled. 'So was I. Many years ago. Not this king, of course, but the king of a far distant land. I too was a king's vessel. My husband was a great king, my country a …' She stopped what she was about to say and her eyes travelled over the Eternal Sea to somewhere far away. Then she looked back at the child. 'Have you ever heard of the land of Israel?'

Isha-Ashtoreth nodded. Of course she'd heard of the southern land. She knew of the people and of their one god called Yahweh, but she was suddenly afraid of this woman, for now she suspected who this woman might be, and the word in Phoenicia was that she was not alive, that she was dead and buried.

'Israel is a far-off land. A dry and joyless land. But what is my life to you? I talk of another time, another king and another country. Unlike you, I was more than a vessel to please the gods. I was a queen. And more than that. Much more.'

7

Isha-Ashtoreth frowned. She was now too frightened to say anything else.

'Do you know who I am?' asked the older woman.

The child shook her head, pretending she'd never heard of this woman, wanting to be away, to pray to Asherah, to make her peace with the world, and then to enter the temple and begin the life which had been chosen for her. She didn't want to be with this woman, whose name she knew but didn't want to pronounce. Yet she was held captive, overwhelmed by the woman's beauty, her regal bearing, her painful honesty. She couldn't move.

'My name is Jezebel.'

The name had been said! It was a name which mustn't be pronounced. But the look in the girl's eyes was one of recognition.

'Yes,' said Jezebel triumphantly, but also sympathetic to the girl's fear. 'I am very much alive.' Jezebel was delighted that she was still known, even in a young woman's alarm. For years in Phoenicia, her name had become a curse, and she was afraid that she was all but forgotten. But not in Israel, where she was still a blight, a plague, anathematised by those loyal to Yahweh who forgot the joys she had brought to the people in their worship of Ba'al and Asherah.

Yet how many truly knew her? How many knew her story? Her name, once glorious and sung on the lips of the multitudes who loved her, would, she knew, soon be forgotten, as dry as the sands of the desert.

'Many years ago, I was young and innocent and beautiful like you. Remember this, child. Be very careful in whom you place your trust. Always ask yourself, "*Who is plotting behind my back to destroy me?*"'

8

Isha-Ashtoreth nodded, not understanding why Jezebel was saying these things to her.

A sudden anger overtook Jezebel. Being faced with this young innocent, she was forced to accept how far she herself had fallen. Jezebel looked up to the sky and screamed, 'Why have you done this to me?'

Isha-Ashtoreth shrank back terrified. She wanted to run, but something rooted her to the spot. Jezebel breathed deeply, attempting to control her fury. She looked again at the girl.

'The gods have played terrible games with me. Yet all I wanted to do, all I ever wanted, was to serve them, to love them and be loved by them. But they've conspired against me, and turned me into this,' she said, pointing to her body. 'I should still be Queen. I should be sitting on a throne and have nations bowing down to me. Once, there was a time when my dancing brought the entire world to a halt; when my beauty was so great that poets wrote songs just about me; when I would stand outside the walls of a great city and the whole population would crowd around just to see me; when men of wealth and power came to me to listen to my every word. I was the centre of the world. Yet today I am alone, friendless ...'

Jezebel was sad that she was frightening the girl, and so she said softly, 'Always look behind you, child, as you walk the corridors and pathways of the royal house. And know your enemies; for though I held this power, even I was brought low by a shrivelled up madman and his woman-hating god.'

Isha-Ashtoreth wanted to run; but strangely, she was attracted to this woman. She wanted to hear more, to learn everything about this fabulous being, but she was terrified that someone might come up the path and see her talking to Jezebel; for the law said that Jezebel had died long ago, and she knew she would be punished just for being here. She would be forbidden to be His Majesty's concubine, her parents would lose their land, and at eighteen she was already too old to find a suitable husband – she would have to marry an old widower instead of becoming a priestess.

She wanted to get away, to continue up the hill to the asherah. In a dry and frightened voice, Isha-Ashtoreth said, 'Lady, forgive me, but I have to …'

'To pray,' said Jezebel. 'Yes, child, soon you must go and pray to Asherah. Soon, you will lie before the sacred pole and offer yourself to her. And when you see the plaque of the goddess riding on the back of a lion with her son and lover Ba'al slithering up her legs into her body, think of the pleasures you'll be enjoying with my brother the King.'

Isha-Ashtoreth couldn't move. Something about this woman, this woman who was once a glorious queen, held her transfixed.

'Soon you will pray. But why rush headlong towards your destiny? Command the moment, child. Take charge. I tried, but ultimately … but that's a long story.'

Isha-Ashtoreth bowed, and began to walk away. But Jezebel caught her by the arm. 'Tell me, what do they say of me? Do they still speak of me in the towns and villages of Phoenicia?'

The girl nodded. 'Yes, Lady, they speak of you.'

'And do they say how beautiful I was, how powerful I was?'

Isha-Ashtoreth shook her head. 'No, they only say

how you allowed your kingdom to be taken from you – and that you are dead!'

'No, I am very much alive!' sighed Jezebel. 'Ah, there's so much they don't understand. Come, sit with me for the moment. Sit down and be my companion. There's plenty of time before you give yourself to my brother. Sit with me and listen to my story, for there's much that will benefit you. There's no need to rush to lose your innocence. When I was about your age, I was too eager to lose mine. I'll tell you the story of a woman who held the whole world in the palms of her hands, and who lost it to an evil old man, and an unseeable god.'

CHAPTER ONE

THE CITY OF SIDON, PHOENICIA

The potter immediately realised that he and his work were being viewed, and that every movement he took, every nuance of his body was being scrutinised by the clear eyes of a young woman, little more than a child, standing in the shadow of his doorway.

It was a crowded doorway to be sure, and as she had done on a number of occasions in the past, the young woman had somehow found a way to insinuate her lithe and nubile body in between the columns of pots and jars and storage vessels so that she thought she was obscured from his sight.

The potter knew who she was. He had seen her in the temple dedicated to the worship of Ba'al and when he had visited the royal palace. She was a pretty child who, in the past year, had begun to change into a beautiful and beguiling young woman. One day soon she would become a priestess, or maybe even the wife of a king.

He'd never spoken to her. Potters didn't speak to people such as her in the royal palace, but he wondered why she was so interested in his work. Was it the mystery of the kiln or the wheel?

He knew that there was no mystery in what he did, though he understood why others were so interested. His work wasn't like that of the diviners and soothsayers and priests and doctors when they performed their arts. He had been a potter since his father taught him the craft when he was nine. He'd learned to fashion the dull clay of the earth into majestic pots, colourful vessels and sturdy dishes; yet he also knew that it wasn't him, but the gods and the heat of a fire which transformed the dreary and lifeless vessels into something strong and solid from which people could eat and drink or into an object which became an idol for prayer.

Unlike he who worked with his hands, the diviners and men and women who spoke with the gods performed in intriguing ways: mumbling strange and hidden words into their perfumed salves, healing ointments and macerations; making miracles; and communing with the deities.

These diviners and soothsayers were people whose work deserved to be studied, whose activities could teach a young person things. So why was she wasting her time observing a mere potter whose only expertise came not from the gods themselves, but from a lifetime of copying the skills of his father? Try as he might, the potter couldn't define the moment when the dull wetness and weakness of the clay shapes were transformed by the gods into the shining and brittle things which the people valued so highly.

The potter glanced up cautiously so as not to disturb the young girl. She was the fawn, he the hunter. She was standing there, her face hidden by

13

her hood. That was all he could see; that, and one of her feet which a large vessel, one that would be used for storing olive oil, had failed to obscure.

But he knew who she was. When she first began to visit him in secret he'd been told of her presence by his wife, who herself had watched in fascination while the young Princess Jezebel crept surreptitiously into his workshop and hid behind the columns of pots. The young Princess was still a child whose body had only recently begun to bleed with the moon, yet she would stand for ages in the half-light of the doorway watching him as he stroked and massaged and fashioned the wet clay into pots. His wife, not trusting her own observation, had once followed this mysterious girl back up the hill to the massive walls of the city and had seen the guards stand stiffly to attention as she walked past them. The wife returned and told her husband, who was certain that the visitor was a princess of the royal blood, for he'd seen the child when he had delivered pots to the palace.

But why would a princess be so interested in the work of a humble potter? Should he ask her? That might drive her away, and there was much that a princess could do for a poor artisan.

He and his wife had determined on a particular approach days earlier, shortly after her previous visit. The potter, Ishbaal, coughed, and stood. He pretended to reach for a tool on a shelf, a knife wire made of the keenest strung bronze with which he cut the wet clay, but clumsily he dropped it.

Looking down at the ground, and mumbling complaints to himself, he suddenly brightened, faced the tall olive oil jar and asked quietly, 'Could you pick it up for me, please, Lady?'

14

He sensed the figure in the shadows suddenly stiffening. She seemed to slink further into the half-light of his workroom.

'For me to pick it up would mean I have to come around the wheel, and that is bad luck for a potter. A potter should be behind his wheel, not in front of it. You would be helping me appease your goddess, Asherah, if you did me this kindness.'

Slowly the fawn emerged from the shadows. She was tall for a girl of thirteen, almost as tall as he was. He couldn't make out her face as it was still covered in the cloak she wore over her tunic. The girl bent down and handed the wire cutter to Ishbaal. The potter thanked her and continued silently with his work, kneading the clay and pressing it with his palms to expel all the air in the mix, then folding it and repeating the process time and time again.

He said nothing. She had revealed herself after all this time. That was progress. To ask her questions would have made her run back to the palace. And anyway, he was curious as to what she would do next.

Cautiously, the fawn moved from the doorway, and stood closer than ever before. Now she could see much clearer in the dull light of the hut. She didn't retreat back to her hiding place. That was good.

'Why do you keep pressing it like that?' she asked. Her voice was that of a child, but it had the lilt of a singer or a storyteller, strong and confident. It was a clearer voice than that of his own daughter, Taliba, now sixteen years of age and living with her husband, Ehud the swordmaker.

'I press the clay in order to squeeze the air out. If there's air inside the clay, then when I fire it in the furnace, it will cause cracks to appear and the vessel won't hold water without leaking. If there's a lot of air, it will explode when it becomes very hot, and the shards could break the other pots in the fire.'

He continued to work while the fawn looked on in interest. She was following every movement of his body. When he kneaded the clay with the heels of his hands and flattened it, she smiled. Then he gathered the corners, folded it over onto itself, and used his feet to press the pedals whose strings turned the table. He wet the clay, and shaped it into a tower. She smiled as it took on the familiar shape of a man's penis. She'd seen many penises, but only occasionally had she seen a member stand firm like this penis in the hands of the potter. She laughed, unselfconsciously.

'Where does clay come from?' she asked.

'From the ground.'

'From the ground here? In Phoenicia?'

'Yes. And from other places. Some comes from the banks of the rivers which flow through Assyria, some from the upper reaches of the River Nile in Egypt, and the very best, the richest, comes from further north, up the coast, where whole hillsides are made of the densest and most wonderful clay. That is very expensive and I use that to make pots for the great King Ethbaal so that he, his sons, daughters and wives can have wonderful vessels in which to store their grains, flours, oils, wine, dates and water. And so I'm told, the King and his family use my pots on their table, even when they're entertaining an ambassador from lands far away.'

Ishbaal thought that she'd next ask about how the pottery on her father's table came to be coloured differently from the dun coloured pots in his workplace. Then he would have told her about the dyes, pigments and paints which he purchased from merchants who came all the way from Africa and India. But, strangely, she didn't ask, instead she looked closely at his hands fashioning the clay tower into a higher and higher shape, before flattening the top with his palm, and then indenting the centre so that it began to take on the form of a large cup, or a vessel for fruit or meats.

For the first time the potter glanced up at the young woman to see her reaction. But there was none. Instead, she was concentrating on the way in which his hands were kneading and massaging the clay.

'What words do you use to ask the gods to change the earth from the ground into these pots and plates and jars?'

The potter looked at her, wondering why she was asking these questions. She had been watching him for a long time now. Surely she knew the answers. Surely this was a test. But he would play along with her game, because she was a princess of the royal blood, he had no alternative. Indeed, a single word from her lips could affect his trade – an accusation of … of … *anything* could force him and his family into exile or even cause him to be put to death. Or a word of praise could reap fortunes from the palace. So he determined to answer her politely.

'Before any words come from my lips to the gods, much has to be done. First I prepare the clay by pouring water all over the crude earth which I receive from the merchants. Then I mix it carefully and stir it. The sand and stones which are heavy drop to the bottom of the vessel, and I pour the clay liquid off

17

down a channel and into another vessel so that it doesn't settle with the sand and stones. I keep doing this until all that's left is rubbish which I throw away. Then I allow the clay to settle, and I pour off the water and I place it in the sun to remove even more water. I cut it into bits as big as my hand and do to it what I'm doing now, pressing it smooth and firm, and removing all the air.'

'But how do you make the pots and jars?'

Ishbaal smiled. 'You've seen me do it. I've watched you looking at my work. I throw the clay onto this turning wheel, add some water to soften it, and while the wheel's turning, I mould it with my hands. When it's in the right shape, I put it into the sun to dry, then I coat it with a thin solution of clay water to close any holes, and I let that dry. Then, to make it hold liquids and to seal it, I put onto it a mixture of egg, mica, sea sand and salt and I fire up my oven until it's as hot as it can be, at which time I put in the pot or plate or jar until it's hard and ready for use.'

She stood listening, enthralled as Ishbaal continued to work. Eventually she asked, 'But when do you pray to one of the gods to make sure that the pot comes out properly? And which god do you pray to in order to ensure the pots come out perfectly? Is it Ba'al and El and Asherah you pray to while you're working?'

He looked at the girl in surprise. 'To them all, of course. Every move I make is guided by the gods. When I make a mistake and have to throw away a pot, it's because of some sin I've committed, or some fault in me. It makes me a better person.'

She smiled. And then, suddenly, Princess Jezebel turned and left without a word. Ishbaal looked at her disappearing from his sight and prayed that she would return. His luck might change and riches come his way if he had the Princess as a friend.

Jezebel lay on her divan as her Ethiopian slave fanned her with the feathers of a Syrian ostrich bird. The day was achingly hot and twice she'd been to the sea in order to be refreshed by its cooling waters. But by the time she climbed out of the warm broth the sea became in summer and had walked up the sand to where it met grass and the slaves had poured river water over her naked body to wash off the salt, perspiration was already beginning to form again on her forehead.

She hated the smells which came from her body when she sweated beneath her arms. A physician from Egypt who had visited her father's court the previous year, one who had healed the pharaoh when a wound he suffered had turned evil and become full with black spirits, advised everyone to grind the pods of the carob tree into a paste and smear it in their armpits. Jezebel had been doing this all season, and was now instructing her servants to mix in fresh moringa oil and three drops of frankincense along with four drops of the essence of cypress bark; the perfumed aroma didn't make the carob work any better, but it made her smell nicer.

The heat of the day was becoming unbearable, and because she'd been scratching her head for most of the morning, she was sure that there were lice in her hair, despite washing it carefully the previous week with lemon and lime juice, and ensuring that her apartments were freshly dusted with fleabane and sprinkled with natron water.

She lay back on her bed, too exhausted to move, too exhausted, even, to pick up the vial of oil from the exotic Asian sandalwood tree and smell it. Normally it would refresh her, but she was just too tired. The heat was draining her very essence.

Tonight, she would have to attend one of her father's receptions. But this afternoon she had told people she wanted to sleep and rest and protect herself from the hot sun.

As she lay on her bed, she mused over the activities of her recent past. One part of her life was over. She would no longer go and play games hiding from the potter. He was no fun any more. Anyway, he wasn't attractive. He'd looked interesting sitting there in the half-light, shaping clay into the shapes of penises, but the moment he'd spoken to her, she had quickly lost interest in him and, instead, had become absorbed by what he did with his hands. He shouldn't have spoken to her, now the allure of secretly watching had gone.

No, she was smiling to herself because of her other exploits. At first, they'd been painfully exquisite. When she'd first stolen away from her apartments and dressed up like a peasant to go down from the palace into the huts where the artisans made their things, the thrill had suffused her whole body. Sneaking away from the palace, past the Nubian guards who were busy looking through the wagons of the traders who visited the palace every morning, had been a joy beyond expression. But when she'd done it a number of times, and the Nubians recognised her as a regular comer and goer, the fun began to disappear, and so she tried wider fields of exploration.

She'd tried to steal out of the palace using different techniques, but soon even the most inventive became boring. So she contented herself with the thrill of knowing that she was wandering the town without her father's knowledge or permission, and mixing with ordinary people – with merchants who visited exotic lands, and with peasants whose bodies were hard, and with dirty children who scavenged around looking for food. Yes, it was thrilling being with the people of Phoenicia and outside the ordered world of the palace.

First she went to the street of the butchers, but was repelled by the vivid blue-red colours of the carcasses, the stench of rotting meats on the ground, and the stink of innards suppurating in the heat. The constant buzzing of blowflies and yelping of feral dogs frightened her. And the people also upset her. Their hands and clothes were covered with dried blood and the guts of animals. They were so different to the priests whose white tunics, when stained by the blood of sacrifices, were taken off and never seen again. No, these people who cut up meat were horrible, and she wanted nothing to do with them.

Her next adventure took her to the huts where the jewellers, coppersmiths and gold and silver workers made their amulets and charms and necklaces. This was a much better place, although there was a definite smell in the air from the liquids and powders they used when putting flame to the metal; a smell which assaulted her nose, and occasionally made her sneeze. Sneezes were signs that the gods were upset, so whenever she felt like sneezing, she would walk away quickly, and the gods would be appeased. But when she didn't sneeze, Jezebel watched in wonder as they put tubes in their mouths or used bellows to blow air into their furnaces making their fires glow white-hot and the once-strong metals would glow in the bottom of the combustion pots until they changed into gleaming liquids which hurt her eyes when she looked at them.

What intrigued her most was when they poured the brilliant molten metals, as shining as the noonday sun, into a mould, and suddenly it changed colour from brilliant gold or silver into the angry red of blood pouring from a wound. Then, when the melt had solidified, the jeweller would turn the mould over and he would beat the metal until its shape became that of a bracelet or an amulet or a necklace or a bangle. And while it was still hot and had the texture of unbaked bread, he would press into the metal precious stones like blood-red garnets from the mines of Moab, or green emerald from Upper Egypt.

But the days grew long and increasingly boring as she watched the same men make the same jewels, and soon Jezebel was seeking new and more exciting adventures. Which was when she discovered the art of pottery making and especially the name Ishbaal about whom everybody spoke as though he was guided by the very hand of Ba'al himself.

She found the huts of the pottery makers easily. They were stationed at the foot of the mount where her father's ancestors had built the palace of the city of Sidon. These days, there were many different buildings at the base of Sidon, the tents and huts of potters and armourers and jewellers and incense makers, and the owners of caravans with their snorting and growling camels and heehawing donkeys, and spice sellers and flour makers and charcoal burners.

There were so many that they had arranged themselves into enclaves so people from Sidon and Tyre and other cities could find them more easily.

And Jezebel would look out of her window high in the palace and listen to the noises that the tradesmen made and smell the aroma of bread baking and incense burning and fats being melted down for candles.

But the place which she had only ever visited once in her expeditions, and had never visited again, was the Valley of the Lepers, which was beyond the hills and on the other side of the range of mountains which hid the city of Sidon from the rest of the world. She had been told of the Valley of the Lepers from people who had seen it from a distance. She was told that it was a place of death and horror, closely guarded by suspicious and speechless men who were stationed there morning, noon and night. There were signs on the roadside leading to it proclaiming that anybody who stepped inside the valley and touched a leper would never be allowed back into the town. Food was left for them every night, which had disappeared by morning.

It was a place which had fascinated the young girl and so one day, telling her servants that she was going alone to pray to Asherah, she had ridden her horse to the valley. The guards recognised her, but even so, warned her not to go beyond the edge of the valley. '*Even a princess may not return from here,*' they warned.

And so she had stepped off her horse and looked down. There in the valley were huts and simple dwellings and the snaking trails of smoke from fires. And there were people wandering around aimlessly, or lying down, waiting for the relief of death.

Jezebel reeled back from the horror of the place. They were so isolated from the colour and life of Phoenicia. These people were outcasts, excluded and banished and shunned by their own people. There was a finality about them, as though they were dead, yet still living.

Was this the true meaning of being dead? To be cast adrift and alone, yet knowing how isolated and lonely you were? She shuddered at their fate. Could there be anything worse in life than being an outcast? Did the gods visit the valley? Who looked after outcasts? Asherah? Ba'al? El?

As days wore on, Jezebel forgot about the Valley of the Lepers, and for a time it was the potter who captivated the girl's days. Ishbaal's was a small hut, and the pots and vessels he had made were stacked up inside and outside, some stacks as high as the roof. Here was a place which fascinated her, indeed the entire spectacle of the potter's art excited her. She told her servants in great detail about the times when the potter used his two hands during the moulding of the clay, and built it into a small tower which looked exactly like a man's penis. Then his hands became wet and brown, holding the column, massaging it, grasping it, shaping it, making tiny indentations in it which became rings, then collapsing it so that it became flaccid and puny like she'd seen men after they'd spent themselves within a woman slave. But unlike the men who often took a whole day before the gods put height and strength back into their members, Ishbaal could re-perform his magic immediately. After making the clay tower small and fat and flaccid, he could build it up again with his two hands until it was tall and strong. Her maids burst out laughing as she imitated the process.

Of course, the more she visited Ishbaal, the less of a mystery pottery-making became for her. But, even so,

Jezebel determined that she would spend at least one morning every few days standing in the demi-light of his doorway, continuing to watch him.

Why had he broken her thrill of secrecy by speaking to her? Why had he broken the mystery? He was so silly. Didn't he understand the rules of her game? He knew she had been standing there; she knew he knew. It was unwritten, desired by both; yet this last time, something had made him break the invisibility of her illicit behaviour, the furtive bond which tied man and girl together. And now the magic was no more, the bond destroyed forever.

She lay on her bed, and thought back to the morning when he'd spoken to her. For the first time, Jezebel had been able to come up close and in the open, and could see in great detail what was being done to the clay. The excitement of the act had disappeared and many of the thrills she had covertly experienced went out of what she was doing. She saw the clay for what it was, nothing more than wet earth; the shapes she'd seen from across the room were no longer images of penises or breasts, but were the rudimentary objects which she ate and drank from every day.

Jezebel looked around her room and thought how dull it was. The painted walls of yellows and reds and greens, the ceiling imitating the night sky, the glazed vases with their motifs of men and women, the statues of her Goddess Asherah in union with her son and husband Ba'al, the bowls of pomegranates and oranges and melons, the flasks of wine … all were here today as they'd been here yesterday and the day before. Nothing ever changed in her life. Today was yesterday and would be tomorrow. So today, as the sun descended into the Eternal Sea, she would have to find a new adventure.

THE CITY OF SAMARIA, ISRAEL

He had been into this square before, but he still disliked cities. He was happy in his home of Tishbe in Gilead where there were few people, and little noise. He was happy in the inner sanctum of the Temple of Yahweh, where the noise of the crowd praying and worshipping and the chanting of the priests was a distant murmur, and where he could lay down before the altar and be as one with his God.

But in his heart of hearts, he had to admit that he was happiest in the desert, where there was absolute quiet, and the noisiest thing was the sibilance of the sand as the winds whipped it into the air like clouds of seaspray, until it fell back to the ground and slipped down over the dunes, like gentle waves on an evening sea. There were no people in the desert, unless one counted the nomads who were there, but not there.

Yet, the Lord Yahweh had commanded him to come to the towns and cities of Israel and Judah and to bring the fickle people back to the worship of God, and that's what he would do.

Elijah stood on the makeshift platform he'd constructed on the wagon, and looked down at Rizpah; there was a sadness in her eyes. She was missing their two children, just as he was, and just as she missed them every time she and Elijah went away to preach the word of God. But the children were well looked after by their neighbours in Tishbe and, in a month, he and Rizpah would leave Samaria and cross the Jordan and return to their home. Then they'd all be together again. He thought of his children and a warmth came over him, an inner warmth, hotter even than the hot sun of the middle of the day.

Sometimes, he wondered why he had been chosen above all others to carry out the work of the Lord. He was a good man, yes ... a man of faith and belief ... yes! But only Yahweh could make him a prophet, and ever since he'd seen the vision in the orchards of his youth, people far and wide had recognised him as a prophet, and so he had been forced to lead a lonely and often difficult life – a life which would have been so much more difficult without his rod, his support, the staff of his life, his Rizpah.

He looked down at her and the feelings of love for his family swept over him, threatening to wash him off the platform and back to his home, where he could rest forever in the love and joy of his family.

But this was God's will they were carrying out, Yahweh's work was of greater importance than he himself, his wife or his children.

Rizpah was a good woman, a decent and honourable woman. In her words she was Elijah's staff and right arm, but in her heart, he knew that every time she kissed the children goodbye, she began the journey doubting the mission they'd been given.

She glanced up and saw him looking and smiling at her. She smiled back and nodded in encouragement. For the entire morning, she'd been going up and down the streets of the city of Samaria, into and out of the houses and the stalls and bazaars telling the citizens and merchants and tradespeople that Elijah, the great prophet of Yahweh, God of Israel, would be preaching in the early afternoon in the central marketplace of the city.

Many had come, yet not as many as she'd hoped. It wasn't the sea of faces she expected to see. Not that Elijah noticed the spaces in the crowd, for he was lost in his thoughts, and she was confident that as soon as he began to speak, the people would begin to gather into the central square, as they did whenever her husband began preaching.

She nodded, and he smiled. Then, in a loud voice, he shouted, 'People of Samaria; men and women of Israel; lovers of Yahweh the one true God, draw near, for I am the vessel of the Lord, and I have a message to bring to you, which was told to me by the Lord in my dreams.'

And the people began to gather. Those at the front who had been standing there for some time drew closer, and the crowd at the rear pressed forward. Rizpah looked up towards the balcony of the second floor of the palace. There were guards up there who had been standing looking at the proceedings. Rizpah noticed with a slight degree of pleasure that one of them had disappeared inside. Would he return with the King of Israel, Omri? Would that evil man who ruled over a divided kingdom come out and hear what her husband had to say?

Omri hated Elijah and the truth he spoke. Now, perhaps, with Elijah speaking at the King's doorstep, Omri would have to take action. Then Yahweh would intervene and defeat the dynasty of the House of

Omri, and Israel and Judah would once more be joined, and all of the people of Israel could worship in the Temple of Jerusalem ... then all would be well with the world.

CHAPTER TWO

THE CITY OF SAMARIA, ISRAEL

The ambassador looked around the throne room to which he and his delegation had just been admitted, and did his best not to let the sneer on his face show too obviously. It was the first time he'd travelled south from his rich and glorious and colourful land of Assyria to the land of Israel, his first visit to this hovel which was called a palace. On the walls of this building – he could hardly bring himself to call it a palace – were dull hangings and carpets and rugs, but none of the painted decorations to which he was used in his own wondrous Palace of Nineveh or the Palace of Nimrud, or which he'd seen in other palaces of neighbouring countries such as Syria, Phoenicia and Babylonia.

Except for the hangings, the walls were bare! Where were the scenes of triumph, or the intricate designs or patterns which made for beautiful surroundings in which people of elevated rank could live and enjoy themselves? Where were the decorated walls, using the expensive dyes of seashells or the barks of exotic trees? Where were the patterns which pleased the eye, or the mystical obeisances to the gods to show that they were omnipresent?

This wasn't a palace, thought the ambassador, it was a burial chamber, as bare and sparse and unwelcoming as the entire land through which he'd travelled when he'd left Nineveh in Assyria to reach Israel and its capital, Samaria. It was almost as though the moment he crossed the borders of the land, the light in people's faces disappeared, as though happiness suddenly evaporated like water left out in the middle of a summer's day.

The Ambassador of Assyria looked piteously at the King of Israel. He'd been sent to treat with many other kings in his time of service to Sarkin-Ashurbanishpul, the greatest king in the world. He'd seen many lands and monarchs while representing his majesty; but never in all his days had he seen a king like this, dressed in the drabbest of robes, the most ordinary man in a court of ordinary men.

What kind of a land was this? Where was the colour? Where was the richness of surroundings to strike awe into the hearts of visitors? Where were the ornaments and gifts which foreign kings had sent in reverence to the strength and majesty of the kingdom? Where was the joy? Where were the wall paintings depicting the greatness of the monarch? The decorations? There were none here in the palace, nor adorning the walls of the buildings as they did in the city of Nineveh or Nimrud or Ashur. Here, there was only drabness, ordinariness. What a kingdom! He would have much to report back to his monarch.

Omri, King of Israel, was irritated by the contemptuous sneer on the face of the ambassador. He'd been noticing his attitude since he'd entered the throne room, and knew what was going through the man's mind. It went through the minds of all the ambassadors. And it both infuriated and surprised the King. Why weren't ambassadors briefed on the religion of Israel and the demands of Yahweh before they entered His land? After all, there was enough trade between Israel and the rest of the lands of the region for word to have spread, even to the land of Babylonia and further north.

Omri decided to deal harshly with this arrogant man. If these ambassadors came to his court, they would learn that Yahweh was the one true God; that Yahweh of the Hebrew people forbade the making of idols or images and painting on walls and false imagery to detract from His greatness. Holy, holy, holy was the majesty of the Almighty Yahweh. Nowhere in Israel would this presumptuous ambassador find a painting; nor would he find paintings in the sister land of Judah to the south where Yahweh also reigned and where the temple of the great King Solomon had been built high on the hills of mighty Jerusalem, the city of inheritance, the city of peace. For painting and idolatry were sister and brother, and Yahweh was the only God, the invisible presence who was everywhere and nowhere.

The ambassador's sneer made King Omri sit stiffly on his throne, as though he were at attention like his soldiers before a battle. But regardless of the fool who had just entered the throne room, Omri felt strangely ill at ease, a feeling of being uncomfortable within himself, as though he were a part of yet somehow removed from these surroundings.

Everything had been well, until this morning. Then Elijah began to preach, and suddenly Omri's life had been disturbed. Elijah! Would the House of Omri, would Israel, never be rid of these ranting and raving prophets?

This feeling of discomfort seemed to overcome him whenever Elijah was in the city. Why did Yahweh, such a demanding, unforgiving and stern God, have to punish Omri even further with a blight like Elijah the Tishbite? What had Omri done to make Yahweh so angry? He had inherited a divided kingdom, and nothing he could do or say would reunite the two lands. It had been King Jeroboam who had divided the kingdom when he rebelled after King Solomon died. Yet it was Omri who was being blamed.

Omri had done everything to appease the Lord. Yahweh didn't allow images of idols and paintings of people and other such decorations as they did in Egypt, Assyria and Phoenicia, but the buildings which had been erected to glorify Him in the southern land of Judah were great indeed. And Omri had worked hard to create such buildings in the northern land. He'd built cities and temples in Israel of the north to rival those of Judah of the south in order that the people of Israel would be happy and so that Yahweh would be pleased. Did that satisfy Elijah and the other priests of Samaria? No, all they wanted was to pray in Jerusalem, to reunite the two nations. But things had gone too far – there was too much anger and loathing between the two royal houses for that.

And so day in, day out, night and morning, the barefoot madman would walk through the land and rail and scream and point his finger and shake his stick and threaten Omri and the royal house of Israel with the most dire warnings and predictions. Since the division of the one kingdom into two, all the kings of Israel in the north had been severely criticised by the priests of the temples, Omri no less than his predecessors.

By far, Elijah had been the worst critic. Elijah couldn't be appeased by rich gifts made to the temple; his head couldn't be swayed by banquets in his honour, nor presents of rich cloth, gold and jewels. No, he was unswerving in his condemnation of Israel, and of all that Omri tried to do.

Twice Omri had locked him in the palace cellars; twice the priests of the temple had whipped up the fury of the people to stand at the gates screaming and threatening and demanding their prophet's release. And twice the great King had been sufficiently humiliated to have to release the madman in order to avert a civil uprising.

Omri shuddered with the agony of the problems which the prophet Elijah was causing him. The people were divided between their King and their temple. Omri wanted to raise more taxes so that he could build bigger and better buildings for the people – Elijah screamed and fulminated that it was all vanity and that everything must be done for the glorification of Yahweh. Yet when Omri had built a magnificent temple, Elijah had been the first to scream that only Jerusalem's temple was truly fit for the worship of God.

Every day brought new reports of trouble with the prophet. If Omri had his way he would have rid himself of Elijah and the other priests of the temple years ago ... but that would have led to the destruction of everything he'd built.

Getting rid of Elijah would be such a delicious

achievement. And it became even more appealing as he looked at the sneering and contemptuous ambassador who kneeled at his feet, going through the motions of respect, but in whose heart was contempt at the unworthiness of the palace. Without Yahweh and Elijah and the priests of the temple, Omri could decorate his palace and make it grand and beautiful.

Yes, thought Omri, Elijah was the real problem, not this silly and ridiculously overdressed representative of the Assyrian King Sarkin-Ashurbanishpul with his gold earrings and his bangles and beads, and hair beaded and threaded, and his beard plaited like the hair of a girl child.

Omri tried to listen to the sycophantic words of the Ambassador of Assyria, but was distracted when the image of Elijah, barefoot and wearing little but a loincloth and a rough cloak kept appearing in his mind.

Not that Omri hadn't tried to reason with Elijah. But like all the men before him who heard the voice of God, Elijah blamed Omri for dividing God's kingdom into two, and for the loss of Jerusalem. Why couldn't they accept the inevitable – that the land of Yahweh was now and forever divided, Judah in the south and Israel in the north?

Omri was in a constant state of fury with Elijah. Hadn't he done everything to appease the madman? Hadn't one of his most important acts as the King been to pay two talents of silver to the farmer, Shemer, for the hill on which Omri had built the new capital of Israel away from the accursed capitals, Shechem and Tirzah, which King Jeroboam had built on partitioning the lands? And hadn't Omri willingly agreed to remove the hated golden calves from Bethel and Dan which Jeroboam had installed as a way of drawing the people from Judah's temple in Jerusalem?

But nothing would appease Elijah the madman. The more Omri bent in the storm of his words, the more furious the prophet became.

But it wasn't just Omri whom Elijah blamed for dividing the kingdom ... no, that priestly madman went all the way back through time and pointed his holy and bony finger at everybody who preceded Omri – at Zimri before him, and Elah before him, and Baasha before him and Nadab before him, and ultimately the great demon, the man who had partitioned the nation of Israel from the nation of Judah – Jeroboam.

The thought of killing the prophet kept coming back into Omri's mind when he heard Elijah, day and night, outside his bedroom window, screaming abuse at the King. Why was he doing it? What could Omri possibly do about the division of the two kingdoms? It was too late. They could never be rejoined. It was a fact. The kingdoms were divided. The ten tribal lands had gone to the north in Israel, and the tribes of Judah and Benjamin had remained loyal to the king of the southlands in order to pray at the temple in Jerusalem.

Once in his fury, Omri's advisors had begged him to get one of the guards to take Elijah into the desert and kill him, blaming his death on the Philistines or the Syrians. In a moment of weakness, he'd nearly agreed, but Omri came to his senses and knew far better than they what the consequences would be. He couldn't allow a war to happen now, not when Omri had ensured that for the past ten years there had been a state of peace between Israel and its brother kingdom Judah in the south. And it was this peace which had enabled Omri to collect the taxes and tithes of the people so he could afford to rebuild cities which had been torn apart by a vicious past war. Never had the people of Israel or Judah been so prosperous, so content. Even in this time of drought, the people had food and oil from the King's granaries and storerooms.

And this madman, this voice of God, was trying to ruin all of this in order to reunite the two kingdoms, just so that everybody could worship in the Temple of Jerusalem.

Wealth, he reasoned, would eventually put paid to Elijah. The people would no longer listen to him when they were content, when they had great and awesome buildings, when they loved and respected the temple he had built for them, and when their bellies were full of bread and olives and cheese and meats.

Of course, peace with Judah was also essential for another reason. There were now growing threats of war with the Syrians to the north and the Philistines to the coastal south, and the last thing he needed was an adventurous monarch of Judah joining forces with these brigand nations.

Omri's mind was clouded with worry. As he sat on the throne trying to concentrate on what the ambassador was saying, thoughts of war and the growing drought which could lead to panic and a possible raiding of food stocks in the royal granary, all caused by the strident voice of Elijah, ran through his mind. A silence descended on the throne room. Omri looked around, and saw that all eyes were on him, especially those of the delegation from Assyria.

'What?' he asked.

Omri's battle commander came forward, and whispered into his ear. 'The ambassador from Assyria wants to know how many men will be sent from Israel.'

The King was pulled back from his musings to the dangers of the present, the here and now. The delegation had come to his court to enlist Israel's support for Assyria which was intent upon waging war against Syria in order to stop the aggressors from a pre-emptive strike. Many of his men would be killed. It would cost him a fortune. But if he refused, then the Assyrians would take it as a statement either of war or of weakness, and Israel would find itself attacked by Assyria; or it might leave itself open to war from the Philistines of the coastal south, who would see Israel's unwillingness to support Assyria as a sign of incapacity, and were looking for any excuse to attack the north.

Omri cleared his throat. 'How many men will your King be sending against Syria?'

The ambassador, naturally, had anticipated the question. The process of bargaining began, as of now ... 'Great King, we will send as many men as are necessary to defeat our enemy and make eternal and everlasting peace. The number of men we send will, of course, be governed by your Majesty's commitment to the cause of war and its brother, peace. If your Majesty sends a thousand, then my King will send a thousand.'

'But Ambassador, how many men shall I commit

when I am unaware of the size of your army and the strength of your men?'

The ambassador looked discomforted; he'd practised the look many times, until it was just right.

But before he had a chance to give his answer, King Omri continued, 'In the songs which come from the mouths of your people, they sing of your great King Sarkin-Ashurbanishpul as being invincible. Of having an army of ten thousand brave men, twenty thousand in some songs. How can I possibly match that host amongst nations?' he asked.

And then, in what appeared an afterthought, he said casually, 'And why should your mighty King Sarkin-Ashurbanishpul need my assistance when, according to his people, he has so strong an army? My country is small, yet my men are strong and my army valiant. But who, Ambassador, could equal an army of twenty thousand invincibles? And I don't know how many men of Israel are needed to equate to a thousand men of your country, Assyria. You kneel before me today and tell me one for one; yet your songs say that I should send twice, or even three times that number. Why, out of the mouths of your people, I am told that your men are twice as brave and three times as strong as any other.'

The ambassador from Assyria began to speak, but the King of Israel foreshortened him. 'Tell my brother the King of Assyria that I shall send as many troops, chariots, horses, war carriages and spearsmen as are necessary to help an army which cannot be defeated. Tell him that I believe the words of the songs which are sung of him, and that if I need to send ten men, or even twenty simply to watch his invincible army in battle, then I shall. Tell him that King Omri of Israel has spoken. That Israel will send a single chariot and a single man to observe the might of Sarkin-Ashurbanishpul. Now go.'

The Assyrian ambassador looked up in surprise. He was trying to follow the logic of the Israelite King's mind. But just as he was beginning to formulate an answer, he'd suddenly been dismissed. How could that be? These sorts of discussions took days, sometimes weeks. Yet this was only the beginning of the negotiation. He expected it to last at least until nightfall, backwards and forwards, as was the custom. Then to continue the following day, and the day after until eventually the Israelite King agreed to send his army, as all knew he would. But to be peremptorily dismissed when he'd only begun to speak was worrying. And to be told that the King of Israel would only send ten or twenty men ... or just one man and a chariot ... no, surely this was a joke.

Or was it a clever plot? Was the Israelite King being very clever? The ambassador had heard from others how skilled a negotiator the King was, despite the mediocrity of the surroundings in which he lived.

Quickly the ambassador reviewed what had been said. The King had failed to make an offer, and then cut short the discussion without allowing the ambassador to get him to commit to numbers. No serious offer had been made, nor was one able to be consummated because he was relying on the songs of the Assyrian people.

This meant that when the ambassador returned to Nineveh where the Assyrian King Sarkin-Ashurbanishpul was wintering, criticism would fall on him for failing to secure reinforcements for the Assyrian assault against the Syrians the following summer, and knowing Sarkin-Ashurbanishpul's temper, the ambassador and his entire family stood a good chance of being killed in a sudden rage.

'Perhaps, Majesty, before I depart, I might rest here overnight and seek another audience with your Majesty tomorrow, when your mind might have determined the true meaning of the songs, and will have thought through how many men might go forth from here.'

King Omri smiled. 'I understand the true meaning of the songs. You might pray to your gods and sing songs which extol the valour of your King, but we in Israel have a different god, and my people sing songs of Him, not of their King who is mightier than all others, but still a servant of Yahweh. Our ancestor, King David, felled the giant Philistine Goliath with a mere stone from a slingshot, but it was Yahweh who guided David's sight and gave him a mighty hand and an outstretched arm.

'Now leave my kingdom, Ambassador, for the roads are dangerous at night, and robbers might attack you. For your own comfort, Ambassador, why not sing to yourself the songs of your own people. Console yourself on the journey by wondering how many Assyrians you'd need to protect you from robbers. And take my message back to your king. Tell my brother Sarkin-Ashurbanishpul that I stand ready to send to him whatever he needs, but I know that being invincible, he will need nothing; tell him that I know the songs his people sing, and that my judgement is based upon them. But first he must tell me what he himself seeks to send against the Syrians.'

41

The King dismissed the now terrified ambassador with a wave of the hand.

Suddenly, the Nubian girl's massaging irritated him. The perfumes she had brought from Egypt were unpleasant in his nose. The joy he'd experienced when he first lay down to let the child's experienced hands wander over his body had ceased. He turned, and let his towel fall to the floor, exposing himself before her.

'Go!' said the King.

The child looked frightened, as though she had done something wrong.

'Isn't your Majesty ...'

'You're not at fault. Go,' he said, trying not to sound too harsh.

The girl looked at the King's member. 'Shall I ...?' she asked, pointing down to where the King lay.

Again he was distracted thinking about how to deal with Elijah.

'What?'

'Shall I use my hands? My mouth? Shall I do what the Nubian girls do? Will your Majesty lie down and let me ...?'

'No! Go, I said.'

And the girl began to walk away from the table towards the door. But as she walked, the King noticed that although she was little more than a child, her body features were already defined. Beneath her robes, she was tall and had a round and sensuous bottom. The King's interests stirred. There was so much modernity, so much beauty and strength in Egypt. He had been told by merchants of the colour and vitality of the court; of the reds and blues and yellows and vivid shades of the sky and the green of the trees which decorated the palaces, both inside and outside. He'd been told of the fountains which played inside the palaces, of the temples and monumental buildings which were so high their roofs were invisible from the ground; he'd been told of the sumptuous foods which were served, and delicacies which were kept cold by the snows brought from distant Ethiopia, even in the height of summer.

One day, before he died, he would travel to the land of Egypt. Yes, he knew that the pharaohs looked longingly eastwards towards the lands of the Fertile Crescent, lands which their ancestors had once conquered. But one day, he would find an excuse to visit Egypt and see for himself, see the beauty, the power, the splendour. For despite his power as the King, Omri was restricted from any adornments by the priests and the men of Yahweh, who called such decorations an abomination and a vanity in the sight of the one true God. And so he and his people lived in the absence of colour, their homes and palaces the shades of the rocks and the desert.

Perhaps a union with colourful Egypt rather than warlike Assyria? But why would the Pharaoh form an alliance with Omri? From the beginning of time, the pharaohs looked upon Judah and Israel and Philistia and all the other lands of the Crescent as eternally belonging to Egypt, theirs by right, and only temporarily under the suzerainty of kings like himself. One day, Omri knew that Egypt would regain its strength and once more send its armies to spread the mantle of its civilization and its pantheon of animal gods over the entire Levant and north Africa and as far south as the unknowable jungles. Omri mused on a union with Egypt in preference to a union with Assyria.

'Wait,' he shouted to the slave girl. 'Return.'

The child looked back in surprise. But when she saw the increased size of the King's realm, she smiled in gratitude.

THE CITY OF TYRE, PHOENICIA

King Ethbaal of Phoenicia lay on his bed, cooling towels on his forehead, his masseur finding all the points of stiffness and soreness in his body. The ride had been slow and sedate south from his residence in the city of Sidon to the King's other capital of Tyre, but it still exhausted him. He hated travelling, yet he was obliged to visit the cities and towns of his realm, to show himself to the people, to dispense justice, to punish lawbreakers, to plan new buildings and roads, and to ensure that he was sung about. That way, the kings of Israel and Judah and Syria and all the rest would know that he continued to be important both to his people, and completely in control of his land.

Whatever a king did, he was safe as long as the people sang about him. When they stopped singing, that was when he had to cut off a few heads and put down a potential rebellion. These were lessons he'd learned from his father, who had learned them from his father before him. They were the reason for the success his family enjoyed. But during his reign, he'd not had to execute anybody. He showed himself to his people, and they loved him for it.

But that was before the days of this drought, which was making the people unsettled and restless. What would happen when the crops failed for the second year, and people started to die? That was why he was visiting mountain villages as well as coastal towns and cities. So that his people could see that he was a compassionate and merciful ruler.

King Ethbaal had ridden a horse from Sidon to Tyre, normally he would ride in a wagon or on a camel. He despised camels as slow silly lumbering animals but because of their very slowness, they allowed the body to adjust to the rhythm of their walk and a full day's riding didn't exhaust him. A horse, on the other hand, even one with a back covered by three thick blankets, walked or cantered at a pace which was unnatural and so, after only a short time, his body was usually sore and stiff with the effort of trying to adjust to the animal's movements.

But a camel couldn't climb a mountain or traverse rocky roads, and so he ended up on horseback at the city of Tyre stiff, sore, in an evil temper, yet unable to rest and relax as he wished; for he was the King, and any sign of weakness, such as falling asleep in the reception in his honour, or yawning while he was inspecting the city fortifications under the eagle gaze of his officials, would be reported by spies to the kings of Syria and Assyria and Israel. Then his kingdom would be in jeopardy.

It was Jezebel who rode ahead as the walls of the city came into view. At first, Ethbaal didn't understand why, but it became obvious when the city guards stood stiffly to attention and blew trumpets and banged drums and strummed harps to fanfare him into the city. Ethbaal thought that it was a lovely gesture on his favourite daughter's part, but what he didn't know was that she had ridden quickly through the gates, and given instructions that the formal welcome on the steps of the palace was to be foreshortened. Normally it was a ceremony which took an interminably long time as the city dignitaries and merchants recited his honours and successes and formally acknowledged his rule. Yet Jezebel had arranged things differently.

Jezebel had begged the city dignitaries to forgo their welcome so that her father could attend immediately to an urgent matter of state on his arrival. She didn't, of course, tell them that he needed some rest after the arduous journey, but she had also privately arranged for a masseur to be brought from the temple to minister to her father's aches and pains. She also organised for one of his servants to masquerade as an emissary from a distant kingdom and pretend to engage her father in a secret meeting. In this way he would maintain his potency in front of his people, and at the same time be able to rest.

When he had kneaded and pummelled every sore and wayward spot of the King's body, the masseur took his leave, and Jezebel brought fresh cold towels for the King her father's forehead.

'It was very kind and thoughtful of you, child, to arrange this. But there are dangers in what you did. Refusing a formal welcome, even for the reasons you gave, could still be construed by my enemies as a sign that I'm growing old and weak, and incapable of managing the affairs of Phoenicia. Just the look on my face would have told my enemies that I'm not the man I used to be. It might have been better to allow me to do the things which the city had planned for me. This might not have been such a good idea.'

Jezebel nodded, appreciating her father's point of view. 'I know a way to overcome their concerns. Tonight at the temple, why not spill your seed into one of the youngest and most active prostitutes, and when the people see it spilt onto the ground they'll cheer and celebrate you. Once they see proof of your vigour, all thoughts of your weakness will be forgotten,' she said.

The King nodded. It was a good idea. But he knew his daughter suffered the misconceptions of youth. It wasn't a young sacred prostitute he needed, but an old and experienced one. All the older men in the city would appreciate his strength and manhood if he took one of the better known and more respected of the temple prostitutes. He would speak to the chief priestess, and arrange with her to be given the one prostitute in the temple who satisfied the needs of older and wiser men, one who more closely resembled their wives. Were he to be given one of the younger ones, pre-emptive passion might get in the way of duty and the sacred coupling could be over too quickly.

He had one of the prostitutes in mind. Her name was Meenah. She was a desert woman with skin as dark as the night sky and ample breasts. He was the first man she'd ever had inside her all those years ago, and he still remembered the shocked look of pain in her young eyes, quickly transmuting to intense pleasure as he'd thrust his penis time and time again into her body; he still thought of the way her lips opened and her tongue played with her teeth as he thrust and thrust until he'd yelled in ecstasy and exploded within her. He also remembered the stiffness his penis had once been able to achieve, so different now to the limp and often unresponsive thing between his legs.

Meenah had been captured during a battle inside the borders of Moab many years earlier and brought back to Tyre to be sold by the captain of the army into slavery. But she'd been purchased by the high priestess, now long dead, as a curio because of the jet black colour of her skin, or perhaps even because the high priestess lusted after her herself.

But the young King, only three years on the throne, had seen her during his stay in Tyre, and it had been Ethbaal who had first known her as a woman. He could still remember her smell, the heat of her body, the way she moved like an animal. And his seed had poured out of him and onto the sacred ground of the temple, to be dug and removed and planted in obedience with the commands of the God El.

Ethbaal remembered when he had a lot of seed to spill. Now ... well tonight with Meenah, he would again show his virility.

'Majesty,' said Jezebel, interrupting her father's musings, 'are you able to talk to me?'

He looked at her in love and regard. She was so young, so beautiful; yet she already had the breasts of a woman, and her thighs were spreading and developing. He had seen the triangle of hair and knew that soon he must find her a suitable husband, for soon, she would be ready to bear a child and continue the dynasty. He lifted his arm and beckoned her over. Jezebel walked across the room; Ethbaal noticed with surprise that she walked in a seductive way, yet it was her natural way. He knew, of course, that she enjoyed herself with the boys of the town, but with the way she walked, and with the development of her body, she would soon be a prized catch for someone.

Jezebel nuzzled into the crook of her father's arm, and he stroked her lustrous black hair. He remained silent. He knew her so well. When she wanted to ask her question, she would.

'Father,' she said after a long moment of silence, 'how would you feel if I became a priestess?'

The question was so preposterous that he didn't really understand what she had said.

'You see, the love of Asherah is very strong within me. My mother and some of my sisters don't love her as much as I do, but when I go to bed at night, I see her in my mind. I hear her talking to me, and she tells me what to do. My goddess is closer to me than ...' the girl tried to think of an analogy '... than all the other gods and goddesses.'

Ethbaal remained silent. When Jezebel spoke, it was with a purpose. But what she was thinking was completely unpredictable. And unacceptable.

'I want to be one of Asherah's priestesses.'

The words hung in the air. And Ethbaal felt a great sadness suddenly overcome him. He regarded his daughter, sitting on the floor at his feet. He knew her body well; she was often naked in his apartments, and he felt pleasure whenever he looked at her. Yes, she was tall for her age, nearly mature with beautiful breasts budding in their development, and long lustrous black hair. Her skin was unblemished and radiant, especially after the long ride they had taken through the mountains and in the cedar forests to get to Tyre. He'd seen her run naked from their encampment through the tents of the admiring retinue and down into some mountain lake and there she screamed as she hurled herself into the freezing water and had swum naked and free like a beautiful fish.

She rode with the strength and certainty of a man. When she attended banquets for visiting kings or ambassadors or generals, she would sit at the separate table with her mother and the other senior women of the Phoenician court and would converse with confidence and sophistication. She spent much of her time in the temple, and the priests and priestesses informed Ethbaal of his daughter's devotion and sincerity. And, most pleasing of all, Jezebel was the most loving and affectionate of all of his many children. It was she who would run to his side when he returned from a hunt or from a battle or a visit to another nearby kingdom, to find out what had happened, and who and what he had seen. And she would force him time after time to repeat the stories of what he'd witnessed and what he'd done, never once becoming tired or listless.

And now she was informing him that, for the rest of her life, she wanted to devote herself to the service of the goddess. For any of his other daughters, it would have been a wonderful event, a momentous turning point in their maturity. Because most of his other daughters were more concerned with luxury or fun or eating or sports.

But this was not a path which he had determined for Jezebel. She was a fine and determined young woman, and she would make a powerful match in an arrangement with some future prince or king. Yes, there was a youthful wildness about her, like when she crept out of the palace and into the town, thinking that she was doing so unobserved. But her father the King revelled in her curiosity, and knew that these were experiences which would make her a better wife and future queen.

Through Jezebel, Ethbaal could secure his borders. Through Jezebel, he could ensure peace and prosperity for his people. And the thought of denying her broke his heart.

CHAPTER THREE

Jezebel, Princess of Asherah, Friend and Knower of Ba'al, Consort and Connubist of El, Most Beloved and Revered Bride of the Moon and the Stars, Light of the Sun and Knower of All Things, Ruler and Helper Who Sits Beside the Supreme Ruler of Tyre and Sidon and all the Lands and Cities of the Empire of the Phoenicians, Overlady and Mistress of the Rulers of all the Lands and Domains of Egypt, Philistia, Israel, Judah, Syria, and Assyria, and Most Adored of the Gods who Rule from the Euphrates to the Nile, tried to stifle her yawn.

She had been standing, watching the procession of supplicants for so long that her legs were aching and her shoulders were beginning to sag. She glanced over to where her father was sitting on his throne, and looked at his ageing countenance and body. Yet she was suddenly suffused by the wonder of him, by a warmth and a love. How did he do it? How did he manage to receive so many subjects for such a long period of time, yet still make it seem as if every one was as special and as important as the very first who had bowed and genuflected and prostrated himself in the early morning when the thousands and thousands of subjects filed in through the doors of the palace to lay gifts at her father's feet and prostrate themselves before the Ruler of the world?

Her mother and the King's other wives, her brothers and sisters, and stepbrothers and stepsisters were all standing beside her. She glanced at them to see whether they, too, were bored and wilting under the heat of the palace and the weight of the day. Was she the only one who reacted so badly to these long, drawn-out spectacles of adulation and obsequiousness? Her father had told her how important sycophancy was to his people, and to his rule. Yet she couldn't but feel that it demeaned both the people and the King. All these words! All these gifts! For what purpose? As soon as another pretender arrived, the people would divide immediately between those loyal to her father the King, and those attracted to the pretender. So why was the show of sycophancy so important? It was a mystery which one day, when she was the wife of a king, as now seemed certain, she might understand.

To distract her from the unending line of supplicants, her eyes moved upwards to the ceiling of the throne room, where the blue and green and yellow triangles and swirls and circles of the painted wall decorations met the golden suns and red moons of the roof. She followed each and every line of the different colours, blues from the northern coast, reds from the desert lands, and yellows and greens from the lands far to the east, as they ascended and descended in continuous patterns along and up and down the walls. The entire room was a rainbow of colours and shapes and forms, much like looking up through the canopy of the forest on a hot summer's day and seeing the vivid blue of the sky while bright insects and brilliant birds intersected the trees.

And as the insects flew through her mind, she gazed upon a young man, the eldest son of one of the supplicants, who bore a resemblance to a man she had enjoyed recently, her teacher of court etiquette. And as she gazed at the lovely young man, her thoughts flew to the many men whom she had enjoyed in the past few years. Reaching the age of fourteen had been a great and wonderful turning for her; at that age, the priestesses determined that, as a princess of the royal blood, she was ready for knowing men. And she had entered into her learning with great enthusiasm. She'd been talking about sex with her slaves and her handmaidens for so long, that she was impatient, almost to the point of despair.

Jezebel fought back a smile as she thought of her etiquette teacher. He had been so proper at first, but after only a few lessons alone with her in one of the antechambers, he'd been so overwhelmed by her beauty and seductiveness, that he'd begged her to touch him.

And then her mind wandered to the memory of her first partner, a friend of her father who was chosen by both her mother and father because his member was not too big, and because he was old and tired and wouldn't hurt her when he penetrated her body for the first time.

Jezebel bit her lip at the thought of what had happened the first time she had made love; it was so funny. The priests and priestesses were there, gathered around the divan in the temple, all waiting

54

for him to perform the act. Jezebel had been dressed in the red robes of womanhood and her breasts had been specially painted by the women of the court who attended her mother. Her stomach was washed with laurel leaves dipped in milk as a symbol of fertility, and her womanly parts had been smeared with a paste of honey and cloves to perfume the entry way for the man.

She had entered the bedding chamber, and smelled the perfumed air; a delicate scent of roses and hibiscus flowers filled the room but beneath the aroma the air was heavy with the burning of a bouquet of thyme for the sweetness of her youth and myrrh for the bitterness of childbirth.

Her father the King smiled and nodded his encouragement. Her mother the Queen had kissed her, and said the prayer which all mothers recited to daughters when they had their first sexual experience on attaining womanhood: *'This moment for you will be your greatest moment; this feeling your greatest feeling; as your body is entered for the first time, you and Goddess Asherah will be as one; as you receive the seed, it is as though you were being coupled with the God Ba'al. Be fruitful and multiply, and may the blood of your childhood and the spilling of your first man's seed on the ground cause rain to fall and crops to multiply.'*

Then her mother had led her gently over to the divan, strewn with the petals of winter jasmine flowers. Jezebel lay down, and looked upwards to the ceiling, covered with paintings of the gods and goddesses coupling and doing the things which her handmaidens told her that ordinary men and women did and which she was so eager to experience. The gods were doing things with their mouths and hands and their other parts which had been described to her by giggling handmaidens, yet which she had never seen until now as she lay on the divan in this most adult of rooms. From nervous girl, she suddenly became an expectant woman, eagerly looking forward to her first encounter with a man. She remembered clearly how her breasts began to tingle, how her womanly regions between her legs had started to ache and throb in expectation.

And then the man had been led in, accompanied by his friends, his wives and his children. The entourage was singing songs and throwing laurel leaves into his path so that his route to the bed was covered with the signs and symbols of fertility. His chief wife had slipped off his robe, conscious of the honour the King and Queen had done to him and his family; she had covered his private parts with oils from Nubia, and she had massaged them into his penis so that it began to stand stiff and erect.

Jezebel had looked at the man's growing member in sudden disquiet. She had seen her father's and many others of the men of the court, but never one of this size. And although she knew fully well what was going to happen, for it had been explained to her in great detail by her handmaidens, she hadn't realised that a penis could be so big and hard and throbbing and ... and ... *vertical*. But it was her lover's eyes which caused her the most concern. For they were the eyes of a madman, a man full of lust, of passion. She'd seen those eyes before, in the face of a warrior who was fighting with another man who had insulted him in the courtyard. And suddenly Jezebel was scared. Scared of the man's eyes.

She drew back in fear, her young and innocent face

showing the features of a startled animal. The man had looked at her, his own eyes widening in shock at her expression, and immediately his erection began to decline. He tried to hide his deficiency with his hands, and had walked over to the bed. Jezebel looked over at her mother, who smiled her encouragement; suddenly she felt less concerned.

The man lay beside her, on top of her, underneath her, with the voices of encouragement from the court calling out to him. He kissed her, felt her breasts, placed his hands in the triangle of hair between her legs, but although his body was rigid with expectation, nothing else was stiff.

Try as he might, his member wouldn't obey his desires. It withdrew in fear into his body. And Jezebel had just lain there and waited for something to happen.

And waited.

And waited.

The old man kept looking around him and playing with himself and mumbling prayers to El and Ba'al and everyone else ... but still nothing happened. His member remained soft and useless, and no matter how much he rubbed himself against her, he kept on flopping and flapping like a fish landed on a boat.

In the end, one of the priests of Ba'al had been co-opted for the young Princess's benefit, and he only took moments to increase the size of his member and to grow into the biggest erection Jezebel could imagine. Even now, even so long after the sacrificial opening of her body for the benefit of the gods, even now she remembered with a shudder of pleasure the young man's erection and the feeling of him entering her and opening her body to a lifetime of adult pleasure. She smiled every time she thought of his huge member, and the way she'd first seen it, the admiration and wonder she'd felt as it disappeared – painfully at first, but then joyfully – into the womanness of her body.

Even today, it was better than anything she had come to know. The young priest's penis was bigger than the one she'd seen on her father last time he'd conjoined with a yellow-haired and blue-eyed slave girl from the dark lands of the north, and her father, even at his age, was renowned for the size of his penis.

Oh, what a moment her first time had been. After the nonsense of her parent's old friend, the young priest's entry into her body had caused her surprise. She'd expected far more pain, and there had been a moment of shooting discomfort, but not the pain of which her mother had spoken. Jezebel remembered how her body suddenly went rigid at the feel of a man inside her. Fear? Pleasure? It was so long ago … three years … that she couldn't remember all of her emotions. But she did clearly remember the pleasure on her mother's and father's faces as the young priest rocked backwards and forwards and within only moments of beginning, suddenly arched his back and yelled out a thanks to Ba'al, and then collapsed on her as though he was in a dead faint. As he lay inert and flaccid on top of her, the whole court clapping and cheering, she had looked over to the old man who had tried so hard to be her first; there was a look of infinite sadness in his face. Jezebel was deeply upset for him and determined to go to his bedchamber later in the week so that he could finish his supplication to the gods.

And now, so long afterwards, Jezebel would, from time to time, try hard to remember whether her first feelings were fear or pleasure, but today, she could remember her feeling of disappointment as she felt the young priest's penis slowly disappear from inside her, right at the very time when she was adjusting to the joy of his being there. There were things which her body told her to do, things like arch her back, like move her buttocks backwards and forwards, like get him to feel her breasts, like have him kiss her fully on the mouth. But too early he had come and gone from her, withdrawing and mumbling his thanks and turning to her parents for their praise and gifts.

Jezebel was distracted from her thoughts by her father's steward who banged his staff on the floor as the last of the supplicants prostrated himself before the King and the royal family. Then she watched as her father the King stood and indicated for all present to leave the throne room. The entry door was shut, and as the last supplicant wandered from the room, the exit door was closed with a definitive bang.

The noise and smells of the populace began to disappear. The entire royal family, all sixty-two members, remained standing absolutely still as silence descended where noise and commotion had been only moments before. She could sense that her father the King was immediately less formal, sitting less stiffly on his throne, arching his shoulders from the weight of his crown and other regalia.

There was no movement in the room. No sound. Everybody was waiting for the King to move from the dais on which his throne had been placed, so that they could relax their own formality. And then he started to descend the few steps, rubbing his bottom, and said, 'Well, the duty of the King is done for another year. The people have seen me and made their wishes known. Let's eat.'

And he walked out of the throne room to the banquet hall where a table of meats, breads, leaves, pastes and spices had been laid.

Jezebel was surrounded by a sudden noise and babble of whispered conversation, comments by older and younger brothers and sisters and stepmothers about how dirty the people were, or how much they stank, or their appearance, or their scars or the blisters and pustules on their faces. It was all so disparaging, so unworthy. It angered her, and rather than joining in with their comments on the awfulness of the people of Sidon and Tyre and the countryside between and around, Jezebel instead followed in her father's footsteps and went for something to eat.

She had always been popular with the people who lived inside the walls of Sidon, and even with those tradespeople who lived and worked in the valleys and hillsides which were in the shadow of the city. Ever since she was a young girl, when she'd made illicit excursions from the palace, and down into the town to where the artisans worked, even going out of the walls to where charcoal burners and hide-curers plied their trades, Jezebel's open and welcoming manner had done much to bring the people of Phoenicia closer to the people who ruled them.

She offered simple gestures, such as asking one of the fishermen if she could help him mend the nets; or providing the muscle to blow the bellows of a metalworker or an armourer; or helping a baker in the early hours of the morning to grind the flour to make dough or axe wood into pieces small enough to feed his fires, enabling him to make bread for the hungry people of the city.

She loved the bustle of the city in the early morning. She loved going among the people and understanding their lives. Because the lives they lived were so different to the lives of her stepbrothers and stepsisters in the palace, who were pampered and who did nothing but swim and laze around and eat and play games. Indeed, except for her father the King Ethbaal, and his advisors, especially Hattusas, who all worked hard, nobody in the palace seemed to do anything.

At times, Jezebel was worried about the way in which her father and his advisors worked. They always seemed to be talking at the beginning of the day, and continued talking, even when the sun sank into the Eternal Sea and the day ended. Hattusas, Ethbaal's chief advisor, worked particularly hard. He was always walking quickly through the corridors of the palace carrying tablets or documents, or dictating letters to his secretary. So if her father and his advisors worked so hard, why didn't her brothers and sisters do any work at all? Why didn't they do things in the city? It was a mystery for her.

Many years ago, when she used to wander into the city, her father told her he knew what she was doing and asked her why a Princess of the royal blood, even one little more than a child, wanted to work with the peasants and artisans of the town. She had not understood the question. She liked to help. She liked to assist the cooks in the kitchen, and watch the gardeners attending to the fruit and olive trees. She loved being part of what was being made, to take delight in holding a vase or an amulet and say to her parents, 'I made this'.

So the idea that princes, or princesses of the royal blood, did not work with ordinary people was unusual to her. And what was her alternative? To be like the other princesses and princes, and to sit around all day, playing silly games; or creating mock wars which they played out with wooden swords and clay daggers in the safety of a nearby field; or to ride through the town on horses and donkeys, just so the people could look at the splendour of their clothes and marvel at the life they led. Nothing that her brothers or sisters did interested her, although, because of her popularity with her father the King, they always tried to curry her favour and get her to participate.

And neither was she trying to be like the peasants and the artisans in the city and beyond the walls. Jezebel loved the luxury of where and who she was, and revelled in the act of being cleaned by slaves when she returned from the dirt and the grime of everyday life. She loved the ministrations of her slaves; she adored the unguents and perfumes and salves they used to make her feel refreshed and beautiful. She enjoyed being washed and adorned with oils and precious spices brought from far away by traders, and having her robes put out for her every morning; and she especially enjoyed not having to do things for herself or others, such as she'd seen the wives of the craftsmen do, like washing their linens in streams or changing the reeds and straws for floors and beds.

She'd smelt the straw used for bedding, straw that hadn't been changed for weeks because of shortages and famine. She knew the smell. It was like the smells from the barns in which the horses and donkeys lived, the animals that serviced the needs of the royal family. The work of these women in cleaning their homes and changing matting and bedding wasn't nice work. It didn't produce things. It merely kept things the way they had always been.

These women, these peasant women married to artisans and tradesmen, seemed to spend their lives working, yet not making things. Their days were mundane and ordinary, spent in ensuring that things didn't get any worse than they were: that clothes didn't fall off their family's backs because of disrepair, so they were always sewing and mending; that there was always food for their family when they returned home in the evening, so they'd spend their day picking food from the fields or buying meat from the butchers or they'd go down to the quay and buy some of the catch when the fishermen returned in the early morning; that the house didn't get any dirtier or smell any worse than it had the day before, so they'd spend their time filling the bedding with fresh straw and grasses, or sprinkling natron water throughout the house to keep down the lice, or they would clean out the hearth so that the evening fire burned brightly and smoke from the cooking didn't fill the entire house.

In many ways, Jezebel felt sorry for the women. The women and daughters prepared food in the morning and the afternoon for the men and boys to eat in the evening. And when the families had eaten and were full and satisfied, the women of the house then had to go out to the troughs near the river and wash their plates and cooking utensils for them to be ready the following day to repeat precisely what they had done that day, and the day before.

Jezebel tried to make every day different. Half the fun in life was planning the adventures of the following day; sometimes, she could hardly sleep for the excitement of what she knew the morning would bring. But these women ... they would go to bed, knowing with absolute certainty that they would have to get up in the early morning to carry water from the river and light the fires of the house and begin the process of baking bread and mixing the pastes which their menfolk would need to take with them when they went to the fields or the orchards or their stalls to make or sell things. What a terrible life, Jezebel always thought when she watched these women. Knowing that every single day when you'd finished whatever it was that you had to do, the following day would dawn and you'd be doing exactly what you had done this and previous days. Where was the fun in that? Why did Asherah, such a kind and generous goddess, allow this to happen? Couldn't Ba'al and El and Melkart and all the other gods find better things for people to do? The gods ruled all existence – why then was life so dull and difficult for so many people?

And how could the people themselves lead these lives? Couldn't they, like she, do the things they wanted? She'd seen them, spoken to them; and they didn't understand what she was talking about. The women knew that they would have to clean the house, and put fresh leaves and branches down every day to keep away the flies and lice and mice and cockroaches; and they would make and mend clothes for their husbands and children and themselves; and they would help their husbands in whatever it was that they made to sell so that they could buy food for the table.

It was all so ... so ordinary, so monotonous. All so different from the relationship her mother enjoyed with her father. Her mother would attend to the running of the court and the kitchens; she would prepare her husband the King to meet delegations; she would be by his side at banquets; she would participate in temple worship and encourage her husband if ever he found difficulty in entering one of the sacred prostitutes. She was a woman who was busy all the time, but who didn't do the things which the wives of the farmers and the craftsmen and the bakers and lamp makers did.

And in her time, Jezebel knew that when she married she, too, would be like her mother and minister to her husband's needs. For it had been decided that she would be married, and to a king. The idea she had suggested to her father so many years ago of becoming a priestess of Asherah had been rejected outright. Her father had not even allowed her to mention the subject again. She'd cried her eyes out, wailed at the waning moon, begged the priestesses to intervene on her behalf, and after half a year, accepted the impossibility of ever becoming Jezebel, Chief Priestess of Asherah.

And since those days, since those first passionate stirrings, she had enjoyed her life of freedom. She now realised, three years on, that her father had been right. A life confined to the temple, even worshipping Asherah daily, would have been too restrictive for a woman of her passions, enjoyments and inquisitiveness.

But above all else, Jezebel wanted riches. Not for herself, because she had all the richness in life which she could possibly want; no, she wanted riches for the townspeople and the country people of Phoenicia. It was her father's wish, and so it became her wish too. The richer and more peaceful the people, the less chance that he could be overthrown, as the King of Syria had recently been overthrown by one of his generals at the behest of an unhappy mob who hated paying one of his newly imposed taxes.

And the happier the people, the less chance that an invading country would succeed in gaining control of Phoenicia, for the people would rise up as one and the army's ranks would swell overnight if the King were beloved. Yes, the people would flock to his side if Phoenicia were attacked. And he'd seen what had happened to countries where the King was hated. Hadn't that been the case with King Zimri of Israel, who was detested by the people, and had been overthrown by General Omri after only seven days of his reign, cheered on by a people who welcomed the rise of another to take his place?

More than her brothers and sisters, Jezebel realised that the absolute power of the King was an illusion. Despite the songs which were sung; despite the way in which the people lined the route whenever the King passed in procession; despite the words of the priests and the ministers; despite the tributes paid by other monarchs, Jezebel knew that a tax which imposed too high a burden, or an incursion by some raiding brigands over the border, or an insult which wasn't properly addressed, could cause rumours to spread throughout the land. Then the King would have to quell any unrest with force ... kill an outspoken village leader, salt fields, destroy crops by fire in punishment ... even put to death an entire village. That would make the people hate and resent what the King had done, which meant that even more force would need to be used ... and that would lead to further hatred of the King and the constant threat of uprising or invasion, which meant that the King would have to spend all his time trying to keep the throne instead of ruling his people.

Jezebel had been tutored by her father Ethbaal that even with a strong army, a King could rule safely only when he was loved by the people, when he built great buildings for their temples and gave them marketplaces to sell their wares, and made the priests and priestesses go out into the towns and villages and spread the worship of the gods – for then they would pay taxes and produce more.

In all of her time in the palace, Jezebel had known the people, and had been one with the people of Sidon and Tyre and of the villages of the country.

One of the things for which she prayed most earnestly whenever she entered the Temple of Asherah, was for sufficient wealth in the royal treasury to provide each family in Tyre and Sidon and all other places in Phoenicia with at least one, and possibly even two, slaves. Then the women wouldn't work so hard. Then the men would be happy.

As she explained to one of the priestesses of Asherah, a young woman called Memtebaal, it was a simple concept to explain to the goddess, and then to her father if she had Asherah's approval. For then Asherah should enable Jezebel's father the King to conquer Philistia or Egypt or Israel or somewhere, kill all the men in the land, take all the women and children into slavery, and then none of the women of Phoenicia would ever have to work again. Then they could all be like Jezebel, who didn't have to work. But they could come and go as they pleased, and they could swim in the sea in the middle of the day, or wander into the forests, or go to one of the sacred groves and pray. It was to Asherah's advantage to organise for King Ethbaal to win a major war.

The last time Jezebel was in the temple, she'd said this to a priestess. Memtebaal had smiled and agreed with the young woman, and promised to spend all of her time praying to Asherah for just such an eventuality.

Jezebel's maidservant came running into her bedchamber in a state of excitement.

'Your father the King has commanded your attendance, Princess.'

Jezebel looked at her in surprise. The King only ever commanded her presence when she'd done something terrible. Like the time she put aloes into the food of the cruel and vain Queen Elohabel on the night of her wedding to her father, the night when Jezebel's own mother no longer enjoyed the rank of Principal Queen. The new Queen spent the entire evening and all the way through to the following day vomiting. Despite Jezebel's protestations that she hadn't done it, the King her father knew very well it was she; she had been indiscreet and told her older brother that she intended to ruin the day for a woman who was rude and aggressive to her from the moment her caravan had arrived from the land of Edom to the south. Jezebel had, on instructions, given the Queen flowers as she alighted from her camel, but the flowers in the centre were dead and the Queen took it as a bad omen and spent the next three days before the marriage criticising her. Which was why Jezebel had spiked her food and drink with aloes.

So if the King her father was now commanding her to be present, then it must be something serious. But what had she done that was so bad? To her knowledge she had been good for at least the past couple of weeks.

Perhaps it was her behaviour on the day of the supplicants. But she had been completely proper, even refusing to join in her brothers' and sisters' criticism of the people. Perhaps it was one of the priests or priestesses who had complained that her prayers to the gods weren't fervent enough. But how could that be? She was devoted to Asherah, loving her and everything she did. No! Of that, Jezebel was absolutely certain. There was nothing to criticise there.

The young Princess stood up from her divan and, heart pounding, followed her maidservant from her room into the antechamber, past the two guards who immediately stood rigidly to attention and banged their spears on the marble floor as she went through the open archway. She walked quickly down the colonnade, past the throne room and the banquet hall, past the kitchens which supplied the banquets and past the King's bathing room, and the room where the secretaries and amanuenses drew up the King's orders of the day, until she came to the huge bronze doors of the King's private apartments. Four massive Nubian guards blocked her path.

'Go back to my chambers and wait for me,' Jezebel told her maid. The young woman's heart was pounding faster now as she approached whatever it was that would be her doom. Throughout the walk, she'd been desperately trying to remember what she might have done to stir the King her father's anger. But try as she might, she could think of nothing.

She stood waiting and waiting, the Nubian guards standing impassively, awaiting a signal from inside for the doors to be opened to admit her to the King's presence. She heard a barely perceptible knock from inside the room, just the gentlest tap, but it was enough to breathe life into the guards and impel them to the action of opening the doors, the weight of which took all four men to perform.

Jezebel saw her father, sitting on the chair on his raised dais, surrounded by his advisors, ministers and attendants. He was busy reading a tablet, some communication from an ally or an enemy. His face was pinched in the act of concentrating. Silently, Jezebel crept forward until she was standing in front of his chair on the dais. He seemed not to notice her entry. In every other room in the palace where she entered, her arrival would be announced by the recital of her titles ... in every room save that occupied by her father the King who naturally took precedence over her and everybody else in the kingdom.

One of his advisors was explaining the meaning of the communication. It was Ethminhak the Egyptian, a man who, along with her favourite Hattusas, had been the King's advisor for all of Jezebel's seventeen years on earth. She listened to a voice she knew well, a voice which not only advised her father the King, but also advised her whenever she needed help. It was Ethminhak who picked her up when, as a little girl, she fell on the floor; it was

70

he to whom she addressed her questions about the ways of the court and what was expected of her, when she was twelve; it was Ethminhak to whom she'd come last year when her monthly bleeding didn't materialise and who had organised for one of the midwives to give her a potion which, two days and much pain later, caused the blood to flow. She loved his black skin, his deep and gentle voice, his calming and intelligent ways, just as she loved the more austere and more fatherly Hattusas, the chief priest turned counsellor to the King, turned friend to her in her growing up. With these two men at her shoulders, she had grown into a fine and noble woman, a daughter who pleased her father the King.

'Great King, the letter merely states that if our army ...'

'I know what the letter says, Ethminhak. But I don't know what it means. Why is Omri warning me when I have made no moves to the south in ... in ... I can't even remember when last my eyes were turned to the south. Our enemies are to the north and the east, in Babylonia and Assyria and ...'

Ethminhak interrupted, 'King Omri of Israel is merely stating that if our army ...'

'But why?' thundered the King. 'Why suddenly does his ambassador come unaccompanied by attendants and deliver a letter which is clothed in the words of affection and brotherhood, yet whose intent is as sharp as a sword? Why send me this letter? Is he testing my resolve? Is he goading me to some precipitate action? What?'

'King Omri of Israel merely wants ...' And the advisor suddenly stopped talking, his voice trailing away in the silence of the room. The answers which he had so far given, which had obviously failed to satisfy the King, stopped flowing from his mouth. He looked up and saw that Jezebel had entered the chamber.

King Ethbaal looked up at him, wondering why he was suddenly silent.

'It's his way of seeking knowledge of whether or not you would agree to a treaty, Great King,' the old man said quietly. It was almost a whisper, as though he had suddenly divined some inner meaning.

The King looked at his advisor in surprise. 'A treaty? He has a funny way of asking if he seeks a treaty. Why is he threatening me with retaliation for things I haven't done, if he wants an alliance?'

Without the usual preambles of 'Great King' and 'Knower of All Things' Ethminhak said suddenly, 'If Omri were to ask for a treaty without testing your resolve, you might think it a sign of his growing weakness. We know that he has no money left in his treasury because of all his building work. So the knowledge is no stranger to us; we and all the kingdoms in the region know that he needs an alliance.

'Yet by posturing and threatening and puffing out his chest in pride, he's saying that if you are strong, I too am strong, and we together will be stronger than both of us are now. And if the two of us are together, then we will be mightier than Philistia, Assyria, Edom, Syria, and Babylonia, and all the kingdoms from the Euphrates to the Nile. That, Great King, is what Omri is saying.'

Ethbaal picked up the letter and glanced at it. Then he began to smile, and looked at Ethminhak. He nodded, and once again scrutinised the wording of the letter the ambassador from Israel had brought to the court. Ethminhak coughed and whispered in the King's ear. Ethbaal looked up and noticed Jezebel for the first time.

The King beamed a smile, much to the relief of the Princess, who now realised that she was not the cause of his anger.

'Ah, Jezebel, Princess and daughter. I've asked you here because the ambassador from Israel has arrived unaccompanied. He needs a companion for tonight's feast to the God Ra, in honour of the many Egyptians in our land. You will be his companion.'

Then the King, her father, looked back at the letter, still scrutinising it for hidden meanings and messages. But the look of relief on his face matched the feeling of relief in Jezebel's body as she realised that she had done no wrong.

The ambassador was an Israelite. She had never been companion to an Israelite before. She wondered what they were like.

His name was Bengeber. He was of the tribe of Asher, of the clan of Abimelech, of the family of Macheler. He could trace his family's lineage from the time of a man whom he called Jacob, one of the men in his religion who spoke directly with their God, Elohim who he also called Yahweh. This man, this Jacob, it appeared, had been a man who had lived in the land of Egypt with his family of brothers and his aged father and who had risen high in the service of the Pharaoh to become the second most important person in the land.

The ambassador was a tall man with black hair which had some greying within it, and an attractive smile, though he had a scar on his cheek which, he claimed, was from a battle he had fought in Moab, but which, after two cups of wine, he admitted was caused when he fell from his horse. He had three wives, all of whom he liked very much. He said this, Jezebel thought, because he wanted her to know that Israelites were men who didn't couple with women who weren't their wives and, even when they were on caravans to distant parts, or away from their homes for many days, never enjoyed the flesh of other women. And, he said pointedly, they never ever went to the temples of foreign gods, and never coupled with sacred prostitutes which the priests of Yahweh called an abomination in the sight of the Lord.

But that wasn't all that was strange about Ambassador Bengeber of Tirzah, son of Ahilud of the same town. During the banquet, he refused some of the dishes which had been prepared in his honour, dishes such as goat's eyes in lemon balm and milk stew, and the sweetbreads of pig in figs and yogurt. He said he could not eat meats and milk together and the flesh of the swine was forbidden to him.

And neither, to her complete surprise, did Bengeber eat the centrepiece of the table, stuffed loaf from the northern shores of Egypt which had been specially prepared in honour of the feast by a kitchenman who had recently joined the service of her father, the King.

'I cannot eat this for it contains meat mixed with cheese,' he told her.

'No!' Jezebel lied, because she was so keen for him to taste the delicious food. 'I made this myself, and there's no meat in it. Let me tell you how it's made. Our kitchenman and I made the Egyptian loaf from

74

flour which I sprinkled with water and vinegar and made into a paste; then I hollowed it out and put in ground pepper and honey and fresh leaves of mint and garlic and cucumber and fresh coriander which we obtain from the land of Philistia. Then it's filled up with salted cow's milk cheese. I cooled it with the ice which was brought in the early morning from the mountains. When it was all put together, I placed it in the ovens on a low light for most of the day, and it's now wonderful,' she said, adding, 'and it contains no meat.'

She looked at him earnestly, enthusiasm in her eyes which persuaded him to taste the Egyptian loaf. He ate morsels with his fingers, licked them, and then tore off another chunk, nodding in appreciation. He told her it was delicious. And she was pleased, even though she knew quite well that one of the ingredients was the meat of a lamb. But what he didn't know couldn't damage him. She particularly wanted him to eat it because the cook had said to her that the diced cucumber was a love potion when mixed with lamb's sweetbread.

But when she looked at him brushing the crumbs from his beard, she realised that she wasn't particularly attracted to him. So why, when he had made it perfectly clear to her that he was beyond her grasp, did Jezebel take conquering him as a challenge?

When he'd feasted, she pointed to the goat's meat in milk, urging him to taste it. But the Israelite smiled gently and told her, 'Unfortunately Lady, as I've explained to you, this is a prohibited meal for me. Anyway, I have feasted very well tonight, especially on the loaf from Egypt. The pomegranates and dates and figs and melons and breads are unsurpassed to my taste. Your table bends under the weight of your father's generosity and hospitality. Any more food and I shall not be able to walk back to my quarters.'

Jezebel sighed. She was suddenly frustrated and bored with the Israelite and wanted to be somewhere else. He was so stiff in his appearance and manner. He didn't relax her, and try as she might, she couldn't seem to get him to relax either. But her main reason for wanting to be rid of him was that she didn't yearn for his body, and so she would satisfy herself on a slave tonight.

A new man had been bought by the head of the household and it was rumoured that he came from beyond the mountains and the deserts, from far to the east where the Sun God rises after he has murdered the god of the moon each night. She hadn't seen this slave yet, but from the gossip of the maidservants, he wore a strange headdress and was tall and very strong with beautiful muscles and very dark smooth skin.

But it wasn't to be, because the banquet went on for a long time after the Egyptian loaf had been eaten. That night, when she returned to her bedchamber, her head aching from the long and boring speeches of the King her father to the ambassador on behalf of King Omri of Israel, and the ambassador to her father the King, and from one nation to another and speeches in favour of eternal harmony and other speeches in support of the gods of Phoenicia and on behalf of the Israelite god Elohim who is also known as Yahweh, she retired and went straight to sleep. Normally her servant would rub her body with a mixture of juniper oils, cinnabar and the essence of white lotus leaves. The fumes made her sleepy and she usually awoke feeling refreshed and happy. But tonight she was so exhausted that she ordered her maidservant away, and she fell on her divan and went straight to sleep.

She dreamed. She dreamed of the ambassador. Of walking with him beside the shore of the sea on a moonlit night. Of sitting with him on a blanket as the waves of the Eternal Sea gently lapped at their feet. She dreamed of how he lay back on the blanket and she fed him the meat of a cow, cooked with cloves and olives and capers. And he smiled at her. She dreamed of how he turned to his three wives looking on at the scene, and then he kissed her and fondled her breasts and made love to her. And in the height of his passion, he cried like a baby. And as he lay spent and exhausted on the blanket, his three wives clapping and nodding in approval, Jezebel heard herself say, 'Phoenicia conquers Israel'.

CHAPTER FOUR

TISHBE IN GILEAD

He had been home for not more than a week, returning exhausted from preaching in the towns of Judah, when the Almighty ordered him to leave again. Although he was weak and tired and thin from his seven months of wanderings, he knew that he had to obey the voice of Yahweh. Rizpah, his wife, had also lost the glow in her cheeks from their time on the road, but she was robust and he knew that she would quickly recover.

In the evening, when they'd eaten their fill, he gathered his children and his wife Rizpah around him, and told them the news.

'Last night in my bed, I heard the voice of the Lord Yahweh. The Almighty One, Blessed be He, came to me, and said: '*Elijah, do not rest in sloth and comfort with your wife and children, for there is much for you to do. You must leave your beloved home, and go into the towns and cities where my chosen people have turned their faces away from me and are worshipping false idols, where dancing and lewdness and lasciviousness are rife, and you must*

raise your voice against it so that all Israelites will
bow down to me. I am the Lord your God.'

Rizpah looked at him in shock. She had been resting for only a few days, had only touched and kissed her children for a few brief and glorious moments, and now he was going to demand that she follow him again on one of his wanderings. Seven months she had spent travelling the hills and valleys, the fields and woods. She hardly recognised her children when she returned – they had grown, and there was something in their manner which seemed to give them greater comfort in the neighbour they had lived with than in her, their own mother. She needed to spend much time with them, finding out how they had spent their previous seven months, what had happened, what injuries they had suffered ... she needed to be a mother again.

So how could she leave already? She was exhausted, and once again the children would grow up, unnoticed by her. She was becoming less a mother to her children than was the village neighbour who had taken in her orphans.

Elijah saw the shock in her face, and understood immediately what was wrong. He reached over and touched her hand, telling her, 'God said nothing about you following me, my wife. His words were for my ears, and his instructions were only for me to go to the towns of Judah and Israel, and even into Egypt to preach to the Jews there where they are said to worship the strange animal gods of that land. Yahweh has spoken. I must go. But you are a mother and must stay with our children ...'

Relief swept over her exhausted body and she felt tears welling up inside her. She loved her husband;

she even loved his love of Yahweh, and she prayed fervently that one day, the love he felt for Yahweh would spring up inside her and she would find the same inner exhilaration which she often saw in Elijah's face.

Rizpah looked at her husband and smiled, her lips betraying a silent prayer of thanks to the merciful Yahweh.

Elijah the Tishbite was a troubled man. These days, his head was full of fury, his ears full of the sounds of anger. He was a man riven by disparate and conflicting forces: by his love of his God Yahweh, and his hatred of the way in which the minions, the evil curs and hyenas who were in command of the land of Israel, were ruining the nation of the one true God; by his feelings of warmth and tenderness towards his wife and children, and his hatred of the way that the women of his nation and in other nations behaved, with their loose ways, their painted lips and their seductive walks.

He loved his children for their fear and reverence of Yahweh their God, yet he hated the way in which the children of his land were so easily seduced by forces which were opposed to everything that was good and right and proper. They turned away from the worship of Yahweh and they were so easily tempted by other pleasures, such as pleasures of the flesh and the sight of a woman's ankles. And the girls were no better, always giggling and laughing and whispering some crude silliness into their companions' ears.

He loved the worship of Yahweh in the Temple of Jerusalem, yet he hated the fact that he had to worship

Yahweh in the Temple of Samaria because God's nation had been split into two after Solomon died.

He loved the awe and majesty and decency of the religion of Moses and Aaron, and he hated the sacred prostitutes and idolatry of Moloch, El, Ba'al and Asherah, and all the other false gods which were a parody of the one true God, Yahweh, who had created the heavens and the earth and all the majesty which was in them.

Why was life so different today from when he was a boy? When he was growing up in the town of Tishbe in Gilead, he had played like every other child had played; but his father had ensured that his play was conducted and governed by worship and that his actions were always in the sight of Almighty God who governed all things. His father demanded that all play must be for the glorification of God; all play must be worshipful and righteous; no play must involve girls or nakedness or lewd thoughts. Any lewd thoughts were punishable by beating, and nor was there safety in failing to confess the lewd thoughts, because God saw into the hearts of all people, and God knew when lewd thoughts were coursing through a boy's mind, and the boy had to admit it to the father, or God's punishment would be a thousand thousand times worse than the punishment meted out by the father.

And any touching of those parts of the body which had to be hidden and which were only used to void waste or for the purpose of procreation was punishable by immersion for the time of daylight in the freezing mountain streams, even in the depth of winter.

Six times a year, Elijah and his father and brothers would journey from Tishbe through Bethel along the high road to Jerusalem where they would pray at the temple, paying their tithes to the priests and surrounding themselves with all those appurtenances which were of God, by God, and for God.

From his very earliest moments of remembrance, Elijah had come to know with absolute certainty that there was only one God, Yahweh, a God of great potency and majesty, creator of all things, yet a God who was to be worshipped and loved and feared all at the same time; for if the people loved Yahweh, then God would care for, and even love His chosen people, Israel, just as Yahweh had loved His servant Moses and the great kings, David and Solomon.

And so Elijah's youth became his adulthood as the boy grew up into a man who feared and loved God. As he played in godliness during his time as a child, so he lived his godliness as an adult. There was no such thing, for Elijah, as eating or breathing or walking or seeing outside of the sight of God. Every action he took, every thought he had was known by God, was directed by God, was created for him by God. He was God's man to do as the Almighty chose. That was his life and should he contravene the laws of God, so that would be his death, as it would be the death of those who turned their backs on the face of God.

And lately God's voice was becoming stronger and stronger within him, and when he talked to his wife Rizpah about whether or not she could hear the voices which were so clear in his head, she said that she couldn't. Sometimes she looked worried for him, but mostly she appeared to be happy that the Almighty God Yahweh had chosen her good and kind husband as His mouthpiece. She was Elijah's rod and his staff, she was his helper, the woman who journeyed with him when he went around preaching the word of God. She was the woman who made him his food, mended his shoes, patched his cloak when it was snagged, and bathed his feet when he had walked too far.

She was with him at his rising up and his lying down in the night; she gathered the people to listen to him, and was there with a drink when he had finished.

And now he had walked all the way to Samaria alone. Rizpah was back in Tishbe with their children, for Elijah knew that she was tired, and that this new call, this journey deep into the troubled lands which had turned their backs on Yahweh, would be difficult. He knew that if he commanded her to leave only a week after arriving back home, she would become ill on the journey, a burden to him, preventing him from doing God's work. Yes, he thought, it was right to leave her at home. This mission would be too soon for her. But not for him, for he had to obey the word of God.

The people saw him enter the city. Many of them who had heard him preach in the marketplace the previous year recognised him and greeted him with reverence. Some came up to him and gave him money for his food and journeys; for this, he blessed them in the name of Yahweh, and told them to turn their backs on false idols and to tell their neighbours to do the same.

Followed by a small and curious crowd, Elijah found his way to the temple of the city of Samaria, and walked in beyond the door to the inner courtyard. Involuntarily he shuddered as he walked upon the path. This was a mockery of the Temple of Yahweh in Jerusalem built by the great Solomon. This temple – he could hardly bring himself to call this building a temple – this structure was built by King Omri to appease the anger of the priests. Nor could he blame the priests for using this building, for the true believers in Yahweh must have somewhere to worship the Lord.

He looked up at the huge cedarwood gates and smiled as the chief priest, Jonathan, came out to greet him, kissing his cheeks and his hands.

'I heard you were returning. I'm so pleased to see my brother. But why do you return to Samaria? You were here preaching only last year.'

An acolyte came out and gave Elijah a glass of herb water.

'I am ordered by the Lord of Hosts to return and to preach His word. I don't know why He commanded me to return so soon, but who am I to question His bidding?'

Jonathan led him inside into the coolness of the vast building. There was still a smell of smoke in the air from the sacrifice of the previous night. Flies circled the altar hysterically. As he walked deeper into the building, the smell of roasted sacrifice reached his nose, and his hunger became insistent. Soon, he would eat well for the first time since he'd left home.

Elijah and Jonathan walked down the length of the building and turned into the inner sanctum, where the priests met to dress in their sacred raiment – the mantles and ephod, the upper garment which hid secret words; the headdresses and breastplate, or Hoshen, which contained a pouch for the sacred methods of divination; the Urim; and the Thummin. It was here that the priests prayed before a service. The chief priest motioned Elijah to a seat.

'I suspected that the Lord would speak to you and command you to return to us for another reason,' he said.

Elijah didn't understand.

'You haven't heard then …?'

Elijah shook his head.

'An ambassador left Israel a month ago. He travelled to the northern land of Phoenicia. There are rumours that he has gone on a secret mission. That he's there to arrange a marriage between the daughter of the King of Phoenicia and Ahab, the son of King Omri.'

Elijah looked at him in incomprehension. 'But that's not possible. In Phoenicia, they worship …'

'I know,' said Jonathan. 'And it appears that the particular daughter whom King Ethbaal is giving to our Prince Ahab is a young and wilful girl who is a devoted worshipper of one of their cursed goddesses. The girl's name is Jezebel. Her goddess is Asherah.'

Elijah felt himself suddenly become weak; was it exhaustion from the journey, or the evil news he'd just received?

'I must go to see Omri. I must tell him that Yahweh will never …'

'I've already been to Omri,' said the chief priest. 'He's told me that this treaty must be concluded for the safety of Israel, and that Jezebel will not be allowed to worship her gods and goddesses in public. He reminded me that many Israelites worship false gods in private.' Jonathan looked down at the floor, almost in shame. 'There's nothing he will do to prevent it.'

Elijah stood. He felt himself shaking with anger. Yes, he knew that many Israelites had turned their faces from Yahweh. But to have false gods in the palace ... no, that was something he would never allow.

'I am Elijah, Prophet of God,' he shouted at the startled chief priest, who drew back when he saw Elijah's eyes widen as though he were possessed. 'I am Elijah,' he shouted again. 'I will never allow this evil to happen! I will go south to the land of Judah and command the people to rise up and overthrow the House of Omri and all his sons and daughters. No Phoenician princess will ever marry into our land.'

Elijah stood on a rocky outcrop above the desert as the sun, which had spent its day beating down on the parched land as if it were a metalworker's furnace, slowly sank behind the buildings of Bethel. Despite the heat of the day, the people had come out to hear the words of the mystic, of a man who spoke with God and who knew God. Time after time, he had stood on this and other rocky outcrops throughout the lands of Israel and Judah, abandoning his children in order to obey the command of God which he heard so clearly in his head, and yet which could not be heard by other men. So many who should be faithful seemed to be deaf to the voice of the Lord. And deep in his heart, he knew that amongst them must be counted his beloved Rizpah.

Rizpah! What a wonderful and complex woman. Simple, honest, loving of her children, perfect in every way – a Sarah or Rachel or Leah – Elijah was as fortunate in his choice of wife as were the patriarchs Abraham, Isaac and Jacob. But he knew deep in his heart that the flame of God didn't burn as brightly in Rizpah as he ... or she ... would wish. She often seemed distracted from worship of Him, caring more for her family's needs than for spreading the holy commands.

Thank the Almighty, he thought, that the voice was strong in him. Often, especially in the early days, he'd fallen to his knees in fear, trembling with the awful noises within his head; and on many occasions recently, he'd cried aloud in the wilderness, asking God, 'Why me?' And for the sin of doubt, the Lord made His voice stronger and stronger.

Life was so hard being a prophet of Yahweh. He was an unmerciful God who demanded much of his servant Elijah, but the prophet knew that his reward would be eternal and that the trials and tribulations of this life were as nothing compared with the joys of sitting, close to Moses, for evermore at the feet of the Almighty.

And so Elijah had been ordered, and indeed he had made it his life, to go out and tell the people of their sins, warn them of the danger of their ways and order them to turn their hearts and minds back towards the face of God. But they were a stiff-necked people, and many of them were proud and unafraid of the countenance of the Lord. And worse, for even though many people of Israel had heard His word and had moved over to stand in the shadow which Elijah's body cast in the sun which God created, and who were in fury against King Omri and his court for the evil and the corruption which was in his temple, there were just as many in the villages throughout the land of Israel who had strayed from the path of Moses and Aaron. Elijah knew that although these foolish people continued to worship Yahweh, in their hearts they also sang praises to other gods, to false gods and to idols from Phoenicia, Moab, Edom and Philistia. And now he knew that an evil princess of a false goddess was coming to the land of Israel, to marry into the bosom of the ruling family. And he would travel to the land of Judah to raise the fury of the people.

Elijah looked at the crowd, restless now, and waiting eagerly to hear his words. He raised his wooden rod and held it in both hands, pointing in the distance to the temple of Bethel built by the accursed Jeroboam, son of Nebat the apostate, the evil doer who had conspired to split into two the land of the Hebrew people given by God to Moses as an inheritance. Now the nation was weakened because of the schism caused when the two proud men had split the one kingdom of God into two. Most of the tribes went with their inherited lands to Israel in the north, but two had stayed loyal to God as Judah of the south. Apostasy and immorality reigned in Israel of the north.

Jeroboam, evil man and cursed in the sight of God, had proclaimed himself the first king of the northern nation of Israel. It was he who had built the corrupt temple with its false idols in order to seduce the people and weaken their resolve.

More than any other, more even than King Omri, Elijah hated Jeroboam the most, for the festering pestilence of the two nations had started with him; in his reign began the evil undoing of the work of their forefather, Moses. Elijah's predecessor as prophet,

Ahijah the Shilonite, had accosted Jeroboam one day before the schism, before the split of one nation into two, had taken place. Ahijah, knowing what was in the proud mind of Jeroboam, took his coat from his shoulders and tore it into twelve pieces, pointing out the danger of his plan which would have made him lord and master over ten of the twelve tribes, warning him of the danger of tearing apart the land which was the birthright of the people of Israel. In fear, Jeroboam had fled to Egypt when Solomon the King realised what he was doing.

But on Solomon's death, Jeroboam had returned to Israel and so the revolt had started. Only Judah and Benjamin in the south had remained loyal to the word of Moses. In order to appease the people of the ten tribes of the north, Jeroboam had built a new centre of worship at Bethel, a temple which was a hideous parody of the real Temple of Solomon in Jerusalem. The false and vain King had even taken winged cherubim and other items from the temple and set them up in Bethel to be worshipped by the people as a sort of mockery of Yahweh.

Consideration of the two kingdoms, and how he could blend them together again, was always at the forefront of Elijah's mind. The key was getting rid of the House of King Omri and for the people to rise up and demand their reunion with their brothers and sisters in the land of the Almighty One, Yahweh, God. But even though he was a simple priest, Elijah was wise enough about the grand designs of countries to know that he couldn't put his plan into action until he had fomented more hatred in the people of the kingdom of Israel in the north. And that was what his life was directed towards, for the sake of Yahweh.

Elijah stood on the precipice, watching more and more people arrive. He had not yet begun to speak to the multitudes. He always held his wooden staff up high to call for peace and order and silence. It allowed him to reflect on his purpose, on the prostitution of the history of his nation. It allowed his anger to ferment and boil up like a stinking cauldron.

The hood of Elijah's robe shielded his eyes from the setting sun. The people became quiet and a hush fell upon the assembly as Elijah put down his staff, then raised it again and pointed to the temple.

Other young men were in their homes, enjoying their lives with their wives and children, working in fields during the day and then enjoying the pleasures of a family at night. Only a few times since their marriage had Elijah and Rizpah enjoyed the knowledge of each other as man and wife, even though they had been married for seven years.

Rizpah was a good woman. She understood Elijah's mission. When she travelled with him, she suffered the torments of the body's call for closeness and comfort, for just as at home he forbade them to be as husband and wife when they were on the road, travelling from town to town. For when they travelled, they were on God's mission, and even though God encouraged husbands and wives to be fruitful and multiply, Elijah was not like other men. He was a prophet, and his work demanded that he put aside the pleasures of the body. But like Rizpah his wife, he suffered in his ministrations throughout the length and breadth of the country where he trod.

Now he'd told her that she must remain alone in bed, unsatisfied in her own home, for the Lord had said that she could no longer travel with him, that this was his ministry and his alone.

When he'd parted and he'd kissed and blessed his children, Elijah walked with Rizpah beyond the fields. And he had said to her that even though their lives would be hard from this moment to the end, Almighty God would reward them in *Gan Eden*, the Garden of Paradise, and they would be reunited, just as Adam and Eve would be forgiven their sins and reconciled with the Almighty and reunited at the end of time.

Elijah sensed that the crowd was ready; he cleared his throat and began to speak.

'Listen to me, men and women of Bethel, of Tirzah, Shechem, Ramoth-Gilead, Jezreel and all the cities of Gilead, Amon, Judah and Israel. Listen to the voice of Elijah the prophet who speaks through his mouth with the words of the Almighty Yahweh, Blessed be He. Listen to my words for these are the words of the Almighty, your Lord who brought you out of the land of Egypt, out of the house of bondage and servitude, for He brought you out with a strong right arm and He slew the Egyptian host and made them nothing in the eyes of the world.

'Soon I will travel south from the land of Israel into the land of Judah and there I will cause the people to rise up in anger against your King Omri. For Omri will prostitute our land and make our land into a land of prostitutes.'

He heard the gasp of the people. They were used to his injunctions against their wickedness in worshipping false idols, but these accusations against the King were different. This was treason, and men had been put to death for inciting the people to rise up against their King.

'Soon, travelling south into Israel from the idol-worshipping land of Phoenicia in the north, will be a painted harlot, a woman whose lips are red, who dresses her hair in adornments and whose breasts smell of perfume. Vanity. All is vanity in Phoenicia. All is worship of Ba'al and Asherah and gods who demand the sacrifice of children. For this is what this harlot woman of Phoenicia will visit upon you. Soon all Israel will become like whores and prostitutes and men will sell their bodies to satisfy the evil lusts of idol worshippers and your wives and daughters will open themselves in fields and beside streams to any stranger who passes. And the land will be as though it were salted by a marauding enemy, as though it were stripped bare by a plague of locust.

'For Jezebel will destroy you all, she of the wicked ways. Jezebel will turn your wives into ways of idleness and your daughters into the ways of whores and harlots, and they will speak openly against you and refuse to do your bidding; she will make your sons lust after the flesh instead of working in the fields. Remember the name of Jezebel, for I curse her name today, and you will rue her name tomorrow.

'But why, people of Israel, is she coming? Because of you! Because you have danced in the black of night with evil idols and have worshipped unclean spirits. You have turned your faces away from the true path of Yahweh. You have been loose and lazy and immoral. You have become whores and idolators, like dogs scavenging in the field of hope, and your vain and evil King Omri knows of your wrongdoing and encourages it, for he and his descendants are cursed among all men. And to curse you further, he will marry his son Ahab to this foreign princess called Jezebel whom I curse among all nations.'

He paused for breath, and saw that they were white-faced in terror. Yes, he had shown them to themselves, and they were distraught. Now he would bring them back.

'But there is salvation at hand. It is here, in this land and everywhere that Yahweh's goodness and kindness and love of His people shines forth. For Yahweh will save us all from the evil of those who rule this land. For just as the Almighty smote the Egyptians in the time of Moses, so Omri will be spat upon by the nations of the world. He will be the vomit of a dog.

'But if you follow him, then Omri and his kin will lead you into a great undoing and they will cause pain and suffering and misery amongst you, and leprosy and plague will visit this accursed land while ever Omri and his family of dogs sit upon the throne and cause it to be separated from Judah in the south. But not if you return to the ways of the Lord and expel the idols from your homes, and instead go to the temple and cleanse yourselves and worship the one True God.

'For some it is too late, for Yahweh has already turned away from you. And unless you repent of your ways now, it may be too late for the entire nation; because when was the last time that the ministering waters of His goodness fell upon your land? Two seasons have you been in drought, for God is unhappy. You are doers of heathen things and worshippers and lovers of false idols and gods. But you are promised by God, the one true God, that you will be forgiven and rain will fall and crops will grow and children will be born whole and women will be fertile and cows will have issue and your enemy will be stopped at your borders if you return to the path of God. My people, return to Yahweh now, before it's too late and we are all doomed.'

Elijah looked at the assembled crowd. There were more today than yesterday, but there were still not enough. Tomorrow he would go into the city of Bethel and risk arrest and death at the hands of Omri, for the King hated him and all like him, as did the King's son, Ahab, himself a dissolute, drunkard man and a womaniser who had sinned greatly in the eyes of the Lord. And if he lived beyond tomorrow, he would continue his journeys from the north of Israel through to the southern border with Judah, and he would continue to preach against the House of Omri until it was no more. And he would stop this Princess Jezebel from coming to Israel. Even if he were to be killed for his actions.

It was a hot day, hotter than yesterday. And by the look of anger in the deep blue sky, unrelieved by white clouds, tomorrow would be just as hot. Neither Asherah nor her husband, son and consort Ba'al were listening to the prayers of the people of Phoenicia, nor to those of Jezebel. And neither were they listening to the prayers of her father, Ethbaal, who had spilled his seed many times on the ground and given sacrifices to the gods. They remained deaf, for still the rains from Egypt and the flooding of the Nile had not relieved their northern lands.

Jezebel had swum twice in the tepid waters of

the Eternal Sea, and when she emerged, her maidservants had washed her body with waters and perfumes. It was cooling and refreshing, but not for long. Only a short time afterwards, even by the time the towel had finished drying her feet, her face was hot again and so was her body. And when she was hot, and especially when her handmaidens were drying her breasts and her stomach, it was at moments like these that her body began to ache for the feel of a man. Now that the Israelite ambassador had returned home, and no other ambassadors or emissaries were expected, the palace was quiet and dull. And worse, the townspeople weren't fun any more because they were all so worried about their crops dying. The King's granaries and oil stores had been half emptied, and if the drought continued and the food supplies were completely used up, then nobody would have anything. If the crops died, there would be no food in the marketplaces. People would go hungry, and children and the elderly would begin to die. But she knew from the drought seven years earlier, that the death of people wasn't the worst thing which could happen to the land of Phoenicia.

It all began innocently enough. When there was no food because of the failure of the crops, her father would open his granaries and sell food to the people. That gave them grain to make bread; but people weren't always satisfied with bread, and they began to steal chickens and goats and sheep from farmers, and take them into the forests to kill them.

Farmers and livestock owners who lost their animals began to murder those who stole from them. And when the granaries were completely empty, Jezebel's father the King would have to impose an additional tax on the people so that he could send his captains to buy food from other countries and prevent starvation. Then there would be no money for the people to buy pots and pans and jewellery and charcoal and skins and everything else. Which meant that the potters and the craftsmen went without. Their families became hungry. And so it went on. It was a miserable time when there was drought.

Jezebel was lying in a field between the city gates and the sea, staring up at the insects wheeling in circles around her head. Her thoughts flew from the coming misery of the land to her body. She felt an ant crawl on her skin and lifted her arm to take a closer look. Ants were funny things. Their bodies seemed to be divided into three parts, each part working in unison. There was a large head, a middle part and then a big end part joined to the middle by a slender waist. In many ways its roundness and slenderness reminded her of a woman.

She flicked it off with her fingernail. It was the most exciting thing that had happened to her since her last swim. She longed for some real excitement. At least when the Israelite ambassador had arrived she had used her womanly guile to have a brief flirtation with him when the feast had finished. That was fun. But since then, nothing at all had happened in her life. She had woken, swum, gone to see some of the tradesmen and artisans, said goodbye to a caravan that was travelling to Damascus, ridden a donkey along the seashore, played games of war with two of her brothers and sisters, eaten and slept. In the height of summer there was little else to do.

They said that the summer rains came to Phoenicia

because the snow in the mountains of Africa, south of Egypt in a country called Ethiopia, melted in the heat. The meltwater travelled down the hillsides in huge cascades, and collected at the foot of the mountains where it became the Nile River, sacred of the Egyptians. For some reason the rain clouds above Phoenicia always rose when the Nile flooded with the meltwater from the snows. The clouds drifted north over the Eternal Sea, and fell over the lands of Judah, Israel and Phoenicia. Or so the wise men of the court told her. One day, she decided, she would travel to the lands of the south and visit Egypt. There, she determined to see for herself the snows of the mountains melting. She would look at the cascades plummeting down the sides of mountains. She would bathe in the icy waters of the upper regions which gave water to the river of Egypt. One day.

But now it was summer, and the rains had not yet come. People fell into a lethargy in the summer, and a torpor in a summer drought, as though the god of sleep was suddenly impelled towards daytime worship.

And then, just when her mind was idling and she was about to drift into a midday sleep, Jezebel heard the creaking of a cart. She looked up through the heat haze of the day, through the long grass in which she was lying, her head just poking above the top of the grass. In the distance a woodcutter was pushing his cart uphill towards the palace kitchen. Poor boy, she thought. If only he were richer, he could have used a horse or a donkey to pull his cart. Instead he was the donkey. But then she looked closer. He was a young man, her age, seventeen, maybe eighteen years old. His body was straining and sweating in the heat but his muscles were strong and beautifully

97

defined, his skin was glistening and his perspiration held his thin cotton robes closely to his chest.

The more she looked at the boy, the more interested she became in him. She hadn't seen him before. One of her servants the other day had told her that because of the drought, the eldest son of one of the charcoal burners in a small village two days from the city had been sent to stay with his uncle in the city to earn extra money. But she didn't know for certain whether or not this was the boy. If it was, he could stay for as long as he wanted. The closer she examined him, the more interested she was, especially when she looked at his straining legs and his taut buttocks. The one thing that Jezebel liked about a man was taut buttocks. She could drive her fingernails into them when he was thrusting inside her, and she could squeeze them and hold their muscles firm in her hands ... her lips felt dry in anticipation.

He had black, curly tousled hair and a face which wasn't unattractive, already with a dark growth of beard masking his cheeks. But it was his legs which she found most interesting. No. That wasn't quite true. It was also his arms. They were powerful arms, arms which could hold her in a firm embrace while she struggled to get free and on top of him ...

She sat up, still obscured by the grass and the trees so he didn't notice her. But she could now see him clearly as his cart trundled towards her, climbing the hill towards the palace gates and the kitchen. How on earth was he going to have the strength to push the cart uphill, groaning and laden down with chopped wood for the kitchen fires?

And then the boy's forward momentum seemed to slow as the cart tipped slightly uphill at the long road which led up towards the gate. It was a steep hill and even she, a young and healthy woman, sometimes felt the exertion as she climbed towards her home. The boy stopped the cart. Jezebel felt disappointed. She had hoped he would have the strength to push it, and then she saw that instead of pushing, he wheeled the cart around so that he was now the real donkey and he was pulling it. He took a strap from the back of the cart and tied it from one of the cart's handles around his head to the other handle. And then, with the strap strained around his forehead, the boy pulled, and she could feel the strain as the cart slowly and painfully began to move up the hill. Now she stood in awe and wonder at the young man's strength. By the God Ba'al and the Goddess Asherah, this boy-man was strong, unbelievably strong! The cart must have weighed as much as ten men, yet even though he was straining and his feet were slipping, he was still managing to move the cart forward.

And then a thought came to her, spreading from her groin to her mind. She would have this boy. She would know him. She would know him now. It was the excitement which she craved.

She stood suddenly to the surprise of her servants and ran out of the field and quickly along the road and then up towards the palace. He was only a quarter of the way up the hill when she met him. She stood close to him, and saw him covered in the sweat of labour ... but what she saw most especially was his strong and muscular body.

'You are the woodcutter who has just come to the city?' she asked imperiously. His face was etched in strain and stress, the strap biting into his forehead.

He could hardly turn. His mouth was set like stone, his teeth clenched in what he was doing.

'Yes,' he hissed.

'Stop taking that to the kitchens. It's wanted by the sea for a sacrifice.'

Painfully and slowly, he turned his head towards her. 'But ...'

'Do what I tell you,' she said. 'I am Jezebel. I am a Princess of the royal blood. You will follow me.'

The boy carefully turned and released his grip on the strap, grasping instead the handles and being impelled down the hill as the cart, suddenly released from its uphill walk, nearly ran away from him to the very bottom where the boy used all his strength to stop it from going further off the road and spilling its load into the grass verge.

Jezebel walked quickly after him. 'Follow me,' she said and walked in front of him. She could hear the wheels of the cart rolling along the level road behind her and she came in sight of the rampart where sacrifices of animals were carried out and a small altar was built for the gods of the air and the sea.

'Take the cart into the fields and unload it over there, ready for tonight's sacrifice,' she said.

Diffidently, almost unwillingly, the boy mumbled, 'But my uncle told me to take it nowhere but ...'

'And I am telling you now,' said Jezebel. 'You will do what the Princess of the royal blood says and you will do it immediately or I will have you punished.'

The boy knew instantly that there was no argument. He spent much time unloading the wood and stacked it neatly where he was told in the field. Jezebel enjoyed watching his beautiful body straining and tiring with the weight of the wood. And she began to feel guilty for playing a silly trick on this innocent peasant.

'You are a good man,' she told him. 'When you've finished, I shall reward you with a purse of money. And I shall send to your family a cart loaded with meats and cheeses and eggs and honey. There, isn't that nice?' she asked.

He looked at her, but was utterly confused. So he continued with his work. By the time he had finished, he was sweating profusely, body water pouring off his forehead, down his neck and off his chest in tiny rivulets. Jezebel had watched his every movement and each one was more and more erotic. In some ways he was as delicate as one of the temple dancers, lithe and beautiful and desirable. In other ways he was like a wrestler who used his balance and strength to overcome opponents. And beneath his sweat, the boy was beautiful. An adorable looking wild peasant with rough crude hands and achingly strong muscles. When he was close to her, she could hardly breathe in her excitement.

'Go for a swim in the sea,' she said. 'Wash yourself and then return.'

The boy, exhausted and grateful that his work was over, walked the fifty paces to the sea and there he washed himself and swam in the waves before he returned to her, dripping wet, his tunic sticking to his body.

'I lied to you,' said Jezebel. 'I wanted to see if you would believe me. The wood is required up there,' she said pointing to the palace gate inside which were the kitchens. 'Now you will have to load it all up again and you will be punished for being late.'

The young man looked at her in disbelief. 'But ...' he mumbled.

'Or,' said the Princess, 'I can get four of the guards to load it and pull the cart up and it will be delivered on time, and there will be no punishment for you either from my father the King, or your uncle the woodcutter.'

The boy frowned. He was frightened of this powerful person. He had never met a woman like this. She was different from his mother and sisters and the other girls from his village. He didn't understand what she was doing or why she was doing it.

'Go down on your knees and beg me to get my servants to help you.'

The boy looked as though he had just been smacked across the face by his father, but not knowing what to do, he fell to his knees.

'Kiss my feet,' she said.

He was now in her thrall, and so he bent down and kissed her feet.

'Now take off your clothes.'

He stood and looked at her strangely. 'But ...'

'Do what I tell you. Take off your clothes.'

'I can't. I must not. My mother ...'

'I can have you beheaded instantly if you disobey me.'

'But my father also said ...'

'I am your god. I'm your Princess. I'm your father and your mother. I'm your ruler. Take off your clothes now or you will die.'

She knew she was being horribly cruel to such an innocent, and was desperately trying not to laugh, especially when she saw the boy's eyes widen in shock. Wisdom and kindness told her to stop it immediately and tell him she'd been joking; but her sense of mischief prevented her and she wanted to see how far she could go. But should she relieve him of his misery and tell him the truth? That she was only having fun with him? No, she would have a few additional moments of amusement and then relieve him … in more ways than one.

The boy swallowed and he untied his tunic and took it off. He stood there in the light of the hot sun which made his body glisten. He was wonderfully naked except for his loin wrap.

'Everything,' she said, pointing down to his groin. Now his eyes bulged like white shells on the shore. She was on the verge of bursting out in loud laughter, and bit the inside of her lip to prevent the wonders of what she was doing from ending.

The boy looked as though every misery on earth was suddenly at his feet. He gazed up at the sky so that she might not see the look of shame on his face. Then he undid the knot at his hip and let his loin wrap slip to the ground. He stood there naked. Completely naked. His manhood was flaccid in the fear that he now felt. He was even more beautiful out of the clothes than he was clothed. He was strong; his stomach was flat and firm. His chest was muscular. His legs were those of a messenger.

'Lie down in the grass, boy. You are about to make me very happy.'

He did as his Princess commanded him, but nothing he could do made her happy. She slipped off her wrap and stood there naked. She positioned herself on top of him, underneath him, beside him, but all to no avail. No matter what she did to him, with him or for him, he simply lay there, rigid with fear. But rigid with nothing else. She thought back to her first experience with the old friend of her parents – eventually she'd made him happy when she visited his room on her own and had encouraged his growth and manhood – but on the day of her becoming a woman, his place had been taken by a young and virile priest.

This young woodcutter's lack of ability surprised her. His penis remained small and flaccid, insignificant. The youth lay on the ground staring up into the canopy of the trees, the whites of his eyes like those of a hunted animal. He was petrified! It was obvious that he had never known a sophisticated woman of the city before; that all of his coupling had been with crude and unattractive girls from the countryside. So she used her hands, her mouth, and every other part of her body to excite him, to increase the capacity of his body to pleasure her, but he was so frightened and tense, it was like attempting to couple with a tree.

Eventually, frustrated and bored, she asked, 'Why are you so frightened of me?'

For the first time since he'd lain down, he looked at her. He shook his head imperceptibly.

'You don't know, do you? Why can't you relax and enjoy me? Don't you think I'm beautiful? Aren't I the most beautiful girl you've ever seen?' She drew back from him so that his eyes could take in her whole naked body. She cupped her breasts seductively. 'Isn't my body the stuff of your dreams?'

He nodded imperceptibly.

'Can't you speak?'

Hoarsely, he told her, 'You're beautiful. I've never seen … never touched …' And then he lapsed into silence, looking away from her and upwards into the canopy of trees.

'Then why won't your penis stiffen? You're the first boy who hasn't stiffened when he's touched me. Is it me?' she asked gently, now as concerned for the young man as she was for her own satisfaction.

'No,' he said. 'But where I come from, women don't ...'

And then she realised with a shock that the youth was a virgin. It hadn't occurred to her that this could be a possibility. In the royal household, and especially in the city, the moment a boy reached his thirteenth birthday, his parents immediately introduced him to the Temple of the Sacred Prostitutes for the prostitutes would teach him everything he needed to know about sex. Some boys stayed in the quarters of the prostitutes for a night, some for a week, but in the end, when the prostitutes were satisfied that the boy knew enough, they would deliver him back to his parents' house with gifts of seeds and flowers and pots of honey and statues of the God Ba'al in a state of coupling with the Goddess Asherah. It had never occurred to Jezebel that some boys and girls in her country weren't introduced to the joys of the body by prostitutes. And to find a boy who was already a young man, especially one who had the body of a god, who had never known the pleasures of sex was astounding.

Jezebel looked at the youth, and said, 'You need to learn about women. I'm going to take you to the Temple of the Sacred Prostitutes right now so that they can teach you what you need to know.'

The young man looked at her again, his eyes boring into hers. 'The temple? But I have no money for that ...'

'You are a guest of a Princess. You need no money. What you need is lessons.'

She stood, dressed again in her summer robes, and the boy sprang up beside her grabbing his clothes.

'Come. Walk with me to the Temple of the Sacred Prostitutes, and I'll introduce you to my friend.'

'My cart?' he said.

Jezebel told him that she would ensure it was safe until his return. She led him up from the road which ran at the base of the hill on which the city of Sidon had been built and through the gates of the Passageway of the Cooks. As they passed through the gateway, the guards came to attention in the presence of the Princess.

She said to one of them, 'At the bottom of the hill in the field is this young man's cart with wood piled on the ground. Go down and put the wood back, and bring the cart up here. Take it to the kitchens, and return the cart to this gate.' The guard saluted to show he'd understood, and Jezebel and the boy walked into the city; he was astounded by her ability to command men to do her will. Was this the power of a queen? he wondered.

Further up the hill, the narrow city streets opened out into the first of four vast public spaces before the palace. These spaces were used for markets, discussions, victory parades, games and contests, as well as for the trial and punishment of criminals. The closer to the palace, the more the square was valued for its authority.

As the boy – Jezebel still didn't know his name, nor was she particularly interested – walked beside her, he became increasingly awestruck. He had only ever been through the gates as far as the Passageway of the Cooks. Once, when the load was light and he finished unpacking early, he had crept to the corner and been amazed by the way in which there were a multiplicity of streets and small braziers high on buildings (which

106

he was later told were lit at night to illuminate the streets for safety and comfort), and crowds and crowds of people. In the village where he lived near the sister city of Tyre with his parents and five brothers and sisters, there were almost never people who walked around in the middle of the day. And the idea of people walking out of their houses after dark was something which he couldn't comprehend. How could they see where they were going? Did the fires on the tops of buildings provide enough light?

But never had the boy been deeper inside the city than the Passageway of the Cooks. Neither had his parents, nor any other member of his family, nor any of his neighbours, even though his village was two days' walk from the city. He stared wide-eyed at the surroundings. People were everywhere, wearing robes the colours of which he had only ever seen in the sky or in the bushes where he lived. Robes which carried the colours of flowers or the heads of crops which the farmers grew in their fields. A confusion of colours, blending one into the other. And the patterns. How did they put the patterns into the garments, he wondered.

He couldn't wait to return home and tell his parents and brothers and sisters of the sights he was seeing. But then he looked down at his own clothes, and suddenly felt dull and awkward. His tunic was made of rough flax and string held the ends together. Yet the men and women who walked nonchalantly through the streets wore clothes which looked like the plumage of birds – brilliant reds, greens, blues, oranges and yellows; and not just all over, but in patches and swirls and lines which zigzagged across the fabric, and variegated lines like the leaves of bushes; lines which seemed to travel up and down a garment. And the robes and tunics which the people wore were fringed with cloth of different colours, or had tassels on them similar to some of the tassels he'd seen on the backs of camels travelling past his village in a caravan.

The city was noisy, with the shouts of men and women and children, and the barking of dogs and the belching of camels seeming to come from all sides of him. He looked to see where some of the noises were coming from, but his sight was obscured by the corners of buildings. But what shocked him most was the light. It seemed somehow to be dusty; like the light above a field of corn in the spring when winds blew the dust of the flowers into the air. Yet there were no crops or flowers here. Only people. But when he looked to the other side of the square, or up into the sky, the air seemed clouded. Dull. How could this happen, he wondered. He'd seen something like this last year when a desert wind blew from the east. Then he couldn't see the next houses in the village. But here, there was no wind; here there was no howling painful grains of sand blowing into his eyes and nose. Here the wind was quiet, and all that there was were people and these buildings ... so how could the air be full of dust? He would ask his uncle when he returned to his home.

And then, for the first time since following the Princess into the city, he stopped looking at the crowds of people, and started to look at the buildings. Now that he was in the square and could see further than the narrow confines of a passageway or a road, he was able to see the buildings properly. And he was staggered, so surprised, so overwhelmed, that he nearly stopped walking.

In his village, the buildings were low. A central door, and four walls which supported a roof. But here, the buildings seemed to rise and rise into the very sky itself. It was as though the buildings were built one on top of the other. The roof of one was the floor of the other. But how? How did they build buildings like that? Didn't ... wouldn't ... couldn't the people ...? He wondered why the people on top didn't fall upon the people down below, as he had once fallen out of a tree from a branch which overhung his father's house. He had damaged the roof thatch and was forced by his father to repair the mess.

'Come on,' said Jezebel sharply as the boy was falling behind her, dawdling along as though he'd never been to a city before.

She turned into the Street of the Priestesses, and came in sight of the temple where the sacred prostitutes lived and worked. It was their job to have sex with the King and other members of royal blood to ensure that the crops were fertile the following season, and also to have sex with any other man who paid for their services. The more sex they had on the sacred stone of Asherah and the more male seed which spilled onto the stone, the greater the chance of there being rain and abundant crops in the future.

And their secondary role, though just as important, was the reason that she was taking this young man who was so urgently in need of their lessons. Only the other month, she had joined her mother and father when they took the son of one of the rich merchants of the town into the prostitutes for them to teach him all about women. When the boy first began to sprout hair around his penis, and when his voice became deeper and lower, his mother and father came to the palace and asked the King and Queen for permission to take him to the temple for the prostitutes to teach him everything he would need to know to enable him to marry well: where to put his penis, what to do with his hands and lips, which parts of a woman's body best responded to touch and feel and rubbing. Normally it cost the parents a month's tithe to the temple, but because this family supported the King with money for building, he was allowed free access to the temple.

Jezebel slowed down and waited for the woodcutter, who had obviously never been shown what to do by any of the people of his village, and who would now be taught by the priestesses. So who was it that taught young men who lived in the villages of her country what to do when they needed to learn about sex? She determined to find out.

And for now, Jezebel would pay for this boy's education, and instruct him to return to her the following day, so that she could reap a return on her investment. And she would talk to her father about how boys in the country were educated about women and sex. Knowing her father, he would joke that all country boys had to do was to watch a bull and a cow and they would know all they had to know. But that wasn't the point. Jezebel felt sorry for country boys. And country girls. Their life was hard and primitive enough. She determined to do something to alleviate their condition.

CHAPTER FIVE

Furious beyond words, shaking with an anger which he had only rarely felt during his life, Prince Ahab, heir presumptive to the throne of Israel, was held down by invisible hands and prevented from standing and drawing his sword.

The man standing at the foot of the dais knew but didn't care that his life was endangered, for God was standing with him as God had stood beside Moses before the fury of the pharaoh. And his courage didn't desert him, not even for an instant. Instead, the visible fury of the arrogant young man impelled Elijah to even greater heights of rhetoric. For Elijah knew that the moment the young man lost control of his reason, and stood to threaten the prophet, his father Omri would command him to remain seated. And if he didn't, if the King lost control of his son and the Prince's sword cleaved Elijah's body, all would still be well because then the people of Israel would rise up in fury and overthrow the House of Omri and the divided kingdoms would be reunited, and Yahweh's will would be done.

And so the prophet continued to point his accusing finger at the King and all Israel. 'And for how long, Omri, do you believe that you can live like a whore in the brothel which is your country Israel, and in the whorehouse which is your capital Samaria, without paying the price demanded of any loose and wanton man who abandons the ways of the Lord? How long, Omri ...' He fixed his stern gaze on the young man seated near his father, '... And you, Ahab, how long can you continue to defile your temple with graven idols and images?

'Is this what Israel has become? Are we to begin again the practice of murdering children to appease the evil God Moloch? Are we to have sacred prostitutes defiling the temple as they do in the harlot nations of Philistia and Phoenicia? Are we to have sodomites as they had in Judah before the great King Asa thrust them onto the dung heap of Jerusalem?

'I warn you, Omri, defy the ways of the Lord for another day, and it is a day which will hasten your end ...'

But before Elijah could continue any further, Ahab released himself from the restraint of Omri, and with a shout of anger and hatred sprang up from his subordinate chair, a position which, for this confrontation with the prophet, had been placed just behind and lower than that of his father the King. Omri looked up in shock and distress at his son, who stood shaking as though in a fit. This outburst from the House of Omri was precisely what he had commanded Ahab not to do.

It was all the young man could tolerate. Up till now, he had obeyed his father and restrained himself from standing and killing the man, but Ahab suddenly shocked the court when he paced towards Elijah and shouted in the man's face, 'And how much

112

longer, Elijah, do my father and I have to suffer your insolence and your meddling and treasonous ways? What you have said would be death for any other citizen of this land.

'Now listen to *my* voice, Elijah, because it might be the last voice you hear before you go to God and speak with Him directly, for soon I'm going to kill you. Listen carefully to me. If you ever come back into our lands and stir the people to revolt, if you ever rouse the people to complain against their Lord and King, if you even set foot on any rock or road, or bend one blade of grass or eat one grape from the land of Israel after your banishment, your life will be forfeit ...'

Elijah, anticipating the onslaught and completely unbowed by its vehemence, suddenly stretched out his arm, pointed his finger towards Ahab's heart and boomed, 'Stop! Silence! Arrogant boy! Obey the commands of your father the King. I am a prophet of the one true God. I am ordained, anointed with the holy oil. Do not dare to raise your voice to me or you and your house will be struck down by ten plagues and buried underneath fire and brimstone like Sodom and Gomorrah.

'Foolish and intemperate boy! I know that you have been ordered to remain quiet in my presence. Sit like a puppy while your father the King and I discuss matters of which you have no understanding.'

Uncontrollable anger impelled forces inside him, and Ahab reached down to unsheath his sword. Never in all his days had anyone spoken to a Prince of the royal blood and heir to the throne of Israel like this. Never. And no matter who Elijah was, no matter what the consequences, the prophet would pay for the insult with his life. Ahab now completely unsheathed his sword, and strode forward like a lion, holding it aloft, about to bring it smashing down on Elijah's skull, splitting him from top to bottom, side to side.

But King Omri stood quickly and placed himself between the Prince and the prophet, barring the young man from his potentially catastrophic move. He turned to his son and shouted, 'Sit! Immediately! You will never raise your sword against a man who speaks with the voice of the Almighty God.'

Father and son looked at each other, the younger man's fury not abating. Now he was insulted before the entire court by his very own father. But to strike the King, even if he was successor to the throne, was treason punishable by death, and not even he could avoid the penalty which would be carried out by the palace guard instantly and without a moment's thought. Indeed, in the background, he heard the palace guard beginning to draw their swords. It was a confrontation he couldn't win.

But for long moments, Ahab stood there breathing deeply and trying to control his fury, sword raised, only his father preventing him from marching forward to his own destruction. It was an evil stand-off between father and son, and Elijah, frightened and mumbling the name of the Lord, attempted to control his own emotions and looked on in eager anticipation of what would happen. Although terrified of the Prince's sword, the prophet's heart was rejoicing. It was precisely what he'd come to the court to do ... to drive a wedge between the cold-hearted but responsible father and the high-handed and tempestuous son.

The younger man, the Prince of the court, slowly returned his sword to its scabbard, as did the relieved guard. Still with fury in his eyes, he turned, but instead of sitting back in his subordinate chair, he strode off the dais and the crowded court parted to allow him to leave the throne room.

All of the court's eyes followed him, but before he walked out of the room, he stopped for a moment, turned and shouted, 'Be warned, Elijah. My father cannot live forever, and when he dies, then guard yourself very well. For on some dark night, on some dark highway, someone will forget that you are a prophet of God, and will cleave you from top to bottom with a sword. And then your body will be eaten by dogs, ants will eat your innards and your bones will bleach in the sun.'

And with the final victory song, Prince Ahab strode away back to his chambers, leaving the throne room quiet. Nobody dared move or cough or clear their throats. There were only two people in the crowded room who would make the next move, King Omri or the voice of God, Elijah, the mystic and prophet.

It was Omri who broke the silence. Calmly, to show the court that he was still in control and command, despite his wayward and impulsive son, Omri sat and said softly, 'Elijah. Do you see what you do? You divide house from house, son from father, brother from brother. Can you not see the division you cause with your wild accusations and your intemperate ways? The land of God was divided in two before our time; now you seek to divide us further!

'You are a man of God. Yahweh surely doesn't want the chosen people of Israel to fight amongst each other. Why can't you accept that the land of Israel is strong and the people are happy and rich beyond measure? Why can't you understand that one nation has become two and as allies are richer than before ...?'

'Richer? Richer, Omri? Rich by whose measure? Is a man rich who has much money but dies the following day? Is a man rich who has land but whose sons refuse to work the land because they are all seeking the pleasures of the flesh and the land lies fallow and useless? Is this the richness of which you speak, Omri, for if it is, then to me you speak not of richness, but of dire poverty and misery. Israel will never be rich and loved by Yahweh until it is reunited forevermore with Judah.

'Richness comes from God. *Is* God. It is the love and the fear of God. A man can have nothing but the clothes which cover his back, yet be rich beyond measure if he is in the sight of God. You can dress in fineries and yet be poorer than the poorest leper because your eyes are closed to the sight of the Almighty One. And the poorest leper of Israel is richer than the King of Phoenicia because Yahweh is with us.

'You and your people will only be rich, King Omri, if you come back to the worship of the one true and Almighty God. If you cleanse the Temples of Bethel and Shechem and Samaria. If you remove from them the hideous idols and winged cherubim which are an abomination in the eyes of the Lord. And if you go to the King of Judah on your bended knee and ask him to forgive you and those who came before you and reunite the kingdoms of Israel and Judah, as was ordained by Moses the Lawgiver.'

Omri shook his head. He hadn't wanted this audience. He had known precisely what the prophet would say if he gave him the opportunity. Elijah had said it a hundred, a thousand, times in every city and in every town and in every village throughout the land of Israel. And he'd been screaming imprecations and dire threats against the land of Israel from over the border in nearby Judah, much to the delight and approval of old King Asa.

Omri shuddered when he thought of his brother king in the southern nation of Judah. Asa was a fearsome monarch, and was inspired to new and religious heights by Elijah and other prophets who promised him everlasting peace and love in the sight of God if he cleansed the temple in Jerusalem of false gods. And he'd done it with a vengeance.

First of all he had marched down to the temple in the middle of a service and had picked up and broken an idol of the Goddess Asherah made by Queen Maacha, the King's very own mother. Yet despite his closeness to his mother, the King's action was taken as a mighty insult which had nearly caused a war within the country because Maacha was of Aramaean descent and was of the royal blood. Then King Asa, encouraged by the priests of God and the prophets of Yahweh, had purged the temple of all other idols and symbols of worship of all gods other than Yahweh himself. And not content with smashing and expunging the idols, he had even marched down to the quarters of the *qedeshim*, the sacred male prostitutes, consecrated men, and kicked them and beaten them and thrown them out onto the streets to be spat upon and ridiculed by the priests and prophets. It was a day of greatness for Elijah and the

117

other priests of Yahweh. Omri had heard of their rejoicing.

But the last thing that the King needed or wanted at this moment in time was an audience with a fanatic and stiff-backed man of God. However, he had no choice, because his spies had told him that with the drought and the fear of famine in the land, there was a mood of revolt among the people, and that unless he came to terms with Elijah, his very authority as King might be undermined. Nor was Elijah's murder a possibility, for that would mean a war with Judah, and Philistia and Judah would form an alliance and Israel would be defeated.

For some reason, despite the peace and wealth in the land of Israel, Elijah had convinced the people of the villages that the way of the Lord Yahweh was richer than the way in which Omri governed the country. If Elijah's words were believed in the cities, then there would be a full-scale revolt. Of course, the King could easily put it down, but it would show him as a weak king, and other kings from nearby and adjoining nations would look keenly at the internal dissent and plot and plan an attack. Even though every country was suffering the failure of the rains, Israel was in a better position than most to survive; but there were still strong lands and strong armies which would love to take advantage of Omri's problems.

And right at this moment, he was beset by problems. Even without Elijah's prophesying, war was brewing on his northern border with Syria. Assyria wanted a union with him, but that in itself was a problem because the very act of signing a treaty would be a source of threat and could precipitate a war; Asa in the south was echoing the words of the prophets and declaring his nation to be run by and for God. He was becoming fanatical enough to go to war against Israel in the north to cleanse the land of other forms of worship – worship which was demanded by the people of the countryside.

And as though that was not enough, there were rumours coming to him that Egypt was again on the march, and that would compel Moab and Edom to join forces. Should he join with them and attempt to defeat the mighty, and for so long sleeping Egypt? Or should he not tempt fate and take no part? Should he join as an ally to Egypt and attack Moab and Edom? Would that cause Syria to attack? Problems. His life was beset by problems.

Sensing his master's rising concern and anger, his principal advisor leaned forward and whispered into his ear, 'Remember, Majesty, that it is Elijah's intent to unite the two kingdoms of Israel and Judah. Show weakness and you will aid him in his mission.'

Omri turned and hissed, 'I don't need to be reminded of that by you.'

Elijah knew that he was risking death at the hands of either the father or the son, but he also knew that at this pivotal moment, with a drought in the land and the people soon to suffer from hunger, Yahweh had chosen him to unite the divided lands. All he could think about was cleansing the temples of Israel and returning the land to the exclusive worship of Yahweh, as though this would cower all the rival nations into quiescence.

Omri looked up and saw that the prophet was staring at him in contempt. 'How can you, Omri, control your country if you cannot control your son? How can you stop the people rising up in support of

Ba'al and Asherah and other false gods and overthrowing you and your kin, and befouling the land which Moses the Lawgiver willed to us through the hand of Almighty God himself? Let me tell you, Omri, what will happen if you fail to heed my words ...'

And he did. For much of the morning, Elijah didn't stop telling him of the evils which would occur unless Omri did precisely what Elijah told him. And he continued talking until Omri's head was bursting and all he wanted to do was to be surrounded by silence.

'He, not Yahweh, nor Asherah, nor Ba'al, nor El, nor Moloch, nor all the other gods put together, but he, Elijah the Tishbite, will bring down the House of Omri! How could you let him deal with you in such a way ... in front of your whole court?' screamed the young Prince Ahab. 'How is it possible that the greatest King on earth could be humbled by a man who lives in a hovel, who wanders the desert, who has no shoes, and whose only weapon is a wooden staff? And you, Father, have a thousand chariots and ten thousand men at arms.'

Omri's head was pounding, but he needed to quell the civil war in his own family. Before he could utter a word, the tirade continued, 'And how could you allow me, your son and the heir to your kingdom, to be belittled by this man?'

'You belittled yourself,' Omri said quietly. It was such a hot day, made a thousand times worse because of the desert wind, the hamsin, blowing in dust and covering the rugs, cushions and carpets with its fine sand and making it impossible to breathe. And whenever there was a hamsin, Omri's head felt as though it were about to burst like an overripe melon. The very last thing he wanted now was an argument with the heir to his throne, his eldest son Ahab, a young man who seemed to be learning the lessons of kingship too slowly.

Omri worried about the future of Israel. Clear-minded as he was, the land was in trouble. All those years before, when Omri was a general and had overthrown the weak and vacillating Zimri, the path of the future, though still strewn with boulders, had seemed clear. But now the path was rockier than ever, and he was without shoes. He looked closely at his son; tall, handsome, the plaything of all the girls in the court and the town, a young man who knew how to hunt and enjoy his life ... Would he ever be ready to don the mantle of the King? To wear the crown of authority? In body, he was so strong and capable, but in mind, he had the temper of a petulant child. What was needed in these troubled times was a man with the wisdom of his ancestor Solomon – but Ahab was no Solomon.

'Ahab, listen to me carefully. When the kingdom of Israel separated from the kingdom of Judah, we claimed the greater part of the land of Moses. We had the riches, the sea, the crops, the grazing fields. The remaining kingdom of Judah, so my predecessor Jeroboam believed, would become impoverished and become the prey of other nations. He thought it would capitulate within a few years and beg to be brought back into one nation and then the tribes of the northern kingdom would be in control of the land of Yahweh.

'Yet Jeroboam was the first to recognise the power which Jerusalem holds over the Hebrew people. And when he set up temples in Dan and Bethel, he ensured that golden calves, like the winged angels of Jerusalem, were placed on pedestals to give the people comfort. What he didn't do, what he couldn't do, was to have the Tribe of Levi or the Cohanim within the temple. They stayed in Jerusalem. Without them, the religion was cut in half. Our services were less godly. And it is for that reason that Elijah and other prophets raise their voices against us. Because they are a barricade between the temple and the people. They are the priests and the attendants of the priests. In our way in Israel, we have none of them. We have our own priests. And because of this, they are frightened of the people worshipping God directly, and not through them. They are scared that God will turn His eyes, and look directly at the people, rather than through the eyes of the priests and the prophets.'

Ahab's anger hadn't abated. 'But Jeroboam was wrong. Judah did not collapse. It is looking to the east and to Moab and Ammon as allies to conquer us.'

Omri nodded. 'Which is why we have to make an alliance with Phoenicia. Which is why I sent an ambassador there. Because we must have a permanent and friendly ally in the north to protect us against Syria and Assyria so that if Judah marches north, especially with Moab by its side, then we will not be attacked on two borders.'

Ahab looked at his father and knew in his heart that some momentous news was about to be delivered, something awesome was about to happen. He realised that was why his father had explained so carefully what he already knew.

'And that is why,' said Omri, 'I have decided that you will marry the Princess of Tyre and Sidon. This girl is the daughter of King IttaBa'al. In his own country, he prefers to be called by the local language and his name in Phoenicia is King Ethbaal. This is how he is known to the Syrians and the Babylonians, as well as to his own people, the Phoenicians. The girl's name is Jezebel. She entertained our ambassador recently. He says that she is a delightful girl, full of fun and intelligence. She is very pretty, dances beautifully, has a strong and developed body, wonderful teeth which the ambassador says is because of her habit of chewing the skins of grapefruit and lemons, and she has wide hips. The girl is seventeen years old and knows much about men and the ways expected of women, so that from the first night of your marriage, you will experience the joys of being a husband.'

Ahab looked stunned. 'But …'

'It is decided. I signed the marriage treaty this morning before Elijah arrived. The ambassador is already back on the road to Sidon, Phoenicia's northern capital. He will be there by nightfall tomorrow.'

'But Father … I can't marry this girl. I'm already pledged to be married. You know that. You've given your consent. I love Hazah. She already shares my bed. She is my wife in all but ceremony.'

'And you may keep her as your servant and your concubine. Even as your second wife if she'll accept the position. She will be good for you when Jezebel's body is unavailable to you because of the passage of the moon. But Hazah will not be your first wife. You will marry Phoenicia and peace will come to Israel's northern lands. I have spoken.'

Ahab looked at his father in anger. He shook his head in concern, which quickly changed to incomprehension. Only that morning, Hazah had been talking to him about the colour of the gown she would wear beneath her robes on their wedding day. How could he now tell her that she would never be anything more than a second wife? He bowed to his father, and turned from the private chamber to return to his own quarters.

Omri watched his son leave the room. His head was becoming worse and worse. And it would continue to ache and pound until the hamsin was over, and that could be days, or even weeks. The only relief was to ride out of Samaria until he was out of the path of the desert winds. Or climb a mountain and wait there for the wind to blow itself out. He had done that the last time there was a hamsin. He'd watched the dust in the air obscure everything below. As he stood on the top of the mountain above the Sea of Galilee, he'd seen the surface of the water disappear and the buildings of the city of Aphek seem to be swallowed up by the yellow dust. And then, just as suddenly the following morning, when he awoke and left his tent to relieve himself, the air was clear, the sky was a brilliant blue, and the surface of the water of the sea was reflecting the clouds.

Omri remembered his feeling of joy that the desert wind had blown itself out to the Eternal Sea and disappeared from the land. He smiled. These days, he only rarely remembered feelings of joy and exultation. How difficult life was these days, now that he was a King.

When his army had fought the Philistines at Gibbethon, life was so much easier. But then his brother commander, Zimri, had murdered Elah the King of Israel at Tirzah, then the capital city. Omri still remembered the shock which shuddered through the entire land. It was as though a huge boulder had suddenly fallen from the sky and landed in the middle of a crowded square. When the news was brought that the King of Israel had been murdered, the army considered mutiny. And it was Omri who held the competing forces together. Because of his strength and the love which his men had for him, they rejected Zimri and elected Omri King of Israel in the fields where they were camped.

That, Omri remembered, was the greatest and most wonderful feeling he had ever felt, being held aloft by a hundred men, and hearing them roar his name while toasting him with wine and ale. The feeling of sudden power had gone to his head and he had felt as though he was floating on a cloud for days afterwards.

Despite the ache in his head, Omri smiled at the memory of how he had been suddenly elevated to the kingship.

But as with everything, his quarrel with Elijah and his difficulties with Ahab receded into the background as he closed his eyes to shut out the pain of the day. He needed to recapture those glorious moments of his life. So, as he often did at these moments of great tension, Omri thought back to the events immediately after his crowning. He and his army had marched on Tirzah to wrest the throne away from Zimri. They laid siege to the capital for seven days, and, just when they were about to storm the city and force Zimri's abdication, the fool, thinking it was a method of escaping the blockade, had set fire to the palace, but forgotten to ensure an escape route for himself and he'd burnt to death in the flames.

And then Omri was King. Oh, for the first few years, another man, Tibni, had tried to usurp the throne and actually called himself King, but he had no following and was nothing more than an irritation, and he'd died six years ago and that put an end forever to any rival claims to the throne of Israel.

The early days were the best. But on the death of Tibni, Omri felt it important to move from the old capital of Tirzah and to buy a hilltop from Shemer the shepherd and landowner, so that as the crowned monarch, he could build a new city which, by agreement with Shemer, he called Samaria.

The first thing he'd done was to build a huge terrace enclosed by a massive wall as thick as a man was tall, which acted as a retaining wall for all the houses which he would build in his new city. Then he'd built a magnificent temple and palace, an arcade of shops for merchants and an open space for people to meet and listen to visiting speakers and for parades. And the building work continued as he ran his kingdom. And with the building, people came from all the lands nearby to see what was happening. And they spent their money and bought their goods, and Israel prospered.

Yes, in the early days all was good. The people were happy, especially as he allowed visitors to the nation of Israel to worship their own gods in their new country. The worship was looked upon with interest by the Israelite people who had, if truth be told, always kept idols and deities in their homes. Now, some of these new gods were even being worshipped openly in private houses where people met together. And why not? He still worshipped

Yahweh and loved Him. But the people wanted to worship other gods as well, and despite Elijah and his brotherhood of prophets, Omri couldn't now take away the people's pleasure.

He sighed. His head felt awful. He picked up a flannel from the water pot, and wrapped it around his head, water dripping down onto his tunic. He banged his staff on the floor, and the door flew open. His guard commander looked at him expectantly.

'Order my slave to come and bring a fan. I need cool air over my body. And have my bath prepared. I must bathe to cool myself.'

The guard commander nodded, bowed, and left the room.

When would this hamsin end? When would his problems diminish? Was this kingship? Suddenly, he longed for the life of the army, where all he was expected to do was to fight and kill his enemies, and to win battles. But how could he possibly win a battle against an unseeable and perpetually angry God? Especially one who had sent to earth a prophet like Elijah whose voice was like nails which spiked his body and mind and gave him no peace.

Maybe Ahab was right. Maybe he should risk an uprising of the followers of Yahweh and have Elijah taken out into the desert and killed. There would be war with Judah, but he knew he could win that. And that would be an end to his troubles. Or would it? For he knew that in the midst of the battle, Philistia would ...

It was so hard to think. The hamsin suddenly started to blow louder outside his apartment window whistling like a demon. Was it Yahweh God making him suffer for his thoughts?

The entire court, her father the King, her mother, the King's other wives and children and extended family, as well as guard commanders, royal advisors and their families, and specially invited guests who looked around the banquet hall in awe of its decorated walls and the splendour of the appointments, listened to the man who stood on the carpets in the centre of the tables.

The room had been laid out so that the tables followed three sides of the hall, and the fourth side was left open so that the Babylonian could stand and perform and would be heard and visible from all sides. The members of the royal household and their friends and followers lay on their divans and couches, listening to his mellifluous voice. Some were still eating fruit, some the meats and flavoured ices made that morning from the snows of the nearby mountains; but most had eaten their fill and were listening intently to what the Babylonian poet was saying.

Only the King was seated on a throne so that he was higher than everybody else, and in the centre of the room, around which all, except the man who was performing, revolved.

Ethbaal nodded when the Babylonian poet looked towards him, waiting for permission to continue with his epic saga. Sensitive to the easy boredom from which people suffered when he recited the *Enuma elish*, he had informed the King that he would continue each verse, pausing just long enough for the King to nod or shake his head if he wanted him to continue or cease. But the King was enamoured of the poem, and willed the poet to continue. In his deep and practised voice, the poet sang:

Discord broke out among the gods although they were brothers, warring and jarring in the belly of Tiamat; heaven shook, it reeled with the surge of the dance; Apsu could not silence the clamour, their behaviour was bad, overbearing and proud.

But still Tiamat lay inert till Apsu, the father of gods, bellowed for that servant who clouds his judgement, his Mummu,

'Dear counsellor, come with me to Tiamat.'

They have gone, and in front of Tiamat they sit down and talk together about the young gods, their first-born children; Apsu said,

'Their manners revolt me, day and night without remission we suffer. My will is to destroy them, all of their kind, we shall have peace at last and we will sleep again.'

When Tiamat heard, she was stung, she writhed in lonely desolation, her heart worked in secret passion, Tiamat said,

'Why must we destroy the children that we made? If their ways are troublesome, let us wait a little while ...'

The poet from Babylonia was suddenly interrupted by King Ethbaal bursting out in loud laughter. All eyes in the room moved from the poet to the King.

'Forgive me, master poet, for interrupting. But this is a wonderful story. What was that ... *why must we destroy the children that we made?* How wise are your gods in Babylonia that they understand the heartache and difficulties that children cause their parents, but also that parents cause their children. Couldn't we say just as easily, "*Why must the children we make destroy the parents who made them ...?*"

The Babylonian poet looked at the King, clapped and nodded eagerly, agreeing with every word, though he really didn't understand what King Ethbaal was talking about. But then the poet saw the look on the face of the Princess Jezebel and decided to remain mute, for she looked at her father sharply. She suddenly worried that, in front of the King's other wives and their children, the King might recount the argument which she had had with him earlier in the day.

But to her intense relief, the King nodded for the poet to continue his recital of the epic of his Mesopotamian history, explaining how Babylonia and the earth were founded at the same moment and how Babylonia is the centre of the earth.

Of course, as was his habit before reciting the poem, the poet knew that he must beg forgiveness of the court of Phoenicia. He readily assured the royal court that Babylonia was in decline and was not the power it once was, and that the tale he had come to recount must be viewed not as truth, but as a story to be enjoyed; that there were eternal lessons to be learned from the wisdom of the gods, just as there was wisdom in the tales of the Egyptians.

And that was how the story was received. The Phoenician court welcomed many storytellers; some had indeed come from Egypt to amuse them, and told stories of their gods Ra and Isis and others who were crocodiles; some came from India and told of even more strange gods who had the heads of strange gigantic beasts called elephants and the bodies of orange beasts called tigers and of divine birds called peacocks whose great tails contained eyes and were the fans of the gods themselves; others were from Akkad and Judah and told stories of different gods and their manifestations.

And Jezebel listened to them all, and found comfort that in the pantheon of gods who strode the earth and the heavens, the only gods who were consistent and who loved mankind were Ba'al and Asherah and El, and they were the gods who favoured Phoenicia.

Soon the poet finished his recital of the epic, and the court clapped, and her father the King gave him a purse of gold, and the Babylonian bowed humbly and gave his blessings to everybody in the room. And then people began to stand and scratch their bellies and say goodnight and drift away.

But before Jezebel could leave and return to her apartments to go to sleep, the King her father caught her by the arm, and said, 'Well?'

'Well?' she replied imperiously.

The King became angry. 'Have you changed your mind?'

'I won't marry him. I won't marry an Israelite. Not unless I can take my gods and my priests and priestesses along with me.'

'I've already explained,' he said, trying to restrain his recurrent anger and to keep his voice low so that no one overheard his displeasure, 'the ambassador said that you could worship our gods in the countryside, but that priests and prophets of their god, Yahweh, are causing problems for King Omri, and if you bring our gods into the city of Samaria, you'll cause him great difficulties. And it's not as though our gods aren't worshipped in Israel and Judah. It's only within their cities and their temples that images of our gods must not be placed. Surely you can go outside the city walls and worship your gods without too much inconvenience, and then there will be no problems, and you'll be loved by the people ...'

She interrupted him, 'I'll be loved by the people anyway. But I want Asherah and Ba'al with me in my palace. Without them, it would be like walking without my legs, or being without my arms. I won't do it, Lord my father, and that is final.'

Ethbaal sighed, and looked at his daughter. She was a woman now, not the little girl who had sat in his lap while singers sang at banquets and storytellers thrilled the court with their tales of the battles between the gods and mankind, or soldiers returned from some distant battle and recounted their deeds of heroism and bravery.

How Jezebel had clung in fear to his clothes and sometimes his beard when the soldiers told of hacking off the heads or arms of captives, or of chaining and enslaving whole towns which resisted the onslaught of their army. And when she was older, Ethbaal remembered how Jezebel had taken such pleasure in performing songs and dances for the court, even when a delegation or an ambassador was being entertained.

Now he looked at her beautiful face, firm in its resolve, haughty in its determination. He could command her obedience. He would have to in order to make her bend to his will. Now that she was a woman, she was making life so difficult for him. He had just signed a marriage treaty with Israel. Soon he would sign a treaty of friendship so that the two countries would be brothers in peace and united in threat.

He sighed. Maybe he needed a peace treaty with Jezebel; or at least a skilful negotiator.

'Five hundred!'

'What?' The high priestess of Asherah shook her head in disbelief. 'Five hundred. But that's ... we'll never be able ...' And then she was utterly lost for words.

'Not all from the Temple of Asherah. I want half that number from the Temple of Ba'al. Maybe even some who attend to the worship of El. But I need many,' said Jezebel.

'Majesty, this number is impossible. It would denude the temples throughout Phoenicia of all the acolytes and priestesses and priests and prostitutes and ...'

'Nonsense, High Priestess. I know as well as you how many priests and priestesses there are in Phoenicia. There are many times that number. And anyway, my father has agreed to raise a special tax against the people so that your sister priestesses and your brother priests will have enough funds to train more priests and priestesses. There are many worthy young men and women who would love to be part of the temple and spend their days worshipping the gods.'

'Majesty, dear Jezebel, why are you doing this?' asked the high priestess quietly. She had known the young Princess all of her life. She'd admired her colourful and youthful spirit, her enjoyment of bodily pleasures, but mostly she'd been impressed by the girl's love of Asherah. It was a devotion which had once, four years earlier, nearly drawn her into becoming a priestess, had not King Ethbaal stood in her way and forbidden the induction. But her demand for so many priests and priestesses to accompany her on her road to becoming the future Queen of Israel was more than devotion. It sounded like panic.

'Lady,' said the Princess, 'I do this because Israel is a primitive and barren land. Because in their temple, they only love their one god, Yahweh, and he is a very stern god who demands much of the people. I need to introduce the joys and beauty of my Asherah to the people of Israel so that they can see how kind and welcoming she is. So that they can see how she makes the crops grow and the land become fertile. So that mothers who are barren will conceive babies.'

The high priestess nodded. 'Yes, I know all about this god Yahweh. There are other gods worshipped in Israel, but he is the master god. His word is the word by which all act. All other gods are small in comparison. And his prophets and priests say that he is the one true god.

'But if Israel has only one true god whom the people now own to be above and beyond all other gods, then I don't understand ... How can you, as their future Queen, enter their country and introduce Asherah to the people and risk offending this god, Yahweh? In a year, maybe in two or three years, once you are Queen, you can set up some shrines in the gardens of your palace and worship Asherah. When the people are ready to accept her. But to do so now, when you are about to enter a foreign land ... that, surely, would be an insult to the priests and the people of Israel and, more importantly, to your husband the

Prince. You stand the risk of being reviled. Their priests might even rail against the marriage.'

Her father had used the same arguments. But in the end, and after many nights of anger, he had given ground because it was the only way he could find to make her agree to marry Prince Ahab without absolutely commanding her. Since the treaty had been signed, Jezebel had done everything in her power to dissuade her father. But nothing she said would overcome his insistence; no threat she made would concern him; and no argument she used negated his much-repeated claim that her marriage would ensure secure southern borders and the future peace and prosperity of the people of Phoenicia.

After days of arguments, and days when she refused to come out of her chambers, she suddenly demanded an audience with her father.

'I will go to Israel.'

He sighed in relief.

'I will marry Ahab.'

He nodded.

'But I demand three things ... First, the right to worship my own gods in my own way; secondly, the right to my own counsellors and advisors; and thirdly, the right to my own court, my own friends. Agree to these conditions, and I will do my duty as your daughter, and as a future queen of Israel.'

Ethbaal looked at his daughter. He regretted that soon he would have to separate from her. If only his son and his future successor, Jezebel's half-brother Abimel, had even a part of the spirit and courage and fire with which Jezebel was blessed.

He nodded, and said, 'I will instruct the scribes to write this into your marriage contract.'

Jezebel smiled, and kissed her father. She was pleased, because she knew that continuing her opposition would not work. And the thought that she would be Asherah's handmaiden and spread the worship of her to new and unconquered lands pleased her. And further, she had begun to remember what the ambassador had told her about Prince Ahab. Yes, he was apparently a very good lover, and had a reputation among the women of the palace for being very proficient in the bedchamber; yes, he was good looking and tall, and had no diseases, and his skin was clear; no, the evil spirits had never infested his mind, and even though he had a temper, he'd never been known to strike a woman or a maidservant; and yes, he was a brave warrior who led charges and was skilled in chariot fighting and with the bow and arrow, the sword and the catapult. And the ambassador assured her that even though there were other women to whom he was either already married or who were his concubines, her position as a princess of the royal blood of Phoenicia would ensure her of primacy as his one true wife. And then, when she was properly married, she would be queen of a great and noble land, Queen Jezebel of Israel.

Jezebel sought out merchants in the city who had done business with or who had been to Israel, to determine whether anybody had yet seen Prince Ahab. Only one man had actually done so. He had been in the crowd as King Omri and his son Ahab had ridden in from visiting border encampments. The crowd gathered around their horses, and cheered, especially when the trumpeters riding ahead of them blew their instruments for attention and to clear the way through the crowded marketplace in Samaria, and threw victory coins into the crowd.

The merchant described Ahab in much the same terms as the ambassador had done the previous day – tall, handsome, strong, manly.

Ethbaal was somewhat surprised when Jezebel sought him out after a meeting of his council some days later.

'Do you remember my three conditions of marriage to Ahab?' she said.

He nodded.

'Well, there's one more condition which I want to impose. I want to take five hundred priests and priestesses to Israel to introduce the worship of Asherah as part of the official religion.'

Ethbaal looked at her in amazement. 'The King of Israel will never agree to such a large number,' he said.

'Then I won't go,' she replied.

'And then I'll lock you in your room for the rest of your life. Push me too far, Jezebel, and I'll forget my love of you and deal with you in a manner you'll regret as you rot in your room and die painfully, remembering the life you could have led.'

She smiled at his empty threat in the way she knew always softened his heart. She knew she'd win.

Reluctantly, her father the King said that he would add this last, and final, demand to her wedding contract, but warned her that such a huge number of holy men and women who attended to a foreign god and goddess could cause trouble; but it was a negotiating point which he was willing to concede for a greater glory. After all, when Jezebel crossed the border between Phoenicia and Israel, her retinue would be Omri's and Ahab's problem, and no longer his.

CHAPTER SIX

The procession left the city of Tyre with a fanfare the like of which the citizens had never before heard. It sounded as though all the heavens had opened and all the gods were looking down at the land and shouting in one voice. The noise spread from where the procession had assembled, and then it seemed to rise and cover the city, it could even be heard out to sea where the fishing boats were drifting with their nets in the becalmed waters.

One hundred trumpeters stood on the walls of the citadel of Tyre as the Princess Jezebel passed beneath the vast wooden lintel of the Samaria Gate at the head of her retinue, leaving the city on her way to becoming queen of her own realm. A further one hundred drummers stood a step beneath the trumpeters on the ramparts and made noises which sounded like the wildness of a winter's storm. And on the ground, as the procession passed by, one hundred harpists on one side of them, and a hundred lyrists on the other, strummed their instruments sounding like the voices of the gods rejoicing in the majesty of what was passing before their eyes.

Following Jezebel on her horse were fifty men of

her personal bodyguard, each with a new shield specially crafted for her entry into the city of Samaria, capital of her future kingdom of Israel. The shields had been specially designed by Jezebel and were round with metal ribbing forming a cross over the leather facings. In the centre of the shields, where one gleaming strip of the burnished iron crossed over the other, Jezebel had instructed that an image of the Goddess Asherah should be emblazoned. On each of the fifty shields, the goddess stood proud and naked on the back of a horse with her son and lover Ba'al, in the body of a snake, crawling up her leg to be joined with her as man and wife. Jezebel had been warned against this imagery by her father who was worried about its potential to insult the people of Israel and their god, Yahweh; but she had gone ahead anyway, convincing him that she needed to assert her status as a royal princess of Phoenicia and not merely as the wife of a future king of Israel. In some trepidation, he had finally agreed.

Behind the bodyguard walked her priests and priestesses, all dressed in reds and whites and greens, and gold tunics; and the Princess could feel the excitement of the crowd for she had instructed the priestesses to bare their breasts as they walked. This wasn't only for her own people in Phoenicia, but also because she had heard that the women of Israel were enjoined by their god Yahweh to be modest and not to inflame the hearts of their men and so distract them from their worship.

Yes, she knew that it would challenge the women and the priests, but she also realised that if she could win over the men of Israel, she and her retinue would be accepted more easily.

From the moment she knew that she was going to become the future queen of the southern land, she had planned the seduction of the nation's men. She and her priestesses had conspired, schemed and created an entire landscape of seduction. Every traveller, every soldier, every merchant who journeyed northwards from Israel to Phoenicia was questioned by Jezebel about the attitudes, the behaviour and the ways of the men and women of Israel. And the retinue which left Phoenicia was like a perfumed arrow, aimed directly into the hearts of the Israelites.

The one thing she knew she had to do was to inflame the hearts of all the men of Israel; Jezebel had learned that the easiest way to conquer a nation was to make the men fall in love with her. Had not the Ethiopian Queen Sheba conquered all of Israel when she landed at Eilath? Had not the men of Israel fallen to their knees in awe of her beauty? And had not the King Solomon of Israel become like dough in her hands when she arrived in Jerusalem? So it would be with the arrival of Jezebel in Israel.

Of all the things which she'd recently discovered about the habits of the women of Israel, the habit of their being modest – covering themselves and turning away from the pleasures of the body – was perhaps the most peculiar. How did they wash? When they bathed, how could they ensure that nobody looked at them? Were they supposed to be invisible to their friends and neighbours, in the same way as the gods were invisible to the people of the earth? How did they undress at night without being seen through the windows of their houses? It was absurd. And it was one of the first things which Jezebel intended to set about changing, priests or no priests of Yahweh!

Following in the wake of the five hundred priests and priestesses of Ba'al and Asherah were her personal slaves and maids and manservants. In all, it took a very long while for the procession to pass beneath the Samaria Gate, so much so that by the time the last of the slaves had walked through, most of the curious onlookers, and those who had come to cheer the retinue, had already gone home. As the great gate was shut and bolted, as the last trumpet sounded its song to the hot dry air, Jezebel had already ridden her pure white horse around the nearby hills which masked the city and was out of earshot of the fanfare.

She relaxed for the first time in days. Leaving Sidon several days earlier had been difficult, with her father obviously unhappy to lose her from his side, and her brothers and sisters squabbling about who would be allocated her rooms within the palace. Even her mother, with whom she rarely spoke, came out to pay her greetings and homage to the future queen, and to wish her speed and fortune.

She and the captains of her bodyguard knew the road from Sidon to Tyre very well, and when they'd left the northern capital city, there was a mood of excitement and anticipation. They'd camped on the first night where they all had camped many times before. Food was plentiful, as was wine and ale and fruits. The King had sent along a bull which was slaughtered to mark the first night of her leaving, and huge fires were made in the centre of the encampment. Prayers were said to the gods, and the bull's tail and testicles were cut off and sacrificed respectively to Ba'al and Asherah.

One of the priestesses was given the task of placing them in a sacred grove in the hills above their camp. During the night, there was much laughter and singing, the priests and priestesses, who had been worried about leaving their temples, were quickly excited by the prospect of adventures on the road ahead. A captain of the guard had engaged Jezebel in conversation and, as she drank more wine, he convinced her that it would be good for the men if she were to dance. This she did, in front of the roaring fire. She swirled and twirled to the voice of the harps and the lyres and the beating of the drums and the singing of the flutes. She clapped her hands, she jumped perilously over the fire, she swayed her hips seductively and excited the passions of the men at arms. And then, laughing at the top of her voice, she took herself off to bed in her tent, leaving the soldiers aching for more. Whether or not the priestesses managed to get any sleep that night was something Jezebel wouldn't find out until the morning.

The following day was arduous, but they covered a lot of ground, and camped for the night only a half a day's ride from Tyre. They spent three days in Tyre, resting, swimming and restocking their food wagons.

Now they were on the road again, and by nightfall the following day they aimed to camp within sight of the white cliffs and chalk rocks of Ras Nichrah which marked the northern border of Israel and the southern border of Phoenicia. And then they would make their triumphal entry into the northern Israelite city of Ak-Kah.

When they stopped, one of the captains of the guard, who had accompanied a Phoenician ambassador on an embassy to Israel, told Jezebel about the city of Ak-Kah and the majestic sweep of bay on which it was situated. He said that the bay was reputed to have been carved out of the land by the fingernail of the god Mot, the god of drought, sterility and death. The Phoenicians who lived at Ras Nichrah believed Mot visited the area one day in ancient times, before mankind walked the face of the earth. He came from his home in the sun-blistered deserts and wastelands and the region of the underworld, because he feared that the mighty God El would take pity on the land because it was so dry from Mot's jealousy; and El did! He made it rain torrentially, and in his fury, Mot dug his fingernail into the land and warned El not to trespass any further on his territory. But El pulled all the land inside the god's fingernail into the sea and made a huge island over the horizon. Mot was so furious he had inadvertently lost so much land that he killed all the trees and grasses beyond the mountains, and to this day it remains desert to the east and the south of the Fertile Crescent and the King's Highway.

Jezebel had listened in fascination. She lay prone, her hunger satisfied and her tiredness from the hard ride evaporating as her manservant massaged her back and legs and buttocks. She asked the captain what he knew of this god of the Israelites, Yahweh.

'Is he related to our chief god, El?' she asked.

'To be honest, Lady, I find it hard to understand their god. Sometimes he is called Elohim, sometimes Adonai, sometimes Yahweh. But these are not three separate gods, these are some of the many names of the one god, and the true name of God is known only to the high priest.

'With Ba'al, Asherah, Anat and Yam, and especially with El, our worship is easy. If we want rain, we sacrifice and pray to Ba'al, the Lord of the

Earth, the Eternal to all Generations, the Lord of Heaven and the Rider of the Clouds. His voice is thunder. He is the god of fertile things. Without our constant prayers to Ba'al, and if your father the King did not spill his seed in the priestesses and then have it buried in the ground, the land would soon become infertile, arid and sterile, and of no use.

'Anat is the same. As the goddess of love and war, she and Asherah are those to whom we pray for fertility and to conquer our enemies.

'But the god of Israel, Yahweh … He is nowhere. There are no idols to him, the temples are bare and if he is there, then he is hidden in a box which the high priest stands over, much like one of our sacrificial altars. Indeed, when I was shown into the temple in Bethel, a priest was sacrificing a week-old lamb to Yahweh. I looked everywhere for the god, but he was nowhere. I asked, and was told that he is in the heavens. When I asked whether he ever came to earth, I was told that he is always on earth. I asked how he could be in heaven and earth at the same moment, and I was told, *"Because He is Yahweh, and He is omniscient and He is everywhere"*.'

Jezebel sat up, and looked directly at the captain. He found it difficult to look into her eyes without looking at her beautiful and naked breasts.

'But how is he?' she asked. 'Why is he? What makes him so different from our gods? Why are Israel and Judah reputed to be so dull and lifeless? Is it because of him? Because he's invisible and the people can't understand what he looks like? Why does their Yahweh forbid the worship of other gods and the use of idols in the temples and in homes? What do the people take into their homes when they leave the temples? What do they worship? And why are the women so frightened of the men, for that's what I've heard. The men are the priests. There are no women priests. And the women of the court take no part in the government of the country. Why is this, Captain?'

He shook his head. 'I don't know, Lady. It is a very strange country. And worse, they have prophets there who shout and scream at their King, or so I've heard.'

She looked at him in amazement, which quickly turned to horror. 'Someone shouts at the King?'

The captain nodded.

'And he lives?'

Again the captain nodded.

'What's a prophet?' she asked.

It was as she descended the cliffs of Ras Nichrah, from the highlands of Phoenicia to the seashore of northern Israel, that Jezebel found out in no uncertain terms precisely what a prophet was, although she had been warned by her father's advisor, Hattusas, who had been assigned to travel with her and stay in Israel until she was comfortable remaining on her own.

She encouraged her horse to follow a trail into a gully which led down to the sand of the sea road, on which she would travel and enter Ak-Kah. But as her descent levelled out, and she found she could again ride on the horse's flanks instead of the blanket slipping towards its neck, a voice suddenly filled the air, like the terrifying scream of a lunatic, or a dog baying at the moon. It was a voice which turned Jezebel's blood cold. The moment they heard it, her captain of the bodyguard unsheathed his sword and rode forward urgently to protect her. Her advisor Hattusas looked around in fear, shouting for a bodyguard to come immediately to the head of the column to protect their Princess.

The entourage stopped immediately they heard shouting, and the guards all looked around, drawing their swords, arming their bows and preparing themselves for attack.

'Whore of Phoenicia!' the voice screamed, echoing off the walls of the canyon, amplified in hatred and fury. 'Evil and idolatrous heathen. Loose woman of Sidon and Tyre. Get you gone from the sacred land of Israel and return to Phoenicia and your false gods and idols. Hide your nakedness which is an abhorrence in the eyes of the Almighty. Wash off your perfumes and your precious oils. Cover your skin and remove your shoes, for you are treading on the holy ground of Israel. Turn around, and do not dare to enter our land with your painted women, your sodomites and your graven images and hideous statues.'

When he stopped speaking, his words continued to rebound over the rocks, and became magnified in the still air. Even the crickets and cicadas stopped their summer chirping. Jezebel looked up, but she was no longer frightened. Words, not arrows, rained down upon her. Having lost her trepidation she kicked her horse in the flanks to move him closer to the rockface so she could get a better look at who was shouting. Her bodyguard assembled behind her.

The captain looked at the shadows in the cliff side and breathed easier when he found no trace of men or weapons. Like Jezebel, he realised quickly that there was no immediate danger of attack, and resheathed his sword. He took his bow from off his back, and slotted in an arrow from his quiver. This was the voice of a single man. The captain instantly pulled back the loaded arrow and scanned the hills and vantage points of the valley. He had been assured by the captain of the Israelite army that the way had been made clear for their progress, that bandits and robbers would not bother them. He would have things to say when he arrived in the capital, Samaria.

He squinted in the brilliant reflection of the sun on the white cliff face, and tried to make out where the man was hiding. But the voice seemed to be formless, as though it had come from the very rocks themselves. And then he saw the slightest movement, high up on the cliff. It was a lone man, or so the captain's first glance made him believe. The man, dressed in a blinding white tunic with a grey hood emerged from his hiding place, what appeared to be a cave high in the walls of the cliff. He stood on the edge of the precipice; one step forward and the lunatic would fall to his death.

The captain made a quick assessment. He was sure it was a single man, but even if he was wrong, there could be no more than a handful of men up there, the rock ledge wouldn't hold any more; of course, there could easily be others hidden in the valley walls, but it was unlikely because, having given away the element of surprise, they should now be in a full-scale attack. Rocks, arrows and spears should be raining down on them. And if that happened, the men of the bodyguard knew to race to the side of Jezebel and erect a canopy of shields over her head to protect her. Yet the only weapon this man seemed to be hurling was anger.

He began his insane attack again. 'Be gone, Jezebel, harlot and whore and queen of the night. Be gone, back to the land of idols and false gods. Be gone, scarlet woman and woman of painted lips. Take back with you your priests and priestesses and ...'

The captain let fly an arrow. It flew up into the air with a hiss, and hit the rock wall beside the madman. His troop also let loose with their arrows. Hundreds of them in rapid succession. They heard a cry of surprise, of disbelief, and the man in the white tunic disappeared inside his cave. More arrows, more anger, the arrows making tiny chirping sounds as they bit into the rock, and then fell back to earth. Jezebel kicked her horse forward, her face a mask of fury.

'Who is he? How dare he talk to me like that? Climb up to the cave and bring his head to me.'

The captain dismounted, and ran towards the cliff face. As he climbed, he suddenly realised who the enemy was. He had been told of this man, Elijah, by the Israelite captain of the Samarian guard, but was assured that he would be detained during the arrival of the Phoenician Princess. The captain began climbing rapidly, but slipped on the loose gravel and stones. Eventually he managed to ascend halfway up the cliff face, but Jezebel shouted up to him to return.

He stopped his ascent, and turned to look back at the Princess. 'He has just disappeared over the top of the cliff and by the time you reach there, he will be long gone. Return Captain, and let's continue our journey. But believe me, somebody will pay with his life for this insult to the royal blood of Phoenicia.'

Her advisor, Hattusas, came towards her. 'Jezebel,

I know this man. His name is Elijah. He is a prophet of the god, Yahweh. They say that the King himself heeds Elijah. I'm afraid that this is not a good beginning to your reign.'

But she turned to him in anger. 'I am not the one who should fear, Hattusas. That man who has disappeared like a thief into the desert will quickly learn to fear me.' And she kicked her horse and continued her journey into Israel.

Hattusas noticed with concern that instead of subsiding, Jezebel's fury grew with every step of her progress. A formal delegation should have greeted her at the gates to the town of Ak-Kah, but when she arrived in the middle of the following afternoon only the town's governing fathers were there, and a mere four trumpeters. It was more insult than welcome. And it was deliberate, for a proper and fit reception had been negotiated between her father the King of Phoenicia, and Omri, King of Israel. Yet the formal reception was nowhere. Again, she thought, someone would pay with his head.

Garlands of herbs and flowers were placed around her neck by the officials of the city, and her path was strewn with petals, but nobody from the royal family of Israel had bothered to turn up. Indeed, had it not been for the calming words from her father's chief counsellor, Hattusas, Jezebel would have instructed her retinue to turn on their heels and return northwards to civilisation.

'Most high and mighty Lady, glorious in the light of the sun and the moon, beloved of all your people, and soon to be beloved of ours, you who are the blood which flows between our two great bodies, you who ...'

'Where is my reception?' she said interrupting him. He looked at her in surprise, but behind the surprise, Jezebel discerned a knowing smirk, a surreptitious grin. Another head, she thought. But in a calm voice of authority and command, she asked, 'Why is my future husband not here to greet me?'

Hattusas looked at her in surprise. He'd expected rage, but she was cold and calculating in the way she handled this minor official. What had been done was an obvious and profound insult, and surprising because of the desire of King Omri for the marriage treaty. Hattusas had determined to make his anger known to the officials of the town, but now Jezebel herself was dealing with the matter. Yet she was inexperienced in the ways of diplomacy and he feared she would start an incident which would lead to the nullification of the treaty.

Jezebel dismounted from her horse and stood with two feet solidly planted on Israelite soil. She placed her hands on her hips while the governor of the city ignored her earlier question and continued with his set speech. This time, though, he glanced at her warily. He'd been told by Prince Ahab that she was a slight thing, a young and silly girl who would probably burst into tears. He hadn't been prepared for the sort of face-to-face confrontation which he would have expected from a man.

Again Jezebel interrupted and demanded to know where her official reception was, and again the surprised official continued to recite the list of titles and sycophancies he had carefully written the previous day.

Another man, equally drab, stepped forward. He put up his hand to silence the sycophant, and told Jezebel, 'Our city is busy with its work, great Princess, and despite our entreaties, nobody was able to join us to greet you. A thousand apologies. As to His Royal Highness, the Prince Ahab, His Majesty sends to you his deepest and most profound apologies for not being here to greet you, but he was prevented by the urgency of palace business. However, he sends his devotion and affection, and commands me to inform your Royal Highness that he and his father the King Omri, look forward with unsurpassed zeal to your arrival at the gates of Samaria.'

Jezebel listened to the words, and quickly thought through their hidden meaning. It was obviously an insult designed to make her feel unwanted and unwelcome. It had been carefully constructed and calculated by the Prince to inform her and her retinue that she was secondary in his life, and that her place would always be inferior to other things in the governing of the country. Hattusas looked at her, wondering how she would react to this most visible of snubs. Her guards and captains, her priests and priestesses listened carefully. They were certain she would flare up in fury and order an assault on the delegation. Some of the soldiers pointedly moved their hands to their scabbards in order to draw their swords quickly if necessary.

She delayed a moment before answering. Then Jezebel said softly, 'I'm sorry that His Royal Highness is too busy to greet me and my retinue. Because he is so very involved in his work, the last thing I would wish to do would be to further compound his difficulties. We will rest here overnight, and then my retinue and I will travel the countryside of Israel, looking at your cities and villages, your mountains and your valleys, until Ahab sends me word that he is not too busy to greet his future wife at the gates of Samaria. Please convey this message to His Royal Highness, my future husband.'

Her guards looked at her in surprise; the captain in admiration. It was an impressive and diplomatic insult for one so young. They had trained her well. Hattusas could barely restrain his smile. He had left Phoenicia with a girl and arrived in Israel with a woman.

That night, Jezebel made it known to the city officials that neither she, nor any member of her party, would attend the hastily arranged official banquet to be held by the apprehensive headmen of the city of Ak-Kah. She was, her maidservant reported, too tired after the strenuous ride south from Tyre.

The banquet was cancelled, but the city was awakened late that night with the sudden eruption of singing and music and shouts and laughter from nearly a thousand Phoenicians, camped at the foot of the city walls. Jezebel had made it clear shortly after her arrival that she would not like to lodge in the home of the headman of the city council, but preferred instead to stay with her own people until she arrived in her new home of Samaria and became his Queen and sovereign overlady.

The revelry began late in the evening, when nobody was in the streets, and only a few guards were walking the parapets of the walls to ensure that all were safe behind the locked gates of the city. But when the noises started, men and women suddenly emerged from their homes, ignoring the curfew, and walked towards the walls to see what was happening. They heard a long and monotonous drumbeat and the sounds of harps and lyres and the singing of voices, ululating in the warm night air.

The noises seemed to surround the city and to invade every corner of every building. Then trumpets cleaved the night air. People who had ignored the drums couldn't ignore the trumpets which sounded like a clarion call of the heavens. The moment the trumpets sounded, every citizen of Ak-Kah poured out of his house and scaled the walls of the city to see what they could see.

Fearful of an attack, the guards screamed for help from their commanders, who came out from their sleeping quarters and shouted orders for everyone to return to their homes and to obey the curfew, but nobody took any notice.

And then the explosions began. Loud and roaring explosions which lit up the night sky and sent colourful sparks high above the rooftops. At first, there were screams of fear from people who had never heard such noises, but when they saw that they were only coloured lights in the sky, like the sort which Yahweh occasionally sent from heaven through the firmament, they began to enjoy themselves.

With every explosion, there were screams and cheers and peals of laughter. Men lifted up their children so that they could see the sparks which flew into the night sky. What was causing the explosions, nobody knew. But every time a priest threw some liquid onto a fire, a boom like distant thunder could be heard, and a plume of coloured flame rose up.

Those few citizens of Ak-Kah who were still indoors, stunned by the sudden noises which tore at the night-time serenity of the city, finally emerged out of their homes, and ascended the battlements of the thick walls to join curious neighbours. Dogs in the city, suddenly terrified, started to howl and bark.

No one, of course, could leave the city through the gates, which were firmly locked and bolted at sunset. But they came in their hundreds to the north facing walls to stare down into the plain where the friendly army was encamped.

And there they saw sights the likes of which they had never seen before, nor knew existed. On the vast field in front of them there was a blaze of fire and colour and movement. And in the distant background, the luminous sea reflected the strange rainbow of colours from the fires on the land. Some of the campfires were burning a brilliant orange red, some a deep and mysterious blue, others green, yellow and vermilion.

And just as their eyes became used to the fires and the spectacle of colour, suddenly dozens of women slowly and sensuously walked out from tents and appeared to bow to the citizens. They stepped in front of the fires and began dancing to the beat of drums in a sensuous and provocative manner, knowing that their entire bodies were clearly visible through their transparent veils. On their fingers, tiny cymbals were making erotic, bell-like noises, as were the anklets on their legs and bangles on their arms. In the eroticism and preoccupation of their dancing, they seemed to forget that a large crowd had gathered and was watching them from the balustrades. As though in a trance, the priestesses weaved in and out of the light of the fires, their arms mimicking the act of lovemaking, their legs intertwining and prancing, slowly and seductively stepping as though in front of them lay men tethered to the ground and in their thrall. The citizens of Ak-Kah looked at the young women, but the dancers' minds were lost in the concentration on their dance.

But what captivated the citizens of the city even more than the dancers was the enormous pit which had been dug in the centre of the encampment. It took up almost as much space as a house, and the coals in the base of the pit were glowing red-hot. On top of the pit, four spits had been built, and each was roasting a different animal. On one, there was a huge cow, on another two lambs, on the third were threaded dozens of birds, and on the last were three pigs. The smells were sensuous in the warm evening air. Men edged forward over the balustrade for a better look at the glorious women and priestesses who were dancing in the firelight. Women became concerned with the way in which their men stared at these sensuous and lustful creatures.

And then, when virtually all of the town's citizenry, except the crippled and the infirm, and including the guards, the counsellors and the priests of Yahweh, were gathered speechless on the tops of the walls watching the spectacle, a thunderous crash of drums announced the arrival of a young and mysterious woman. A line of soldiers holding flaming brands walked to the doors of her tent, and laid a wooden platform in front of it. The young woman emerged as if in triumph from her tent and stepped forward until she was on top of the platform; nobody could make out who she was, nor what she was wearing, for she appeared to be wrapped up in a cape. But she stood on the platform, which was then lifted onto the shoulders of the guards. As they did so, their brands lit the four corners of the platform, which exploded in dazzling balls of fire and flamed violently into the night sky.

A gasp from the throats of all the men, women and children present rose into the air. As the fires roared upwards, the small figure seemed to grow in stature, and she cast off the cloak she was wearing. Another gasp from the Israelites. This was the Princess Jezebel. She was young and tall and lithe and beautiful. And she was naked. Her exquisite body moved fluidly on top of the platform in the firelight of the brands, and she seemed to insinuate herself upon the night.

Princess Jezebel looked upwards at the citizenry of Ak-Kah. She stared at them for a long and uncomfortable time. Many of them began to squirm in her withering stare; her displeasure at the people and government of Ak-Kah was palpable. But then a slight smile crossed her otherwise impassive face. Suddenly she threw her head back, her raven-black hair appearing to float in the firelight, and laughed at the top of her voice. It was a laugh which told the people that she was not in the least bit concerned about the insult done to her, that she was Jezebel, and nobody was important enough to upset her.

The guards carried the platform forwards towards the sunken pit, and lowered it so that the Princess could step off. But as she walked forward, moving closer and closer, languidly, erotically, towards the wall, it became obvious to those with good eyes that she wasn't, in fact, naked. She was wearing gossamer clothes; in the firelight her body could somehow be seen – the contours of her breasts, her hips, her legs – yet when she moved from the front of the fires she was swathed in robes which had the lightness of feathers; robes which were at once shimmering with the blue of a morning sky, then the red of an evening sunset, then the greens and golds of flowers in a field.

It was as though she had turned into a goddess come to earth and was wearing the exotic plumage of a beautiful bird.

Not only the men, but also the women were staring at this mystical apparition, this being from another world, this goddess of loveliness and sensuality.

She stood in the space between her encampment and the city walls, and again appeared to look up at the people. No! Not up, but through. As though she were staring beyond the high city walls, beyond the people, beyond even the night sky, and into the realms of Yahweh; as though challenging Him to come to earth and prove to the Israelite people that He was greater than she. Could this be true? Could Jezebel be tempting Him to defy her, as she was defying Him.

And there she stood! Alone and in complete command of who and where she was. The people's eyes were fixed upon her, despite the loud and sexual music in the background, the orgiastic dancing of her priestesses, the many-coloured fires which set the evening ablaze; the erotic aroma of ale and wine which the cooks were pouring over the rotating meats; and the eerie singing which seemed to be coming from everywhere and nowhere.

And Jezebel continued to stand and stare through the people until she suddenly laughed, turned and retraced her steps back into the tent.

The display was over; the main event at an end. Jezebel had conquered the city of Ak-Kah without a single arrow being loosed.

'She just stood there?'
   'Yes, great King.'

Omri looked aghast. 'She did nothing, said nothing? Just stood half-naked before the city walls and laughed?'

The captain of the guard of Ak-Kah nodded. 'Just laughed, Majesty. As though she had suddenly thought of something funny, something known only to herself and communicated to nobody. Then she turned and walked back to her tent. She wasn't seen for the rest of the night, but in the morning, when the people arose and went up to the city walls to see what was happening, the entire Phoenician encampment had disappeared, as though it had never been there. Only the pit was left. And scraps of meat. And bones.'

'Where did they go?' asked Prince Ahab.

'Nobody knows, Royal Master,' said the captain. 'Naturally we sent men after them, but by the time the scouts returned, all we knew was that they were heading in the direction of the Jezreel Valley. I sent more scouts after them to determine their exact location, but ...' The man hesitated.

'But ...?' demanded Ahab.

'But they'd disappeared. We spent two days searching for them. But it was as though the valley had just swallowed them up. We questioned villagers who reported having seen and heard some great army in the middle of the night, but nobody knew where they camped. We have no idea where they are now, Great King and Master.'

Omri looked at the captain in astonishment. 'A thousand men and women. Five hundred priests and priestesses and a command of guards! And they've just disappeared?'

The captain, mortified by his patent failure, just nodded. He knew that he was about to be punished;

relieved of his captaincy if he were lucky, disciplined or banished if he were unlucky. But neither happened. Instead father turned to son, and hissed, 'You're such a fool! If I'd known what you were going to do, I'd have forbidden it. What game are you playing with Phoenicia? Don't you understand the importance ...?'

His words trailed off when he realised that he was reprimanding his heir in front of the entire court. He coughed and turned back to the captain.

'Have you continued to search the area? It is my duty to apologise for this unfortunate incident and welcome her and her retinue officially into Samaria.'

But before the captain could answer, Ahab, stung by his father's rebuke, angrily retorted, 'I'll go and look for her, Majesty. This Princess needs to be taught a lesson in manners if she thinks that she can ignore an official reception from the city ...'

Omri turned and hissed, 'You thought that your stupid little insult would tell this girl your true feelings towards her, and teach her a lesson. You have taken her for a fool, Ahab, and she is no fool. She knows how to hold our people in her thrall. Word will now spread of the display she put on outside the walls of Ak-Kah. The same will be expected of her in every town and village which she visits. She will become the celebration of Israel. Crowds will gather whenever word comes of her arrival. She's made a fool of you, Ahab. She already wears the crown more securely than you. You will stay here and do nothing. I will deal with this from now on.'

The young Prince looked sternly at his father; but then his gaze softened, and he nodded. 'If that is your command, Majesty, then do so. But she has insulted me and that is something which I won't forgive. What I will do, though, is to ride north to the Jezreel Valley and find her. There, I'll greet her and make her welcome … as welcome as she would expect from one who's forced to marry her.'

Omri shook his head sadly. Soon, the crown of Israel would be upon Ahab, and that was something Omri feared, for his son was arrogant and headstrong and understood nothing of kingship.

'Ahab,' he said softly so that the court didn't overhear what he was saying. 'Don't be hasty. This is good for us, for when word spreads of her beauty and sensuousness and the richness of her retinue, the voice of Elijah will be dulled in comparison. You were wrong to insult her. She is worthy of being your wife if she can win a people over even without being by your side. If you think that you can put your petty jealousies to one side, then by all means, go and ride out to her and greet her properly.'

His jaw set in anger, Ahab bowed, excused himself, and walked from the throne room. The King dismissed the grateful captain of the guard of Ak-Kah with a wave of his hand. And in his place, the King's counsellor walked forward and bent over to whisper in the King's ear.

'Even with my old ears, I overheard what your Majesty said. You're right, Great King. With the noise of Jezebel's arrival, Elijah will have to shout much louder to be listened to.'

Omri turned to the old man. 'I hope so! Much of what I said was to make Ahab see reason. But I'm not so sure about Elijah. Now that she has arrived in Israel with her naked flesh and her public dances, Elijah will have much more to shout about.'

The King thought for a moment, and then continued, 'And how long before the young girls of Israel will be locked in their houses by their fathers, and before Israel's women will stop their menfolk from greeting this Jezebel? Yes, it was an amazing performance, but if she offends Yahweh too often, then all Israel will turn against her. And when she's Queen, that means that the people will turn against us ...'

CHAPTER SEVEN

Elijah returned to his village of Tishbe in a state of increasing tension. When he was up on the cliff at Ras Nichrah, when the arrows had rained upon him and the soldier began to climb to his ledge in order to kill him, he'd been terrified; then, as he scaled the top of the cliff, he'd been certain that the men below would let loose a volley of arrows and one would find its way into his back and he'd die plummeting to the ground like an eagle shot from the sky. But when the arrows no longer thudded into the rockface he was climbing, Elijah realised that the men below were restraining themselves because of their fear that they might hit their compatriot climbing after him. God, once again, had saved the Tishbite. Great was Almighty God. Yahweh was good.

When he escaped, he hid until the sun began to darken in the sky. He was sure that they would follow him to put him to the sword; but they didn't. Then he returned to the cliff face and peered over. There was no sign of the damnable woman's entourage. She had disappeared into the landscape like a hyena in the desert. Again, the Lord God had saved him.

And so Elijah the Tishbite journeyed home to be with his wife and children again until the Lord God showed him the way. And the closer he got to the Jordan River, and his home of Gilead, the stranger the sky began to appear. Sometimes, it was so strange that he would stop his walking and look. Suddenly in the day sky he would see strange shapes and bright lights. He would look up and they would be there … and then not there. He couldn't ascertain what these shapes were – one looked like a plough being pulled by a man bent over in the labour; another one like a ewer of water but it was empty; and one he thought looked like the chariot of an army. But each was presaged by a brightness in his eyes which was coloured the hues of flower petals or berries, sometimes red, sometimes tinged with blue.

He was nervous at first, but when he heard the voice of the Lord Yahweh his fear came to an end; because in his head he heard Yahweh telling him to put an end to Jezebel. It was when he heard this instruction that he knew these lights and noises and symbols in the sky were to be his instruments. One day, when he had chased her away from the land of Israel, the entire sky would erupt and the hosts of heaven would descend to earth with a roar and with the same bright lights which people said surrounded Jezebel.

And so Elijah returned to Rizpah and his two children. On the way, he had preached at every town he came to, telling them how the Lord had saved him from the merciless hands of the evil Jezebel, and he told them of the noises and the lights in the sky, and the people fed him and gave him charity because he was the mouth of the Lord and the conscience of the inhabitants. He slept in fields or in barns with cows and goats and sheep or, if he was fortunate, in the home of a religious man who welcomed him in as an antidote to the poison being spread by those who did not follow the words and the ways of the Lord.

Word continued to assail his ears of the immoral display which Jezebel had put on for the people of Ak-Kah, but when the most evil and lascivious details were told to him, Elijah refused to believe it. Whatever her immorality in praying to false gods, no Princess of royal blood, betrothed to be married to a future King of Israel, could have danced naked all night and taken a dozen men to be her lovers in front of the entire population of the city. So he discounted the rumours as just that, rumours and gossip.

When he arrived back at Tishbe, tired and ravenously hungry, his mood had sharpened against the foreign Princess. The voice of the Lord was sometimes weak and inaudible, but at other times loud and deafening in his mind. And the Lord's voice had been getting stronger and stronger in his head as he neared his home. The lights had become more oppressive, and sometimes they were so bright in his eyes, flashing like the sun off a white cliff face, that he squinted and averted his gaze.

As he entered the outskirts of the town, the message from Yahweh became very strong and insistent; indeed, Yahweh's voice was rarely out of his head. The Lord was telling Elijah, His servant, that anyone who shot arrows to kill a prophet of God was guilty of the greatest of all crimes and must be sought out and destroyed. The people must be made to listen through their laughter and through the seductions of this damnable woman to the dangers which were upon them. The name Moses kept entering his mind. Moses had been ridiculed by the Pharaoh and the court of the Egyptians. Nine times he'd been rebuffed by the evil monster who sat on the throne in the land of the pyramids. But on the tenth occasion, on the occasion of the slaying of the first-born, nobody had been laughing.

And nobody would laugh at Elijah. Not Jezebel, nor her captains, nor her priests and priestesses; not the people of Israel who were so quick to turn their heads when something seduced them from the sight of the Lord; and certainly it would not be the King of Israel when Elijah slew the first-born son of the King Omri, as were the first-born of Egypt who were slain in the time of Moses.

Rizpah had known of her husband's arrival for most of the day. A boy shepherd had told her while driving his flock to another pasture near to her home. At first she was delighted. It had been fifteen days since he'd last been home. She would welcome him back and comfort him with the food and the drink he liked. Then she and the two children would gather at his feet and he would recount for them his adventures: who he'd seen, where he had been, what he had done. She and her children were so proud of their father, and the love of Yahweh was strong in all of them. But still she worried about him. And about herself.

In the privacy of her own mind, she had to admit that she enjoyed life more when her husband was away from her house, when Yahweh didn't command her to travel with him as on this occasion. On these rare journeys when Elijah left her alone, his long absences were a time of peace in her household. It was when the children and she were at their closest. But on his return, especially in these most recent years, times were difficult for her family. Now that he was travelling more often on his own and returning unexpectedly, it was – she begged forgiveness from Yahweh for having these ideas in her head – as though a demon were in the house, pulling and pushing and tugging and shouting and complaining and wailing at the moon.

Whenever he returned, Rizpah greeted Elijah with respect, with affection, with pleasure, but within a few days, she couldn't wait for the Lord to descend from on high and to speak within him, and for her husband to be off again, visiting another city or town or village.

In trepidation of what state of mood he would be in when he appeared, Rizpah waited and waited for her husband's return from early morning till just before the sun went down. She knew that he was close to his home, yet he hadn't returned to his wife and family. That could only mean that his head was again filled with the voice of the Lord.

She feared for the next few days. This was a time which she dreaded the most, even from the first few days of her marriage all those years ago. She knew that he was a holy man, and that many of the things he did were not of his making, but were the Lord's. Yet despite her attempts to accommodate him, to be a good and God-fearing wife to him, his increasing rages scared her and terrified their children.

It had been only in the past year that things had become really bad. When she'd been travelling with him, he'd been kind and considerate to her and loving to their children when they returned home.

But lately, there were times when she didn't even recognise Elijah her husband, when his mood was strange and distant, and when he talked to himself as though there were somebody else in the room. Sometimes, she would wake in the middle of the night, and find that he wasn't in their bed. She would rise, and find him outside their door, bent over, holding his head and moaning. Or she would look for him in the cattle barn or the nearby fields, and he would be stretched out, sometimes naked, his body cold to touch, shaking and mumbling in some incomprehensible tongue.

Today, she knew, was such a day. From what the shepherd boy told her, Elijah should have been home by noon. Rizpah went out from their house and told Sharai, her daughter, to prepare the table and to serve her brother with his lentil and barley stew and bread for she was going out to greet their father. A look of concern passed over Sharai's face for she knew what her mother meant, and determined to hide it from her brother. Rizpah left the house and walked on the Shechem road.

She had walked only a few hundred paces, when she detected a movement in one of the barley fields which belonged to Nahmun. It was only the slightest of movements, little more than the wind blowing the tops of the stalks, but enough to make her stop on the road and look. And then she saw the hands and arms of a man waving amongst the heavy ears of the crop. She left the road, and walked towards the figure, knowing with certainty that it was her husband.

She lost sight of him as she entered the field of tall plants, but as she walked in his direction, she began to hear his voice. And the closer she walked, the more certain she was that it was Elijah. She saw him and was frightened; he looked as though he were possessed not by God, but by some evil and malignant force. Rizpah drew close enough to understand his words.

'Yes, Lord.'

A long silence.

'Yes, Lord.'

More silence.

'Now, my Lord and Master? Now? But I am tired and weary and don't know whether or not I am capable of the task.'

Then she heard her husband cry out. She was tempted to run towards him, but restrained herself.

'But my wife. My children. I must see them ...'

And then he shouted.

'Yes, Lord. Yes, I am unworthy. Yes, I am as the dirt of the fields, as the dung of animals. Yes, Lord. Now. I go now.'

He turned and saw Rizpah. He smiled, and she wanted to embrace him, for he knew her and recognised her.

'My love!' she said. 'Elijah, Master, welcome home. Come with me and I'll give you some food ...'

He nodded, and walked over to her. 'Rizpah, dearest and most loyal wife.'

He put his arms around her and they embraced in the barley field. He kissed her long and hard on her cheek, her neck, and her head. She felt his body, and was surprised at how thin he'd become on the road without her to cook for him.

'Come, husband, let me take you inside into the house and there you can rest.'

He started to follow her out of the field.

But suddenly she realised that he'd stopped walking. She turned and saw again the look in his face, the look of fear and hatred. And he was looking at her ... He bent double and grasped his head, screaming in pain. Rizpah drew back, terrified. Then he straightened up and suddenly he came crashing towards her through the stalks of barley, passing within touching distance of her. She smiled at him, tried to reassure him and shouted out his name. He looked at her, the pain of death in his face, white now, contorted in agony. She was horrified. Like a child wailing for his mother, he gasped, 'Rizpah ... help me ... the voice of God is so strong ...'

And then he looked through and beyond her and his face began to relax, as though the pain had suddenly been spirited away. Rizpah knew that for some reason, God had blinded his eyes and he couldn't see her. He began to run towards her. She yelped in fear but Elijah ran straight past her, and shouted as he went, 'Whore! Spawn of the Devil. Be gone, foul and filthy whore!'

He ran out of the field and onto the road where he again stopped, gripped his head, and shouted in agony. Rizpah went over and tried to comfort him by putting her arms around him. She felt his body relax somewhat from its wooden rigidity and she managed to gently lead him away from the road. She wasn't frightened any longer, but she was still shocked. How could he speak to her like that? Was this his voice, or the voice of God who accused her of these vile and hideous things? In her heart, she knew that it wasn't her husband speaking, but another within him. Though if it were the Lord who looked at her through her husband's eyes, and spoke such words to her through her husband's voice, why did He call her a whore? It distressed her horribly, because she had lived a pure and holy life from childhood, only occasionally having lascivious thoughts which she quickly buried deep within her. But who could understand the ways of the Lord?

Rizpah followed in the path of her husband, fearful that her children might be frightened by seeing him in this condition.

Jezebel was the major topic of conversation in Israel. When people gathered in marketplaces or on streets or in the stalls set up by wandering merchants, the name Jezebel dominated the conversation.

The people flocked to her whenever and wherever she and her entourage emerged. It was a royal procession the likes of which nobody in Israel had ever seen. Not even the Egyptian Pharaoh would have created more of a sensation. Her arrival was compared in the minds of the people with the arrival in Ezion-Geber of the famous Queen of Sheba, who had bewitched the King Solomon. Jezebel, though not black like the Queen of Sheba, was just as exotic and mysterious in the eyes of the people of Israel, and everyone was waiting anxiously for her arrival in their town.

Her regal progress had been staged twice but the second event was not the same as the first. In Ak-Kah, Jezebel had stood beneath the city walls and laughed. After consulting with Hattusas, Jezebel now realised that it was wrong for her to be so derisive, so dismissive. She had been angry with her husband-to-be and with the audacity of the townspeople for not giving her a splendid official welcome.

But from then on she determined to change her style. When she and her entourage suddenly appeared beneath the walls of Megiddo, a city high in the Carmel mountains, people flooded into the city from extensive surrounding areas. As the sun was setting over the Eternal Sea, the people waited on the tops of walls with bated breath. Her appearance this time would be more to the delight and excitement of the citizens because she had decided that her performance must be changed.

Nobody told her to change what she did, but her knowledge of how to perform to crowds and how to please people had been developing for many years. She was a favourite in the court of her father the King of Phoenicia and her performances of song and dance at royal banquets were always well received.

This time, when the citizens of Megiddo should have been in their homes and the only people on the streets of the city were supposed to be the watchmen and guards, there was no silence of the night, for there was a murmur above the city, a noise of people anxiously awaiting a performance. And so, to be heard, the crowd noise had to be overwhelmed by the loud beating of drums. As with Ak-Kah, those of the citizenry who were still in their homes, those too proud to be bothered, suddenly poured out and rushed up the ramparts squeezing into whatever space was still available.

In the seven days since the performance at Ak-Kah, word had spread throughout the towns and the countryside. Nobody knew where the huge caravan had disappeared to. Some had seen it but by the time people gathered to witness the spectacle, the assembly had moved on and disappeared again.

The people of Megiddo stood on the walls of their city and, for half the night, watched the sensuous undulations of the priestesses and the erotic movements of the priests thrusting their manhood and flaunting their bodies. But what all were waiting for was the appearance of Jezebel; and she did not disappoint. She danced, she walked, she promenaded before her newly conquered people. She ensured that she walked in front of the fires so that her body was visible through the flames which made the material of her apparel transparent.

She knew the effect, and her calculation was correct, because every time she walked in front of the fire, men would cheer and clap, and women would laugh and, following the lead of their menfolk, clap too. Quickly the entire city was clapping and shouting in their appreciation. The only voices of contempt were those of the priests of Megiddo who shouted their warnings to the people and who spat insults down at the worshippers of false idols. But the voices of the priests were thin and reedy in the heavily perfumed atmosphere of enjoyment and liberation which the people were enjoying.

But not all of the people. And not all of the women were happy with the naked and sexual cavorting at the base of the walls. Many of the wives ushered their complaining children back indoors and warned their husbands not to look at the women. Some wives even gathered up their entire families and forced them away from the walls of the city, muttering in their disgust about the harlotry and immorality which was going on at the base of their city. But most were revelling in the spectacle, breathing in the richness of the cooking aroma and the provocation of the perfumes which filled the summer air.

And at the end of the spectacle, Jezebel walked forward to stand at the foot of the walls, and looked up at the evening sky, her face impassive; once again, she did not engage people's eyes, but looked beyond what was on earth and into the very realms of the gods themselves. Nor did she laugh as she had during the previous event. Instead, her impassive face suddenly took on a golden glow, as though a goddess were revealing herself to the Phoenician Princess. Her eyes suddenly came alive, her lips parted slightly as though she were about to kiss a lover, and her arms moved slowly upwards as though at any moment she would link hands with the goddess and be transported to the stars.

And as she stood there in a trance, unseen by the citizens of the city, hidden by bushes, two priests with lighted tapers lit a liquid in a carefully concealed trench which suddenly burst into flames, the line of fire spreading from both sides into the middle just in front of where Jezebel was standing. To the citizens of Megiddo above on the ramparts it looked as though the very ground itself was on fire. Never had anybody seen this happen. It was magic from the heavens, the stuff of idolatry.

The citizens gasped in astonishment and drew back in wonder as the flames licked upwards between themselves and the Princess. Their view of her was obscured by the sudden appearance of fire and smoke, and by the time the liquid – called by the desert people 'the breath and fire of damnation' – had burnt itself out, she had disappeared.

This time, there were no gasps. Only silence. Questions were in everyone's mind. Where had she gone? How had she disappeared? What was the liquid fire?

Jezebel had conquered another Israelite city.

CHAPTER EIGHT

Elijah lay on his bed, ashen white, as deathly pale as the sun-bleached cliffs of Ras Nichrah. And hot! His skin felt like the wall of a house which has stood all day in the summer sun. The bandages Rizpah placed over his head, soaked in cold water from the village well and mixed with a soothing and perfumed balm she had saved in a jar since she last gave birth, became warm almost as soon as she lay them on his forehead.

On previous occasions when he had returned home from preaching the word of God, she had known what to do. He needed rest and comfort and the ministering touch of his wife on the first night home. A bland, well-cooked meal of roots and leaves with small amounts of fresh meat, but not made with spices which might affect his stomach, was what he enjoyed most. A meal such as the one she had in the pot over the fire, lentils and barley stew, into which she would cut some squares of the sheep meat she'd purchased the moment she'd heard he was on the road home.

She knew that Elijah would be suffering stomach cramps from the crude and simple diet which he ate on the road during his absences. At best, and especially when he was journeying on his own while she remained at home with their growing children, Elijah only ever ate simple food of bread and olives, and Rizpah knew from previous experience that to make her husband food which was blended with herbs or spices could make him sick.

After he'd eaten his simple meal and drunk some ale or wine, he would usually smile at the children and give them God's blessing before sleeping until well past sunrise on the following day. Rizpah would keep the children very quiet, ushering them out of the house the moment they woke, and only attending to those of her duties which she could do outside or took her into the village so that Elijah could continue to sleep. She would gather water from the well, knead bread dough outside and leave it to prove in a special spot which was shaded from the harsh heat of the sun; or she would gather those fruits which were ripe on the trees, press olives and filter the liquid to sweeten the bread and to cook the meat or fish, go to the merchants of Tishbe and buy what she needed with the small amount of money they were given by followers and supporters, and then sit outside and mend the clothes until she heard Elijah cough or move in the bed.

Then she would gather up her children, and they would stand at their father's bed and bid him a good and blessed morning (even if it was well into the afternoon), asking him where he'd been and what he'd seen.

But that was on previous occasions. This time it was very different, and for the first time since she had married Elijah ten years previously, she was seriously concerned that the voice of God was so strong within his head that it was shutting out all other voices, even her own. He'd even called her a whore and that, more than anything else, worried her.

Was this Yahweh's image of her? How could it be?

It had been late in the night when she had heard the strange sounds at her door. She was immediately frightened, as she often was when Elijah was away doing the work of the Lord Yahweh. She sat up in her bed, and then stood, walking softly to the door, the candle guttering noisily as wind blew in through the window. Was it the sound of the candle she had heard? Or an argument from a distant house? Or perhaps an animal in a nearby field?

And then the noise again. A scratching noise. Right at her door! A dog? A cat? Perhaps a lion or lioness, driven to enter the town in its hunger, suffering as much from the drought as were the villagers. The scratching continued and she couldn't move, so she sat silent and terrified on a bench. And then she heard the moaning. The voices of the dead. Her hair stood on end and she could hardly breathe in fear. It called her name. Softly as though carried on the foul breath of a demon, she heard her name through the wooden door.

She stood and uttered prayers to the Almighty One, Blessed be He. Rizpah went to the window, her knees shaking in terror, as though she were walking in the middle of a hideous dream. She looked out, and saw the body of a man lying face down at her door, his hands scratching at the wood.

Rizpah ran to the door, helped her husband stand, and carried him into the house. Was it her husband? It was his face and his hands and his body, but the man who lay on her floor was barely recognisable. Perhaps he'd been beaten by robbers and evil men; but there were no marks, no blood on his body. Perhaps he was sick. But although his body shook, it was with cold ... yet his head was hot against her breast.

It was her husband. The last time she'd seen him like this was two weeks earlier, when he had run past her out of the field, like a whirlwind in the desert, calling her whore and slut and demon. She'd followed him and led him back to their house, but after he'd been inside for just a short while the strange and distant look had come over his face once more, and he'd run screaming from the house. She watched as he had run into another field with the speed of a horse, but try as she might, she hadn't been able to find him since. Neither had the townspeople seen him.

And now he'd returned to her like a spectre in the night, his face so hideously distorted it looked as though a bull had trampled on him; yet there was no blood, no torn skin. No, his was the face of a man who has seen the very demons who skulk in the darkest corners where not even God's light is able to shine. She nearly cried for his terror, his pain.

She lay Elijah on the bed, and took off his sandals. Though she tried, she could not persuade him to take a drink of water or eat a morsel of bread or meat. He just lay on their bed, his head aflame, his body cold as though it was winter. His eyes were wide open, the whites red with tiredness. Yet he saw nothing. All he did was whisper her name, as though he was talking in his sleep.

'Here, husband. I'm here for you. You're home and safe. I'm Rizpah, your wife. Can you hear me?'

she whispered so as not to wake the children who were sleeping in the other room.

And she cursed herself for her selfishness, for when she'd journeyed with him, this had never happened. Then she'd been able to care for him, to feed him, to protect him from the crowds. But for some time now she'd remained at home – at her husband's insistence – and looked after her family. And in that year, he'd become more and more distant, his mind wandering in areas which were closed off to her. Never again would she allow him to leave the house without her. Of that, she was determined!

For the rest of the night, she ministered to him, but there appeared no movement in his body, except for his shaking. Then she stood to change his bandage as she had done many times during the night; but suddenly he grabbed her arm. She screamed in fright and in pain, for his grip was very strong. It was the first time he'd moved since he'd lain on the bed.

Rizpah turned and looked at her husband. His eyes told her that he had returned and that the Lord or the demons who had held him, had released their grip. He was back with her, back in the home of his wife. Wherever he had been, his eyes told her that he was now back in Tishbe. She stood silently as he tried to formulate words, his dry lips and flushed face a mask of confusion.

'Woman?'

Still she said nothing.

'Rizpah? How are you come here?'

'This is our home, Elijah. You're home. In Tishbe. In Gilead. You returned in the middle of the night. It will be morning soon. You have a fever.'

Her husband sat up painfully, trying to support himself on his elbows, but slumped back on the straw in exhaustion.

'Has she been here?'

'Who?'

'The harlot of the north. The whore of Phoenicia. The wife and mother of Ba'al. Has she been here?'

'Jezebel? No, Elijah, she hasn't been here. Nobody knows where she is. She arrives at the gates of a city ...'

'I know what she does,' he said aggressively, dismissing his wife's attempted explanation with a wave of his hand, spending even more of his limited energy. 'She is the very Devil herself. She appears and disappears. She is here and she is gone. She comes on a cloud of fire and smoke and disappears within it.' He licked his lips, and looked at Rizpah. 'I tell you this, woman. If she marries Ahab, Israel will be cursed in the sight of God for ever. Like the people who laughed at Father Noah before the earth was flooded, like the citizens of Sodom and Gomorrah whose immorality led to their destruction, we will all be washed away in the fury of God's flood. Water and fire and lightning will be our end. We will be burnt to ash in the conflagration and the fire which will rain down from heaven as God turns His face from the abomination which Israel will be committing.'

She turned white in fear. What her husband said, he said with the voice of God. 'But what can we do? How can we save ourselves?' she asked, her voice weak.

'Do? We can stop this accursed marriage. We can drive the heathens and idolators out of God's land. We can implore Asa, King of Judah, to send a mighty army against Israel and rid us of this blasphemy of the House of Omri. We can ...' he fell back on the bed, coughing, all energy having gone from his body. Rizpah looked at him in concern. He was shaking his head and mumbling.

Softly she asked, 'Where have you been, Elijah? You have been away for many days. I had no word from you. We were told of the progress which Jezebel makes through Israel, of how she appears and disappears like a spirit, but no word came to me of your whereabouts. Then I saw you two weeks ago in a barley field and you called me whore and harlot.'

He looked at her quizzically. 'I haven't been in a barley field. I was in the north of Israel with her. With the whore of Phoenicia. I was the shadow of her sun.'

His voice was dry and rasping. 'Wherever she went, I followed her to see what magic she was weaving, looking from the crags in the rocks, hiding behind trees, standing in the shade of a mountain. I followed her from the north of Israel, from Ras Nichrah to Ak-Kah to Megiddo to Shunem and then to Jezreel. I, a prophet of Yahweh, was forced to hide from the power of her magic. I feel shamed, yet until the voice of the Lord entered my head, I didn't know what to do ...' Again he coughed.

Rizpah cradled his head and tried to give him some water, but he turned his lips away, too intent on speaking of the fear he held for the future.

'She is like an animal of the night, preying on the dying carcass of our people, feasting on the body of Israel. She would arrive at a city in time for the evening curfew, hiding from the guards in their towers. The air would be full of the perfumes and ointments of her breed of whores and libertines. She slaughtered the animals she'd brought with her, even transgressing the law of God by killing pigs on our

181

sacred land. But it was her dances and incantations which mystified and made the people spellbound, like Lilith held Adam in her thrall.

'You should have seen her, Rizpah,' he said, a frown creasing his brow. 'She is the most evil and brazen woman I have ever seen. She sullies my eyes with the sight of her, she dirties my body when I tread where she walks. She is the essence of evil. She must be stopped. God has spoken to me. He has told me to speak out against her in all the rooms and public spaces and marketplaces of all the towns in Israel. God has commanded me ...' He began to cough again, and lay back, his body flaccid with exhaustion.

Once more, Rizpah lifted her husband's head and tried to give him something to drink. Since Elijah had arrived home, she had gone out and plucked some herbs from the nearby field, and some buds from the fig tree to make Balm of Gilead, which was for coughs and colds and to give a sick person strength. But by the time she had lifted the cup to his lips, he was fast asleep. She lay beside him, and tried to fall asleep herself so at least she would be awoken by the dawn and she wouldn't be too exhausted to do her work in the morning. But she didn't sleep straightaway, because her mind was tumbling like a rock falling off a mountain.

How evil could this young woman be? How much damage could one woman do? If she was truly the seed of the Devil, then she alone could destroy Israel. But her seed was that of Ethbaal, known to be a good man, and a King who treated his people well. He wasn't a despot or a tyrant like other kings in other nations. So how could this girl, only seventeen years old, be so evil that she could bring down a nation? Perhaps she was possessed by these Phoenician gods and they were commanding her actions. But if Elijah was right, there was only one true God, Yahweh, and all the other gods didn't exist; if that was the case, who was possessing Jezebel to do these terrible things? And how could a young woman be so destructive?

A king with an army was only a man, but he could destroy an entire country, and lead the people off to slavery and a life of misery. But from what Rizpah had been told, Jezebel came with no army. Just a bodyguard as would befit a princess of royal blood, and priests and priestesses. Yet her husband was talking of this woman as though she were an avenging angel; as though she were as mighty as an Egyptian pharaoh or an ancient Hittite marauder. How could a woman, a young woman at that, be so powerful? What could her husband mean? Rizpah tried to work out the words of the Lord, as spoken through the mouth of her husband. But she was unable.

And then something occurred to her which was so audacious that she nearly laughed out loud and disturbed her husband. She dismissed the thought, but it returned, and so she gave it careful consideration. And the more she thought it through, the more it became her path.

She determined to see Jezebel for herself when she came near to Tishbe or to any part of Gilead. And so curious was Rizpah to see her that, just before she eventually drifted off into a light sleep as the sun was about to rise, she determined that if necessary she would travel beyond Gilead into Israel itself. But of course, she couldn't tell Elijah. And that in itself was a sin. '*Ah, well,*' she thought as she drifted from exhaustion into sleep, '*if Jezebel is evil, then her evil is beginning to work on me.*'

Jezebel sat on her cushions in the royal tent and listened with increasing pleasure as the spy told her more of what she most wanted to hear. So far in her progress she had hardly spoken to one Israelite, yet the country seemed to be at her knees, each city begging her and her entourage to grace them with a visit. So intense was the curiosity concerning this young woman Jezebel and her mystifying dancers and priestesses that the King, Omri, had put about a warning: work must continue in the fields and people must not waste their time travelling from city to city in idle speculation about the Phoenician.

'The fire which makes me disappear,' she asked. 'What of the fire? Do they have such a fire in Israel? Do they know what it is? Are they mystified?'

'It is the talk of the nation, great Lady. The people of Israel have never seen such a spectacle. They have never seen water which burns. They say you are a miracle worker. Or in league with their God Yahweh himself.'

'So they don't know about the desert water which burns?'

'They have no trade with the people from the great southern desert lands. They have never seen the liquid which rises from the very ground itself and which can be set on fire. The people of Judah and Israel trade with many other nations, with Gilead and with the northern people of Assyria. But even so, the water which catches fire is unknown in this country. They see it as a miracle. And when you disappear ...' He left the sentence unfinished.

184

'And what of Ahab? What of my future husband? What does he say of my progress around my future country?'

The spy smiled, but before he could speak, Hattusas, whose admiration of the young woman's developing diplomatic talents increased daily, warned him, 'Tell Her Majesty the truth. You aren't her sycophant. The Princess Jezebel needs no praise from a spy, only knowledge of what is happening in the towns and cities. Now, tell us of Ahab ...'

The spy nodded and turned back towards Jezebel. 'Great Lady, word has it that he is bereft. He is both furious with you, and fascinated by you. A rich merchant at a royal banquet two nights ago reported to me that at the end of the dinner the Prince grew into an increasingly sullen mood. It appears that at the beginning of the night, he was merry with wine, but then dancers from the northern desert land of Ammon began their entertainment. He was happy to be distracted from the cares of his life and applauded them greatly, throwing their leader a purse of gold. But when they had left the banqueting hall, one of the guests said in an unsubtle voice, "I was in the city of Aphek on the shores of the Sea of Chinnereth two days ago and I saw Jezebel dancing. Let me tell you that her beauty and grace and seductiveness are far greater than these Ammonite women. She is a true woman with a body more beautiful than any I have ever seen, and she weaves her arms and legs ..." but Prince Ahab interrupted the guest with an imperious shout and told him that he would cleave his head from his neck if he, or anyone, mentioned the cursed name of Jezebel again in his presence.'

Jezebel burst out laughing. She turned to Hattusas and nodded. He was her chief counsellor, and she'd known him since she was a child, but she knew that he was also travelling with her not as part of her entourage, but as the eyes and ears of her father's command. She asked him, 'Well, what do you think?'

'I think, great Princess, what I have thought since we arrived in your new country. Your answer to Ahab's deliberate rudeness when we first arrived in Israel has been wonderful. But from this point onwards, I feel that you should proceed with caution. This man Ahab is not a pampered merchant or a crude soldier. This man is a Prince of the royal blood. He is vain and mighty as befits his rank. And at this moment, he is bemused and mystified. He set about making your arrival unpleasant so he would upset you and make you subservient to him on the wedding day. His plan has failed and the people are under your spell.

'At the moment, Ahab doesn't know which way to turn, nor which path to tread. We know that Omri is furious and ordering him to seek peace with you. We also know that on the second day of our arrival in Israel he rode from Samaria to the north to greet you and present himself, but couldn't find us; our spies told us that he was fascinated by a woman, a Princess who danced before the walls of Ak-Kah. But by hiding from him, we have also frustrated and embarrassed him before his father the King.

'When he couldn't find us, he was forced to return to Samaria and feel the scorn and ridicule of the entire court. Push him too much further, great Princess, and his fascination might turn to hatred. It might bode ill for you and your future happiness.'

Jezebel heard what her father's counsellor said, and smiled.

'Hattusas, your words are wise. But you know nothing of the hearts of men. I know men such as Ahab. I have slept with them, played with them, made them grovel and beg at my feet, made them cry with frustration and laugh with happiness when I threw them bones. I know Ahab and how to treat him.'

But the counsellor shook his head sadly. 'Proud woman. This is not some plaything, some woodsman with whom you want to spend an afternoon. This is a Prince. A warrior of great bravery. A builder of cities. He is not a man to be treated like a child's toy. Jezebel, you are not here for your own private enjoyment, but to fulfil a contract which my Lord, your father the King, entered into with Omri in order to protect Phoenicia's southern border and to warn off Syria and Assyria. I warn you, don't let your games with this man endanger the lives of Phoenicia,' Hattusas told her sternly.

She was momentarily angry, and was inclined to shout at her father's counsellor. But she had played on Hattusas' knee when she was a baby; his daughter was her close friend; and what he said was right. She had made Israel fall in love with her, and brought Ahab to his knees. Now this Prince knew how mighty and clever she could be, he would never insult her again. On her wedding day, she would stand as tall as he. Now was the time to travel to Samaria and to be received into the court of Omri.

She nodded and smiled at the counsellor. 'Send word to King Omri and to my future husband Prince Ahab that I wish to come to the court of Israel in Samaria. Ask the permission of their Majesties for me to bring my entourage into the city. Beg His Highness Omri to receive his future daughter in law.'

The counsellor smiled, bent, and kissed her feet.

For the first time since Jezebel had travelled across Israel's northern border, Ahab felt himself relax; he breathed a sigh of relief as he listened to the Phoenician Ambassador asking their Majesties for permission to enter the royal court of Samaria. He nearly burst out laughing with satisfaction when the Phoenician finished speaking. Ahab looked at his father the King, and saw that the old man, too, was smiling.

'Tell the Princess Jezebel that I will welcome her with open arms into my court; tell Her Majesty that here in Samaria she will experience hospitality like none other. We will be to her as her father and mother; we will be sun to her day, and moon to her night. We will feast for two full days and nights and we will slaughter ten cows and twice as many sheep in her honour. Go and tell her this.'

But the ambassador did not rise. Instead, he turned to Ahab. 'And you, mighty Prince, will you also welcome my Princess when she arrives? Or will you, again, be detained in the business of the realm and too busy to be here to greet her?'

The insult by the ambassador went deep, but Ahab had been previously warned by his father to be silent and courteous, and not to let his arrogance or temper rule his wisdom. And so he answered, 'I will be here. And tell my future wife that my body is full of urges to see her. Reports come to us of her beauty and grace and ability to dance. Tell my future wife and Queen that after our wedding night, I will expect her to dance for me as she dances for my people in Israel.'

The ambassador smiled. It was precisely the reaction which he wanted. He stood and bowed to the King and the Prince. Everyone in the court was smiling as the ambassador prepared to take his leave; everyone except Hazah, a woman of Israel, daughter of a rich merchant in the city, who had been Ahab's bed companion and wife in all but name for the past year. She had been told by Ahab that he would marry her and make her Queen beside him; but now his face was turned from her and even though she still occupied his bed, his mind was on another woman, as he was enthralled by this idol-loving and false-god worshipping Phoenician whore.

Hazah, hiding behind a column in the audience hall, watched the ambassador and wondered what she could do to regain her place in Ahab's heart.

But Hazah wasn't in Ahab's mind. Instead, he was trying to determine what attitude he should take to his new wife. She was the celebration of Israel; she was the word on the lips of people in the cities, the towns and the villages. Jezebel was a goddess; Jezebel was the Devil himself come to earth as a woman; Jezebel was the most beautiful woman who had ever lived; Jezebel was a white Queen of Sheba; Jezebel was going to ruin Israel with her idols and her seductive ways, she was going to make each man unhappy with his wife and make all of the people of Israel turn away from the paths of righteousness. Jezebel this ... Jezebel that ...

But only Ahab would know the real Jezebel, and he was fascinated by the prospect. He had underestimated her badly. He'd thought to show her that he was her Lord and Master, and that her status as Queen would be in title only, that she held no real power. That his real wife was Hazah, and while she might pleasure him for a few days after their marriage, the rest of her life in Samaria would be cold and barren. How wrong he'd been. His musings were interrupted by his father the King.

'Tomorrow or the day after, as word arrives of her progress, you will ride out and meet her. You will go to her as her consort and her equal. You will be alone, unaccompanied, you will take no bodyguard; you will be wearing the crown of a future King. You will bow before her, and offer her yourself and your future kingdom. You will …'

Ahab interrupted. 'Bow? You expect me to bow before my future wife? I bow to nobody except you, Father,' he said in a voice loud enough to be heard by the entire court.

Omri sighed. It had been a long day, and he was still exhausted from the effects of the hamsin wind which had only blown itself out after eighteen hideous days. The wonderful news of Jezebel's final acknowledgment of the majesty of the House of Omri was now being tempered by the short-sighted stupidity of his son and heir. How could Omri possibly leave the nation of Israel to a man such as his son, Ahab? Yes, he was a valiant warrior and a great captain of his men, as well as a man who could build great buildings as he had in the cities of Shechem and Jezreel where his temples were still being talked about. But he was also a man whose limited vision would prevent him from seeing the dangers which surrounded him.

Furious, Ahab saw the look of contempt in his

father's eyes and said, 'She has given in, Father. She comes before me as my future Queen. I have won. She has acknowledged my standing, and now begs to enter our capital. And yet you think I should go to her on bended knee, and ...'

Omri held up his hand, concerned that his son's outburst would be reported back to the Phoenicians.

'I desire to call this audience to an end,' he said suddenly. He turned to the Phoenician, 'Ambassador, please convey our undying love and respect to Princess Jezebel and tell her of our earnest desire to welcome her and her entourage into our court. She has already won the hearts of our people ... now she will conquer its ruling family. Forgive me, but I must return now to my apartments. The recent hamsin has given me a sickness and I must rest. Ahab, would you follow me to my chambers ...'

The King stood and left the audience hall in silence, followed by his courtiers and his son. He dismissed the attendants and shut the door to his private bedchamber, turning on Ahab and shouting, 'Stupid idiot of a boy! Fool of a son that Yahweh has cursed me with. How could you have said those things about Jezebel in front of her ambassador and her spies in the throne room?'

Ahab drew back in shock at his father's vehemence. Omri continued, 'So you think we've won, do you? You think that just because she asks to come to Samaria, it's our victory? Idiot! Imbecile! This young woman could have travelled around all Israel and Judah and even Egypt for the next ten years, and the people would have voluntarily handed over their lands to her, she would have ruled in my place and taken the kingdom of Asa and all before her, had she but wished. This isn't a victory for Israel, Ahab. This is the worst defeat imaginable. She comes to us because she wants to. She comes at a time and in a manner of her choosing. We are her vassals.'

The Prince began to speak in his own defence and to argue with his father, but Omri, shaking with anger, shouted over his son. 'Ahab! You will bow before her. Without even meeting you, she is more than your equal in the eyes of the people, and they might even look upon her as your overlord. A girl of seventeen without an army has captured Israel without a battle; she's won the people without any casualties, except for you. Are you so blind that you fail to understand what this girl has done in only ten days? She holds us in her thrall. She is ruler in name, if not in fact. The people leave their fields unattended just to see her, their pots unfired, their furnaces cold, their orchards bursting with overripe fruit. The priests report a turning away from Yahweh and a turning to the worship of Asherah and Ba'al in her wake. Are you so stupid that you can't see where this could lead?

'So you *will* bow before her, and you will take her in your arms, and you will love her and make her welcome in her land. If she annoys you, you will turn away; if she insults you, you will ask why you are at fault; and if she displeases you, you will smile and tell her that she is the most wonderful creature of God. You will do this, Ahab, not because I command it, and not because it is the right thing to do, but because you have no choice.'

Ahab looked at his father. These words were an admission that the House of Israel was suing for peace; that the Phoenician Princess had clearly outmanoeuvred his son and himself, and that she could enter the kingdom on her own terms. Now he heard them from his father's lips, he realised that he was right.

But still the words hurt Ahab. He thought he understood why his father had said them; so that when Jezebel entered the court, there would be no other wives which would be before her. That she was as an equal with her future husband; so that Omri's actions of cutting short his son's outburst would be reported back to King Ethbaal of Phoenicia and would counterbalance the report which Jezebel would have sent her father about Ahab's snub; so that the treaty which the two Kings had signed would remain intact and in force, and Ethbaal would not rescind his contract and withdraw his daughter; so that Israel would be safe on its northern border and King Asa would think twice before deciding to attack Omri.

But despite his knowledge of why they had been said, the words hurt. Ahab could feel the contempt of the men and women of the court, standing there as observers to his further humiliation, as he was forced to walk out and follow in his father's footsteps. He could envisage them all, secretly laughing at his disparagement.

And then an image of Hazah came into his mind. He knew that she'd been in the audience chamber. In his mind's eye, Ahab saw her, standing next to a distant column at the back of the room. And even though she was far distant from him now, he knew within his heart that there were tears in her eyes.

* * *

Ahab stood on the parapet alongside the captain of the guard. The sun was burning as it reached its zenith. He had begun standing on the top of the defensive walls of Samaria when the sun was only halfway towards the top of its arc and his eyes were burning from the glare of the distant mountains.

The captain had told Ahab that if he wanted to return to the coolness and safety of the palace he would call him the moment the messenger arrived, but Ahab wanted to know immediately what the answer was. And at last a puff of dust in the far distance announced the return of the man.

Exhausted, the red-faced messenger pulled up his horse to announce himself to the guards standing to attention at the Damascus Gate, but before he was allowed to enter the city, Prince Ahab shouted down, 'Well? What did she say?'

The startled messenger looked up and smiled. 'She will greet you, Majesty …'

He didn't finish the message. Instead, he watched the unusual sight of the Prince laughing and shouting out a loud, 'Yes!' before disappearing from the wall.

As the sun began its journey to the Eternal Sea, Ahab rode out of the Damascus Gate in the direction of Tirzah. Only a few people saw him leave in such a hurry. One of them was his mistress, Hazah, who smiled bravely, but whose heart was breaking. For she knew that all her power was disappearing as Ahab retreated from her into the distance.

Kicking the flanks of his horse, Ahab determined his route. He would journey to the south of Jezreel and meet up with Jezebel somewhere on the road to the capital Samaria. Reluctantly, his father had agreed to delay Ahab's journey for two days to allow a messenger to announce the Prince's desire for an audience. Her reception of the messenger and her agreement to a private audience was good news. It meant that there was no possibility that he would be ridiculed in front of her entourage, that she had forgiven him his snub, and that she wanted to make a move of conciliation so that their lives together could be lived in harmony. And when she saw him and his majesty, she would realise that her role as Queen would place her at his feet.

Ahab had never ridden so fast. Even the horse seemed to sense the man's urgency. Although it was a normal half-day's ride, Ahab arrived long before nightfall to the surprise of the city leaders who had not been notified of his visit. But he did not stay in the town. Instead, he changed his horse at the stables, washed, ate some meat and bread and drank some ale, and thundered out of the northern gate in the direction of the city of Dothan. He would arrive there after dark, and knew he would have trouble identifying himself to the commanders of the locked gates. But he also knew that his word was law and he could command the guards to open the city gates. And in the morning he would be gone so that he could meet the caravan of the Phoenicians north of the city. He had no idea where they would be. All he knew was that they would be somewhere on the road between Dothan and Jezreel.

The following day, just after midday, he found them. And for the first time, he knew why the people of Israel were so enamoured by the procession. There seemed to be a thousand people, two hundred horses, twenty wagons groaning with food and wine and ale and folded tents and clothes. Oxen strained along the road pulling the carts while men and women walked four abreast in front of the supply wagons. How had they managed to conceal themselves in the early part of their journey through northern Israel, he wondered. It looked like an army on the move.

But when Ahab saw the women, he stopped wondering about concealment and immediately understood why men in their thousands were flocking to see the Princess of Phoenicia. The women ... priestesses ... were bare-breasted. They were walking along the road with nothing to cover their breasts. They wore headscarves to protect their heads from the heat of the sun, but on their chests was nothing. Was it an insult to the modesty demanded by Yahweh? Or was it the custom of Phoenicia? Either way, the effect of over two hundred semi-naked women made Ahab draw his horse to a standstill on the crest of a hill, and look at the entourage as they approached him.

But his eyes were drawn from the mass of women's bodies to the front of the assembly. For there, riding imperiously at the head of her people, like a queen herself, was a young and startlingly attractive woman. She was raven-haired, dark-skinned and even from this distance he was drawn towards her and her beautiful eyes. But it was her body which captivated him, swathed like some exotic bird in shimmering clothes which seemed to dance in the sunlight.

He was transfixed by her image. He had seen more beautiful women; some of the prostitutes whom he visited were more beautiful. But none was as regal, as confident of herself; none held themselves with such assurance, such dignity and confidence. The young person riding her white stallion was a woman in every sense of the word. She was seductive and alluring, and he wanted to ride down and touch her, to feel her body, to let the rainbows she was wearing slip between his fingers and touch his face.

Suddenly Ahab felt crude. He looked at his clothes, a grey tunic which he always wore when he went riding in the countryside, and immediately he was embarrassed because he recognised its roughness. He looked at his hands, the hands of a soldier, pitted with dirt which he had barely washed off in days; he reached up and felt his beard. It was untrimmed, and hadn't seen a knife in over a week; and worst of all, he felt his hair. It was unwashed and felt damp with sweat and heavy with oil. He felt deflated and unwilling to ride down to a woman who looked as though she had just spent an entire day in her bedchamber being prepared for her wedding night.

He narrowed his eyes to see her better, even though she was riding slowly towards him and her image was getting clearer all the time. Had she noticed him, astride his steed on the top of the hill? If so, she made no indication of it. Perhaps he could ride away without her noticing, and find some village where he could get his hair combed and cleaned and his beard cut and trimmed, and change his clothes to suit a Prince of the court of Omri.

But he knew this part of Israel well, and the villages nearby were full of peasants and workers of the land who had never heard of the refinements to which he was accustomed in Samaria. He was not a vain man; he never spent anywhere near the amount of time that other princes and princesses of the court spent on their clothes and preparations. Instead, he spent his time in sport, in visiting his future realm and in the creation of buildings and cities.

Now he felt that he should have spent more time attending to himself, for he would soon have to ride down to Jezebel and announce himself; and he would appear to be like a farmworker to the entourage. He could already see their smirks and hear the remarks they would make about him behind hands placed in front of mouths. He felt unworthy. But he had no choice.

Reluctantly, he kicked his horse in its flanks, sped down the hill, and wheeled around in front of the procession. A tall and virile man, obviously the captain of Jezebel's personal guard, suddenly drew his sword and rode quickly to place himself between Ahab and Jezebel. Ahab brought his horse to a stop.

'I am Ahab. Prince of Israel.'

The captain frowned, unwilling to believe that such a ruffian could be of the royal blood. But the rider's bearing and confidence told him that he was no robber and so the captain nodded in respect, sheathed his sword, and retreated from the front to allow the Prince and the Princess to see each other.

He saw the look of disappointment in her eyes and it annoyed him.

'I've been riding for two days to get to you ...' he said angrily.

'And I've been riding for two weeks to get to you,' she retorted.

He bristled. She had not addressed him by his titles, nor shown him any respect. She was on his land, yet she was making him feel inferior.

'Perhaps you'd prefer it if I returned to Samaria

198

and bathed and pampered myself. I'm not like that. I'm a soldier and a builder. I don't have time for perfumes and barbers.'

'Not even time to bathe in the two weeks I've been visiting my future realm? No time to cut your beard? Is life so busy in Israel?'

'Jezebel ...'

'You will address me as your Highness,' she shouted. She was furious that her future husband was treating her with such disdain. And she could feel Hattusas cringing three rows of horses behind.

Ahab's eyes widened in fury. He was about to wheel his horse around and return to Samaria when the words of his father entered his head. Breathing deeply, he said, 'Your Highness. I apologise for my custom and my manner and for not dressing properly to greet you, but I was eager to meet you and to escort you back to our capital of Samaria.'

The entire entourage paused, waiting on Jezebel's response. Hattusas especially was praying to his god that she would say the right things.

'Your Highness. Husband. There is much that each country can learn from the ways of the other. Phoenicia is a great and mighty land and my people understand the needs of the body and are trained from birth to obey the gods who protect us. We bathe often and those of us who have wealth use perfumes and unguents and salves so that our gods will appreciate the beauty of our odours and the care which we have taken in our worship of them.

'Israel,' she continued, 'is also a great and mighty land and I will enjoy learning of the things which will be new to me. In the meantime, we will rest here for the day. You will enter our tents and if you allow us, we will show you how Phoenician women look after their Phoenician men.'

She wheeled her horse around without waiting for his response. Jezebel saw Hattusas looking at her. His face was impassive, but he nodded his approval gently. She had passed yet another test as a future Queen of this strange country.

CHAPTER NINE

Prince Ahab fought to restrain his irritation. He'd been embarrassed before the Phoenician retinue, ridiculed by a young girl, and made to feel unkempt and unmanly because of his appearance. But his father's words were reverberating in his head like echoes off the walls of a desert wadi. If he did not curb his anger, if he followed his heart and rode away, then the treaty would be broken, and all Israel would be imperilled. So he contented himself to play the fool, to allow these Phoenician girls to pamper him and pull him into the hastily erected tents and lay him on cushions, as though he was a bridegroom visiting a house of prostitutes before his wedding.

Yet ... yet there was something about these Phoenician women which fascinated him. He'd never before experienced a Phoenician woman – or women! He'd had Moabite and Edomite and Egyptian and Assyrian women before and Israelite women too numerous to number. But there was a quality of sensuality in the way these priestesses moved and touched him and seduced him which was ... he struggled to find the essence which made this experience different from others, and slowly came to the realisation that these women were truly enjoying the experience, and were naturally seductive, rather than trained in seduction, and acting out their parts. He found all women seductive, from the youngest to the oldest, and he'd experienced the joys of many. But these Phoenician women were more feminine, somehow, more determined and alluring and more in control of him than he was of his emotions.

He had smelled perfumes before – those worn by the wives of rich merchants or prostitutes from eastern cities – but he'd never smelled aromas before like these. They were the very essence of night-blossoming flowers on a balmy summer evening, the delicacy of newly plucked petals, the mouthwatering refreshment of herbs and the erotic flavours of oriental spices. He could smell roses and hyssop and jasmine and oleander, as well as the tantalising aroma of the buds of figs, heavy with the dew as the sun rose and the webs of spiders could be seen knotted with droplets of water.

And the food! He'd eaten well at banquets both in Samaria and in foreign capitals when he'd been on a mission for his father, but he'd never eaten meats or pastes or breads like these. It was as though he were sitting at the table of Yahweh, God Himself, dining in the clouds. With each mouthful, he repeated the questions, 'What is this?' or, 'How is this made?' or, 'How did you prepare this feast so quickly?' For that was what amazed him so much. In his capital of Samaria, it took an entire day for the cooks to slaughter animals, skin and salt them, mix up the pastes and herbs with which to cook them, cut them up so that they could become stews, boil the crushed ears of wheat, make the breads and the sweetmeats, and filter the ale and the wines so they could be drunk.

But it had taken Jezebel's servants just a short while from the time in which they erected their tents to the moment when a slave whispered into the Princess's ear that their banquet was prepared and ready.

Yet she made no move. Instead, she waited for her husband-to-be to indicate that he was ready to eat. And so they sat inside her tent on the softest of cushions his body had ever sunk into, and as Ahab breathed in the heavy and erotically perfumed atmosphere, Jezebel simply smiled at the obvious joy he experienced in the luxury in which she lived. But at last the aromas from her mobile kitchen insinuated themselves into his consciousness, and he said that he would now like to eat.

From the time she'd insulted his dress and cleanliness on the road, to the time when they went to the banqueting tent to eat, Jezebel's metamorphosis was complete – from the outraged Princess to the loving and obedient woman who wanted to marry him. Where she had first been a commanding and arrogant ruler of her entourage, now she was observant and respectful and coquettish. Ahab tried to understand the motives behind the change, the subtleties which she was using to undermine him, but he couldn't. He knew she was playing games with him, but he didn't understand the rules.

Jezebel's smile became even more pronounced when they left her private apartments on the roadside and wandered to a large and solidly built tent in which he could see frantic movement. As he entered the tent, his curiosity was aroused, for suddenly the movement stopped and there he saw a table strewn with flowers and cushions for them to sit upon, but nothing else! There was no food on the tables as there would have been in a Samarian banquet.

And her smile couldn't be contained as she saw Ahab's jaw sagging in wonder as stews and platters of meats and fruits and breads and drinks were carried in by semi-naked priestesses. He was truly astounded by her magic. What seemed to be only moments earlier, she and her entourage had been astride horses, her baggage and pack animals strapped down tightly for the rutted and uneven roads, completely packed for the long and arduous journey from city to city, accompanied by enough people to inhabit a town; and the next moment the procession stopped, the wagons were unloaded, and shortly after he'd washed himself and drunk a cup of honey and wine, he was invited to sit in the dining tent, and an entire intricate meal was being served to him. In the space of time it had taken him to shake off the dust of his journey, Ahab was being treated like a king and feted in the manner of a potentate in his own palace by his own sycophants.

He asked her how she had managed to create and serve a banquet of such magnificence so quickly after his arrival. She demurred and didn't answer his question, telling him only that there was much magic which Phoenicia could teach Israel, advising him simply to enjoy the fruits of her people's labour, rather than wondering how such menial slavish tasks were performed. She told him that kings and queens shouldn't be interested in the preparations of the kitchen, but that their minds should be absorbed by the affairs of the nation. And this she did to each of his questions; she simply answered with a smile, and a deferential bowing of her head.

What Ahab didn't know was that three wagons were trundling down the road behind and out of sight of the main party, in anticipation of the imminent arrival of the Prince of Israel. Her cooks had been working since early morning in their preparations, complaining and cursing because of the difficulties of creating a banquet on the move for an eagerly anticipated Prince; and not only was the choice of food important, but their preparations had to be done while on the back of an ox-drawn cart lumbering along with the stability of a drunken camel, and constantly in danger of the flames spreading and incinerating the wagon, the food and the cooks. The slowly-moving wagons had rolled up to the rest of the caravan when it stopped, and by joining the entourage, it looked as though the meal had just been prepared.

The miracle of the cooks was now being enjoyed by Ahab as he dipped a piece of bread into a bowl of red stew and withdrew a chunk of lamb, his fingers coated with the richness of the juices and spices. He ate the meat, the bread, and then licked his fingers. It was, perhaps, the most delicious lamb he had ever tasted. The red paste with which it was covered, was both hot and spicy, and made the flesh of the animal almost glow as he ate it. Wiping his hands on a cloth, he picked up a glass of ale and drank deeply.

'Your Highness, I must apologise for my rudeness when you first entered my country. I was …'

Hattusas looked at the young Princess in concern, but smiled to himself when Jezebel held up her hand to stop his talking. 'Ahab. You were busy. I understand that. You are a man of importance, and I was not offended. But rather than disturb you, I decided to join you in the service of our people, my future husband. So

I determined to visit my future subjects, as is the right of any future queen. For that, I ask your understanding.'

Any animosity between them was nearly put to rest.

'And as to my dress when I arrived at your caravan, please understand that it wasn't my intention to insult you. But in Israel, dress and appearance aren't things which occupy us as much as they do the rulers of our neighbouring lands. Our God, Yahweh, believes that we should be modest in all things. He believes that vanity is a sin, and that instead of spending time on fineries and other indulgences, we should instead pray to Him.'

Jezebel frowned. 'Then when does your Yahweh allow you time to enjoy yourselves? If you're always praying, when do you sing and dance and make love?' Before he could answer, she continued, 'Our gods understand the needs of the body. They appreciate our desires to look our best for our husbands and wives, to spend time when work is finished in enjoying ourselves. They demand sacrifices and prayer, but we are still able to laugh and play and enjoy the sunshine and revel in the night. Your Yahweh sounds an irritable and ill-tempered God. He sounds as though He needs a goddess to keep Him company in the heavens.'

Ahab looked at her in astonishment. 'We're told by our high priests that there's only one God, and that's Yahweh alone.'

'Yes,' replied Jezebel. 'My ambassadors have told me this. And they've also told me that you don't decorate your palaces or paint your women's faces or adorn your bodies with tattoos and that you aren't permitted to do many of the things which give us

Phoenicians pleasure. This, my husband-to-be, is something we need to talk about if I am to sit on a throne beside you ...'

He looked at her in disquiet. He should tell her that her position as a Queen was that of mother to his children and partner in his bed. Yes, she will sit on a throne, but it would not be *beside* his ... But again, his father's words were loud in his head, and he remained silent. He retreated back into himself and allowed the contentment of the Phoenician banquet to please him. He knew he'd made some wrong moves at the beginning, that he'd been brutish and slow-witted; he'd thought that with his apology and riding to greet her, things would be put to right. But there was much which needed to be sorted out if this arrangement of marriage wasn't to be the bane of his life. And this he would do when they arrived in Samaria and he was within his own territory, not one recently conquered by Jezebel.

She saw the look of disquiet on his brow. 'Husband-to-be, try the figs. They're soaked in wine and then dried. We eat them with yogurt, a kind of soured milk, which softens them and aids their digestion.'

He picked up a fig with his fingers, and nibbled the outer edges. He'd eaten dried figs when he was on a campaign with his army and the field kitchens were running short of food. It was a meal for country people, peasants who could not afford real food so ate such things as dried grapes and fruits and meats. So he was surprised that the Phoenicians ate them as a delicacy. But they were delicious. The white thick milky covering she called yogurt was slightly acrid to the tongue, like goat's milk which had fermented in the sun, but somehow it offset the tantalisingly vivid sweetness of the figs; the taste in his mouth was one of sheer joy.

Again she smiled at his obvious enjoyment of her gifts. 'The yogurt comes from a land far to the east. Knowledge of it was carried by the ancient Hittites from the furthest parts of the world, and brought to the people of the Great Sand Desert who use the milk of their goats to make the yogurt. We use the milk of sheep and the milk of cows to make ours. It is less bitter and acidic to the tongue,' she told him.

He listened to her with his mouth half open, as a child listens to an instructor. She liked this way with him. He was obviously strong and manly, but there was an innocence which appealed to her. In some ways he was very much like a child, unsophisticated and unused to the manners of adults. She looked at him carefully, examining his face and neck and body and legs. She liked strong legs on a man. She liked being captured by their embrace, struggling to free herself, but ultimately having to give in to a man's stronger muscles ... yes, she liked them very much. And Ahab had strong legs, though he smelled of horses and his face was rough and he looked as though he needed a bath. But he had a pleasant face and Jezebel knew that once she and her maidservants set to work on his outer being, she could transform him into something spectacular, someone who would please her eyes and satisfy her body.

Ahab knew he was being scrutinised, and again realised that this young woman was making him feel ill at ease. There was something of the harlot in Jezebel; the woman of perfumes in a house which was redolent of sex and the odours of the body. But there was another person within Jezebel, a much older and wiser person than her youth revealed. Within her coquettish being was a woman of all ages, someone who understood the ways of older men, who seemed to know instinctively their desires and thoughts. Her eyes were boring into his very soul, as though he was a rabbit being transfixed by the stare of a snake. Would she suddenly pounce on him, as snakes darted their heads forward and sank their fangs into the body of a hapless animal? What lay behind the youthful and open smile, the look of innocence? Was he being snared by some superb huntsman who had just set a perfumed and invisible trap, a gossamer web of spider's breath?

'Husband. You're not eating?'

'Husband?'

'Soon-to-be-husband, then. Soon-to-be-lover. Master of my household. What should I call you? Highness? Ahab? Prince of princes? Or would my husband like me to call him something known only between the two of us? Something which we will both share and nobody outside of our bedroom will ever hear?' Her voice had dropped to little more than a husky whisper as she leaned forward so that she could only be heard by him. 'When we're alone, Ahab, tell me of our bedroom. I'm sure we'll be spending much of our time in there, when you're not working, of course.'

Ahab felt a stiffening in his groin. She was wonderful. She was everything he'd ever sought in a woman ... a wife and a whore in one. Certainly, Jezebel was good to look at. She had eyes as black as a jewel of jet, hair which was glossy from some perfume which she brushed into it, a skin which glowed in radiance like the surface of the sea on a moonlit night. And Ahab could tell from the way she positioned her body on the cushions in front of him that she was lithe and nubile and that she knew how to move when a man lay on top of her. Perhaps, like the prostitutes he visited in foreign temples, she would also ride on top of his body.

Jezebel glanced down at his groin, knowing he was growing an erection from the way he repositioned his body on the cushions. Silken cushions tended to do that to men, for some reason. She, too, liked the fabric from far in the east, brought to Anatolia by caravans and made into carpets and material for dresses by the skilled women of the mountain villages in that far-distant country, or in caravanserai to be sold in trade. But no matter how she liked the feel of silk, she didn't find it as erotic as she knew the men found it.

'Is my Prince growing in manhood?' she asked innocently, nodding down towards his manly arena. 'If you desire a woman, I have many priestesses and prostitutes who would be honoured to service a man of your ...' she hesitated a moment, '... stature.'

He looked at her in utter amazement and shock. For a Princess of the royal blood to speak so openly about matters which were not spoken of by women in his court, only by prostitutes in foreign temples and brothels! This woman was brazen. Immoral. Perhaps Elijah was right. Jezebel was uttering the words of men, the sort of things which soldiers said to each other in camp, or which friends said in playful banter. But coming from a woman, a Princess of the royal blood, addressing her future husband and Lord and Master, was unheard of.

Yet! Yet her face was that of an innocent. He

frowned in his astonishment. Jezebel immediately knew the thoughts in his mind. 'Ahab, my ambassadors tell me that in your country these things are not discussed openly; they are whispered. I know that you have no prostitutes in your temples, and that women who give their bodies to the service of men are considered contemptuous and are shunned by good citizens; and I know that the houses where these women work are on the outskirts of the cities and the towns. And I also know that you do not love your bodies as we do.

'That is your country. In mine, we are happy to see our men in a state of pleasure with another woman, just as we women look admiringly at men and, provided there is no anger or jealousy or close ties to family, we have them. That doesn't make us an immoral people, deserving of the derision and contempt of men like your prophet Elijah. Why does Elijah find whores evil? A whore is a woman whose life is given over to the pleasure of men and the instruction of young boys in the art of loving. We in Phoenicia have male prostitutes who pleasure widows and women whose husbands have gone to sea or are away from home at war or are merchants in a distant country. Would you rather that these women stayed at home and suffered from the aches of their bodies? Or that in their frustration they sought out and separated a neighbour from her husband? Is that what your people want? Is that what Elijah and the other priests and prophets are condemning Israel to? A lifetime of frustration?'

Ahab was in a state of confusion. He agreed with every word she said, yet it was against all that he had been taught since he was a child. And it was contrary to what the priests in the temple shouted from the altar. Yet, for all that, Ahab knew in his heart that she was right. When he was frustrated, he had three, sometimes four women to whom he could turn. Omri his father have seven wives; one for each day of the week or so he joked. The great King Solomon was reputed to have a thousand women in his palace in Jerusalem, seven hundred wives and three hundred concubines.

But what of the poor farmers and merchants and townspeople, who could only afford one wife? What did they do when their wives were cold in the middle of the month? And as Jezebel quite rightly said, what did the women do when the men were away from home? He knew that women's bodies also reacted to being deprived of love as did men's. He had been told so by one of his women, a widow of one of the King's courtiers whose husband was killed when she was in her middle age and on whom he had taken pity when he found her one day crying in her room, curled up on a divan like a baby. At first he'd been shocked by what she'd told him, about her loneliness and the nature of her dreams; but then he'd been happy to take her to his chambers and give her what she missed now that her husband was dead.

Jezebel smiled at her future husband. She wondered what was going through his mind. 'Ahab. When you have finished eating, do you wish me to bring in some of my maidservants? Or some of the priestesses who accompany me? Let me tell you what they'll do for you.' She nearly laughed out loud as his eyes began to stare wide like that of a child for the first time seeing a man and woman coupling.

'They'll bring in fresh warm water, and infuse it

with perfumes and the sap of lemongrass, and then they'll wash your hair and your beard and your face and your body. And while they're doing that, my barber will come in and will trim your beard and your wet hair with the sharpest of knives so that you'll hardly feel what she's doing.

'Then, when you're clean, my servants will take your clothes and wash them in the brook which runs in the valley beside this road. You will be naked, my Prince. And when you are, we will anoint your body with oil which has been steeped in the most expensive and glorious perfumes and spices from the shores of Lake Urmia in Mesopotamia.

They will rub your body with silks, my Prince, silks taken from the furthest regions of the east and formed into cloth which is so soft and tender to the touch that it is like the skin of a newly born child. Two women, my Master, will cover your chest with their warm silks, as they weave their soft breasts over your heart; two more women, my Lord and Master, will rub and massage your manhood until it is hard and firm and ready for the delights of a woman; and then two other women, the most experienced and beautiful in my retinue, will enter your tent, and will straddle your manhood, just as you straddle a horse. And they will take turns in riding you as though you were a rampant stallion, galloping across the hills, firm and strong and muscular. And these wondrous women will continue to ride you, my love, until the milk of the gods bursts from your member like an eruption from a volcano. And as you burst and shout your delight, these women will smother your face with kisses and bless you for the wonders which you have performed. They will rise up and stand in front of the assembly of my people, and your milk within them will drop out of their bodies and fall to the earth, and all Israel and Phoenicia will bow down to your manhood, for the place where your seed falls will be fertile, and the fertility will spread throughout the land and in the next season there will be grass for the animals and the fruits will grow on trees and the crops will be bountiful in the fields. And all because we have taken your manhood and spilled it on the ground.'

Ahab's face looked as though he'd just seen a vision of Yahweh. His eyes were wide, his mouth agape, lips dry, his breathing shallow and barely audible; if Jezebel had touched him, he would have rolled over and out of the tent. She bit the inside of her lip to stop herself from laughing.

She glanced over at Hattusas, whose eyes were also bulging out of his head, whose mouth was also agape in memories of pleasures past. Then she turned back to Ahab.

'May I do these things for you, my Prince? My husband-to-be?'

Ahab tried to speak, but his throat and lips were too dry and his voice had disappeared. So he simply nodded. That was the only thing for which he had the strength.

She had been called whore and harlot and temptress. Her own husband had told her that she was evil and wanton. Well, not really her husband. For when he spoke these words, she knew that it was only his mouth speaking, and not his heart. For at these moments, he was only a mouthpiece, and it was Yahweh who had called her these things.

Rizpah was still bereft that Yahweh should believe her to be lascivious; she, a woman of the hearth, a woman who had raised two beautiful children in the sight of God; who had buried three others and sent their souls back to the Almighty and who had understood why God had recalled those beautiful children to Himself. And most especially a woman who for years had abandoned her two remaining children and who had journeyed with her husband doing God's work; who had travelled from town to town gathering food from nearby fields to feed her husband, found him fresh straw for a pillow each night, wakened early each day to prepare him his morning meal so that he'd have the strength to preach to the people with the words which the Almighty put into his mouth; she who had gone to each town and village and gathered up the people so that Elijah would have an audience to listen to His words.

Yet Yahweh had seen fit to call her whore. Why? Since this Jezebel had entered the land of Israel, Yahweh had turned His eyes towards Rizpah and found her to be loose and immoral. Yet she knew she was a good woman. Yes, her body often craved her husband's comforts and although sometimes she looked longingly at the bodies of young men on the road or in towns, these thoughts were buried deep within her, and she continually prayed for their removal from her mind. And she had never, ever, strayed from the path of righteousness which Yahweh demanded of His people.

Which was why Rizpah had made a decision she knew would shock Elijah if ever he found out the truth. For unless Rizpah saw Jezebel, and understood this Phoenician whore, gained the measure of her, and was aware of what made her so evil, Rizpah knew that she would never understand why Yahweh had changed towards her ... why He put these words into her husband Elijah's mouth.

It was far from Tishbe, and Rizpah could think of no reason she could give her husband for the journey she had to undertake. She did not want to lie, but to tell him the truth would infuriate him and make him scream and shout at her. How could he ever understand that unless she saw Jezebel, she would forever wonder about her? How could she tell Elijah that she was so curious about this whore of Tyre and Sidon that she was compelled to travel for seven gruelling days in order to see her?

'Your cousin Sharaz? But how do you know she's sick?' he asked when she told him in the morning. He was drinking his favourite brew, crushed leaves of chamomile with red juniper berries in the juice of young red grapes that had been freshly crushed. She had risen from out of their bed well before dawn to make him his favourite bread – wheat flour and yeast cooked with honey and raisins. She'd hoped it would make him more amenable.

'I saw her face in a dream in the night. She was calling to me from her home in Samaria. She said to me, "Rizpah, come to me and look after me while I am sick." I must go, husband. I cannot let her down.'

Elijah looked worried. 'Our Father Joseph dreamed dreams, but that was the voice of God in his mind. Are you saying that Yahweh speaks with you?'

She smiled and said, 'No, of course not. I often have dreams. Dreams of you and where you are

216

when you're away from me, dreams of the children and their safety when they play by the river. These aren't important dreams. But that's why this dream of Sharaz is so important. I've never dreamed of her before and I'm really concerned.'

Elijah nodded. 'There will be many people with such dreams while the whore of Tyre and Sidon is in our midst. Perhaps this wasn't a dream of Sharaz. Perhaps this was a dream from God, telling you that Israel is sick, and that it is our duty to pray for the expulsion, or death, of Jezebel.'

Rizpah shook her head vehemently. 'I have no such dreams from the Almighty, Elijah,' she told her husband. 'A woman such as me isn't blessed as are you. The face I saw in my dream was my cousin, in great distress. I must go to her.'

Elijah finally agreed. Rizpah hated herself for lying, and she would indeed call upon her cousin while she was in Samaria. Indeed, she would stay with her rather than in a traveller's lodging house, both to save money, and to prevent further lies. But while she was in Samaria she had to see Jezebel for herself, and understand why she was so evil, and why the Almighty One, Blessed be He, equated a simple Tishbite woman with the greatest whore in the world.

What was it that Elijah once told her? 'The only way we can defeat the enemies of the Lord is to know them.'

Soon she would get to know her enemy.

The journey to Samaria, the capital of the northern kingdom of Israel, took her seven days of exhausting and numbing travel. She was reminded of why Elijah was so drained when he returned home after travelling alone the length and breadth of the country. Her journey was a mere seven days. Her husband was sometimes on foot for three months. She had only three times before travelled alone and unaccompanied by Elijah beyond the confines of her village. When she went down to the River Jordan, and on two other lesser occasions.

She worked hard in those days when she travelled with Elijah, but, in many ways, they were enjoyable, for she saw much that was new and she was with her companion and husband and they spoke of many things. Now, alone on the road, she felt a fear and a loneliness which never affected her when she was with him.

She was apprehensive as she journeyed to the Jordan. To ease her mind, she thought back to the first time she'd travelled there alone. It had taken her three days of difficult walking to get there and three days to return, but fifteen years later, she still remembered the exciting things she had seen, things which had never been in her own village. Strange rock formations, the colour of the land as it descended into the Jordan Valley, and the tales of travellers whom she passed on the road – tales of unusual animals and mighty armies. Once she had been overtaken by a caravan, and the black merchant – she had never seen black skin – told her of the lands of the east where exotic perfumes and spices and cloths which shimmered like air in the sun were made. Until she married Elijah, she had yearned for the opportunity to travel and see these things for herself. But living in the village was like drinking the juice of the poppy. It made your mind dull and you forgot all the exciting things which life could offer. Then Elijah had married her and she had been wife and mother and all thoughts of journeying disappeared;

until the voice of God told him to travel and preach, and had demanded that she leave her children and help him in his mission.

And now, as the third morning dawned and her head ached from the rock which was her pillow, she dreaded another day of trudging the long, endless and dusty road. She had been walking for the past two days and was approaching the descent into the Jordan Valley. She thought she remembered some of the rocks and mountain formations from the last time she had been here, but it was so long ago that her mind might be playing tricks.

On this, the fourth long journey of her life, she had talked to many travellers who passed her going to places which sounded strange and mysterious. Never once with Elijah was she afraid of robbers or rapists. She knew that God was protecting her. But God seemed to have turned His face from her, and now she was truly frightened of every man who passed her, ever rock and boulder which could be hiding a robber or a rapist. For now she was in a state of sin, she had lied to her husband and she was terrified that the Almighty would punish her.

Elijah had said special prayers for her before she left, and had anointed her with holy oil to ensure that the Almighty smiled upon her. But he wasn't aware of the words he spoke which came from the mouth of Yahweh. Her husband didn't know that Yahweh saw her as an outcast from Israel, a woman of evil. She still shuddered at the words Yahweh had called her ... whore and temptress!

And so Rizpah walked in trepidation, trying to engage other travellers in conversation and appear to be a part of their company. She talked of her husband and children, but their talk was always of Jezebel: *'Have you seen her? Have you heard where she is now? Did you know that Prince Ahab never leaves her tent and that he is bewitched by her? Did you know she worships the demons from the darkest regions of hell, and disappears every night in the shape of a huge crow and flies through the air above Israel plucking babies from their cribs?'*

Rizpah listened and nodded and became more and more frightened of this devil woman of whom all Israel seemed to be speaking, but she was still determined to see her and understand her.

It was in the afternoon of the fourth day of her journey, after she had forded the Jordan, that exhaustion took hold of her and she was forced to sit down to avoid collapse. She was climbing up the western banks of the Jordan Valley towards Tirzah, when she started feeling faint. She was worrying about her mission, and had begun to doubt the reason for her going. She was a wife, a mother and a woman whose life was ordained by the Almighty to be what it had always been. To stay at home and look after her family. It was a man's business to pray and preach and investigate the rights and wrongs of the world. Men went to war and made decrees and sat in councils and decided on things of importance.

Even the mothers of the Jewish religion – Sarah, Rivkah, Rachel and Leah – great as they had been, were wives and helpmeets first and foremost. God had made them mothers, not fathers; God had made them bearers of children to continue the prosperity of His chosen people, not women who should travel the countryside to see things for themselves. So why was she, Rizpah, wife of Elijah the prophet, travelling to the capital of Israel in order to see things for herself?

Rizpah looked around her, and the landscape appeared to shimmer in the rising heat of the day. She tried drinking from her gourd, but the water tasted bitter, and she vomited into the bushes on the roadside. She felt weak. She sat on the side of the road, overlooking the steep walls of the valley, back towards her homeland of Gilead, and began to feel better. It was then that she determined to return to the place where she belonged, to turn around and walk back to Elijah. Rizpah stood and looked into the setting sun. To go back to him now would mean that she must admit her deceit, admit the lies she had told about her relation. But to go on meant that she was entering territory which was at once unfamiliar and frightening. She would have to confront her enemy.

But how could she, a woman, possibly do what her husband Elijah had done, and look upon a great and awful royal procession such as the one which came from Phoenicia, and hope to understand it?

She stepped back onto the road in order to return to Gilead, but something stopped her from walking. It was as though there were a string holding her to the western bank, preventing her from walking down the hill back to the river. She stood, undecided, and noticed an old man walking slowly and painfully up the hill towards her. He carried a long wooden staff which he used to impel himself forward. He was much older than Rizpah, at least as old as her father, and his age showed in his face, florid from the walk and the exertion of the climb, dark and lined from his outdoor life. Yet there was a gentleness about him, the same creased and smiling eyes she remembered of her grandfather when he'd been alive. Indeed, now she looked at him, it could have been her grandfather walking towards her, except that her grandfather had never once left his village, and this man had a world of experience in his face.

She delayed going down the hill until he had reached where she was standing at the top, in case he required her assistance. He stopped and looked at her, leaning on his staff, struggling to breathe.

'You journey from Israel?' he asked, his voice gruff with lack of breath.

'No. I've just come from Gilead. I go to Samaria.'

'Why are you facing into the east?'

'I don't know. I want to go home, but I want to go on. I'm confused.'

He nodded, and invited her to sit on the side of the road with him while he regained his breath and his strength. He told her his name was Absalom. He was a fisherman whose livelihood was on the shore of the Eternal Sea; that he had been visiting his daughter who had married a merchant in precious stones who lived in the land of Ammon where beautiful gems grew in the desert. Now he was returning to his family and his boat.

Rizpah told him who she was, and whose wife she had the privilege of being. Absalom looked at her with interest.

'I've heard Elijah speak. I was in Arsuf many years ago when your husband preached in the marketplace. He was frightening. Many people were scared. His warnings were full of menace. But after he'd gone, the people went back to their old ways.'

He ate some bread which he took from a sack he

carried on his back. She took some on his offer, and she brought a flask of ale from her sack, and they shared that. Absalom asked her why she was going to Samaria. She was about to tell him that she was visiting her sick cousin, but suddenly the truth came from her mouth. She couldn't stop it, as though on the open road, God could see and hear her better. Somehow she could lie to her husband and family, but couldn't lie to this old man, this stranger who so reminded her of her childhood and her grandfather.

'Ah! Jezebel. Yes. She is very beautiful, they say. I haven't seen her, but one day, God willing, I will cast my eyes on her. They say she dances like the Devil.' The old man laughed.

'Doesn't that frighten you?'

He looked at her in surprise. 'Why?'

'Because the Devil is evil. If she is the Devil, or if she dances like the Devil and encourages the evil one to visit Israel, he will bring death and destruction.'

The old man coughed and reached over to pick up Rizpah's flask of ale. He took a long draught before he spoke. 'And do you believe that there is no death and destruction in Israel already? And in Judah and Phoenicia and all around us? Is it the work of the Devil, or the work of the Lord God Yahweh who tests us and our faith?

'I'm not a priest. Nor, like your husband, a prophet. I don't speak to God. But God doesn't speak to me, either. I spend days alone on the sea, being moved this way and that by the wind and the waves. Sometimes, it's hard for me to get home because the wind changes direction, and then I have to sail far out to sea before I can tack towards my port.

'Some sailors and fishermen blame the demons and the gods of the sea when they're pushed off course. The Israelites blame the one God, Yahweh, for storms and when boats sink. The Philistines and the Phoenicians blame Yam and Ba'al and other gods.'

Rizpah wondered what he was talking about.

He continued, 'Maybe these are the Devil, rather than gods. I don't know. But I do know that storms blow themselves out eventually. Seas calm down and are flat the day following a hurricane. Boats which sink don't reappear, but still sailors put to sea and most return safely to shore. I don't know whether God, or the gods, or the Devil comes here and visits us. All I do know is that when I pray fervently to Yahweh to allow me to catch fish, I just as often come home with empty nets as I come home with my nets full; when I pray for a following wind, it just as often blows me backwards.' He looked at Rizpah. 'I've spent a long life praying to Yahweh. And I'm still poor and tired.'

'Yahweh can only hear our words if we're sincere and repent of the sins we commit,' she told him, repeating what Elijah told the multitudes.

He nodded. 'I probably am a sinner. I'm sure I've committed more sins than most. Yet for years now, I can't remember any of the sins I've committed, because in your husband's eyes, they're sins, but in my eyes, they're ...' He searched for the phrase and his eyes lit up when he found it, '... they're the pleasures of the flesh. And now, my eyes are too old to see the beauty of young women, and my body is too weak to satisfy their demands. Even if I wanted to sin, I couldn't. I don't steal and I don't murder. So for what reason would God punish an old man like me? And why does God make innocent children suffer? Are they sinners? How can a child who is born and soon afterwards becomes an orphan, be a sinner? What sin can he have committed to be punished by Yahweh with the death of his mother in childbirth, or of his father if that happens? Or if the child dies before he's been circumcised? Or if it's a girl, and she's condemned to living a life as a slave to a rich family because her parents can't afford to keep her? Why does God punish the innocent who haven't committed sins?'

Rizpah listened carefully. Elijah would know the answers to his questions, but she didn't.

The old man continued, 'As for Jezebel, well, maybe she is the Devil, but I'd rather look upon her beautiful form than have to face a storm at sea.' He stood. 'I have to continue. I must be in Euphrah by nightfall so I can be home in four days.'

Rizpah decided then to turn back and face Samaria, and not to go down the hill to the Jordan River and home. This old man was right. For all that she might be the Devil, Jezebel was a seventeen-year-old woman. Who was scared of a young person? Rizpah knew at that moment that she couldn't return home until she had done what she came for; that she too, like the old fisherman, would like to see the Devil.

She stood. 'I will accompany you,' she said, and began to walk with him in the direction of Samaria and the great Eternal Sea, turning her back on Gilead and her homeland.

She had been the model of modesty and womanhood from Megiddo in the north to Taanach. She had been demure and giving from the shadows of the highlands of Carmel to the lowlands city of Dothan; and by the time they arrived in sight of the capital city of Samaria, Ahab was Jezebel's slave in his mind and in his body.

Though she had not given her own body to him, telling him she would wait to satisfy his desires until their wedding, Jezebel ensured that all of Ahab's wants and needs were met. She deferred, she bowed, she laughed at his funny remarks, she sat for long hours around their campfire discussing politics and the motivations of kings, and when he asked, she danced for him.

But she also quarrelled with him, and encouraged Hattusas to explain many of the aspects of kingship about which his father had never spoken to him. She argued with him about whether Yahweh could be the only god in the heavens; she told him that he was wrong when he said that Israel and Egypt would eventually form an everlasting pact; and both listened to Hattusas' discourse on the need for an agricultural policy which used the land for different crops in different years in order to keep the gods interested in protecting the nation.

And as they journeyed closer and closer to Samaria, Ahab had to admit to himself that he'd never before met a women as fascinating and all-consuming as Jezebel. From the way she understood things so clearly to the way she moved when she danced, Jezebel was the complete woman.

But it was the way she seemed to float rather than walk which excited him the most. It was as though her body were made of the water of the sea, and she moved in waves, her silken dresses the colours and textures of shimmering and multi-hued birds. She would undulate in front of him, ensuring that the light from the fire shone through her clothes revealing all of her body except the final mystery; she would weave intricate patterns with her hands around his head and chest, never once touching him; and when his urges overcame him and he reached out to grab her breasts or her womanhood between her legs, she would instantly withdraw, like a clever fish from a fisherman, laughing as she disappeared in a cloud of blue and green fire to the other side of the campsite. And then her maidservants would suddenly appear as though by magic, and they would lead him away, gently coaxing him from his sitting position into his tent where they would service all of his desires.

In the morning, she would appear at his tent, dressed in a blinding white tunic and burnous, carrying rose-water and sweet cakes freshly baked and the milky-white and slightly bitter yogurt mixed with honey and raisins. Sometimes she would feed him as though he were a baby; at other times, she would lay at the bottom of his bed and stare at him, smiling; and no matter how many questions he asked, she would continue to smile.

She supervised and attended to his needs, as her maidservants bathed him, massaged him, combed his hair and beard and dressed him. But not once since their first kiss – akin to the affection of brother and sister – had she touched him.

By the time they came to the shadows of the walls of Samaria, Ahab was in love. It began on their first day together, when it was obvious that she was enamoured of him; and it grew day by day. It was at its strongest when they were alone together, or when she was ensuring his happiness with the hands and bodies of her maidservants; it was weakest when her entourage was performing their dance and fire tricks at the foot of a city's walls. For that was when she wasn't his, but belonged to both her arts and to her priests and priestesses, and most of all to the people of the city for whom she was performing. And she reacted badly when he told her not to display herself like that for the common townspeople. For then she reminded him sternly that she was his future Queen and that while he would rule the people, she would be loved by them, and that was the way it would be.

Slowly, laboriously, the entourage and the wagons and the pack animals lumbered from the valley up the hill to the capital of Israel, Samaria; and her first look upwards surprised her. It was a new capital, its building having been started by King Omri only a few years earlier. It was very different to the capital cities of Phoenicia, the great and magnificent cities of Sidon and Tyre, which were old and venerable and whose buildings were glorious and beautifully decorated inside and out with the colours of the earth and the fields and the sky. The buildings of Samaria, capital of her new kingdom of Israel, were yellow like the desert sand, unpainted and undecorated, and had no grandeur. They were buildings as she would find in any large village or town in Phoenicia, not in the capital of a kingdom. Her heart sank.

And her mood became no better as her entourage drew closer to the Damascus Gate. It was tall, probably taller than any gate in Sidon or Tyre, but it was just made of a dark wood, probably a cedar from Lebanon; there were no decorations on it, no carvings of gods or goddesses, no figures of demons to frighten away evil or any carvings of men or women. It was just a plain series of planks of wood wedded together by iron bands and great nails. Jezebel tried not to show her growing contempt for her new realm to her husband-to-be.

'How high is that gate?' she asked.

'Fifteen cubits,' he replied.

She had never heard before of this measure, and asked its meaning.

'A cubit is the distance from a man's elbow to his fingertips,' replied Ahab.

'But if the man is a midget, or a giant, it will be a different length,' she said.

Ahab had never considered that point. In the privacy of his chambers, he would ask the city's architect for an explanation.

They passed below the gate, and ten trumpeters, five harpists and four men with drums and cymbals gave them a fanfare as Jezebel and Ahab at the head of the procession passed beneath the gate. The music continued as they weaved between the houses and through narrow and colourless streets until they turned a corner. The streets were lined with people who had come out of their houses to see the famous Princess, and to make up their own minds about whether or not she was a servant of the Devil himself. Nobody clapped, ululated, cheered, threw petals or danced before her progress as they did in Phoenicia. Trumpeters stood on the tops of the buildings which they passed and sounded a tune, but it was more of a funeral march than the entry of a Queen into her new capital.

And the future Queen's heart dropped when they turned another corner and she saw the palace, the temple and the marketplace. It was like one of the smaller provincial towns in Phoenicia, not the capital of a great and important country. Most of the houses were only just higher than the height of a tall man; they had square windows in their square walls. They were unpainted, undecorated, and had no designs like those of the houses in Sidon, which competed with each other for colour and pattern and style. Other buildings had upper storeys, but they were squat and had no architectural grandeur. And as she became more and more depressed by her new home, she became increasingly angry that she had been forced by her father to leave the colour and light of Phoenicia to live in a collection of desert hovels, the biggest and ugliest being her new palace.

Her mood didn't improve when Ahab seemed to take such delight in riding beside her on his horse, and pointing out the nature of the buildings and also nodding to some of the people who had gathered to see her. Some waved, some shouted out their greetings. A couple of little children threw garlands up to her, which nearly frightened her horse.

And as she rode closer to the palace, she thought again of the rudeness of her greeting into Israel; of Ahab's snub, of the petty gestures and nastiness of the council of Ak-Kah; of the crudeness and roughness of the cities she'd seen; and most especially, she thought of that prophet who had screamed abuse at her when she'd first crossed the border. She had tried to put thoughts of Elijah out of her mind, but now that she was in the capital, his image became more pressing in her head. Apart from the ambassador, Elijah had been the first Israelite to speak to her as she entered her new realm; and he had called her *'whore'* and *'evil'* and 'consort of the Devil'. His words must have spread, because the way that the people were now looking at her, there was distrust and curiosity in their eyes, the sort of look which the people of Phoenicia had when a strange fish was washed up onto the shore after a storm. All other towns and cities had heard of her dances outside the walls, and were excited about her appearance. But the people of Samaria seemed cold and distant.

She dismounted from her horse in a foul mood. All the diplomacy she had exhibited to her future husband, all at the behest of her father's counsellors, was now in the bottom of her mind. At the forefront of her thoughts was the rudeness of the people over whom she was now destined to rule and her anger at being removed from her beloved Phoenicia.

Sensing her growing anger, Hattusas also dismounted and hurried to her side.

'Remember the treaty. Remember that this is a land which needs to be lit by the sun of Phoenicia, not darkened by its daughter's fury. Remember your father's instructions ...'

She turned to him, anger in her eyes. But his eyes beseeched her to be diplomatic. And in his gentle and intelligent face, she suddenly saw herself, a young and isolated woman in a strange and hostile land.

Without waiting for Ahab, who was greeting captains and guards and people in the street, she walked quickly up the steps of the palace where an elderly balding man wearing a crown had emerged from within the building to greet her.

'Jezebel. Princess of Sidon and Tyre. Future daughter-in-law and future Queen of Israel. I, Omri, King of Israel greet you in the name of the people.'

He opened his arms to greet her like a father greets a daughter. After the reports he had been receiving about her gentleness and womanly ways, he was stunned when she walked up to him and said, 'I am Jezebel, Princess of Sidon and Tyre. I greet Omri, King of Israel in the name of my father, King Ethbaal of Phoenicia.'

She turned and looked over the assembly. By far the vast majority of people in the square in front of the palace were from her own entourage; only a small number of Samarians had gathered to greet their future Queen. The insult was palpable and she felt it deeply. Gathering her strength, she called out, 'And to you, my future people of Israel, my future subjects, I will treat you with the generosity and love with which you have treated me. As you have planted your feelings in the rocky ground, so shall you reap your harvest in the coming years. Carry this message to all of those whom I will soon rule ... that Jezebel is come; Jezebel has heard the voice of Israel; Jezebel has listened to your prophet and your King and your Prince. Tell your people that Jezebel has listened carefully to the way in which Elijah spoke to me as I entered your lands and that when I am Queen, I will apply the same laws to him as apply to any priest of the gods of Phoenicia. He above all will understand my meaning. Go, people of Israel, in the knowledge that all of Phoenicia will carry your greeting in its heart.'

And she turned on her heels and entered the palace without a further word.

King Omri's jaw dropped in shock. Phoenicia's counsellor was wide-eyed in surprise. He'd feared a petulant outburst, but he'd just heard a conundrum which would take the Israelites a week to understand. And in the midst of the crowd, Rizpah, wife of Elijah the prophet, knew that she had met her enemy who had just threatened to have her husband put to death. She fainted in the middle of the marketplace.

CHAPTER TEN

Omri's fury was threatening to overwhelm him. Never had he been so badly insulted before the populace of Israel, especially by a woman; and not even a woman, a young and unmarried woman who would one day rise to the heights of queenship simply because she was the daughter of an ally.

Well, he decided, this woman would be punished. Even if she'd captured the hearts of many, Omri was King and he would show her his majesty. His advisors had begged him not to send her home and nullify the treaty, and, after a day or two, his reason had returned to him. Instead, he decided to imprison her until she crawled back to him on her knees, in front of the entire population of Israel, and begged his forgiveness. Then, when she was humbled before his subjects, she would truly understand his might. And it would be at that moment of glory that he would inform her that he had forbidden any great formal welcome because of his concern about infuriating the priests of the temple, and especially of igniting the ire of Elijah.

Had she not been so tempestuous, so headstrong, he would have told her these things as they walked together into the palace. But she'd turned her back on him and walked away from His Majesty of Israel, leaving him like some abandoned bridegroom. And now she would never know what he was going to tell her; and he would never explain to her the different ways of Israel. These things she would have to learn by bitter experience and unhappiness. She'd insulted him and now she would pay the price, as would her retinue.

In her bare apartments, those which her servants might have occupied in Phoenicia, Jezebel, Princess of Tyre and Sidon, future Queen of Israel, viewed things very differently. From her perspective of confinement to her chambers, she restrained her anger, but in restraint, it grew and grew within her. She determined that as soon as she was freed she would demand that her father attack Israel, and pull this pauperous palace apart, stone by stone.

She had been deliberately excluded from the royal throne room and told that the reception arranged in her honour had been cancelled because the King had told everyone that she was frail and indisposed after her long and tiring journey. So she ordered her counsellors and the captains of her bodyguard to refuse any cooperation with the Israelites, not to go anywhere outside the palace until Jezebel was admitted to Omri's presence and he grovelled in apology for the insulting welcome she had been afforded on her arrival. She knew in her heart that the people of Samaria were eager to see her, even though they had been instructed by their King to be cold and undemonstrative on her arrival. The Israelite people in all the towns and villages she'd visited had cheered and been ecstatic when she'd performed, so the inhabitants of the capital city would have been charged with excitement. And now they had been disappointed by the stiff-necked King and would continue to be so until he relented and apologised.

In a further insult to her person, Jezebel's priests and priestesses of Ba'al and Asherah had purposefully not been invited inside the palace, and most had been ingloriously ushered from the capital after the disputation on the steps. They'd been forced to leave the city. Right now, most of her entourage, except her personal staff and captains, was camped outside the walls; Jezebel took this as another sign of rudeness, another snub to Phoenicia.

The impasse was broken by Hattusas, her counsellor-in-chief, who had already sent word of the insult to her father and was awaiting a response. Unwilling to allow the ridiculous situation of Jezebel being ignored by King Omri to continue, and Omri telling everyone he had imprisoned his future daughter-in-law, Hattusas determined to resolve the situation and make matters right. After all, in the short time that she'd been travelling through the land of Israel, she'd won over a large percentage of the population, as well as the heart and mind of its future ruler. Hattusas sought a private audience with King Omri which was granted after three agonising days of frustration in which the old man was forced to stand in an airless and seatless antechamber to the throne room, waiting like some miscreant child for his punishment.

During the time she was waiting for the King either to apologise, or to expel her from the country and hence break the treaty, Jezebel was a virtual prisoner in the palace. The captain of her guard was both furious and concerned, and threatened his Israelite counterpart that he would send to Phoenicia for reinforcements unless the Princess was allowed to leave her wing of the palace and travel around the city of Samaria.

After enough time had elapsed to show this girl who was the King, Omri suddenly admitted Hattusas to his audience chamber. The monarch had listened to his counsellors and soldiers who were concerned about the possibility of armed insurrection from the large party of Phoenician soldiers camped outside the walls of the palace.

As the old Phoenician walked in, Omri smiled at Hattusas as though nothing in the past three days had eventuated which strained the friendship of the two countries. The King knew of Hattusas; he knew him to have been trained in Egypt as a doctor and that he was a man of great wisdom and foresight who had guided the fortunes of Phoenicia for many years. But as the old man drew closer to the King's presence, Omri's smile disappeared and the anger of his future daughter-in-law's insult welled up again.

'Well?' he said.

But Hattusas wasn't going to be intimidated by a King who lived in such an ordinary palace, in such an ordinary city and who, he knew, depended on a Phoenician alliance. Without the usual sycophancies and titles, Hattusas said, 'Understand Omri that if Jezebel returns to Phoenicia without a husband, her father, my King, will go to war against you. Nobody can break a treaty with Ethbaal and expect not to suffer dire and evil consequences.'

'And understand this, old man,' Omri shouted at the Phoenician. 'Nobody can expect to insult me on the steps of my palace, in front of my people, and expect to escape my displeasure. And nobody threatens an Israelite prophet with death. Nobody, Phoenician, can say those words to me in Israel and expect to live, princess or not, treaty or none.'

Unbowed by the wind of royal fury, Hattusas continued, 'If Jezebel is harmed in any way, Israel will be no more. Phoenicia and Assyria will lay your land bare; they will salt your fields, poison your rivers and your wells, scatter the grains in your storage houses to the wind, reduce your towns and villages to rubble, and your people will be taken away in chains and will become slaves. Yahweh will have no more worshippers. And be warned Omri, that Samaria will be the first Israelite city to be levelled to the ground.'

The two men glared at each other. Omri had never been spoken to like this, especially by a man who wasn't a king or a member of a royal family. But in his heart of hearts, he knew that the old counsellor was right. Not that he couldn't fight a mighty war, but it would undo all the good which his movements towards peace and harmony with his neighbours had created. All the building work which had been implemented under his reign would be as nothing if he went to war. It would denude his treasury for generations. And that assumed he would win. Hattusas was right! If Phoenicia was badly insulted she would join Assyria, and maybe even Philistia, and then Israel would have to make a treaty with Judah and even Egypt; Israel would become a killing ground and the bones of young men would lay in the fields like fallen crops. And how would a weakened Israel get rid of Egypt if the war was won? Egypt would become Israel's overlord.

'Listen to me carefully, Hattusas. I must have an apology. Without an apology from that girl there will be war.'

'And understand, great King, that Princess Jezebel will not apologise. The insult at the gateway to Israel by Elijah the prophet was great, but we advised her to put aside her anger and face her new people in a spirit of love and understanding. And for ten days, she has charmed your people ...'

'Bewitched ...' interrupted the King.

'Possibly, Majesty. But we have a different relationship with our gods, as well as to the bodies of our men and women, than you do in Israel. Anyway, after that insult by your prophet we set about gaining the love and admiration of the Israelites. We captivated them – Phoenicia is the talk of all the Israelite people. And then we treated your son the Prince as though he were a very king; he was banqueted and feted every night. He is more than happy to marry Jezebel.

'When our entourage arrived in Samaria we assumed that we would be deserving of a proper reception, fit for a future Queen of this land. But when we were received with such ... such ... lack of circumstance and sycophancy by the court of Israel; to be treated as though we were travelling merchants arriving at a caravanserai or some impoverished desert oasis; to be granted the custom of peripatetic camel herders at a wayside inn; to be insulted by such an ungracious and mean-spirited welcome from the King of Israel ... can your Majesty not see the insult done to Phoenicia?'

King Omri shook his head in surprise. 'But you above all know the constraints I am placed under by the command of Yahweh and the demands of his priests. You know what Elijah would do in the towns and villages if I was openly to greet Jezebel as daughter and future Queen.

'The welcome given to you is all I could do. We are a proud people. We are commanded by our God, Yahweh, to be modest, not to exhibit ourselves; not to worship false idols, not to make images or representations. Our priests and prophets have told us that God's word means that our ceremonies must not include wild dancing and exhibitions of lasciviousness, as is the case in other countries. Surely Princess Jezebel was told this before she arrived at the gates of Samaria? If not, then you have served her badly, Hattusas.'

Both men lapsed into silence. Both realised that they had made severe errors of judgement. Only the King felt that he could not resile and show weakness by admitting his mistakes; he had underestimated the importance of the welcoming ceremony. His own advisors had let him down. They would pay for their errors in protocol, but for now he had a crisis on his hands.

How had this all blown up, like a sandstorm out of a clear sky, he wondered. Omri knew, of course, that other countries welcomed visitors in more impressive ways, but ever since the schism between Judah and Israel the kings of the northern land who reigned before him had ensured that the nation continued their love of Yahweh in order to quell the still-doubting people who missed their Temple in Jerusalem. To have extravagant welcoming ceremonies and festivals would have further alienated the priests and continued to unsettle the people. Yahweh did not like immodesty and wanton behaviour; He hated idols and graven images. He would tolerate no such thing in Israel. And with the way His mouthpiece, Elijah, was spreading poison about Jezebel, Omri knew that the greeting he'd given was all he could do. But in the problem, Omri suddenly saw the solution.

'I fail to understand why you Phoenicians are so insulted. Does Her Highness the Princess Jezebel think that the greeting when she first arrived at the Damascus Gate was the welcoming ceremony?' he asked Hattusas.

The old man looked up at the King in surprise. 'Yes … yes' he stammered, and then fell silent.

The King laughed. 'Fool! That was our traditional greeting for tired travellers. When a caravan has travelled all day to reach us the last thing we would do is to delay their rest by a long ceremony of welcome. We are a people who wandered in the desert for forty years before settling in the land promised to us by Yahweh. In the desert, food, drink and rest are more important than ceremony.

'You are a fool, Hattusas, to think that the greeting we afforded the Princess Jezebel when she first arrived in Samaria was our official greeting. I command you to tell Her Majesty Jezebel that the official welcoming ceremony is tonight. A banquet at which sycophants will accord to the Princess all the rights and privileges due to her royal station and her love in our eyes. A banquet in which only her entourage and the royal family of Israel will be present; not the priests and prophets who will be too busy doing Yahweh's work! And before she steps into the banquet, she will show herself to the

Israelite people of Samaria and she will explain to the multitudes how she misunderstood our welcome. She will apologise for her misunderstanding ... Is that clear?'

Hattusas shook his head, unsure of whether to accept the compromise. 'But Jezebel and her maidservants have been kept prisoner in ...'

'Prisoner? Nonsense. We are giving her time to rest until the welcoming ceremonies tonight.' King Omri looked closely at Hattusas and measured his following words carefully. 'Tell Her Highness that before she enjoys our welcome she will bend her neck and apologise for misunderstanding our intentions when she first arrived.'

The King turned his head and picked up a scroll which had been delivered earlier from the King of Moab. The audience was over. Hattusas had his instructions.

She bowed low as she entered the banqueting hall. As did her maidservants. As she had just done on the steps of the palace before a cheering crowd of Samarians. She had said nothing, but everybody knew that the apology was in her manner, her genuflection.

By demand of the King, the priests and priestesses to Ba'al and Asherah were not attending the ceremony to welcome Jezebel to Israel, and although Jezebel had complained bitterly, Hattusas managed to convince her that for the sake of her future, and for peace between Phoenicia and Israel, she should give way on this point.

As she stood she saw the line of Israelite nobles sitting at the head table. Initially only the royal family was to be invited, but there were great demands by counsellors and officials of the court, as well as rich merchants, to be present and see the mysterious and exotic Jezebel. And so Omri had relented and turned what was to have been a small banquet into a large feast.

The King, of course, was sitting on his throne which had been placed so that he was the centre of everyone's vision, his seat elevated on a dais, and on the throne were placed red and blue cushions. To his left were his wives, in descending order of importance. Jezebel had been told all about them by her spies, and knew that, unlike her mother and some of Ethbaal's other wives, these Israelite royal women held no power or potency.

To his right were his children, starting with Ahab, his successor as King. The look on Ahab's face was one of joy and sheer relief. His smile was as the rising sun. He had been forbidden by his father to visit Jezebel, and all the messages he'd tried to send to her wing of the palace had been stopped by his father's guards. For the past three days, he'd been desperate to tell her of his love and adoration, and of his attempts to make his father see reason; but it was as though he had ceased to exist for Jezebel. His silence was taken by her as turning his back. Now, from the look on his face, that of a dog seeing its master, she began to perceive that she was wrong in that regard. Ahab began to stand to greet her, but his father the King hissed a command from the corner of his mouth, and Ahab immediately sat down.

Jezebel continued to walk slowly down the length of the banqueting hall until she approached the presence of the King of Israel. It was the first time she had seen him since turning her back on his face at her arrival in Samaria. He didn't seem as old as he was then; his face seemed to have softened. It was somehow more benign, more like that of her father or one of her advisors. How had she misjudged his face so badly? Why had she seen him as old and horrible, mean-spirited and hostile?

She bowed low as she reached his table, just as she'd been instructed by Hattusas. She continued to bow until the King said, 'Arise Princess Jezebel and be greeted by your people Israel.' And there was a cheer from everyone at the banqueting tables, loudest of all from Prince Ahab.

She stood up straight, and when the shouting had died down, said to the King, 'Majesty, I bring you love and greetings from your brother the King of Phoenicia, my father Ethbaal. With the marriage between your son Ahab and myself, our countries will be wed as well; married into eternity in a union which will reject all aggression, which will repel all invaders. Am I worthy of your son, Majesty?'

The King stood. His response was laid down by agreement between his counsellors and those of the Princess Jezebel. He said, 'More pleasing than the rose, more beautiful than a peacock of India, yes, Jezebel, you are well and truly welcome as a future Queen of Israel.'

Again the people cheered. This time, Ahab stood and reached his arms across the table to where Jezebel was standing. She smiled, and held his hands across the platters of fruit and meats which lay waiting to be eaten. Seeing his son grasp his future daughter-in-law's hands, Omri shouted to the assembly, 'Thus is united Israel and Phoenicia!'

Hattusas smiled in relief. Jezebel had played her part

magnificently. Earlier in the day, it had been a dangerous situation. When he reported to her on the conversation between himself and the King Omri, Jezebel was furious, and threatened to call upon her bodyguard to break out of her prison, and to escape this hideous city. It had taken him a long time to persuade her that her men would be slaughtered, and she would be held hostage against an invasion by her father.

Slowly, she had acceded to his suggestions, and now the fast-maturing young woman was presenting herself as a diplomat and a future Queen, fit for a marriage between the two countries. He sighed, for this was just the beginning of his problems, rather than their end. What was he going to tell Ethbaal about Phoenicia's entry into Israel? He had already sent word that Jezebel was captive in the palace. How could he explain that she had abased herself to save the treaty? To say nothing would be dangerous as there were spies everywhere who would report everything, and more. To tell her father what had happened would invite the rage of Phoenicia, and the treaty would be strained. Even though there was harmony in the room tonight, the insult had been done. Phoenicia had been held captive in the palace for three days. Her priests and priestesses and most of her honour guard were camped outside the city walls. Yes, thought Hattusas, it is a deep and abiding insult; yet he had to write something which would not inflame Ethbaal and exacerbate the circumstances. He determined to sleep on the problem tonight, and send his letters in the morning.

By the time she returned to her home in Tishbe, Rizpah knew that she was thinner and that her features had been coarsened by the heat of the sun and the desert winds which blew up the valley of the Jordan River. She felt utterly haggard. This physical trial helped her understand the exhaustion which Elijah showed when he returned from one of his many journeys; now she understood why he collapsed over their doorway and fell into his bed, and why it was that his youthful face had grown older and coarser than those of other men in her village of similar age to her husband.

When they travelled together, the road was somehow shorter, the journey less arduous, she caring for him, and he, occasionally, ensuring that her needs of warmth and food were satisfied; as they walked and talked, the distances seemed to disappear. But travelling alone from Samaria was harder and lonelier than anything she had previously done, especially as she was bearing such hideous news in her breast.

The moment her home came into sight as she crossed over the crest of the hill and saw the familiar houses nestling in the valley, the brook of Gishon cutting the village into two halves, she burst into tears. She fell to her knees, and spent long moments thanking the one true God, Yahweh, for delivering her back safely to her husband and her two beautiful children. She never wanted to leave her home again; never wanted to climb the steep hills, nor sleep in fields nor beside roadways; nor did she want to feel the thirst of the road, and wonder where the next river providing her with her next drink would be. And when she thought of food, she never ever again wanted to stray more than twenty paces from her home, where she had plentiful wood for her cooking fires and sufficient grains and oils and fruits and meats, and could prepare a meal which made her whole family smile in gratitude.

But more than any of these things, she never ever wanted to see Samaria again. Not just because the painted woman Jezebel had cursed her husband and threatened his life; not just because she had seen the naked breasts of idolatrous women masquerading as priestesses; not just because the so-called priests of Ba'al made her feel sick with their oiled bodies and the flaunting of their manhood and their kissing of other men ... No, it wasn't for any of these things that she never again wanted to go to Samaria.

The real reason she never wanted to see that damnable city again was because it was so big and noisy and crowded and full of anger like a nest of bees, and the pace of the city was so quick compared with Tishbe. She had been a stranger in a strange land, and she had felt uneasy the entire time she stayed in the house of her cousin Sharaz. Although she had visited cities before with her husband, and was familiar with their size and their bustle, as a woman, alone, she felt frightened and out of place. She felt that people were watching her all the time, perhaps even laughing at her for her crude country clothes.

She looked in amazement at the city people's rich garments, the magnificence of their houses, so big and prosperous, and was awestruck by the palace, the house of the priests and the temple which was in the middle of the city. Even the market square frightened her by its size. It was almost as big as a field, but the crop this city grew couldn't be eaten ... No, the crop was more people than she could count, all milling around and talking, or walking urgently from one side to the other as though they were all busy on the business of the King. When she was with Elijah in the large cities she was his eyes and ears, but she rarely explored the city; on her own, she was forced to go into the big public areas, and she was frightened.

And that was the other reason why Rizpah never wanted to visit Samaria again. She had seen the King and his royal family, and all the attendants, and was rendered speechless by the power and authority which seemed to exude from him. Just being in his presence made her feel weak.

And when that whore, that evil daughter of wickedness from Phoenicia, ran up the steps and turned her back on the King and said those things about her husband Elijah, she was completely overcome by a flush of nerves, and she fainted into the surprised arms of her cousin Sharaz's husband. She hadn't fully understood what Jezebel had said, but she knew that it was against her husband's interests and safety.

But now she was home. As she approached her dwelling she saw her children in the house, preparing food for the night. She saw her husband, Elijah, sitting outside the house reading a scroll, and mumbling in between the words he spoke, his lips appearing to kiss each other as he sometimes whispered, sometimes shouted, their content. Something disturbed him and he looked up from his scroll, and saw his wife Rizpah approaching from the distance. He shouted out her name and stood, the scroll tumbling to the ground in his excitement. Her children came running out of the house and suddenly there was mayhem as they all rushed towards each other.

When they had kissed and hugged, and when Elijah had told his children not to bombard their mother with hundreds of questions, he insisted that they all fall to their knees and pray to the Lord God Yahweh for the safe delivery of their beloved Rizpah.

Elijah looked grave as Rizpah explained to him what she had heard outside the palace in Samaria. They stood in a field nearby because she didn't want the children to overhear their conversation. They had eaten and drunk, and Rizpah desperately wanted to rest in bed. But first she had to inform her husband of the danger which he faced from Jezebel.

'Tell me again her exact words, woman. As well as you can remember them,' demanded Elijah.

And she repeated them word for word, as though their meaning might become clearer the third and fourth time.

'But when she said she would apply the same laws to me as she applied to any of her other priests, what did Omri say? Was he pleased? Did he understand her meaning?'

'I don't know, husband. It appears that Omri was at first shocked and said nothing, and then he glared at her as though a cloud was covering the sun. Then she turned her back on him to walk up the stairs of the great palace to go indoors, leaving Omri alone on the steps.

'And then he was gone. He followed her up the steps into the palace and the crowd stayed where they were, as though they had taken root in the ground. Nobody wanted to move. By this time I had recovered, and, although I was feeling ill and faint, I returned to Sharaz's house and rested. The following day in the marketplace, everyone was trying to understand what Jezebel had meant. But there were so many different interpretations that I was just more and more confused. So I determined to return to you and let you work it out.'

Elijah nodded. He was thinking deeply. 'I know exactly what she means. In Phoenicia and other lands out of the sight of Yahweh they worship many false idols. She means that I will acknowledge these idols, that I will bow my head to Asherah and Moloch and Ba'al and all the other obscenities. And when I've done that, and all Israel sees my weakness, she will kill me. You were right when you assumed that it was a death sentence. Now my enemy has spoken, and the fight is on.

'Tomorrow, I will send letters to my brother priests and prophets and all the anointed ones throughout the lands of Israel and Judah. I will tell them of what has occurred. I will tell them that soon I must travel again on the road you have just trodden. Soon, I must go to Samaria and see things for myself. The information you bring is good. Until now, my enemies have been Omri and Ahab. They have turned their faces away from Yahweh, and my God put His words into my mouth and I delivered those words to the unworthy to warn them of the error of their ways.

'But now my enemy is my friend, for we all have a greater enemy – Jezebel. And in her coming is my lifting up. Through her, God's will be done.'

He stood, and began to escort her home. But then a thought occurred to him. 'I don't understand, Rizpah. You say that Sharaz was with you in the marketplace. But I thought Sharaz was sick. Yet she was beside you when you fainted and her husband caught you in his arms. How can this be?'

Rizpah had forgotten her lie, and flushed in embarrassment. 'She was better when I arrived,' she said.

Elijah nodded. 'Good,' he said. 'The Lord's plan must have been to get you to Samaria to hear what Jezebel had to say about me. Maybe, Rizpah, both you and I have become the mouthpieces of the Lord.'

The revolution began quietly. There were no arrows fired in anger, no siege machines groaning against a city's walls, no screams as neighbour murdered neighbour. Instead, a few people looked quizzically at what was being built, and commented upon it to their friends as they bade each other good night.

The first one to be built was within sight of the guards on top of the walls of Samaria. They looked at the young woman and the two men who were helping her, and assumed that they were planting some vegetables, or perhaps making a pen to restrain some animals. Curious, one of the guards left his post and climbed down from his tower, walking through the Jerusalem Gate, down the pathway which led to the copse of trees, and stood on the periphery of the activity, looking at what the three strangers were doing. In truth, one of the reasons he went to where the three Phoenicians were working was because the young woman had removed her tunic in the heat and was bare-breasted.

She stood from bending over the thick staff she'd planted in the ground, and turned to face the soldier. She smiled. A pleasant smile. She invited him to step inside the grove.

'I am Isha-babel, priestess of Asherah, servant of Jezebel. Welcome.'

The guard nodded. Few people, except his commanders and his wife, ever spoke to him. He spent his life in silence, looking from the turrets and walls at the passing traffic which entered and left Samaria, his days unrelieved monotony, his nights exercises in frustration. He had no idea what to say to the young woman. She continued to look at him in curiosity, wondering if he was dumb.

'Do you wish to ask something?' she asked, her voice raised in case he was hard of hearing.

He shook his head. 'No. I was wondering what you were doing.'

She walked over to him and grasped his hand, leading him inside the grove. It had been constructed so that it had a canopy of the branches of the trees, and the walls were made from branches cut from nearby foliage. The middle of the grove had been cleared of all undergrowth and shrubs and grasses, and in their place matting, made of some material which looked like water reeds, had been placed on the ground.

Holding Isha-babel's warm and welcoming hand, the guard was encouraged to walk inside the grove. The most prominent feature within the construction was the staff which had been placed in the ground, its footings excavated to a depth which held it firmly in place and then covered with matting of a different colour.

Isha-babel introduced the Israelite guard to the two men, both of whom she told him were priests of the God Ba'al.

'What do you do here?' the man asked.

'Here, we worship the Goddess Asherah. This is her sacred pole. It has been cut from a two-year-old tree and was selected because its trunk was not marked by any imperfections and no animal had burrowed its way inside the wood. We place this staff upright and link the ground to the heavens. On the staff, we place a golden plaque with messages to Asherah so that if she answers our prayers and comes into the grove to hear us, she will see our devotions and will read our supplications.'

The guard frowned. 'We are told that there is only one God. We call Him Yahweh; we also call Him El Shaddai. He has secret names which are only known to the chief priest in Jerusalem. Nobody knows how to pronounce God's real name other than the chief priest, which he does three times a year and always in secret. In this way, God knows we are calling Him, and will listen to our prayers.'

Isha-babel answered, 'We have no secrets from our gods. They hear our thoughts and our prayers. They control the heavens and the seas and the land. When bad things happen like storms or fires or earthquakes, it is because the gods are angry with us, or because they are fighting with each other. The purpose of coming into this grove is to ensure that Asherah listens carefully to what we are asking, and so will do what we ask.'

The guard nodded. It made sense. After all, he had often wondered in silence how there could be just the one God when there were so many different things happening in so many different places. He had once asked a priest how God could be in Samaria and in Jerusalem at the same time, and had been rebuked for his stupidity. The priest told him that God was omnipresent, and viewed the guard with contempt when he had to explain the word. But still the guard couldn't understand the concept. How could God be here ... and there, at the same time? Was He so huge? And if He was that big, why couldn't He be seen?

The priestess, Isha-babel, took a small idol from her pouch and placed it on the wooden ledge which had been nailed to the staff.

'This is Asherah,' she told him. 'This is the goddess whom I worship.'

'And what does she do?' he asked.

Somewhat surprised by the crudeness of his question, Isha-babel answered, 'My goddess is the god-pair with Ba'al. Together they rule much of the world and the heavens. There are many gods, such as El and Mot, but the reason I worship Asherah is because she commands and controls our loves and likes and hates.'

She encouraged him to stand closer to her ... and then she sat down, asking him to join her on the floor of the asherah, the sacred grove they were constructing. The priestess continued, 'In the beginning of time, when Asherah first came to earth and looked around, we saw her as an unshaped piece of wood. That is why she is called Asherah, because in our ancient language it means "straight". And just as most wood is hard and unyielding, so Asherah demanded much of us, and in ancient times, in the beginning, she was like the wood of her name, harsh and unyielding. We could not make love to a man to whom we weren't married, we could not laugh out loud; we could not enjoy ourselves. But Ba'al, her son, saw how unhappy this was making us people of the earth, and so he seduced Asherah and she enjoyed making love so much that she now encourages us to do so.

'Today we see Asherah in these upright posts we place in sacred groves. We call these groves by the same name as our goddess. And now we are representing our goddess as a naked goddess riding a sacred lion, or sometimes a horse, and holding lilies and serpents in her upraised hands.'

The guard looked on in pleasure. This was a goddess which he could understand.

'And furthermore, Asherah looks after us and protects us when we give birth to our children; she is the force of life in our flocks of sheep and our herds of cattle and she gives sustenance to our trees.'

'But what about droughts?' he asked. 'How can such a good goddess allow droughts and her animals to die?'

'We know that we have somehow offended Asherah and Ba'al when there is a drought. That is when we make most of our sacrifices.'

The guard looked at her in astonishment. He had heard of these people whose evil and false gods demanded the sacrifice of babies. He recalled that the name of the worst of the gods was Moloch. He told the priestess why he believed that they performed this evil practice.

She laughed. 'We don't kill people. Our sacrifices are the giving up of boys and girls to the service of Asherah and Ba'al. They sacrifice their virginity to the King or the Queen. The seed is then spilled on the ground and it is absorbed by the earth, and through the earth offers fertility to all plants and animals. Why would we kill people? Asherah and Ba'al love their people; they wouldn't want to see them die,' she said.

He felt stupid. 'I have to go. I must return to my post,' he told her.

But she held on to his hand. 'Stay with me a while longer. This is the first grove, the first asherah to my goddess. There are to be many more built throughout the length and breadth of Israel for the pleasure and enjoyment of Jezebel's new people. Why not join me and consecrate the first asherah I've built in this new country?'

'What does consecrate mean?' he asked.

When she told him, his eyes bulged in amazement, and he willingly accepted her offer to fertilise the ground of Israel in this holy place.

Later, much later, he returned to his post as it was nearing the end of his watch. The captain screamed at him in fury, but the guard heard little of the reprimand, and merely mumbled an apology. Amazed by the guard's audacity, or thinking him sick from the heat of the sun, the captain asked where the guard had been while he should have been on duty. When the captain understood what had occurred, he immediately went down to the asherah to see for himself; but the priestess who had given her body so freely had already returned to the palace. Impatiently, the captain accepted that he would have to wait till morning before he could sacrifice himself to Asherah and her beautiful priestess.

Word of what had happened spread throughout the city of Samaria like a grassfire in summer, and as more and more asherahs were constructed during the following days, so more and more of the men of Samaria rapidly turned up at the groves in order to learn more of the worship of the gods and goddesses of Phoenicia. Some immediately expanded their love of Yahweh to include the worship of the goddess of Phoenicia, Asherah.

Ahab was told what was happening, and that it was Jezebel who was behind the growth of the harlotry and immorality. Some of the courtiers were offended and tried to put a stop to it; others joined in with great enthusiasm. Omri was told of the building of the sacred groves to the goddess, and was tempted to put a stop to it, as it would offend the priests and prophets of Israel. But his advisors told him that the people of Samaria would soon tire of these things, and to stop it would further offend Jezebel, who, after her obeisance to the King of Israel at the banquet, was becoming loved by the court and the people. Offence might undo all of the good she was undertaking as their future Queen, and might ignite a conflict with Ethbaal which had only just been averted. And so Omri closed his eyes to the further building of the asherahs.

He was visited in his palace by the chief priest of Samaria, Hazarmaveth, who was in a mood of fury.

'Is your Majesty aware of the immoralities being practised at the very gates of your city? Does your Majesty know that guards leave their posts to despoil the sacred ground of Israel with prostitutes of false gods? Can your Majesty ...'

Omri interrupted him. 'Of course I'm aware, Hazarmaveth. Do you think I don't have eyes and ears?'

'Then why are you doing nothing about it?'

'For the same reason as I do nothing about the idols which people worship in their homes. This doesn't affect the security of Israel; it keeps the people happy; there's a drought and the people need to be distracted from their misery and their hunger ...'

The priest's eyes blazed in contempt. 'Yahweh will damn you and condemn you for your lax ways, Omri.'

'If Yahweh loved His people more He'd put an end to this drought.'

'Don't dare to presume the ways of Yahweh!' Hazarmaveth shouted.

Omri rose in anger. During his entire reign, the priests and prophets of Yahweh had been nothing but a source of trouble. The chief priest Jonathan had been terrible, and the prophet Elijah, and now Jonathan's successor, Hazarmaveth, had been sent to plague him. He'd done everything he could to appease them ... built them temples, kept the city dull in comparison to other capitals, forbidden the public worship of other gods ... but now that Jezebel was here he had the treaty to consider, and if the people wanted to worship idols and frolic naked in the countryside and enjoy themselves with bare-breasted priestesses ... well, what harm was there in that? Only the priests were complaining.

'I warn you, King Omri. We will turn the people back to the worship of Yahweh as the one true God. Oppose our will, and Yahweh will strike you and your family down and you will be as dust of the ground and forgotten in the annals of Israel.'

Omri breathed deeply. He couldn't do anything against this priest unless he wanted to invite an insurrection from the people; for they would rise up against him if he moved against the temple. While they enjoyed a dalliance with idols and priestesses, Yahweh was still firmly in their hearts. He'd kept his reign secure by building temples. Now that he was on the point of securing his northern border, the last thing he needed was an insurrection in the nation.

'Listen to me, Priest. And listen well. This fascination with Asherah and the other Phoenician gods is nothing more than the morning dew. When Yahweh's light shines on Israel the appeal of these gods will fade away and the people will return to the temple more loving and faithful than ever. And to ensure that they are properly housed when they do return, why don't we erect a special building for you and your priests near to the temple, somewhere you can pray in comfort and ease ...?'

Hazarmaveth returned to his brother priests in triumph, but the priests and prophets of Yahweh continued to watch in growing horror as the House of Omri tolerated the public frolics and the worship of the false gods and idols. Hazarmaveth and his brother priests welcomed the new building programme. But they retained a deep concern as more and more men – and now many women – continued to visit and take instruction from the priests and priestesses of Asherah and Ba'al.

They had for too long tolerated the worship of false gods and idols in the houses of Samaria and other places of Israel. They knew that in some villages, and in some homes, false gods were more loved than Yahweh and had been worshipped for generations. That was something which they had been forced to accept with quiet resignation. But what the people of Israel did in their homes wasn't nearly as dangerous as what these priests and priestesses of Phoenicia were doing in public. This display of idol worship in the fields and villages of Israel was too much, despite the pacifying words of the King. This was as bad as an uprising in the army. This building of asherahs had to stop, and those which were built had to be pulled down. And the men had to return to their wives and stop seeking bodily pleasures elsewhere, which was disobedience to the word of Moses the Lawgiver.

Word of the spreading immorality and idolatry was sent to Elijah in Tishbe, who read the missive from Samaria and roared in fury as he finished the letter. Rizpah, who had only recently returned from Samaria, came running out of the house, thinking that the voice of God was again upon her husband. But the look in his eyes, one of cold and murderous fury, told her that the rage was caused by man, not God.

'She is not trying to kill me,' he shouted to Rizpah.

His wife froze in sudden horror. 'What?' she asked.

'The whore of Sidon. The temptress of Tyre. She isn't trying to kill me. She's trying to kill my God. She is turning the people of Israel away from Yahweh. They are worshipping false idols in groves at the very foot of the capital. And the disease is spreading throughout all Israel.'

Rizpah tried to understand the reason for her husband's fury. The people of Israel had always worshipped other gods. Even the mother of Asa, the King of Judah, a woman called Maachah, publicly worshipped Asherah. Many people in the countryside of Israel had a small shrine in their homes where false idols were placed and worshipped. And she told him so.

'But this time is different,' Elijah shouted when she had finished reminding him of the realities of life in Israel. 'This time she is setting up temples in opposition to the Temple of Jerusalem. This time she has five hundred priests and priestesses. This is an army. I knew it when first I saw her enter our Holy Land. I stood on the precipice at Ras Nichrah and shouted at her and her minions to return to their damnable land with their heathen idols and their harlotry. I knew it, but I believed God would find a way to prevent it. But the Almighty has put His faith and trust in me, His humble servant, to stop her. His voice will come into my ears tonight or tomorrow. Then I will know what to do. But I now know that it is my mission to stop Jezebel and her legion of damned, and to return the children of Israel to the promise of the land they were given by Yahweh.'

CHAPTER ELEVEN

Rizpah looked at Elijah in utter dread. How could her husband demand such a thing of her?

'You must,' he insisted. 'You will! It is Yahweh's desire!'

It was a command as severe as any he'd uttered to her or either of their children. His face didn't soften despite hers registering first disbelief, then horror. Indeed, the look of distress on her face seemed to impel him to greater demands.

'I'm too sick to travel on my own,' he said. 'This is not just a command from your husband, but from your God.'

'But I'm still recovering from my journey. I need to rest. I've only been home for a short time. How can I leave our children and come with you to Samaria? The journey will kill me. You promised me last year that I wouldn't have to accompany you any more on your journeys. You said that Yahweh would excuse me and ...'

'You can see that I can't travel alone. Now I have this weakness in my limbs, I'm too exhausted to be on the road without help. I need a travelling companion. And we must go today. We leave immediately, or it will be too late. We cannot stay here another moment. The voice of the Lord is strong within me; it has been growing for two days now. I've heard His voice booming in my head and soon I will understand His words and I shall have to obey. Already I know that the Almighty wants me to contest the immorality of this Jezebel and her followers before it's too late for Israel.

'I should have gone when I received the letter from Hazarmaveth the chief priest. This is my punishment: to be a half of a man, and to have to ask my wife yet again to be my walking staff, to lean on her and use her as my legs.'

She continued to question his order. 'But you aren't well enough to travel. Surely God Almighty will spare you this time. There are others who can raise their voices against ...'

He tried to sit up, but the chills in his body prevented him. Exhausted he slumped back onto the bed, but he had the strength to shout, 'You dare to question the word of the Lord?'

She knew she'd gone too far. 'No, husband! But what if you become sicker on the journey? What if you die by the wayside? Will that be fulfilling the requirements of the Lord our God? Does a merciful God want His most faithful servant to die?'

'The Lord will ensure that I die when my time is come. I won't die until I've seen off this harlot and made Israel safe from false idols and harlotry,' he rasped, his voice sore, his throat feeling as though he was being strangled by the ailment. 'Rizpah,' he said sadly, 'why are you questioning the Lord? What if I recover on the journey and am stronger than ever before, and my voice is heard loud and strident throughout the land? Are you able to foretell God's purpose? I'm not. I'm merely the Lord's mouthpiece, the instrument He uses to do His bidding. But one thing is certain: His voice within me tells me that I have to leave, and leave today. I cannot stay in bed any more, despite my illness. I suspect that this sickness was given to me by the devils whom Jezebel worships in order to keep me from telling the people of Israel the true purpose of her coming to God's land.

'Understand this, woman. I must go. I have no choice. Rizpah, I must put an end to these so-called sacred groves, these asherahs where immorality happens; I must end the worship of these idols. Moses died before he reached our land. He stood on the Mountains of Moab, and his heart must have been breaking to be so near to the holy place and yet prevented by the Almighty from entering upon our sacred soil. And why was he prevented? Because of the children of Israel and their worship of idols when they left Egypt; because of Moses' anger. Because, just for a moment in time, for the slightest lapse in his temper, he turned his face from the Lord. I am no Moses, but I am the follower of our Father. Because he doubted the word of the Lord, I shall not. I shall follow the word of God, even if it means my death.

'Since the time of Solomon, foolish Hebrews have worshipped false gods and their idols. Yet Abraham, our Patriarch, was told by God to turn away from the worship of idols. Did not God instruct him to break the hideous idols of his father, Terah? Yet, despite the unmistakeable word of the Lord, we have continued in these abominable practices. Some who call themselves Hebrews have worshipped idols without thought to the anger of the Almighty. Others before me have cleansed this Holy Land of idols, yet again they come back, like some malignant disease which continues to infest our land. Like plagues of locust year after year – just when the crops are bursting with goodness the locust come and make the fields into dust – so it is with worshippers of false gods and idols.

'We followers of the Almighty have been vigilant in exposing and destroying these false gods. We have been merciless when hideous notions grew, spread by false prophets who encouraged the people to wrong beliefs; when the people claimed that our Lord God Yahweh had a consort, a wife. Yet, now this woman Jezebel is openly advocating and encouraging the worship of Asherah, the Devil from the blackest regions. Do you not know who this Asherah is, wife?' he shouted, but then he burst into a coughing fit, and sank down onto his straw mattress.

Rizpah reeled back at the vehemence of her husband whose face had turned red in his fury. She shook her head. In truth, she knew little about other gods from other nations. Lifting himself up on one elbow, he told her, 'She was called the wife of God. Imagine the hubris, Rizpah, the arrogance. This … this pagan idol … this clay thing as the consort of the Invisible One, the Lord Almighty!' He tried to continue but again burst into a fit of coughing.

Recovered after Rizpah gave him a drink, he said softly, 'Like Moses, I am a prophet and a mouthpiece of the Lord. And like him, I shall lead my people from their bondage to these idols, and their servitude to this Jezebel creature, into a Promised Land where the love of God Yahweh is our strength and our breath.'

He coughed and fell back exhausted onto the bed. Rizpah looked at him in concern and fear. And she knew from the sternness of his face that once more, fatigued though she was, she would again tread the path away from her home, away from her beloved children, and into the setting sun of Samaria.

She did not want to see the capital city of Israel again; indeed, when she had left it, Rizpah had thanked the Almighty and one God in heaven that it was the last time in her life that she would need to set foot in that hideous place.

Yet once more she stood in the marketplace of Samaria and, for the second time in a few months, she looked outwards in all directions and saw nothing but people; people everywhere, wearing clothes which were alien and upsetting for her. Rizpah's own clothes were those she wore every day, except on the Sabbath when she changed her dark robes, put on the white dress of purity and went with her husband into the fields to face the city of Jerusalem, and pray as though they were in the temple of David's city.

Rizpah had never been to the temple, but she knew every stone, every archway, every pillar from the descriptions of her husband. She knew of its golden stones which shone in different hues depending on the passage of the sun though the sky, she knew of its entry ways for the descendants of Aaron, and those of Levi, and the separate entry ways for the families of the other tribes of Israel.

So when she looked upwards and saw the mockery of the temple which Omri had built in Samaria so that the people of the nation of Israel could pray like their brothers in the nation of Judah prayed in Jerusalem, she felt sickened. It was a desecration in the sight of the Lord. It was a squat, heavy, ugly building; tall – yes, it was tall, and it was awesome to Rizpah who had lived all her life in a village of only forty homes – and it was crowded with people who came and went as though the Temple of Samaria was some sort of a marketplace; but despite the way in which the Samarians accepted it, she knew it was an abomination.

She stared at the building, so familiar to Elijah, and felt her heart racing. But at the very moment when she was about to follow Elijah, who was rapidly disappearing into one of the streets which led off the marketplace on his way to Sharaz's house, Rizpah's heart nearly stood still. For being carried up the steps of the temple by men clad in white tunics, their legs immodestly showing, was a huge statue. A statue of a woman riding a horse. And in her hand was a serpent. And her face was nearly touching the serpent as though about to kiss it.

An idol in the temple of the Lord! Rizpah felt the gorge rising in her throat, and for the second time in her life came close to fainting in the marketplace. But she managed to turn her face from the hideous idol, and follow her husband.

It had been a hellish journey. And the act of kissing her children goodbye and leaving them in the care of a neighbour was exceptionally hard. When she had returned from her recent visit to the capital, she had made a vow to them that she wouldn't leave them again to travel the lonely roads with Elijah. And she had been forced to break her vow. As she and Elijah had walked away from the village on the long road west, her heart had been breaking because she was suddenly afraid that she would never see her children again. Something told her that this was the last time she would tread the path which led from the village of Tishbe into the fields where the farmers grew crops which brought food for the people and money for them to buy their goods. In her heart of hearts, she knew that she'd seen the enemy of her people, Jezebel, and this Phoenician Princess was stronger by far than was she, a mere woman from Tishbe, even though she was the wife of a prophet.

But the burden of supporting her sick husband had temporarily made her forget the agony of her children and, as they walked the vast distance to the River Jordan, her only thoughts had been on survival. Not only was her own journey difficult and exhausting, but at the end of the day, she was forced to find wood, light a fire and prepare a meal, while Elijah lay and coughed and tried to recover his strength for the journey the following day.

How she had finally found the strength to walk beside her husband and support him on her shoulders, and carry all their packs up the long hills from the Jordan Valley into the highlands of Samaria, she would never know. But each step had fatigued her more than she thought she could bear. But, as with everything in the sight of the Almighty, the walls of Samaria came into view, and when they walked through the gates of the city, Elijah's strength seemed to return suddenly, and he walked quickly through the city to where he would end his journey and could sleep beneath a roof.

And now Rizpah had been left alone to carry their bags to Sharaz's house. She picked them up quickly to escape the sight of the abominable idol and followed in the footsteps of her husband. This really was the worst place she'd ever been to. And as her husband hurried down the streets away from her, she realised that she was completely alone.

'It is not suitable!' shouted King Omri.

'It cannot be returned. The insult would be too great. It is part of Jezebel's dowry,' shouted back the Phoenician Hattusas.

'I will not have idols put back in my temple. Only five years ago I cleared them out to pacify the priests of Yahweh. Keeping that huge horse with the goddess on top would be a disaster for me, a catastrophe. I have been warned by Elijah what would happen if I allowed idols to return to the temple. I've seen what happened to my brother King in Jerusalem. If idols are brought into my temple, the people loyal to Yahweh will revolt.'

The advisor shook his head. 'And you allow priests and prophets to run your country?'

Omri looked at him in fury. 'Watch your tongue, old man, lest it be torn from your mouth. Omri rules in Israel. My word is law. But this is the land of the Almighty One, Yahweh, and His priests are inheritors of the word of the Lord. From their mouths we hear the stories of our ancestors, we learn the wisdom of the ancients. Yahweh is a harsh God and makes many demands of us. But He has chosen the people of Israel above all others on earth to receive the word, and it is our sacred duty to learn it, live by it, and protect it from foreigners.

'No, Hattusas, priests and prophets do not rule this land, but they are mightier than my soldiers and so I listen to their counsel.'

Hattusas realised that he'd insulted the King, and bowed in apology.

'Majesty, I understand your difficulties. But there is something happening in the land of Israel, despite your priests and prophets. The people of your land are turning to Asherah. They are learning to love her.'

'She will not come into my city!' Omri shouted.

'Majesty, you have no choice. It is part of the dowry contract.'

'The contract said nothing about a huge idol,' the King said firmly.

'It said, " ... *the appurtenances suitable and fit for a Princess of Phoenicia* ..." This statue is such an appurtenance.'

'I told Ethbaal that I would accept no idols in Samaria.'

'It's an appurtenance ...' insisted the Phoenician advisor.

The King looked up from his throne. He had come to like Hattusas in the month he had been in the Israelite capital. The man was cultured, intelligent, knowledgeable and accommodating. There had been a myriad of problems, small and large, in the transition of the Princess Jezebel's home from Sidon and Tyre to Samaria, and it was Hattusas who had somehow managed to prevent each one of the problems from developing into a disaster which could lead to war. But the question of the dowry was now threatening to bring down the entire treaty. For the one thing which the King of Israel had said to his brother the King of Phoenicia was that, as part of the dowry settlement, he could not accept idols of Phoenician gods and goddesses in the Samarian Temple. But now King Ethbaal had written to insist.

And the cause of the insistence was Jezebel herself. That, Omri knew with absolute certainty.

He said, 'Hattusas. My word is law. Asherah will not come into the temple.'

Sadly Hattusas shook his head. 'Sire. Your word is law in your country; but these matters go beyond Israel. The word of my King Ethbaal is absolute. The idol will be in the temple. Or the insult to him will make him rescind the contract and there will be war.'

Omri breathed deeply to keep his temper. More than anyone, he knew the limitations of kingship. Those whom he ruled thought that he was in complete command. And, with the power of life and death, he was a fearsome ruler; but because he was so powerful, any decisions which he took had profound effects. The wrong decision, the wrong answer, the wrong move could plunge the country into a war and, if it were lost, he and his entire family would be murdered and his people led away into slavery and captivity forever. These consequences weighed heavily on his shoulders when he was deciding how best to respond to Hattusas – and through him to Ethbaal – and through him to the devilish and manipulative Jezebel, whom he now viewed as so scheming and calculating that he feared for his son once he ascended the throne of power.

On the one hand, if he were to give in to Ethbaal's demand to place the Goddess Asherah in the Temple of Samaria, it would be reported by spies to the kings of neighbouring lands; his concession would be taken as a sign of weakness and dark clouds would gather on his borders. On the other hand, were he to throw the idol outside the city walls, where there were now asherahs in just about every wood and field, and where men and women were now spending more and more of their time in lascivious actions which took them from their work and the care of their families, he would undoubtedly provoke a war with Ethbaal.

He massaged his forehead. 'Here is my word. The idol to the Goddess Asherah will go into the temple grounds. But not into the temple building itself to stand beside the altar to the one God, Yahweh. The idol may be worshipped by the people if they choose, but only within the courtyard which is within the outer walls of the temple. Tell that to Ethbaal, so that he might repeat my words to his daughter Jezebel.'

Hattusas began to speak in argument, but Omri shouted, 'That is my word, Phoenician. You have my decision. Now go!'

Sorrowfully, Hattusas left the throne room, knowing that the word was not the right word, the decision not the right decision.

Ahab took the news to her while she was riding in the fields. She had just visited three groves, placed at three of the points of the earth, and was riding to the fourth and final point upon which the earth rested, an asherah placed on the northern road towards her country of Phoenicia.

Jezebel and ten of her priestesses were riding slowly, enjoying the freshness of the countryside after the stench of the city; and especially the stink which entered her apartments, those directly above the palace kitchens in which she had been placed by order of the King. Night and morning she was forced to smell the odours of the fermentation vats in which the wine and ale were created, the smells of yeast added to bread to allow it to rise, the stench of rotting meats and fishes and vegetables as they were dumped in the yards prior to their collection and removal to the garbage pits by the palace slaves.

Her apartments in her colourful palace in Sidon where she enjoyed living were open to the breezes of the sea, and, night and morning, she could hear the screaming of gulls and the beating of sea waves on the cliffs. These were the sounds and smells with which she had grown up. These were what she most missed in the landlocked hill country on which the capital of Samaria was built. She missed the smells and the moods of the sea, the clouds which formed above it, the gulls which wheeled and circled high overhead.

And the differences between the inland city of Samaria and her own city of Sidon beside the sea, explained her continually bad mood. But despite the complaints of her advisors and guards, and of late her own vituperation, King Omri was completely unmoved by her demands to be relocated to another part of the palace; and so there she stayed.

Getting out into the fresh air of Israel was an increasingly important task for her. And it was bringing her closer to her people, something which she particularly wanted to do. For she liked the Israelites, those that she had met. Not so much the courtiers and their wives in the palace, and especially not the royal family who looked upon her as a wanton and immoral woman. The men, such as the King's younger sons and his brothers and cousins, gave her peculiar looks as she passed them or when she entered a room; the women sneered at her and all but called her 'whore' to her face. And it was all because of the way in which the men and women of Israel were turning to the worship of Ba'al and Asherah.

Jezebel had been told by Ahab that in ancient times there had always been a goddess consort for the God Yahweh. Yet the wife of their God had been expunged from worship by the fulminations of men like Samuel and Saul and Zadok and now Elijah. They had demanded an expulsion of all other gods and goddesses; and they had caused the people to rise up against the worship of what they called false gods. Those who worshipped the gods were forced to do so in private – to build niches in walls and place the idols on these niches, and to ensure that when they worshipped the gods, only their neighbours and friends knew.

But now that a future member of the royal family was openly constructing asherahs and encouraging the worship of the Goddess Asherah, and the priests were constructing their sacred places for the worship of Ba'al, the rulers, as well as the most important merchants and people of the court of Israel, were infuriated that the populace was again openly rushing to worship these gods.

As she neared the northern asherah on the Damascus Road, Jezebel turned when she heard the approach of horses. She saw that Ahab and one of his bodyguards were riding furiously in her direction. She stopped and waited, her horse suddenly shuddering and whinnying, then bending its long neck and head to eat the grass by the roadside. She grasped the horse's body more firmly with her strong legs to prevent herself from slipping down over the horse's head.

'Jezebel. My father has accepted the goddess into the temple,' he shouted as he drew nearer. 'The problem has gone. The idol is already in place. We can worship her together tonight.' He drew his horse to a halt beside her, his face red and sweating from the exertion of the gallop. He saw Jezebel's eyes had brightened at the news.

'He has given way?' she asked. Part of her foul mood was knowing that when she returned to Samaria, the battle over the placement of the idol would go on.

Ahab continued, 'He has admitted the idol of Asherah into the sacred grounds. It is there for all to see as they walk into the temple. No one can miss it. It is to the left of the pillars of the door.'

She frowned. 'It is outside the temple? Yet inside?'

'It's in the temple grounds. We can build an asherah. We can line the floor with reeds, we'll find the most magnificent two-year-old tree, and together we'll build an asherah worthy of your great goddess. And all the men and women of Israel will fall to their knees and worship her.'

Anger began to build within her. Her goddess was outside the house of Yahweh, like some servant waiting outside her master's chambers. How could Asherah and Yahweh possibly form a union if they were separated by thick stone walls? She expressed her anger to Ahab. When he caught back his breath, he looked at her sternly.

'Do not push my father any further than this. He is a powerful and a proud man. He has killed many. He has a thousand slaves who all attest to his power. I warn you, Jezebel. You have already gained more than any other woman. The treaty with Phoenicia is important to Israel, or you would not have lived after your words to my father the King when you first arrived. He has bent further than a reed in the breeze.

But bend him further and he will snap. Accept that Asherah is in the temple and be happy.'

He had never spoken to her as angrily as this. Since the day she'd met him on the road to Samaria he had been like dough in her hands. She had kneaded him into the shape she wanted him to be. He was growing contented on the honey and almond paste which her priestesses spread between their legs, and on which he dined every night. And like a groom at a long and frustrating wedding feast, he looked at her hungrily, eagerly anticipating what it would be like to enter her body once they were married. Yet their marriage could not take place until all the aspects of the treaty had been negotiated and finalised. He was discontent, but soon he would know what she tasted like, what she felt like when he was inside her; when the treaty was ratified, then she would allow him to taste her womanliness and to understand why she was the most desired woman in the world.

But at this moment, she drew back from her normally imperious demeanour. She had miscalculated his strength and his resolve. Suddenly she was confronted by Ahab, the warrior Prince of Israel, a soldier and builder of great buildings; not Ahab, a man besotted by her beauty, and deeply in love with her. She smiled and nodded. 'I shall bow before His Majesty Omri and thank him for the honour he does to me and to my future people.'

Ahab smiled. Even though he hadn't intended it like this, he was very well satisfied with the result. He had won a surprising victory in a game which he hadn't planned. Normally Jezebel played the game of diplomacy well, but when confronted by the strength and power of a man she became just like an ordinary woman. Yes, he thought … he was well pleased.

'Come, Prince and husband-to-be. Follow me to the northern asherah. There is a priestess who waits to service your needs.'

But instead of riding off, he held her back, moving his horse nearer to hers so that the beasts' flanks touched, and so that he was close enough for her to feel his breath. 'Wait,' he commanded. 'Today I don't want a priestess. I want you.'

She was about to refuse, as she had refused since they had met on the road and ridden together into Samaria. But the look in his eyes told her that now was the time for her to give in to his demands.

Give in? She wondered why she had thought of those words. For she now wanted him as much as he wanted her. It had been weeks since she had known a man. Weeks when she'd watched her husband-to-be in the arms of her priestesses, often two or three at a time. She'd felt her body glowing hot watching the way in which his body had entwined into theirs, smelling his manhood, restraining herself from joining in and satisfying her own urges.

But now, in the freshness of the air and the warmth of the sun, she wanted him. Her body ached to be touched by his strong arms, to feel him imprison her in the grip of his legs. And although she had no honey and almond paste, the love potion of the Egyptian women, she would taste his unadorned manhood and he her womanhood, and the Goddess Asherah would smile at them both, and Israel and Phoenicia would come together in more than a mere treaty.

***

Their wedding attracted gifts from Egypt, Anatolia, Macedonia, Syria, Assyria, Judah, Akkad, Moab and most other kingdoms and principalities. The ambassadors attending the wedding brought gifts which ranged in variety from rare African animals to eastern spices, to gleaming precious metals to gemstones whose depth of colour amazed Jezebel.

Yet what they waited for was the gift from his father the King, and her father the King. And from the look on Ethbaal's face it was a mighty gift indeed. So mighty that King Omri, who had ridden to Megiddo, south of the Valley of Jezreel to greet his brother King and escort him into the city of Samaria, was worried about his own choice of wedding present. On their journey together they had talked about many things, sometimes without their advisors, and both men had come to admire each other. Indeed, had it not been for the question of the worship of idols instead of Yahweh, there was much in Ethbaal's views of life which accorded with those of Omri.

Now both Kings were seated on either side of the bridal couple. As custom demanded, Ahab was sitting beside Ethbaal and Jezebel was seated beside Omri, to be welcomed into each other's family. Omri hoped that the gift was not so magnificent that he would be angry. And to his surprise, two Phoenician slaves carried in a huge water jar, an ornately decorated vessel which appeared to weigh heavily.

As the Phoenician ambassador accompanied Ethbaal's wedding gift into the throne room, the audience became still. Not even the animals nor the caskets with gems had caused such a silence. What was this gift, everyone wondered. A water jar as a gift from the father of the bride? Surely not! Only Omri felt a sense of foreboding.

Even Jezebel, who should have guessed the nature and purpose of her father's gift, was silent in anticipation of what the huge water jar might contain. Hattusas stood before it and said in a pompous voice, 'When my Majesty Ethbaal gave me this gift for the future King and Queen of Israel, I begged him on bended knees to present it himself. But he commands me, a humble ambassador of Phoenicia, to present to your Majesties, this jar.'

The jar was placed in its stand at the foot of the plinth, a dais on which Ahab and Jezebel were seated, dressed in their finest wedding gowns. The ambassador took the lid off the jar. Ahab expected a snake to jump out and surprise them, but nothing happened. He and Jezebel walked down to where the ambassador was standing. They peered into the jar, and were shocked. Omri also stood, and walked over. He immediately knew what the liquid was and let out a cry of surprise. The value of the gift was incalculable. The value of a kingdom. Even the tiniest jar was worth a fortune. But an entire vat ...

With a flourish, the ambassador said, 'A jar of the essence of the murex shell, a complete vat of purple dye which has been collected by my Majesty Ethbaal and the beloved people of Phoenicia in celebration of your marriage and the eternal union of our nations. Ever since the first negotiations, the people of Phoenicia have been collecting the shells of the murex in the few places where it is found on the shores of our sea, the only place where the murex shell is found.

'As you will know from the rarity and expense of clothes which have been steeped in purple, clothes worn by only the richest and most important of citizens, much of the income of Phoenicia is dependent upon this dye. Whole villages by the shore of the sea earn their living by collecting the murex shell and processing it so that all that is left is the colour of the gods – purple.

'For my Majesty Ethbaal to present such a valuable gift on top of the dowry he gives with his daughter Jezebel, shows all of Israel the love between our countries and the eternal bonds of friendship which will flow from this blessed wedding.'

He bowed, and the entire throne room transformed from silence into pandemonium as the audience burst into applause. The ambassadors of Egypt and Moab and the other countries which had given lesser gifts shuffled in anger, eager to inform their rulers of the snub which their countries had received at the hands of the Israelites by accepting such a fabulous gift from Phoenicia.

Aware of the growing menace, and furious that Ethbaal had deliberately set out to alienate all the surrounding nations with his reckless and overwhelming gift, Omri said, 'I thank His Majesty Ethbaal for the pleasure our children have enjoyed in receiving such a lavish gift. It will also be my pleasure to discuss with him late into the night the gifts of our brother kings from neighbouring and distant countries who have smiled upon this marriage which will bring peace to our region for a thousand years.'

Omri saw the ambassadors nodding in satisfaction at the rebuff he had delivered to Ethbaal. But he would have to speak to each ambassador in turn and flatter his king on the value of their gifts before the insult of Ethbaal would be extinguished in their minds. Omri sighed. He thought the daughter was bad enough; now he was having trouble with the father. What a family!

Rizpah smiled at the old man from the other side of the marketplace. He looked at her, thinking he had seen her before, but ignored her. In truth, it was because his eyes were beginning to cloud over from age, and although he sensed she was looking at him, he couldn't clearly make out her features. She walked from her side of the marketplace through the assembly towards him.

'I am Rizpah,' she told him. 'We walked together from the River Jordan to Samaria. Some time ago. My husband is Elijah the prophet.'

The old fisherman looked at her, and smiled. 'Yes, now I remember you. My age robs me of my memory and my eyes blind me to your sight. But now you have told me who you are, I remember our conversations. Are you here to celebrate the wedding? I came to see the gifts.'

He pointed into the middle of the marketplace. 'Have you ever seen one of those? I've never seen one before.'

Rizpah looked more closely; the cage had been obscured from her sight, and now she saw the largest, ugliest, greyest animal she had ever seen. It was much longer than a man, and stood half as tall. It had the largest, ugliest nose she'd ever seen. It was like looking at a nightmare.

The fisherman, whose name she had forgotten, told her, 'I have been informed by travellers who are in the crowd that it isn't an elephant, which is much bigger, though as I haven't seen an elephant, I wouldn't know. This,' he said nodding towards the hippopotamus, 'is apparently a horse which lives in mud, though I have seen horses and it doesn't look much like a horse to me. Ah well, another miracle of the Lord. Anyway, this river horse cannot be kept here, or it will die. It must be taken to water, or a river so I'm told, or the King has to build a special enclosure and fill it with water as the animal has no way of keeping cool.'

Rizpah stared at the beast which was snorting and shuttling in anger at the confines of the cage. 'A horse which lives in mud? But what good is that?'

'Who knows the ways of the Egyptian gods? Maybe they ride muddy horses. Or maybe they themselves live in mud and this is their way of riding.'

And then she remembered his name. He was called Absalom.

'Compared to the river horse, the other gifts seem more ...' she searched for the word, '... ordinary.'

Absalom smiled, and shook his head. 'They say that inside the palace is a gift more precious than all the treasuries of all the kings of all the world. It was given to Jezebel and Ahab by King Ethbaal of Phoenicia.' And he repeated to her what the King's secretary had announced to the crowd about the vat of purple dye from Phoenicia, how purple was used to dye the hems and sleeves of the clothes of the richest men and women, how it was responsible for much of Phoenicia's wealth. And why a vat of dye was such a grand and valuable wedding gift.

'But how can the shell of a sea creature be so valuable? Surely I can gather as many as I want from the shore and ...'

'These shells are not found anywhere but in this narrow part of Phoenicia. That's why they're so valuable. That's how they can make the purple, which without these shells only exists in the eyes of newborn babies and sometimes in the setting of the sun.'

She shook her head in confusion. 'How can something which the Almighty gives us be so rare? If Yahweh made the earth, why didn't He put everything ... everywhere ...?' She knew what she wanted to say, but had difficulty expressing the idea.

'Listen,' Absalom said, 'have you ever spiced your meat with saffron from the crocus flower which grows in the Indies? Have you ever eaten the honey from wild bees of the mountains of Cyprus? Have you ever eaten the dream pollen of the poppy from the land of the Hittites? Have you felt the black wood which is like iron and which comes from the mountains of the Etruscans? Have you ever tasted the black flour from the wheat grown in the soils of the volcanoes in Anatolia?'

Rizpah had no idea what he was talking about. She had never heard of these things.

'I told you when we first met that I was a fisherman. I am. But for much of my life, I lived in Phoenicia. In Tyre, where the Princess who is to marry Ahab was born. Only recently have I moved down the coast to live in Israel. Since I was a boy, I've thirsted for knowledge of what lay beyond the horizon, so I sailed all over the great Eternal Sea. But sometimes, I failed to return. Instead, I stayed in places of which you only dream. I was once on top of the highest mountains of the world where the snow is there all the year round. I have been to the Nile River and have seen the pyramids which were built by a race of giants who no longer walk the earth. I have been to more places than you know exist.'

He looked at her and realised she did not understand why he was saying these things. 'Rizpah, there are more things in this world which you don't understand than you could possibly understand.' He burst out laughing at his pun. She wasn't offended, for it wasn't a mocking laugh. 'You open your eyes and behold a horse of the mud of Egypt and gaze in wonder. Yet were you in Egypt, they would wonder why you wonder. You are surprised that purple dye costs so much that men kill for it. Yet if you were rich, you would give away much money to merchants just to own a purple garment. You don't understand why, Rizpah. But the rich man cannot understand your wonderment. Yet both of you are happy in your knowledge.'

Rizpah drew her eyes away from the wonderful objects and gifts in the marketplace, from the crowds of onlookers, and from the magnificent guards in their colourful clothes signifying the many different countries they came from. 'Why are you telling me this? I'm a simple woman. I don't really understand what you're saying. Why not say these things to my husband, Elijah? He is clever, and knows much. He speaks the words of the Lord. You're wasting your breath on me.'

But Absalom shook his head. 'We will meet again, Rizpah. One day in the market or beyond the gates of the city. But there is no purpose to my meeting with your husband. For although he and I speak the same words, we do not speak the same language.'

He turned and walked away, leaving Rizpah speechless.

The music of the wedding could be heard throughout the whole of Samaria. People of the towns and the villages came from far around to crowd into the city and enjoy the spectacle. Dancers, musicians, acrobats, jugglers and singers stood on all the rooftops surrounding the palace and performed from morning to night. The streets were thronged with people who came to buy from merchants and to listen to the amusing storytellers weave their spells and to gasp at the incredible skills of the acrobats who stood on each other's shoulders three men high and somersaulted backwards onto the shoulders of one standing behind. Singers accompanied by cymbalists and drummers walked around all day, and even encouraged boys and girls to join in their songs.

Inside the palace, the celebrations continued after the ceremony of marriage had been conducted. A priest had bound the couple's hands together with a holy cord, and had cut it to signify the fragility of man's tenure on earth. The woman, Jezebel, had lain at her husband-to-be's feet and sworn a vow of respect. He had given her a bracelet to put on her arm, and she in turn gave him the husband's crown to show him that he was a greater king of their marriage than she a queen.

As she placed the crown on his head, the entire assembly, including Omri and Ethbaal and their wives and children, clapped in happiness. They were now one, an indissoluble entity, married and in union, man and wife, nations together!

The moment she stood and placed the crown on his head, musicians began to sing, and the wedding party left the throne room and entered the banqueting room where they sat at tables laden with food and ate delicacies which had been prepared by the many chefs which brother kings had sent to assist in the preparations.

Already full, unable to eat or drink another morsel, Omri leaned back on his divan and adjusted the pillow supporting his arm. He surveyed the scene, and was happy, although irritated by indigestion which he thought might have been caused by eating some lamb which was too spicy for his tastes. He was also disturbed by a small commotion at the entrance to the banqueting hall, where the priests of the temple seemed to be making a bit of a fuss and having words with the guards on the door. King Ethbaal also looked over to the noise of the commotion. It appeared that someone had entered the banqueting hall without permission and was in the company of the priests. A guard was in the process of calling over his captain, who no doubt would sort out the problem. It was another aspect of the minor unpleasantness which seemed to surround this wedding.

Omri had managed to quell the unhappiness of the other ambassadors, although it had taken him all night, and he told the ambassadors that he deliberately hadn't put the vat of purple dye out into the market square with the other gifts as their gifts would overshadow in magnificence the gift of his brother Ethbaal. He told the surprised Ethbaal that the gift he had given was too valuable to be placed out in the streets of the city and would be in its rightful place of honour in the throne room itself. The path he'd negotiated was delicate, but everyone seemed to be happy.

All was good. Omri smiled at the obvious love between Ahab and Jezebel. Even Hazah, Ahab's other wife, seemed to have come to terms with Jezebel's position, and was sitting with the wives of the Kings in a place which gave her prominence without too much respect.

Again his eye was diverted from Hazah and the other wives to the growing commotion at the entry way; he'd placed the priests of the temple at a table near the doorway so that their praying wouldn't disturb the ambassadors and rulers from other countries who did not pray to Yahweh.

The music swirled; the dancers danced. Omri looked around at the happy scene in satisfaction. Now he had a treaty with Phoenicia; now his northern border was secure. The kings who surrounded his nation had sent good gifts and important ambassadors to celebrate the nuptials. Yes. Everything was good at the moment, and perhaps now that this wedding was over and the land again secure, he could resume his building programme, especially the lands between Samaria and the River Jordan, which were sorely in need of a defensive city.

But as he was musing, above the sound of the chatter of guests and the music accompanying the dancers, the commotion at the priests' table suddenly grew to disturb the entire hall, and command the attention of all the guests. Furious that the ceremony and proceedings should be interrupted, Omri was about to stand, when he heard a voice which made his blood run cold.

Someone was screaming above the surrounding noise, someone whose voice was normally heard in the marketplace and in the dry desert wadies and fulminating on the tops of walls and towers, screaming his anger to the mob. The voice shouted:

'You have placed idols in the temple, Omri! Now you drink wine with idolators in the palace! You have taken a viper to the bosom of Israel. Woe to you, Omri. Death awaits you!'

It was the voice of the Tishbite. So he was out of Gilead and back in Israel. Omri should have known, should have told the guards to be on alert. Yet his spies had told him that Elijah was sick and unable to travel.

Now everyone in the banqueting hall listened in horror to the words which interrupted the ceremony. The musicians stopped their strumming, the dancers their whirling. And the voice of the little man with a large wooden staff at the back of the room, dressed like a poor traveller, echoed through the vastness of the hall. He had moved from the place where he'd been secreted by the chief priest Hazarmaveth, and was now standing in the doorway, the light from outside shining around him, making his face look dark and demonic.

Elijah lifted up his staff and pointed it at the table where the royal families of Israel and Phoenicia were seated. 'I have seen her. I have been to the temple of God and seen the abomination which has been placed by your hand in His house. I have sullied my eyes on this goddess from the north, this foul and evil thing called Asherah. I have seen her evil body riding a beast and defiling herself with a snake, the very animal which our forefathers told us brought corruption to the world by its seduction of Eve. Omri, isn't it bad enough that you have built a travesty of a temple in this accursed land and filled it with cherubim and winged bulls and golden cows, evil man that you are?

'But to put a goddess of lust and harlotry in the very forecourt to a place where the people come to worship the one true God, where people journey to bow down to Yahweh! Omri, you are worse than all who have walked the ground before you. And you will go to your forefathers and make them weep in heaven for the sins and the torments which you have made Israel suffer.'

Ethbaal looked at Omri in astonishment. To allow anyone to speak to him like this would have brought immediate death. In Phoenicia, one of his guards would have stepped forward immediately and delivered a blow from his sword which would have sent the head of this madman rolling across the floor to Ethbaal's feet. Yet Omri just sat there.

'And this woman, Jezebel. Our future Queen. A harlot and a whore who comes from a land ...'

Ethbaal could not tolerate another word. Insulting Israel was one thing, insulting Phoenicia quite another. He stood and yelled, 'Aaaaggghhh ...' as he withdrew his sword from its scabbard and began to step forward. His guards immediately unsheathed their swords and started to run across the room to the door. Israelite soldiers quickly drew their weapons, thinking that they and their royal family were about to be slaughtered. Women of the court screamed in shock.

Omri stood and yelled, 'Stop! No one will harm the prophet of the Lord God. Death to the man who strikes a blow against the Lord.'

The Israelite guards now stood with their swords drawn and marshalled themselves quickly in the path of the running Phoenician guards who drew to a halt a sword's length away from the Israelites.

Ethbaal, at the back of his men, turned to Omri and screamed down the length of the hall, 'This man will die for the insult he does to my daughter.'

Omri shouted back, 'His insult is to Israel. He is a prophet of Israel. He will be dealt with by the justice of Israel. It is death to harm a prophet of Yahweh. Yahweh's prophets are sacred. Yahweh speaks through their mouths. Elijah is not your enemy, Ethbaal. It is Yahweh who is the enemy of your gods.'

The Phoenician King looked around the room. Everyone was anticipating the next move. To kill the prophet would be to create a war; to defy Omri would lead to war; to sit down and do nothing would undermine him in the sight of all the ambassadors and make his country vulnerable. The insult to Jezebel must be satisfied, or his stature would be diminished. He looked contemptuously at Prince Ahab who had stood, but hadn't moved. What husband would allow his wife to be so severely insulted?

King Omri shouted again that their swords must be sheathed, but after the first few words, his speech became unintelligible. And as the court looked at the Israelite King, he clutched his chest, and swayed as though he was drunk. Ethbaal tried to understand what his brother King was saying, but something was wrong with the man's face. It was as though he had suddenly swum in the vat of dye which the Phoenician had given the young couple. Omri dropped his sword and seemed to claw at his heart. Jezebel screamed as the King of Israel pitched forward across the banqueting table and fell into the carcass of a lamb. Ahab yelled and rushed over to his father. Suddenly the women of the court of Israel realised that their King was suffering a seizure and began to scream. Even the guards were unnerved by the collapse of their leader and were shouting to each other to bring the Egyptian physician.

Ahab was the first to reach him. Gently, he turned him over, but the King's face was now blue and he was gasping as a fish gasps on a seashore. People were trying to get to him, but most held back, not knowing what to do in such a seizure. By the time the Egyptian physician came running and began tending to his needs, Omri, King of Israel, was already dead.

Realising the catastrophe, the women of the court began to cry. Ahab dropped his head into his hands. Omri's wives began to wail the lament of the dead.

Only Elijah smiled and mumbled thanks to the Lord God, Yahweh. Yahweh had again pointed the way and made safe the path for His children of Israel. Yahweh was great, for in front of the entire world, He had slain Omri and weakened the House of Evil. Great and good was the Lord of Hosts. Elijah quietly moved over to the table of the priests, and sat down.

CHAPTER TWELVE

The high priest of Ba'al who was in the banqueting hall to attend to the needs of his King Ethbaal, was the first man in the room amidst all the screaming and wailing to perceive the unique opportunity which the sudden death of Omri, King of Israel, could present to his own King of Phoenicia. Long schooled in the arts of palace diplomacy and intrigue, and having spent years in the Egyptian court as a diplomat, he knew that this was a moment which could not be allowed to pass; for if it did, it might be months or even years before things would be as good again as this.

Omri had already been declared dead to the shocked assembly by a weeping captain of the guard after the Egyptian physician had placed a shining piece of metal over his mouth and found no sign of breath. Immediately following this declaration, there was mayhem; women wailed more loudly now that they knew Omri's collapse had led to his death.

The high priest of Ba'al walked stealthily past the physician from Egypt and approached Princess Jezebel, who sat staring at the body of her late father-in-law, still sprawled among the platters of food. He rounded the table and stood just behind her, concealing himself from the sight of the mourners.

'Listen to me carefully, Jezebel, Princess of Phoenicia, and now Queen of Israel. This is the time for you to rise up and claim the crown of the Queen; and in doing so strike a blow against the worshippers of Yahweh who have murdered your husband's father, and plant the love of Asherah deeply in the soil of this land.'

She turned and looked at him in surprise, still in shock at the events of the past few moments. He whispered urgently, 'Go over and pick up the crown of Israel which is lying on the ground; carry it ceremoniously over to your husband Ahab, and place it on his head, and when you do, say these words ...'

Jezebel listened, but began to shake her head in disagreement. The high priest insisted, and repeated for her the words he had told her to say.

On legs which shook with uncertainty, she stood and walked over to where Omri's crown had fallen, and picked it up. She held it above her head and slowly, as though in a dance of seduction, walked towards the prostrate form of her husband Ahab, lying across the table, his head buried in his hands, weeping for his dead father.

The commotion in the banqueting hall began to calm as the people sensed that something else momentous was about to happen. Suddenly all eyes were on Jezebel. Women were still quietly sobbing and Ahab took his head from his hands, sensitive to the change in tension within the room.

Omri's wives looked uncertainly at each other in the horror of the event, and the more intelligent realised at that moment that their lives as Queens and people of stature were over. Some looked at Jezebel in hatred, knowing what she was doing. The Palace Guard, looking for leadership, glanced over to their captain to see if he would stop the Phoenician Princess from touching the crown of kingship; but something in her manner of confidence and authority told the captain to remain standing, to wait and see what she would do.

Jezebel continued walking over to Ahab, who now sat back from the table and sprawled on his divan, his body still crouched over in grief.

'King Ahab, Ruler of Israel,' she said in a commanding voice which surprised those around. 'Stand before your people!'

The Prince looked slowly outwards from his sorrow and saw his young wife standing there holding the dead King's crown in her hands.

And then the full understanding of the nature of kingship settled on his shoulders. Ahab stood; the entire banqueting hall suddenly lapsed into silence at the extraordinary sight of a future King of Israel about to be crowned, not by a priest of Yahweh, but by a woman, a foreigner and a worshipper of false gods. Even Ethbaal still clutching his sword and wondering, now his brother King was dead whether to hack this party of conspiring priests to death, looked in astonishment at what his daughter was doing.

Although consumed with uncertainty about the peace treaty, and even his own safety at this moment, in his heart, Ethbaal forgot revenge and rejoiced at the sight of his wonderful daughter poised in the act of crowning the King of a foreign land. The symbolism, the importance, would not be lost on the many ambassadors in the room. Ethbaal would reward his daughter Jezebel with another vat of the dye from the seashells when he returned to Phoenicia.

To gasps from the assembly of ambassadors and royalty of the House of Omri and dignitaries from Phoenicia and Israel, Ahab slowly bent at the knees, and then knelt down to prostrate himself before his wife. The crown was placed on his head.

'In the name of Asherah the goddess who protects all life, in the name of Ba'al, God of All Things; in the name of El, God of All Things; and in the name of Yahweh, God of Israel, I crown you with the sacred crown of Israel and name you King of Israel.'

As slowly as he had knelt, Ahab rose to receive the crown of his country, its kingship and its power. Moments earlier, he had been a Prince. Now, he was the King of Israel.

The priests at the back of the hall stood as one and began to cry out in fury and indignation at Jezebel's usurpation. But Ethbaal marched forward, sword raised high, and shouted at them, 'As you kill a King, so another rises in his place and will quash you and your evildoers like an ant is squashed underfoot. Priests of Yahweh, you and Elijah have killed your King – your days are numbered. Now a new King rules Israel; and a new Queen. And new gods. Prepare, priests, to meet your end!'

They looked at the Phoenician King and at his guards; then at the guards of Israel who stood ready … but ready for what? Before Omri had died they would have sprung forward to defend the priests, but the looks in their eyes, looks of anger and hatred towards the table, told them immediately that there were no friends of Yahweh in this hall. They remained silent. From the other end of the hall, standing in the shadows behind Jezebel and Ahab, the Phoenician high priest could hardly conceal his happiness.

Jezebel, still white and gaunt from the shock of her happiness suddenly being turned to misery, placed the crown on Ahab's head and stood back to allow all Israel to see their new King. Ahab adjusted the crown and walked over to the fallen Omri and kissed him on the forehead. Then the new King turned and faced his people for the first time. Jezebel, Queen of Israel, turned to face the people also.

'Rise, and acknowledge your new King,' she shouted. 'As one King dies, another King is born in his place. Long live Ahab, King of Israel.'

But there were no cheers from the people in the hall. Instead, the captain of the Palace Guard walked into the middle of the floor and ceremoniously genuflected in respect of his new monarch and ruler. And as one, the entire Palace Guard followed their captain, and kneeled.

Ahab nodded in satisfaction, and said, 'Arise, loyal men of Israel. Now, my first command to you as your King is to bring me Elijah.'

His voice was soft, barely audible. No one moved. Not one person stirred at the shock of seeing another King in the place where Omri should have stood. Sensing their mood, Ahab understood that this was the pivotal moment of his new and untested kingship.

He shouted, 'Bring me the prophet of Yahweh. Bring me the man who has brought destruction to the House of Omri. Bring Elijah to me so that he may see the destruction he has wrought. Let his eyes see the dead King of Israel. And let Omri's body be the last thing which his eyes will ever see.'

King Ahab's voice rose with each word, until he appeared to be screaming uncontrollably, 'Bring me the man who has killed my father and who will die this day!'

Ethbaal came forward and laid a hand on the younger man's shoulder. Softly, so that only Ahab could hear, he said, 'Majesty. I mourn the death of my brother Omri. He was a great King. But you will sully his memory if you kill this prophet before the body of your father is even cold. How will your people react if they see that you have given way to vengeance without obeying the customs of burial and mourning? When the period of mourning is over, then kill this murderous prophet.'

Ahab looked at his father-in-law and saw a stranger. 'Customs? The man screamed threats and he committed treason against my father and from that, my father died. Because of this treason, because he is hated by the House of Omri, this prophet of Yahweh will die. That, Ethbaal, is my first command as King.'

The Phoenician King whispered, 'I know you grieve. But the duty of a king is to lead by wisdom as well as by courage. Then people will follow you. Lead by causing fear or by showing your people you cannot control your emotions, and you will be overthrown within the year.'

Ahab appeared to hear, but not to listen. It was as though Ethbaal's voice was one of the mob of people who were still shouting and crying in the nether regions of the room. The young man made no reply. The Phoenician King shook his head sadly, realising that now was not the time for the sort of reasoned argument he might have with one of his counsellors.

Ethbaal turned to his guard. 'Find Elijah. Bring him before Ahab, King of Israel.'

Suddenly the room erupted with movement. The captain of the Israelite guard ordered his men to stand from their kneeling and to find Elijah. They ran through the hall to the table of the priests to seek out the prophet. Where people had stood moments earlier in silent grief and shock, suddenly they were swept up in an outburst of disorder. As one, the priests of Yahweh turned and hurried from the hall; ambassadors who were stunned by the sudden turn of events remembered their duty and left the hall to send messengers to their rulers; servants hurried to clear away the platters of food; and guests left to return to their homes and begin the process of grieving for their dead King.

Guards came forward and lifted the body of the once-King of Israel off the table, and took him to his apartments in the palace where he would be dressed and laid in state to be viewed by the people for the rest of the day and the following day. Then he would be buried according to the tradition of Moses.

At the other end of the room, the search for Elijah was fruitless. The guards looked towards their captain for advice, and he ordered them to scour the city and obey the command of their new King; the men ran out of the doors intent on finding and arresting the prophet of God, Elijah.

But he was gone. They searched the palace, then the marketplace, then they questioned people in merchant's shops and standing in alleyways. They demanded to know where the prophet Elijah had disappeared to when he had left the palace.

Their questions led them into alleyways and into

the temple, but a search of the building showed that if he had been there, he had already left, spirited away by unseen hands. So they demanded to know where Elijah was staying in Samaria, and the guards were led to the house of a woman called Sharaz, who someone told them was a cousin of Elijah's wife. She lived in the metalworkers' alley, close to the southern wall of the city. The guards burst in through the door, their swords drawn, and overturned beds and opened curtains searching for the prophet. Two women screamed as they forced open the door: one was Sharaz, wife of the metalworker, who fell to the floor and hid her face as the phalanx of guards entered her home; the other was a woman called Rizpah who was terrified and cried, but after a beating admitted to being the wife of the prophet Elijah. Their quarry was not there, and neither woman had seen him since he had gone to the palace to complain about the idols in the temple.

A young guard was given the task of escorting Rizpah back to the palace for questioning. He tied her hands together and tethered her legs so she could walk, but she often stumbled and fell to the ground where he kicked her in anger. She cried, but his mood was one of hatred. As he escorted her at swordpoint through the streets of the city, she suddenly appeared to buckle at her knees, her legs collapsing beneath her. She fell to the ground. He kicked her again, but there was no response. He thought she might be dead, but she had only fainted.

When Rizpah opened her eyes again, she was lying on a divan. Her head was thumping, as though a thousand demons were battering her from the inside. She looked around the room. It was vast. And magnificent. Never had Rizpah seen such beauty in all her life. She tried to lift her head but the demons were making it heavy, and she felt that it was being held down onto the bed.

A young woman, with startlingly attractive dark eyes, and hair which looked as though it was shining with the last rays of the evening sun, walked over to where she lay, aware that the older woman had suddenly moved. Recognition dawned on Rizpah like an evil dream as the woman spoke:

'Where is your husband, the murderer of the King?'

Rizpah moaned, her head swimming in a lake of pain.

Again the evil creature spoke. 'Where is your husband Elijah the prophet?'

Her voice dry, Rizpah rasped, 'I don't know.'

With cold menace, as determined as a snake entrancing a mouse, Jezebel said softly, 'I know that your name is Rizpah. I know that you have left your children in a village called Tishbe in Gilead. I know that you stay in Samaria with your cousin Sharaz. I know much about you. I also know that unless you tell me exactly where your husband is so that I might kill him, I will kill you. Then your children will be orphans, I will sell them into slavery and they will be sent to Egypt and will work in the blisteringly hot copper mines until they themselves die young and friendless and without issue. Your family name will come to an end and the name of Elijah will be forgotten forever. Now ...'

But she was talking to herself, because Rizpah had again fainted.

A young and beautiful priestess laid a cold bandage over Rizpah's head. The cool water brought Rizpah instant relief. The woman lifted Rizpah's head from the bed, and placed a cup to her lips – wine mixed with honey. It was delicious.

Painfully, Rizpah turned to look at the young woman. She had seen her before, but couldn't place her. Gently the woman put Rizpah's head back onto the divan.

'Why did you faint?'

Rizpah tried to speak, but the priestess interrupted her. 'Wait. Don't speak. My mistress Jezebel commanded me to fetch her when you awoke.'

The priestess stood and ran out of the room, leaving Rizpah alone. Her mind was still reeling from the pain of the headache, but the clouds of mystery began to clear as the recent events began to make themselves known. The shouting, the soldiers at the door, the weapons, the sword at her throat, the pulling at her arms and forcing her to follow them, the kickings when she lay on the filthy ground. And then she remembered the worst memory of all ... that young demon woman, Jezebel, who had threatened her children with slavery and death.

Her mind suddenly was as clear as a cold mountain stream. She knew where she was, and why she was here. Jezebel abruptly entered the room, full of haste and anger.

'So, you're awake! You fainted so quickly; my doctors thought you might be dead. Do you remember why you're here?'

Rizpah nodded. The movement hurt her head.

'Good. Well, where is he?'

'He?'

'Fool!' she hissed. 'He! The man who killed Omri! Your evil husband, Elijah.'

'I … I don't know.'

'Then your children will be orphans and will die a lonely death.' And the Queen of Israel stood and began to walk away.

'Wait!' said Rizpah. 'Please, wait. Why are you punishing me? And my children? They're innocent.'

Jezebel turned, and said coldly, 'They are the spawn of your husband. No matter how innocent it is in the nest, the egg of a snake still produces a snake. You and all your brood are guilty of regicide and treason and will be killed. That is my final word.'

But before the Queen could leave the chamber, for the briefest of moments, the strength and courage of Elijah suddenly came over Rizpah. She said, 'With my death, comes yours.'

Jezebel stopped, and turned.

'What?' she asked in surprise.

'Make my husband a martyr and another prophet will rise up to fill his shoes. For Yahweh has decreed it. But kill me and my children, and you will have no kingdom. The people will rise up and will end your reign before it begins.'

Rizpah heard herself say these words, but they were disconnected from her, as though she wasn't saying them, but they were being put into her mouth by … by … *No*! She couldn't believe that Yahweh was making her speak in a way in which she'd never before spoken. Not her! Not Rizpah, the wife of Elijah.

Jezebel looked closely at Rizpah. She had never before been spoken to in this way by a woman. She stood there for a long moment, pondering what to do. And then she realised that threats would never work on Elijah and his family. Their God was impelling them ever forward to their own fate – martyrdom – and if she acceded, then she would indeed be the loser. What was it that Hattusas had told her? *'Make the people love you and the priesthood will be yours ...'*

She returned to the divan on which Rizpah was lying.

'My counsellors tell me that I shouldn't threaten you. That you will tell me what I need to know without the fear of death hanging over your head. They say that just the fear of being here is enough to loosen your lips. Is this true?'

Rizpah wondered what was in the mind of this young and evil woman. Jezebel helped her sip the honeyed wine again, which tasted wonderful.

'You feel awful, don't you!'

Rizpah nodded.

'That's because you hurt your head when you fell to the ground as you were being brought here. And I understand that the guards beat you. You must feel much pain.'

Her voice croaking, Rizpah said, 'I do. I feel terrible.'

'Don't try to talk until you're feeling better. Maybe sleep will help you. After you've slept, then you can tell me what I want to know. Rizpah, I will allow you to live if you tell me where Elijah is. I've heard what you said, but you must understand that his life is already forfeit; he is a walking man, but dead in the eyes of Israel. But I don't really want to hurt you and your children. Don't allow yourself or them to suffer because of the crimes of your husband.'

Gently, the young woman placed Rizpah's head back on the pillow and she disappeared, leaving Rizpah amazed. One moment Jezebel was threatening her with the worst fate which could overcome a family, and the next she was helping her drink and speaking to her as though she was in a council of advisors.

Rizpah wanted to argue further, to tell Jezebel that Elijah wasn't committing crimes, but obeying the commands of Yahweh, but she was exhausted and drifted off into a relaxing sleep. She dreamed of flights of angels in a blue sky. Of huge rooms. Of children running around and playing.

When she awoke, the room was darker, as though the sun was no longer shining. Rizpah turned her head, the ache having gone, and saw three young women. They noticed the movement, and one immediately stood and ran off in the opposite direction. Rizpah slowly, and somewhat painfully, swung her legs to the side of the divan and sat there, wondering whether or not she'd have the strength to stand up.

Jezebel walked into the room. Now that she could see her closely, Rizpah was stunned by her appearance. She was tall and slim and young, and very beautiful. She moved with the grace of an antelope. Rizpah knew her better now, and tried to see her as her greatest and most terrible enemy. But she was so young, and smiled with the smile of friendship.

Jezebel asked, 'Are you feeling better? You've been asleep for the entire afternoon. You must be hungry and thirsty.' She turned and issued instructions for wine and food to be brought. 'Perhaps you're still not well. Shall I call the Egyptian physician back to you? He has already been here and he examined you while you were asleep. He tells us that although you need a tincture of cornflower stems as a tonic for your eyes and something which he calls *balanos* for your sallow complexion and constitution, you are otherwise in good health. He also says that your birth chamber hasn't properly healed and closed over from the bearing of your last child, and that your discharges smell, which he says he can cure by a suppository of the essence of a fir tree, juniper berries and hemp.'

Rizpah looked at her in amazement which quickly transmuted to a feeling of horror. While she was asleep, a doctor had examined her in her most private parts, those which not even her husband was allowed to see.

Jezebel immediately understood the look of concern and anger on the older woman's face. 'You're angry that we examined you? Don't be. We were interested in your health. You had fainted for a long time. It was necessary for the physician to examine you. But don't worry, he's a eunuch and felt no feelings of excitement when he was looking into your womanness.'

Rizpah was shocked that this young woman spoke so openly of matters which were never discussed. And she'd never before heard of a eunuch.

Yet there was something about this young woman's openness and confidence which suffused her with trust. Trust? What an odd thought to invade her mind. She was a prisoner in the rooms of her greatest enemy, a woman dedicated to bringing down the kingdom of Yahweh, yet this young woman was treating her as a daughter treats a mother. It was hard for Rizpah to remember that this was the woman in league with the most evil of devils; the woman whom her husband said would bring destruction to their lands.

'Why does your husband hate me?' Jezebel asked simply.

'He says that you are the Devil. You are a harlot and an idolator. That you are consummate evil! You're the instrument by which Israel will be brought undone,' she answered ingenuously, not comprehending the need for diplomacy in such a situation.

Jezebel's eyes flared into fury. Rizpah saw the look of anger in the young woman's expression and shied away, suddenly understanding the impact which her husband's words were having on this young girl. But just as quickly as her anger had erupted at the insults, reason took over and her face seemed to calm down; then she nodded. Jezebel sat down on the divan beside Rizpah.

'I could have your tongue pulled out of your mouth for saying these things to me. Why do you and your husband risk death by insulting the family of your King?'

Rizpah played with her hands; Elijah would know the answers, but whenever she'd travelled with him around Israel and Judah, she had never properly listened to his words, relying on him to think and protect her. Yet! Yet when she had first awoken in this palace, Yahweh had put words into her mouth. Why didn't He speak through her now?

Rizpah sighed and said softly, 'I don't know. I don't understand.'

And Jezebel looked properly for the first time at the woman beside her. This wasn't a servant of

Yahweh, nor some treasonous schemer intent on doing the Lord's work; this was a frail and middle-aged woman who reminded Jezebel of ... of ... her mother. Suddenly the Phoenician Princess, now Queen of Israel, understood exactly with whom she was dealing.

'Rizpah, do you hate me?' she asked.

'Yes.'

'Because I want your husband killed?'

'No, because you are trying to destroy Israel. Because you oppose Yahweh. And Yahweh is God.'

'Why can't there be other gods?'

'Because Yahweh is the one true God. He told us that.'

'Isn't this country big enough to have more than one god? If Yahweh is truly such a wonderful God, then why is He so jealous of other gods?'

'There are no other gods. Only Yahweh!'

Jezebel laughed. 'How can that be? Can Yahweh truly control the seas at the same time as He's controlling the skies? Can He ensure the fertility of the crops of the earth at the same time as He's fertilising women when they couple with their husbands? How can a god, any god, be that powerful?'

Rizpah shook her head. 'I don't know. It's what Elijah told me. It's what I believe.'

Jezebel smiled at the woman. These were matters about which the priests and priestesses and counsellors talked day and night. How could this Rizpah, a simple woman from a simple village, possibly understand what she was talking about? But there was a look of trepidation in her eyes.

'Do you fear I'll be the instrument of Israel's destruction?' asked Jezebel.

Immediately she answered, 'Yes.' But then the older woman looked at the young and beautiful face, and slowly shook her head and whispered, 'I don't know.'

'I don't understand how your husband, Elijah, could ...' she began, but before she could continue, she was interrupted by the arrival of a tray of food and drink which Rizpah accepted gratefully. She was both ravenously hungry and painfully thirsty. She and Jezebel feasted from the tray.

Rizpah knew she shouldn't eat the meats, but she was ravenously hungry and also feared further offending Jezebel. She had never before tasted foods such as these. According to Jezebel, the meats came from deer and from birds of which she'd never heard. And in the centre of the tray was the complete leg of a sheep. Around the meats were breads of various sorts with fruits baked inside, as well as small plates containing powders and pastes of extraordinary colours in which she saw Jezebel dipping her food. Rizpah did likewise, and the brightly coloured additions to her food enhanced the flavours to such an extent that Rizpah began to cough in shock.

Jezebel looked at her in concern, and the older woman held up her hand to reassure the Queen that she was all right. She sipped from a golden cup which contained the wine in which honey had been dissolved to make the roughness disappear.

They continued to eat and drink in silence, like a mother and a daughter, until Jezebel asked, 'I don't understand why your husband hates me so much when we have never met. What is it about me which he calls "devil"? He says that I am a whore. I enjoy men's bodies, but so do the other women of my country. Does that make me a whore? Does he think that all Phoenicia is populated by whores?'

Before she would allow Rizpah to answer, she continued, 'And why is Yahweh such a special god? Why do the people of Israel think that He's so much more powerful than Ba'al or El or the other gods who we worship?'

Rizpah continued to chew reflectively on some bread in which figs and dates had been baked. It was the most delicious thing she'd ever tasted. Rizpah searched for an answer and thought how stupid she must be that she didn't know. She picked up some more roasted meat from the breast of a bird, and dipped it into a red paste which tasted like a mixture of spicy nuts and berries. She ate it, and noticed that even after she'd sucked them clean, her fingers were still tipped with the colour of the paste, in the way that rich women painted their nails with dyes.

Jezebel explained, 'I worship Asherah. But so do all of the women from Phoenicia ... and Assyria and Babylonia and many other countries. So do many of the women and men of Israel and Judah, even before I came here; even before I began to build my asherahs. Why is that bad? I worship my gods. You worship your God. Why is being an idolator so wicked? I just don't understand.'

Rizpah formulated something to say, but again Jezebel interrupted her own thoughts, 'My husband Ahab rants and raves in fury against your Elijah. He wants to kill him. I want to kill him too for the insults he heaps upon me. Nobody has ever spoken to a princess of the royal blood in this way and lived. Once a man in the royal family of Phoenicia told my father the King that I gave my body too easily to men and that I did it outside of the worship of Ashcrali. My father immediately had him killed. But before I kill your husband, I want to know why he hates me.'

Now Rizpah felt she could answer, but Jezebel simply continued to talk, as though she was alone in the room, 'I know that there are people in the court of Israel who don't like me, for the same reason that your husband hates me. If I can understand why Elijah hates me, then I can understand why Omri's other wives, and Ahab's brothers and sisters also dislike me. Now I am Queen, of course, I could easily have them killed, which is the way of the Egyptians, but Ahab says that this isn't the way of Israel; that I will be hated by the people,' Jezebel told her.

It sounded so reasonable. Rizpah sighed. It was like talking to one of the young girls in her village of Tishbe; a girl who might want to know why she can't talk with a young man she likes because her father has forbidden her to meet with him. Yet this girl was generous in sharing her plate, and at the same time talking about murdering her husband and the entire royal family of Israel. Was she a monster, or just innocent of the ways of the world? Rizpah looked closely at Jezebel and despite every emotion which was coursing through her mind, she couldn't help admiring her lovely face. Her innocent face.

'He hates you because he fears what you will do to our God,' Rizpah said softly.

'But if your God is as powerful as you say, then why is he so afraid of what one young woman can do? Or is your God so weak that a young woman can destroy Him? In Phoenicia, we believe that our chief god, El, became the most powerful of all the gods because he beat the other men gods such as Ba'al and Mot and Yam into submission. He did this when the earth was being created and the gods were vying for supremacy. It was the battle which caused so much dust to rise from the unformed earth that the dust became the stars in the heaven.

'El won the battle, yet our priests continue to worship these other gods, accepting that El is the most mighty of them all. Heaven is a large place. Why can't your Yahweh live together with our gods?'

Rizpah couldn't answer her question. Again she dipped her meat into one of the pastes, a yellow one this time, and nibbled it to see what new and unusual flavour she would experience. This one tasted of the perfumes she had smelled on the women of the court; or maybe, she thought on tasting it a second time, it had the flavour of the inside of a newly opened flower in the early morning. Rizpah had no idea what it was, but knew that it must be very expensive. She put down the meat and looked at Jezebel who was waiting for an answer.

'Why don't you talk to my husband, Elijah?' Rizpah asked Jezebel. The Queen looked at her in astonishment; was this woman from Tishbe so simple that she couldn't understand that she wanted Elijah dead?

But misunderstanding the Queen's expression, Rizpah continued, 'Elijah can answer all of your questions. I'm confused about these things. I do as my husband tells me. What you say sounds easy to understand, but I know you're wrong, because there is only one God. Yahweh. And because there's only one God, there can't be other gods like Ba'al and these others you talk about. Please, Majesty, talk with my husband, and he'll explain these things to you.'

Jezebel looked at Rizpah as though she were mad. 'You expect me to talk to Elijah! I will have him killed. And what nonsense will he tell me, if ever I do somehow get to talk to him? He'll tell me that Yahweh is the only God. How can this be? Of course there are other gods,' Jezebel said with a laugh. 'Who do you think causes droughts and makes the earth infertile and makes us die at our appointed time? Mot!

'And who do you think is the Lord of the Earth and the Eternal of all generations and the Lord of Heaven and the Rider of Clouds? Ba'al!

'And who lives in the farthermost reaches of the north and whose word must be obeyed, even by the other gods? If not El, then whom! How can you say that Yahweh is the only god, when there are so many things for the gods to look after?

'How can your husband and your people believe that one god, Yahweh, can possibly do all this Himself? And if He is alone, then what happened to all the other gods?'

Rizpah was becoming impatient for the questions to be at an end. She only ever listened to her husband, and did not have to formulate answers. She never had to answer questions, or to think for herself. Her husband spoke the words of God; understood what God commanded. Yet she was expected to answer these questions. When matters like these arose, she would turn to her husband and let him answer. Now, she wished she'd listened to the answers he had given, because then she would know what to say. In desperation, she said simply, 'Jezebel, why do you want to kill my husband? If you kill him, then you won't be able to ask him these questions.'

'He has killed our King and he has insulted me. He will die. But for now, he has disappeared. He is nowhere in the city. My guards have searched everywhere, but he is gone. I wanted him to be brought before me; to kneel at my feet. I wanted to feel the pleasure of seeing him humbled and prostrate and begging for mercy; and I especially wanted to see the look on his face when I refused to save his life and he was about to be killed. I was so angry about what he called me that I was going to kill him myself. I was going to slit his throat, or stab him through the heart, or take up a sword and cut off his head. But by his disappearance, he has even robbed me of that joy. That's why you, Rizpah, must tell me where he is … so that I can have the joy of killing him with my own hands …'

It took several moments for the words to make sense. But this time, Rizpah didn't faint. Instead, she dropped the tray of food and drink all over the marble floor.

He lay shivering in the dry riverbed. The night was hot, yet nothing could prevent him from shaking with the fever which was no fever. His body was not hot … indeed it was cold, but so violent was his shaking that he was forced to walk around, despite the dark, and use up the nervous affliction from which his body was suffering.

His escape had been a miracle; and ten times he had shouted his thanks to the Almighty One Blessed be He for delivering him from his enemies. Were it not for the faithful ones in the temple of the Lord, he would never have left Samaria alive.

When he saw Omri's face turn purple, as purple as the liquid in the vat which dyed the clothes of harlots and whores and those who falsely elevated their status in the eyes of the Lord, Elijah knew that it was the hand of Yahweh which was strangling the life force from the evil man's body. At that very moment, Elijah knew precisely where the Lord Yahweh was, for he could clearly see the divine light which surrounded the evil King of Israel as God Almighty took his soul and confined it to the very depths of the lowest regions of a nether world where death is ever present and where the blessed light of the sun never shines.

As the King pitched forward and fell across the table, Elijah felt more empowered than ever before in his life; Yahweh was working through him in more than words. He was Yahweh's instrument, and he could strike down Yahweh's enemies and dash them to death on the rocks of his anger. He had already killed a King. How long before Yahweh made him so powerful that, like Abraham, he could break the strength of the idols, and like Moses, his wooden staff would turn into a snake?

Looking at Omri, Elijah knew that the greatest of his enemies was defeated. He had fallen to his knees and shouted out his thanks to the Lord Almighty for delivering Israel from the hands of the idolatrous tyrant. But suddenly unseen hands were upon his shoulders; hands which pulled him backwards; urgent voices which whispered into his ear for him to leave the banqueting hall, to leave the palace.

And he had stood and gone with them, half walking half running, impelled by their urgency, through the corridors and archways and colonnades

314

of the evil place; a place of death, and one in which, through the death of its master, the House of Omri was no longer as powerful. Now that all Israel had seen the power of Yahweh, the treaty would be rescinded and the Phoenician harlot would return from whence she came with her bare-breasted servants and her idols and her fornicating priests and priestesses. Then Ahab would rule Israel, he was a weak and stupid boy, and Elijah could return and his command would be obeyed.

Elijah had been hurried out into the streets of Samaria and had begun to shout his thanks to Yahweh for what would happen now, but a hand had closed his mouth and pleas to remain silent were whispered into his ears. The hands which pulled his cloak and guided his body were forceful hands. But reassuring hands. They guided him out of the palace and across the marketplace where people still laughed and applauded and adulated the godforsaken gifts from other idolatrous kings and princes; people who did yet not know of the death of their King.

The unseen hands led him into the gates of the temple. As he was running through the courtyard, he saw the monstrosity which defiled the House of the Lord. The staff of wood in the asherah; the statue of a woman on horseback with a snake slithering up her leg; the monument to corruption and the evil instrument of desecration. He resisted the pulling of the men forcing him to flee the palace, and stopped in order to put a curse on the hideous place. He stood there, shaking his fist and gesticulating in his hatred, ridiculing it, taunting the goddess who was no goddess to come out and face him; but the priests who were trying to hurry him from the city shouted into his ear that there was no time, and that he must hurry if he was to live.

It was then that Elijah realised the danger that he was in. But it didn't make sense. The death of Omri was a triumph. The House of Evil was no more. Ahab was so weak in the eyes of Israel now he had married the Phoenician whore that Yahweh would cause the people to revolt and overthrow the royal house. A true King of Israel would then arise, a man of God, who would join together with King Asa, now in his thirty-eighth year of ruling Judah, and the land which Moses was given by God would again be united, and then the entire world would bow before the greater land of the people of Yahweh.

Yet these priests of God were saying that he, Elijah, was in mortal danger, and that unless he escaped immediately from Samaria, he would be killed by the forces of evil. It was madness. It was absurd. He was a servant of God, and God had stretched out His mighty arm and defeated the enemies of the righteous ones. God had spoken through Elijah about the future of Israel. How could God's prophet be in danger?

But here he was, cold and shaking in the dry bed of a stream, alone and abandoned. They had disguised him by dressing him in the robes of a merchant; he had climbed out of a window to escape the view of the guards; and he had fled down the road which led to the Jaffa Gate. Then, with three men who were attendants of the priests of the temple, he had been led along the road, and then southeast towards the River Jordan, where those who hated the King of Israel and his idols lived. But night had overtaken him, and he had been forced to hide in the bed of a dry tributary of the mighty river until it would be safe for him to travel in the morning.

Soon it would be daylight. Soon, the blessed light of the Lord would shine upon him. Then he could leave the riverbed and search out those who followed the path and prayed to the Lord. He could find food and water and sustain himself for the fight ahead.

But still his mind reeled. Why should he be afraid of Israel when the Lord had destroyed His enemy? Unless the Lord hadn't destroyed His enemy! Unless there was another enemy! But who? Surely not Jezebel, for now that Omri was dead the whore of Phoenicia would return to her people in fear of an uprising or would be driven out. Not Ahab. He was a fool, a man driven by lusts and carnal thoughts. He was not the stuff of kings. A new King, not of the House of Omri, would be anointed. So if not Ahab, then who was his enemy?

Elijah walked around in the dust of the riverbed. Jezebel was the true enemy. Jezebel! She wasn't merely a part of the evil, with her painted face and her idols and her naked and lascivious priestesses. She was evil itself! She was the enemy. She was a whore and idolator and he had ordered her back to Phoenicia, but she was still here. He was terrified that she would cause a break away completely from Judah and Yahweh in the south, and create an indissoluble alliance with the idols of Phoenicia in the north. With the gods of the Phoenicians! And that would mean that she would drive the God of the Hebrews out of the land of Israel forever.

Now that he was alone under God's stars, his mind suddenly became clear. Neither Omri nor Ahab had been the true enemies. And nor would Ahab be the enemy of God in the future if the worst happened and he truly became King; for then there would be no future for Israel. No, it was Jezebel who was the enemy. Jezebel who would keep the kingdoms of Judah and Israel divided. It was Jezebel alone against whom Elijah must now focus the blinding light of God in order to destroy her evilness.

For the first time in her life, Jezebel sat on the throne as a Queen. Since she was a girl, she had fantasised about how it would be to have men and women bowing at her feet; to see ambassadors with their fine clothes and their colourful entourages genuflect and pay her the same obeisance as they paid her father Ethbaal; to watch the common people of her cities come to her with gifts and tributes in the hope that she might judge on their behalf in their disputes. Even her youthful desire to be a priestess was to have men bow before her!

And now it was really happening. Now it had come to pass. Here she sat for only the third time in as many days, Queen in her own right, even though the land over which she governed was dry and brown and the city in which she reigned was drab and ordinary and devoid of colour and patterns. Yet it was, according to Hattusas, a land strategically placed at the end of the Eternal Sea, the gateway to trading routes from north to south and from east to west. So all the while, great kings would pay tribute to her in order to win her favour. It was a prospect which pleased her greatly.

She glanced over at her husband, Ahab, still white with fury and morose with grief; still fulminating about Elijah and ordering searches throughout every house and every village and every city in Israel. As the days following Elijah's disappearance increased in number, Ahab became angrier and angrier.

The funeral of Omri had taken place yesterday. All Israel had been there. Crowds the likes of which Jezebel had never before seen. Vast fields of people who began arriving at the foot of the hill on which Samaria had been built. And then the wailing and the rending of clothes and the women ululating and sounding like a million demons were filling the sky. It began in the early morning as Israelite women, wearing the white clothes of death and with the stains of ashes on their foreheads, stood in an unbroken ring around the base of the hill on which Samaria stood.

Jezebel looked out from the window of her palace and tried to count them, but their numbers deceived her. They looked like a line of lilies standing in rows. She heard them first, their chanting waking her. She'd woken Ahab and told him to come and look. Even he was surprised by the magnitude of the declaration of respect of the people.

But now that she was Queen, now that people called her 'Majesty' and 'Highness' and 'Great One', there was no longer the sense of anticipation. She was Queen in name, but did not feel herself to be Queen in anything else. For all Israel was mourning the death of Omri and all Israel turned its head away from her, and looked downwards into the grave which he occupied, and wondered about their future.

She'd heard them talking. They didn't know that she was close by, but she'd heard their conversations in the corridors of the palace, and in the alleys of the city.

'Is Ahab capable of ruling the kingdom?'

'How soon before Phoenicia attacks?'

'How will we manage now that Omri is no longer with us?'

And what they said about her!

'Jezebel was responsible for his death.'

'There would have been no screaming from Elijah had Jezebel not arrived in Israel with her naked priestesses.'

'She schemes now to take over the kingdom because Ahab is weak.'

Cruel words. And she felt their cruelty with every breath. They were her cousins and mothers and sisters and brothers; they were the family into which she'd married. They were the ordinary people of the city she ruled. Nobody spoke like this about her when she lived in Phoenicia. This was such a foreign and hateful land.

Now, when Israel looked to Ahab for leadership, and when Ahab looked to Jezebel for comfort, now was the moment. She stood from her throne, and said in a loud and certain voice, 'The Ambassador of Moab is here to discuss with the King of Israel a treaty to import wood from our forests in return for copper from her mines. We will admit the ambassador, and hear his words.'

The court looked at Jezebel in astonishment. Never before had a Queen of Israel addressed a gathering. The audience room descended into silence. Nobody moved, frozen as though statues.

'Bring the ambassador before your King and Queen,' she ordered, her voice steady yet commanding.

And suddenly her counsellor, Hattusas, ordered a guard to do the Queen's bidding. Jezebel sat, and awaited the arrival of the ambassador. It had been done! She was Queen of Israel.

***

When he had left, when the treaty had been discussed, Jezebel sat back in her throne, tired from the negotiations. Ahab had hardly said a word. It was she and Hattusas who had negotiated the best of the deal. Ahab looked around at her. Her seat was below and behind his as was the rightful place of a first Queen. She was worried by his look. Was he angry that she had taken the lead on the negotiations? Didn't he understand that she had to take leadership until he recovered from his grief? He looked so drawn and strained. To her, Ahab was a hurt and confused child. She reached forward and grasped his arm to comfort him.

Every night since their wedding he had cried into her breasts, wailing for his dead father; every night, she had consoled him in the only way in which she knew ... she had kissed him and nurtured him and massaged his manhood until his growth told her that he was ready; and without any words spoken, purely for the relief which her body could give him, she encouraged him to enter her.

She grasped his buttocks and pulled him into her, higher and higher, holding him there, capturing him, surrounding him, and refusing to allow him to move within her. And when she felt his potency was at its maximum, she released him and with her arms and mouth and legs encouraged him to climax quickly and manfully. He did, and as he climaxed, he cried and wailed like a baby, his grief first exploding from him, then slowly deflating to whimpers as his sorrow seeped from his body until the last drops of fluid left him and entered her so that she became the parchment upon which his loss was inscribed.

Yet with the relief of the night came the anguish of the morning. And with the grief, the anger. The target of his anger was Elijah. Over their morning meal of fruits and yogurt and cheeses, Jezebel listened as Ahab recited the litany of crimes the prophet had committed; and by inference the weakness of his father who had not stood up to him. Things would be different, now he was King, Ahab rejoiced in telling her. No priest or prophet would insult the House of Omri ever again, he insisted. Jezebel nodded and agreed, empathising with all the things he said.

When he had dressed and gone to the throne room to deal with the matters of running the kingdom, Jezebel also dressed quickly, and went to seek out Rizpah whose continued luxurious tenancy in the palace was enforced by guards on the doors of the apartments of one of the absent princes of the court. This morning's interview had been no different from their discussion of the previous day.

'My husband the King says that your husband the prophet bewitched Omri through witchcraft. That is the only way in which he can explain how so mighty a King as Omri did not have Elijah put to death immediately he began his troublemaking.'

Rizpah considered this idea, but then thoughtfully shook her head. 'Witchcraft is what my husband has been fighting all his life. We who believe in Yahweh do not believe in other gods and goddesses. So how can there be such a thing as witchcraft, for evil magic is the stuff of the false gods, and we say that there are no other gods? Witchcraft is the practice of Egypt and the Hebrew people left Egypt five hundred years ago. Some say we brought witchcraft out of Egypt with us, and that it has stayed with us since the time of the building of the Golden Cow idol in the desert; but I know nothing of this.'

Jezebel nodded, and then said, 'My husband, Ahab, says that your husband deserves to be put to death for raising his voice in anger against King Omri. Why shouldn't he be put to death for the same offence as others are put to death? Why is his being a prophet something which protects him?'

'Because,' Rizpah replied, 'he does not create the words he speaks. These things he says are created by the Lord God, and put into my husband's mouth. So killing my husband will be killing a messenger of Yahweh which cannot be done. God's vessels cannot be killed or broken.'

'Maybe Yahweh can't be killed, but Elijah certainly can. I intend to kill him myself when I see him.'

'But then you will die. Anyone who strikes against Yahweh will be killed him ... or herself. And even if you were to kill my husband, God would open the mouth of another. Kill Elijah, and your troubles will not be at an end. God will send more. You cannot escape the punishment of the Lord God.'

Jezebel was tired of the answers she was given. She had originally intended to use Rizpah as a way of getting to Elijah; whether Rizpah and her children lived or died was of no consequence. But since then Rizpah had been useful in helping Jezebel understand the Israelite people. She had been of more use than the Israelites at court, for Rizpah's answers were without guile and politics. She had learned the truth of the relationship which Yahweh seemed to have with the temple, and through the priests, with the people. And through Rizpah, she had learned many of the customs of the Israelites, their history, their way of doing things.

But now the answers were becoming the same; now Jezebel was learning little that was new.

Rizpah had served her purpose, and she was beginning to sound more and more like her husband Elijah. At first, she'd hardly known what to say, but as her confidence grew, the words flowed like aged wine turned acid. It was time for Rizpah to understand the power of the Queen

'And you, Rizpah, cannot escape the punishment of the House of Ahab.'

Rizpah looked at her in wonder. What did Jezebel mean?

'I intend to announce that you will be put to death in a week from today for treason. You will be taken to the city walls, and thrown off into the ravine, as is the custom of your people. The only thing which will save you is if Elijah takes your place.'

She turned and walked out of the room, pleased that the older woman's mouth had been closed at last.

CHAPTER THIRTEEN

The voice of Elijah had not been heard in Israel for two years. Despite the efforts of her soldiers and spies, Jezebel had not been able to trace him. And so for her, the prophet of Yahweh became a memory, a matter which could be dealt with if ever it arose again. For she and her husband Ahab were too busy in their administration of Israel to worry about the absent prophet of Yahweh. And as the potency of Elijah's voice diminished in the nation, the priests of the temple saw their influence declining, and no matter what they did, they could not draw the people away from their increasing love of the gods of Phoenicia.

Jezebel had been Queen for two years before she began to transform the look of her country of Israel. During the first year of her reign Jezebel assisted her husband in establishing his kingship, in the rules and regulations of command. Hattusas, her loyal and subtle counsellor, was the voice which whispered in her ear just before she entered the throne room to advise her husband on how to deal with a matter of foreign intrigue.

Never was his voice more welcome than when Ahab was forced to deal with complaints from the temple. Only the other day the chief priest of Samaria, Hazarmaveth, had visited him, saying, 'Ahab, Yahweh will continue to curse this land until Elijah is allowed to return and preach the word of God ...'

But before he could finish his sentence, Jezebel asked quietly, 'Does your god, Yahweh, think that Israel should take a snake to its bosom?'

The chief priest looked at her. He knew that she was the brain behind the throne, that she was the true enemy of Yahweh. 'Arrogant Queen. The false gods which you have brought here from Phoenicia are the snakes.'

'And are these snakes evil?'

'Yes, they are evil and must be destroyed!' he thundered.

She nodded, and asked quietly, 'Did your god, Yahweh, create all life on earth?'

'Yahweh is everything. He created the firmament and the earth; the sea and the land; and all the creatures thereon.'

'Then if Yahweh controls everything, why did He create these snakes? What kind of a god creates evil?'

The chief priest had fallen into Hattusas' trap. He looked around and saw the priests and priestesses of Ba'al and Asherah and El laughing. In fury, he turned and left the palace with his entourage.

Ahab turned to Jezebel, and said, 'Be careful, love, how you treat these men. They are powerful in the land.'

But she replied, 'For now, my love ... they are powerful for now. But soon you and I will have our day, and then all Israel will rejoice.'

The priests of the temple weren't the only people who hated the power of the aliens from Phoenicia. King Ahab's Israelite advisors were increasingly isolated from the power they had once enjoyed under King Omri and were only called upon from time to time in a formal meeting to discuss a point of protocol or the drafting of the words of a letter.

Jezebel's name became more of a curse than an accolade amongst the royal family of Israel. And she knew the hatred and envy she engendered in Ahab's relations, as well as in the ruling merchants and other elites who, in the time of Omri, had free run of the palace. Nowadays, the people most often in the corridors, or huddled in corners whispering about this and that, wore the bright robes of Phoenicians, or the pure white of priests and priestesses of Ba'al and Asherah.

Not that the people of Samaria or the other cities of Israel saw much of the intrigue which was occurring in the palace. For them, the drought continued, supplies were reduced even more, life became harsher. Had it happened during the reign of Omri he would have worried about civil insurrection. But now that Ahab and Jezebel were ruling in his place, and the people were happy with Asherah and Ba'al, there was far less dissent.

During the year, Jezebel spent much of her time travelling to the towns and villages of Israel, talking to the people, giving out supplies of grains and oils and wines from the royal stores, and earning the admiration and thanks of the people. Her husband's seneschals warned her that if the drought lasted another year the palace would have nothing to eat, but she assured them that her father, the King of Phoenicia, would come to the aid of his brother kingdom.

She erected asherahs in copses and woods and outside the walls of the towns and villages of Israel.

She had been barred by her husband from undertaking any programme of building during the year of mourning for her dead father-in-law Omri. And nor did she want to, because until she was known and loved by all the people, she didn't want to begin anything which might cause them to rise against her.

The plan which she and Hattusas had formulated was that she would show herself as a modest young woman, and endear herself to her new people. When that was accomplished, then she could begin the process of transforming the land. She would beautify the buildings of the towns and villages of the rest of Israel, paint them in glorious colours and introduce textures to their outsides. And the buildings in these towns which belonged to the royal family would be completely decorated inside with the ceilings becoming the night sky, and the walls adorned with patterns and pictures and shapes and colours. Soon, she knew, the rich merchants of these provincial cities would follow her lead, and then all Israel, except the capital of Samaria where she was not allowed to work, would begin to look colourful and attractive.

Once Israel was colourful it would be easy for her to offer reductions in the taxes people paid to those who worshipped Ba'al and Asherah and El and Mot, and to increase the levies of those who wanted admission to the worship of Yahweh. In this way, Hattusas believed, she would marginalise the priests of Yahweh, and put them in their place. She would appoint her own priests of Yahweh and they would pray side by side in the lesser temples outside of Samaria with those priests who remained loyal to Elijah, although her threats had ensured that their

328

private anger and thoughts remained precisely that ... private.

At first, the people of the countryside happily prayed before another deity. A new trade started between Phoenicia and Israel in which many idols to Asherah were imported and purchased by citizens for the niches in walls of their homes which had formerly held candles and lamps. New prayers were created by the priests and priestesses of Asherah and were given to the people in the marketplaces. Those who couldn't read had them recited to them and learned them off by heart.

But it was the visits to all parts of Israel by the Queen Jezebel after the first year of her marriage, after the end of the mourning period for the dead King, which caused the most excitement. She was always accompanied by a veritable army of priests and priestesses, and they walked in solemn procession from city to city, town to town, with Jezebel riding a white Moabite stallion at the head of the procession. When she arrived in a new city a banquet organised in her honour was always accompanied by the sycophants; and the highlight of the night was the dancing and acrobatics of the performers who accompanied the Queen. After the dreary and solemn year of mourning for Omri, the people suddenly found that music and colour and dancing were everywhere, all led by their glorious young Queen Jezebel.

In the second year of her reign, she now knew with confidence that it was only the silenced priests of Yahweh and the royal House of Omri who hated her. Her gesture of saving the life of Elijah's wife, Rizpah, at the last moment before her execution, hadn't elicited any concessions from them; they should have shown their gratitude, even blamed Elijah for not changing places with his wife and dying in her stead ... but in the end, as Rizpah was ascending the platform to be pushed off to her certain death, Jezebel had shouted out for her to be saved. The people of Samaria had screamed out their relief and thrown flowers in Jezebel's path in gratitude for sparing Rizpah's life, but the priests had remained stiff-backed and seemingly unconcerned whether Rizpah was saved or sent to her Yahweh.

And perhaps, because of the attitude of the priests, people were turning their backs on Yahweh; or was it because the worship of Asherah was so much more pleasing? Asherah encouraged men and women to enjoy relationships with partners to whom they weren't married.

The priests of Yahweh noticed how many immoral and lascivious orgies were taking place in the woods. When some of the braver priests of Yahweh tried to intervene, to march in and stop the lust-filled prayers, men of the village physically prevented them; some were so infuriated that they stoned them or threatened them with weapons. Increasingly, priests of Yahweh were being killed.

The priests retreated back into their temples, at a loss to know what to do. They knew they had to stop what was happening, but they were powerless to fight against the King and Queen, and most of the people of Israel. And, without Elijah as their leader, they lacked the resolve. Their authority came from Yahweh; but if Yahweh wasn't obeyed by the people of Israel, then the authority of His priests was like snow falling on a warm day. And they well knew what happened these days to priests who openly complained about the worshipping of false idols. They knew full well of the many who had been beaten, even killed, on the express authority of the Queen.

Ahab heard the complaints of the priests, but his ears were closed. He knew of the danger of revolt during a time of drought; and he knew that Jezebel's seduction of the people was keeping them entranced and under control. He also knew that their new-found love of Asherah and Ba'al kept them quiescent, these being far less demanding gods than Yahweh. And in his heart of hearts, he was listening to Jezebel whom he loved beyond all others. He also knew that the words she said to him had been informed by Hattusas, a wise and sophisticated counsellor, one who put Jezebel's interests and those of Phoenicia first; and because of their union, that meant Israel's interests were well-served.

Jezebel knew that the time was right to convince her husband that Samaria was a drab and backward place compared to Babylon or Sidon or Tyre. It had taken a full two years of queenship and marriage for the young Phoenician to win her husband over totally to the belief that Samaria listened too closely to the dictates of the Jewish priests. But while her repression of the priests in the country was determined, her husband forbade her to actively repress the priests of the Temple of Samaria. To do so would invite a potential war with Judah of the south. Although he no longer listened to them, he was aware of their power to foment a war with the King of the Jewish people in the south.

While the people of the countryside, simple and ignorant peasants, were happy in their combined worship of Yahweh and Asherah and Ba'al, Ahab was confident that he could control the situation. He was concerned that if the people of Samaria and the other major Israelite cities turned in large numbers from the worship of Yahweh, he might face more than just the anger of the priests. But, as reports were coming to him of the happiness of the people with his reign and their delight in the worship of Asherah, he was inclined to listen more closely to Jezebel about the composition of the temple of Yahweh in the middle of the city of Samaria.

'It's just a boring looking building. There're no decorations on the outside or the inside to please the people,' she told him.

'But our priests don't permit such things,' he said. 'They allow some colour, but we are prevented by God from making any representation of people or animals. We are warned by Yahweh that such representation is idolatry and we are not allowed idols.'

She shook her head, and fed him a slice of melon, chilled by the cold waters she had ordered to be collected every day by despatch riders from Mount Hermon. 'But Ahab, I have been putting idols of Asherah throughout the land, and the people seem to love her. Why can't we do something colourful and with patterns in Samaria, especially in the temple? Surely Yahweh doesn't want to be worshipped in such dull surroundings? Why can't we paint the palace with designs?'

'Because Samaria is the capital of Israel! Because it was built by my father to be a place where Yahweh could be worshipped, so that the faithful who still look towards Jerusalem and Judah could feel happy; so that King Asa of Judah would be less inclined to attack Israel if he knew that the Jewish people were worshipping Yahweh in a temple similar to that built by King Solomon. Yahweh doesn't let us worship false idols, nor paint graven images on our walls.'

He looked at his lovely young wife, and his heart went to her. She was so keen to allow the people to worship Asherah. And he was forced to admit that the people had never been more happy. Yet her face was sad because even though Ahab had turned away his eyes from what she was doing in the smaller cities and towns of Israel, here in the capital he would allow her no such leeway.

'Perhaps a few patterns on the outside of the buildings, such as the red and green and yellow lines and circles my ambassador described to me when he visited your father's palace in Sidon many years ago. But no faces or idols. Is that understood?'

She smiled with delight, and pushed another slice of melon into his mouth with her own lips until they were kissing.

CHAPTER FOURTEEN

17 And it came to pass after these things, that the son of the woman, the mistress of the house, fell sick; and his sickness was so sore, that there was no breath left in him.

18 And she said unto Elijah, What have I to do with thee, O thou man of God? Art thou come unto me to call my sin to remembrance, and to slay my son?

19 And he said unto her, Give me thy son. And he took him out of her bosom, and carried him up into a loft, where he abode, and laid him upon his own bed.

20 And he cried unto the LORD, and said, O LORD my God, hast thou also brought evil upon the widow with whom I sojourn, by slaying her son?

21 And he stretched himself upon the child three times, and cried unto the LORD, and said, O LORD my God, I pray thee, let this child's soul come into him again.

1 Kings 17–21

For the first time in his life, he was convinced that he was going to die. The sun was hotter than any sun he had ever known, its heat burned his skin from the early morning until it had descended at the end of its arc into the Eternal Sea. It was a merciless sun, not a friend as it was in the orchards and fields of Gilead, but an implacable enemy, sent to destroy all that appeared in its light. It did not shine; rather it beat down on a desiccated land, bleached of all colour and life. No longer was it the sun of God which smiled benignly on crops and fruit trees and gave joy to all living things ... this was a sun of death, an avenging sun whose purpose was to make anything within its view withered and caused to die.

And, similarly, for the first time in his life, the prophet Elijah began to doubt the mission on which he had been sent by the Almighty One, Blessed be He. Elijah knew that God was a vengeful God; that He was uncomprehending of human weakness and unforgiving of human frailty. Which is why Elijah forced thoughts of comfort and capitulation from his mind. Even when his mind wandered in the heat of the day, when he thought of the sanctuary of his own home, of the cold water in the nearby brook and the freezing winds which blew at night from the distant mountains in the winter months, Elijah managed to banish the images which skitted in front of his eyes and expunged them.

But over the past few weeks, despite his prayers, the thoughts hadn't gone away, even by the technique he used to banish such immoral and wicked thoughts by biting his lips or banging his head hard with a small stone. No, even with great pain, these wicked thoughts of home and family, thoughts which he knew the demons were putting there to make him turn back, kept coming to him and insisting themselves on his mind.

His life was so hard. For warmth at night, he wrapped himself in a thin blanket which a worshipper of Yahweh who lived in Tananir had given him when he'd sought shelter after escaping from Samaria. He huddled into himself, and tried to forget the cold. But it was a withering cold. A blistering cold. The sort of cold which robbed a man of strength and purpose, so that in the morning, when the sun began to burn fiercely, there was nothing left within him to save. Nothing!

The sudden cold of the desert night began as a blissful counterbalance to the heat of the day. But after the first moments of blessed relief which happened as the sky darkened and cooled his body of the heat of the murderous sun, the moment when the stars began to shine, the relief he felt was short-lasting. It quickly turned to a biting misery as freezing cold seeped into his bones and he wrapped the blanket around himself in the hope of retaining the warmth.

But hope faded and all that was left until the blessed rays of the sun, when it rose again above the distant Mountains of Moab, was a freezing cold which ripped at his skin and tore into his very being. And just as quickly as the cold ate into his body, so the sun rose and drove away the thousand knives and warmed his very being to its core. But the warmth quickly swamped him and drained him of energy, threatening to boil him like his wife boiled lamb in broth.

It had been this way the day before and the day before that, even from the time when he had escaped the hideous Jezebel and her foul and pestilential idols. At first, he had lived in the Kirith ravine east of the Jordan where the ground was gentle and the currents of air were warm and life wasn't unpleasant. But then her troops had begun to scour the valley. And so he had fled from Israel into Judah and the deserts of the lowlands beyond Jericho. From there, he had turned north again.

Some knew he was here. A widow, called Sharai, fed him from time to time. She came along a path, dressed in the black of a raven, the traditional colour of the people who lived in the desert, her skirts full of food and drink. She asked him to bless her, and her son; this Elijah did gratefully and joyously. Sharai even begged Elijah to accompany her back to her home so that she could look after the needs of the holy man more easily until he chose to return to Israel and defeat the evil that infested the land and was being perpetrated against the word of God. Sharai knew that Elijah was a prophet of the Lord and that his presence in her house would bring her great honour and even good fortune.

But kind as her offer was, until now, until this moment, he'd been determined to refuse, both for reasons of security, and for penance. Though she looked like a woman of God, how did Elijah know that her neighbours could be trusted? Who was in the pay of Asa, King of Judah or Ahab, King of Israel, or Ethbaal, King of Phoenicia?

For two years now, Elijah had been in hiding. Not all the while, of course. Occasionally, when he thought that the people might have forgotten him, and especially when he knew that he was least expected, he would arise like a whirlwind out of the desert, and cause a commotion in a town by preaching of the wickedness of both countries; then he would disappear back into the desert like a mirage.

Since he had been forced out of Israel after the Lord had ended the life of Omri, Elijah had been wandering. During the two years, he had lived in many of the empty places of Israel and Judah, hiding in caves and forests and on the tops of hills and in the depths of valleys. But most recently, his place of rest had been the wilderness. And this had taken its toll on his life and his spirit, because at this moment, he was at his lowest ebb, terrified beyond measure that yet another year might go by and still he would not see his home or his family or those whom he loved. He was even questioning whether the Lord had abandoned him.

Despite his hunger for knowledge of Rizpah and his children, he knew that King Ahab's spies were looking everywhere for him at the behest of the evil Jezebel, and that for his wife and children's sake, he must remain in hiding.

During the years, he had occasionally been escorted somewhere safe and preached to gatherings in homes or on hilltops, always one step ahead of the soldiers or the spies. And when he'd finished, he'd be spirited away by those whose heart was with God, and he would be hidden until it was safe for him to leave the town or the village, and escape into the anonymity of the land.

Elijah girded himself against the middle of the day. Used to sheltering beneath the blanket to shut out the heat of the sun, he made a little tent for himself with a stick and sat cross-legged on the ground until his breathing began to calm down. And then he heard the sound of a footfall on the path below him. It was the sound of one man or woman whose step dislodged stones which cascaded further down into the valley.

'Holy one. Elijah. Are you here?' shouted the woman.

It was the voice of Sharai the widow, come with food. Elijah threw off the blanket. He was starving and thirsty. He had eaten nothing but bread and olives brought by the widow three days previously, and the olives provided the only moisture which had passed his lips since the dew of the early morning on the underside of the leaves of a cactus plant.

Elijah stood, and was about to shout out to her, but saw that she had brought no food or drink. His heart sank. Did she not realise that he would starve or perish from thirst unless she aided him? Was this the doing of the Almighty? Had Elijah sinned without knowing it? Why was he abandoned?

'You must come quickly, Master. My son Ahija is fallen into a sleep and won't wake up. He was bitten by a snake while in the fields, and no matter what I do, the bleeding won't stop. He is deathly white. Come Master.' She said the words without giving Elijah an opportunity to refuse. Nor would he if a boy was about to die.

It took them until the sun was high in the heavens and well above the Mountains of Moab before they reached her home. Even as he neared it, Elijah knew that God was present in the house. There was a silence, an air of peace in the valley where the widow lived. Here there were no men of war or malice or intrigue as there were in a city. Here was godliness.

Elijah walked into the house, and smelt the air. It was rancid with the smell of cooking oil hanging in the fabrics and the straw matting. And it was dark. Indeed, it was some moments before Elijah's eyes adjusted to the light and enabled him to see a huddled figure lying on straw in the corner, as though he was a mass of discarded rags. The prophet walked over and stripped the bedding off the boy. He could feel that it was soaked in the boy's sweat. But when Elijah felt his forehead and throat, the child was as cold as a morning stone in the dawn of the desert.

Knowing death when she saw it, Sharai walked over to her son and knelt down beside him. She felt the boy's forehead and wailed in despair. She looked at Elijah and shook her head in anguish, 'I should have stayed with him,' she cried out loud. 'I shouldn't have come to fetch you. God has punished me for leaving my son when he needed me.' And in her agony for her dead son, she began to sing the songs of mourning.

But Elijah shouted at her, 'There is a reason the Lord Yahweh sent you to me. Stop mourning, and place your trust in the Lord.'

He picked up the child and carried him outside of the hut into the sunshine, into the blessed light of the Almighty. He laid him on the ground, and said to his mother, 'Do you have any poppy flowers?'

While she was trying to think, Elijah searched the boy's leg for the bite mark of the snake. He found it, just above the child's ankle. It was a deep puncture, the fangs of the serpent had penetrated the boy's leg to the bone. But it hadn't risen up in pustules and there was a lot of fresh blood which had weeped out of the wound, and that was good.

'There are poppies in the valley,' said Sharai, still crying in the grief of her dead son, still trying to comprehend how her life would be now that her husband and all four of her children were dead, and she was left to fend alone. Who would have her and protect her? All of her husband's brothers were dead and having had children the mercy of levirate wasn't available to her.

Her mind was rambling but she looked carefully at what the prophet of God was doing. He seemed to be bending over her dead son, as though breathing life into his mouth. Suddenly infused with hope, Sharai scurried off to find poppies for him. Elijah kept on breathing into the boy's open mouth. His lips were cold but moist. If he was dead, then he hadn't been dead for long, and perhaps God would return his spirit to his grieving mother. The more Elijah breathed into his mouth, the more the boy's body seemed to respond; at one stage, Elijah could swear that, underneath his hand, he felt a warmth rising from the child's body. Perhaps it was the heat of the sun, perhaps God returning the child's soul. Who knew the mind of God?

Elijah heard the mother returning, scurrying as fast as her frantic legs could carry her. She fell to her knees on the hard earth outside her hut, and opened her bunched skirt. Inside were the heads of a dozen poppies. Elijah told her to bring him a rock. With it, he crushed the poppy heads until white sap came out. Elijah took some of the sap, and spread it over the wound caused by the snake. He rubbed it in carefully, and fresh blood seemed to exude from the wound as he knocked off the scabs which had formed. Sharai looked at Elijah in concern.

'It is necessary for the bad blood to flow. The poisons from the serpent must escape from the boy's body if he is to have any chance to live.'

And Elijah kept on blowing life-giving air into the boy's mouth, filling his body, warming him, tending to his needs.

Slowly the boy's eyes began to flicker. The movement wasn't noticed by his mother who was looking at the wound, now bleeding through the paste which the holy man had spread on the bite. Sharai whimpered, realising that it was too late. 'I know that he is dead.'

Elijah smiled and grasped her hands. 'Say with me: Almighty God ...'

The woman repeated the words after him.

'Almighty God, give life back to this innocent child, so that he might spend his days in honour of You.'

The boy groaned the moment his mother had finished her prayer.

'God has given the boy back his spirit and his soul,' Elijah said gently.

And Sharai fainted.

He was surprised when he awoke. For the first time in months he was sleeping in a bed, under a roof. He had slept well and long and in great comfort; but he was suddenly awakened, and the noises which awoke him were different from the roars of desert lions or the howling of hyenas to which his ears had become accustomed. This noise was a different and menacing noise – the noise of people.

At first, they invaded his dreams. He was in the middle of a cool, clear pool of blue water, a light shone from the heavens and uplifted him, and the clouds parted and a brilliant light shone through, brighter than the light which lifted him. And he saw the Eternal One, Blessed be He, Yahweh, sitting on a golden throne. And the crowds of Hebrews who surrounded the Lord were his father and his mother and others whom he had known in his life but were no longer alive. And they opened their mouths and started to speak to him, but their voices were a babble, a cacophony, and he struggled to listen to their indecipherable words. And then he was shaken by a great heaving of the earth.

He opened his eyes, and he realised that it was Sharai who was shaking him awake.

'Elijah. The people have come to see you. To be cured by you. You are a miracle worker. You are a prophet. You are He, sent by God to save us all.'

Elijah looked at her, not fully understanding what she was saying because sleep was still upon him. But he quickly saw that they were not alone in the house; for at the door, and the windows and as far as he could tell outside the house, was a babbling multitude. Dozens of people were standing there, looking at him, talking about him, and whispering his name.

He sat up with a shock and cried out. The people in the doorway also drew back in surprise, staring at his startled face in horror. One of the women tentatively came forward and asked him, 'Touch my arm. It has sores which won't heal. Touch me, anointed one, man of God,' she said.

But a man pushed past her, hobbling. 'I am a cripple. Heal me first so that I can walk again,' he begged. And the noises of the people grew louder and louder. He heard them shout out their ailments – pains, broken bones, sores, blindness, deafness, aches ...

Elijah jumped out of bed in terror. He looked at Sharai. 'How? I must not be seen! How did this come about? Ahab's spies. Jezebel.' He was too frightened to speak clearly.

'Forgive me,' she said above the growing noise and clamour. 'I told the mother of one of my son's friends that you had brought him back from the dead and it spread like a desert whirlwind around the village. People have come all morning from far around.'

'But I'm not the lion of God! I'm only a prophet. What they're saying is blasphemy. This is the same as idolatry. I cannot be worshipped.'

'But my son was dead and you brought him back to life. This is a sign of the one sent by God!' she said. Sharai looked at him longingly. 'These people are my neighbours. Many of them are sick. Why can't you heal them like you healed my son?'

Elijah was furious. His head was pounding. 'I didn't cure your son,' he screamed at the stupid woman. 'I didn't bring him back from the dead! God cured your son. I blew God's breath into his lungs. I am nothing. I am worthless. I cannot heal these people.'

He grabbed his meagre possessions and pushed his way through the door, forcing a line through which he could exit past the people who parted in astonishment at his sudden and rapid departure. Some reached out to touch him, some to grab his cloak, but most stood aside, unsure of what to do.

Elijah ran from Sharai's house, and through the village. But he didn't return to the desert. Instead, in his fear of exposure, and in his confusion, Elijah headed in the opposite direction from where he'd been living. He knew he had to go away from this village, but he had no idea where. For he was certain that the news of the healing of the boy, of bringing him back from the dead, would alert Jezebel, and within a day, her troops would be in the village, searching for him.

He ran, and then walked, and then ran again to leave the area as quickly as possible. And when he was exhausted and could run no more, he sat on a rock near the top of a high ridge and looked up into the sky. He felt weak and strange, both hot and cold at the same time. He had eaten nothing since last evening when the boy was sleeping soundly, and Sharai had made some bread which he ate with olive oil. Suddenly he nearly fell from the rock, for he was so tired and giddy from his escape from the village that he felt quite ill. His head felt as if it was full of water, and the landscape over which he looked seemed to be undulating like the waves on the sea. His dream returned, and a light shone from the sky with an intensity which made it unbearable for him to look into. And then, for the first time in two years, he heard the voice of the Lord.

Yahweh, the God of the people of Israel, spoke to Elijah on the top of the hill, overlooking the valleys of Moab. God told him that his enemy was Jezebel. God told him that Elijah was ignorant of anything about Jezebel, yet she was pursuing him and would put him to death. God commanded Elijah to know his enemy so that he could defeat her, her evil priests and priestesses, and the gods and goddesses she had brought into Israel.

God commanded him to live in Phoenicia, the land of the evil ones, which was the very last place that Jezebel would ever think of looking for him. And when he was there, he was to study the false gods so that he could return to Israel and defeat them. And then the light disappeared, and the Lord was gone up to heaven. Elijah was to go to Zarepath, near to the city of Sidon, where Ba'al was worshipped. He was to live there in hiding.

Suddenly, it was all so obvious.

***

It had been an evil couple of years. Years of loneliness, of emptiness, of struggle. But what had compounded the misery of the past two years, made her constantly sad in front of the children, and cry in her lonely bed every night because of her fear of the future, was not knowing whether or not she was a wife or a widow.

Elijah had been gone since the heat and barrenness of two summers ago. Alone, she'd lived through a winter, then a summer, then another winter, and now it was summer again. She had experienced the red sunsets of autumn, the dry chill of winter, and the hues of spring without a helpmeet. She had been on her own from the moment the day started until it ended, alone with the children who looked to her for help and advice; she disciplined them, loved them, cared for them, nurtured them ... but they were growing up without a father. They had grown so much in the two years; Elijah would be so proud of them. Yet when he returned – if he returned – would he recognise them? Would he be pleased? Or would he criticise her for not bringing them up properly?

Normally she and Elijah would bless the beginning of each season with their children, going into the fields or onto nearby hilltops and saying blessings and singing songs in praise of the Lord for the promise of what was to come. But for eight seasons she had failed to make the trip, and now she doubted whether she could remember the songs.

Rizpah remembered that she particularly enjoyed the welcome which Elijah gave to the season of growth, the spring. He would bless the blossoms which were beginning to show on the fruit trees, and kiss the earth as the early buds made their way out of

the still-cold ground. Their children especially loved
the blessings over the start of summer because she was
careful to pack a huge basket of new fruits which the
children hadn't eaten all year; then Elijah would
conduct his family to the middle of a field where a
copse of trees grew and no crops were planted. They
would be invisible to the outside world. She would
adamantly keep the basket closed despite the entreaties
and excitement of the children, waiting for Elijah to
finish praising God for having brought them safely to
the season of plenty.

She tried hard to remember the blessing, and
suddenly it all came back to her: '*You are Blessed, O
Lord our God, for bringing your people Israel to
this time and this place in which your bounty is
made manifest and in which the fullness of the earth
is upon us and on your Holy Land so that the sun
shines its warmth and produces for us the season of
food and wine.*'

Then, when she and the children had repeated the
blessing (to this day, she still didn't understand the
meaning of the word '*manifest*' even though Elijah
explained it to her each year) Rizpah would open the
basket and take out each fruit separately. She would
first spread the rug so that the ants didn't interfere
with her pleasure; then she would ensure that she
took out the raisin bread which she'd carefully baked
the previous day. Then she would take the fruits out
of the basket, and cut each one into quarters so that
each of the family enjoyed its special flavours and
thrilled at the newness of its taste. And each year she
tried to ensure that she bought a particular food – a
fruit or a grain or a paste – from some passing
merchant which the children had never before seen.

She would ask Elijah to tell them tales of the land from where the food had been brought, and the children would listen in awe and wonder.

When they had eaten and drunk their fill, she and Elijah would stand and dance a special dance underneath the canopy of the trees in the light of the setting sun, accompanied by the claps and delight of her family.

These were special moments, times which only she knew of, times hidden from neighbours and friends. Times which now, after two years of waiting in the house for any word that her husband was alive, she missed with the ache of widowhood.

When the children were in the fields gathering food, or out collecting wood, or sitting at the feet of the village teacher, she would think back to these times of bliss and joy and godliness, and the ache would become unbearable. Her fear and loneliness overcame her, and she would begin to whimper; then, as her self-pity grew more intense, she would wail in the emptiness of her home. These days, as the seasons passed, she realised that she was wailing more, not less; that her loneliness was becoming worse, not better. And, in the depths of her grief, she had to admit that she wasn't wailing for the fate of Elijah, but for her own emptiness. Who would look after her now? Who would keep her company as only a husband could?

On the third morning following the Lord's Sabbath, the door to her house was suddenly kicked open. Having seen the children fed and bathed and off to the village teacher, she was laying on her bed, musing forbidden and lustful thoughts about the way in which she would one day like to run naked through the fields of corn, chased by a naked man from Ethiopia who would catch her and force her to the ground, when the door burst open and light flooded into the room.

Rizpah screamed, and sat up, automatically straightening her dress. She clutched her nearly bare breasts and stared wide-eyed at the doorway. Standing there was a huge man, a soldier dressed in the tunic and helmet of one of the palace guards, a uniform she had seen two years earlier when she was in Samaria. Again she screamed. The man entered her home and shouted, 'Silence!'

Clutching her bedding around her, Rizpah became silent, her mind tumbling over what was happening.

'You are the wife of Elijah the prophet?' the man asked, his voice deep and husky from the dust of the long journey.

She nodded, but the guard could not see clearly into the dark room, and could only barely make out the figure of the woman on the bed. He shouted his question again.

'I am Rizpah, wife of Elijah, prophet of the Lord God,' she whispered.

And then she realised that she was about to be killed by the man. Why else would a palace guard have been sent all the way to Tishbe by Queen Jezebel, if not to kill her? This woman who had spared her life when she was a prisoner of the palace had changed her mind. She had saved her from being pushed over the precipice and now she'd sent a man to slit her throat. Oh, what an infamous and evil woman she was.

Rizpah immediately thought of her children, praying that they wouldn't return home and be killed as well. *Please God*, she thought, *keep them with the village teacher until this man has killed me and is returned to Samaria ... please, Almighty God, let my children live ...*

'Stand!' he ordered. 'You are to return with me to Samaria. You are commanded to attend upon the pleasures of Jezebel, Queen of Israel.'

Rizpah remained lying on the bed, too terrified to move. The guard looked at her and realised that she wasn't getting out of bed because of her modesty. 'I will stand outside. You pack what you need and come immediately. Are you able to ride a horse? The Queen has sent one for you.'

So she wasn't going to be killed immediately. She might be able to escape. But one look out of her window, and she saw other soldiers, making escape impossible. What could she do?

'Can you ride a horse?' he repeated, louder this time, and in anger at the procrastination. 'Are you stupid, Israelite woman? Can you understand my words?' he demanded.

'A horse? Why would I need a horse?' she asked, bemused, suddenly overwhelmed and relieved by the knowledge that she would remain alive at least until she arrived in Samaria.

The guard didn't answer, but turned and closed the door behind him. Rizpah was immobile on the bed. She couldn't move, she was in such a state of shock. Out of a clear and cloudless sky, a whirlwind had descended on her. Suddenly, Rizpah was commanded by the Queen of Israel herself to travel to Samaria. And for what reason?

What of her children? 'What about my children?' she shouted to the guard. And she immediately regretted it for he might not have known that she had a family.

Through the door, he called, 'I have horses for your children as well. Queen Jezebel has smiled kindly on your needs.'

Rizpah looked out of the window and saw that there were four men on horseback, as well as a number of other horses. There was a horse for the captain of the guard who stood outside her door, and three for her and her two children.

Her mind was in a state of turmoil. If Jezebel wanted her dead, the captain would simply have marched into her home and slain her. He certainly wouldn't have brought horses, worth a king's ransom, to her village to transport her back to the capital in order to kill her. So why would Jezebel want her to be in the palace? Rizpah hadn't seen Elijah in all the time since the death of old King Omri. She had no idea where he was. And why her? It was her husband who was sought by the evil Queen. Why her? And why her children?

Rizpah stood slowly from the bed. She was in mortal danger. She'd once been used as a hostage for her husband's return. Now she was being used again. And that could only mean that her Elijah was alive, for Queen Jezebel would have no interest in a poor widow of Tishbe otherwise.

For the first time Rizpah realised that there was a smile on her face; Elijah was alive. She wasn't a widow! She looked again out of the window of the house, and saw the magnificent horses. Yes! She would be a hostage, but at least for the time being she wouldn't be killed. She would go to the palace and taste again their wondrous foods and titillating pastes. And she would see the tall and muscular men who walked through the palace with their arms and legs showing.

Suddenly ashamed of herself, Rizpah stopped thinking of the food and the men, and tried to come to terms that she was now a prisoner under arrest ... a hostage whose life could be ended at the whim of a sultry and evil young woman who bowed her knees to idols. The peace and quiet and hardship of her life seemed far more appealing than the journey she was about to undertake.

Travelling had little to commend it. When she trudged up and down the valleys on foot, she had sore legs and aches in her back and shoulders. When she rode high above the road on the precariously swaying back of a huge horse, she lost all feeling in her bottom.

With their young bodies and their youthful vigorous legs, her children revelled in their horseback ride from Tishbe to Samaria. When they were no longer terrified of the size of the animals which they rode for the first time in their lives, and became one with their beasts, they would suddenly kick their horses' flanks, and tear off the road to disappear behind a hill or through a field. When they first did it, the captain of the guard thought they were trying to escape, and sent his men after them to bring them back. He chastised them, threatening them with horrible punishments. But within hours, they did the same again, bored with the sedate pace which was all their mother could cope with. Now, when the journey was almost over, the children would take the horses and disappear for long periods of time, racing up and down hills, along tracks to brooks which burbled in the distance, through villages just visible on the horizon. And they would somehow know the precise moment to return; just as the food was being laid out and served.

Each night of the journey they would dismount from their horses, and Rizpah would collapse onto the ground, railing and moaning in agony. At first, the men had looked at her in shock, and one had come over to her, and offered to massage her back. In surprise and revulsion, she had refused, but as her back and buttocks became more painful, he had insisted, assuring her that he meant her no harm. He gently rubbed her aching muscles. Despite herself and the shame she knew that she was bringing to herself and the women of Israel, she enjoyed the sensation of being massaged and touched, and welcomed the relief from the horse's back and the sensation of a man's hands kneading her flesh.

On their second night, the man again asked Rizpah whether he could help her aches and pains by massaging her body. This time her objections lasted not more than a few moments. On the third night, she didn't object any further, but welcomed the relief. The sensation of being touched by the young man's relieving hands at the end of the day was something which she looked forward to during the journey. And she felt shamed at her thoughts.

Not that her feelings mattered, because soon she would be imprisoned and all thought of life and luxury would be at an end. Surely Yahweh would understand these last few days in which she could feel the touch and pleasure, however fleeting, of a man's hands. But even in the dungeon, for however long she might live, she would have a lifetime of memories; of the ride, of being so high off the ground; of the handsome young guard caressing her body ... all things which Elijah would have condemned as being against the will of the Almighty. But if it was so wrong for her to do these things, why hadn't the Almighty struck her dead?

She and her children were escorted through the Babylon Gate and into the city. The guards at the gate stood aside and saluted the captain of the guard, sitting high and proud on his horse. Rizpah looked at her children's faces. Their eyes were wide in astonishment and fear. Yet she felt none of these emotions. She knew where she was going because she had been here before and was already used to the noise and the crush of people; but her children had never been beyond the bounds of Gilead, and had never been to a huge city like Samaria. Rizpah couldn't help but smile at their reaction. But when she looked closer, she saw that she was wrong. Yes, there was amazement, astonishment, but there was no fear in their faces. They were experiencing none of the fear which showed in hers when she first entered the city two years earlier.

Instead their jaws were agape at the wonders they never knew existed. For the first time on this long and perilous journey, their excitement and enthusiasm was muted by their wonder at the sights before them.

The party made its way to the palace where they were helped to dismount. One of the guards took their horses and the captain escorted them up the steps of the palace, past the guards and into the first antechamber. A crash of cymbals, a flourish of trumpets. The children, now suddenly fearful of the inexplicable noises, put their hands over their ears and screamed.

The vast wooden doors creaked open as though some unimaginable force moved them. Twenty huge black men wearing skins of wild beasts were the first to emerge. Then, out marched fifty palace guards in brilliant armour. The children looked, then shut their eyes, crying in terror. In a voice, sounding of thunder, a male attendant shouted to the crowd:

'Attend, for Her Majesty, Queen Jezebel, arrives. Kneel before the beloved of all the gods.'

The door opened wider and Jezebel walked out, surrounded by ten attendants, five women and five men. In fear, Rizpah dropped to her knees. This wasn't the Jezebel she had met two years earlier when Elijah had escaped from the city and the new Queen had been so kind to her. That Jezebel had been a young and ingenuous girl. This woman was an altogether different Jezebel. A woman of sophistication, painted and perfect. A confident woman. Someone who had the world in her hands.

Jezebel seemed to have grown in height, stature, and importance. The woman who strode towards Rizpah was the embodiment of beauty, haughtiness and self-possession. Yet she held out her arms and offered Rizpah an embrace.

'Stand up. Don't kneel before me. Stand and greet your Queen.'

Rizpah did as she was told. Jezebel looked at her, as though scrutinising the changes of the past couple of years. Rizpah knew that she looked haggard; she'd seen her face some months ago when the brook had been particularly still, and had felt shocked by the way her skin and hair and eyes had aged.

But Jezebel smiled, and said, 'I've missed you. I've missed the talks we had when you were so sick. You taught me much about the Israelite people. I've brought you back to continue these talks.'

Rizpah looked in fear at the Queen.

'Your Majesty,' she said, 'am I to die?'

The Queen looked at her in shock. 'No! Of course not.'

'Then why have you brought me here?'

'Your husband is now being called a miracle worker and the hand of God. They say he can raise people from the dead. I need to know whether he's ever done this in the past. Does it mean he's become a sort of god?'

'So Elijah is alive?' she said, confirming the thought which had been growing in her mind since the soldier had burst into her house.

Jezebel ignored the question, and instead looked at Rizpah's children.

'These are yours?' asked Jezebel.

The two children put their hands over their faces in fear of this vision of power and richness, wearing clothes of colours which they had never before seen.

Noting their panic, Jezebel laughed, and walked over to them. 'Tell me, children, do you like to swim in a river?'

Slowly they took their hands from their faces. The little girl nodded.

'I have a river and a pool, which is inside my palace. Would you like to go swimming in it now? The sun is so hot, and the water is so cool.'

The children simply nodded.

Rizpah looked at the Queen of Israel. She was suspicious. Why was she helping to ease the discomfort of these two children? What was it about this woman which was so fascinating?

CHAPTER FIFTEEN

The blue skies and sunshine of the early days of King Ahab's reign were cast into the gloom of sunset as he came to understand the realities and responsibilities of leading Israel.

The kings of neighbouring nations schemed from the earliest days of Ahab's monarchy to wrest the kingdom from him. They were eager for control of the entire area, especially the port cities of Gaza, Ashkelon, Ashdod and Joppa, as well as the fortune the Israelites were earning from the caravans which traversed the crossroads of the world as they travelled the King's Highway. These surrounding monarchs dreamed of conquest, or toyed with ideas of treaties and alliances which would undermine Ahab's security; they planned insurrections among his people, and plotted ways of paying the captains of his army to lead revolts against him. And some even approached the King of Phoenicia to seek his assistance in their conquest of Israel.

Yet the wily King Ethbaal had been the first to recognise the value of an alliance with Israel when old Omri had first approached him, and had married his daughter to the Prince who suddenly and unexpectedly became King on the day of his wedding. But the neighbouring kings of Israel knew that marriages were merely temporary arrangements; treaties could be nullified overnight; permanent and eternal proclamations of the bonds of friendship between neighbouring nations were like the morning dew.

And the man who knew this more than most was the King of Moab, who was the eternal brother of the Israelites, yet who was always looking for ways of expanding his desert kingdom and conquering the lands which would give him access to the sea. His land was to the east of the Jordan River, between the Salt Sea and the sands of the desert, and he longed for the pastures of the lowlands and the trade which ships brought.

But now that Israel and Phoenicia had a treaty, it would need to be broken. The King of Moab had made unofficial representations to the King of Phoenicia about a possible treaty between their two countries and the dissolution of the current treaty with Israel. The arguments had been potent: the young King Ahab was not strong enough to offer the protection Phoenicia needed from Philistia and other southern nations; Israel was riven in its worship of different gods; the priests of Israel were causing dissent which would lead to an overthrow of the House of Omri; a new king could spring up in the place of Ahab and form an alliance with the Egyptians, and that could spell disaster for all the kingdoms of the Fertile Crescent ... But none of the arguments impressed Ethbaal, and he sent back Moab's ambassadors with empty pockets and dashed hopes.

And so the King of Moab schemed and plotted

and vented his fury by attacking smaller, weaker countries to his east. But not once did the grand scheme he'd envisaged fade from his mind.

Rizpah had been completely mistaken about the reasons for her enforced journey from her home in Tishbe to the palace in Samaria. She'd believed from start to finish that, as a hostage, her life would be forfeit if her husband Elijah didn't surrender himself to Jezebel's mercy. Yet Jezebel insisted that all she wanted was for Rizpah to be near her, that she wanted the older woman to be her companion in her days of loneliness. That she wanted to know all about life with Elijah, and whether he'd performed miracles when he'd been at his home in Tishbe.

Rizpah didn't believe her. She might be held by silken threads, but she was still a prisoner. She didn't trust the young Queen, and continually looked for ways by which she and her children could escape. Yet she was accompanied every moment of the day and night by men and women whom Jezebel called 'companions' and her movements and those of her children were restricted to the Queen's private apartments.

She didn't dare complain to Jezebel on the infrequent occasions she saw her, and so Rizpah played the role of demure friend and companion, patiently explaining the Israelite way of doing things, of the sort of expectations Yahweh had of His people.

She had been in the captivity of Jezebel for so long, she had lost count of the days, and had been occasionally quizzed about Elijah's whereabouts. She had even come to terms with the prospect of enjoying the silken threads which bound her to the royal rooms. And she knew that ultimately her life would be at an end, for she had no idea of the answers to the questions she was asked about Elijah; and one thing she knew for certain was that the imprisonment of his wife and his own children was no way of forcing the prophet of Yahweh to return from the desert or wherever he was. He answered only to the call of Yahweh, and the death of his wife and children, while cruel, would not dissuade him from his mission. And so Rizpah was forced to come to terms with her predicament, and when she did, life became more pleasant.

Rizpah had been in the palace for only a few days before the Queen informed her, somewhat casually, of her true status as a captive. It was when Rizpah asked whether she and her children could leave the palace and visit the city. Even though she could see her children whenever she wanted, she was told that she wasn't allowed to leave the palace with them. They could leave in the company of a servant and enjoy the delights of the city of Samaria, but they weren't allowed to show their mother what new excitements they had discovered. Also, while Rizpah lived in the Queen's private apartments, sharing a room with four other servants, her children were kept in a room above the kitchens. Rizpah had seen their room. It was full of exotic smells, and Jezebel had shown the children a passageway from the corridor outside their room to the back of the kitchens; the first day the children were in their room, the Queen had come late one night and told them how she had lived in this room during her first few days in the palace when she'd come from Phoenicia. Then she'd taught them how to steal milk and cream and meats without being caught. The children adored the Queen; and Rizpah knew that she should stop them from breaking one of Moses' commandments, but somehow she'd rather her son and daughter be happy and settled in this strange environment, than continue faithfully the tradition of being the children of God.

When the confrontation with the mighty and growing nation of Assyria suddenly erupted – a potential war which occurred because of Assyria's determination to spread its empire southward – the tension in the nation of Israel arrived with a mystifying ferocity. Assyria was flexing its muscles beyond Israel's northern borders, and men who had once walked quietly, now walked hastily along corridors and spoke in meaningful whispers. The activity made Rizpah's head spin. Her own status as a captive of Israel was forgotten. Utterly terrified by the sudden shouts and commands which rebounded off the walls of the palace, she went in search of her children, and tried to shield them from the violence which seemed all around her.

Even though there was no war in the palace itself, the tension was everywhere. Jezebel and Ahab sought to assure their servants and friends that Israel wasn't being invaded, but that the Israelite army was merely preparing for the eventuality of war.

Rizpah had known of wars before, but only in the distance. In living memory, wars had always bypassed the country in which she lived, Gilead, and her village of Tishbe had never known the crushing heels of an invading army. Of course, in the days of the ancients, the land had been swept by successive waves of invaders – people from the northeast who were called Hittites; people from the southwest who were the Egyptians; Moab had invaded, as had Edom and Ammon – but these invasions had been long before her grandmother had been a child, and so they were part of the lore of the country, and not part of its present.

Yet now she was a part of a war; now, without warning, her life was in greater turmoil than merely being a hostage in a sumptuous palace. Not that it was a war; according to Hattusas, who occasionally gave Rizpah time by speaking to her while he was waiting to be admitted to the presence of the Queen, Assyria hadn't declared war … nor had it attacked anybody.

'So why,' Rizpah had asked, 'is everybody suddenly frightened, and preparing for battle?'

Hattusas answered, 'Imagine a field of poppies. They grow happily in the sun; then one day a vigorous thistle appears on the outer edge of the field. The farmer thinks to himself that he can ignore it, that it will die and wither. But the next day it has spread, until it, and the others it has spawned, become too big and strong and powerful. Then the farmer can't destroy the thistles because there are too many of them. The thistles grow and multiply until the whole field of poppies is swamped and overtaken, and the farmer's livelihood is at an end. That, Rizpah, is why we are gathering on the borders of Assyria; to show this tall and powerful thistle of a King that we are ready to repel him if ever he dares to march against us.'

She had nodded her thanks. When he explained things, they were so clear, so relevant to everything that she understood from her past life as the simple wife of a man who had become a prophet. In Hattusas, she found the comfort of friendship and companionship. And in these ways he was so unlike Elijah, who spoke often in a strange tongue and in words and phrases which she didn't understand. Yet Hattusas was a Phoenician and, according to Elijah and every other Israelite in the palace to whom she had spoken, he was evil and untrustworthy.

But while the Phoenician had reassured Rizpah, still everything around her was madness. One moment the palace was quiet and collected, people walking and talking, laughing and making jokes; but the next moment a delegation of men arrived, followed the subsequent day by another delegation, and then it was as though a battle were taking place within the walls of the palace itself.

Jezebel had arranged this morning for Rizpah to be shown by the barber how to comb and dress the royal hair, but when she appeared at the Queen's bedchamber, her maidservant told Rizpah that she wasn't wanted. The Queen had been called to her husband Ahab's side for urgent business.

It was the beginning of all the troubles. With no royal hair to tend, Rizpah began walking around the palace with little to do to occupy her. The day passed slowly. A mood of despondency seemed to descend on the palace. Everybody was suddenly cautious and guarded.

The following day, she didn't see the Queen. Nor the day after, so Rizpah walked into the kitchen to see what was happening; then she walked into the banquet hall, the biggest room she had ever seen, with more pillars to support the ceiling than trees in a forest; then she walked through the chamber and pushed ajar the heavy wooden doors. She had never been in this part of the huge palace and as her eyes took in the sight, she was overwhelmed by the majesty of her surroundings.

She peered through the crack in the door and heard the urgent voices of men in discussion. She looked, and was awestruck to see the King and Queen, sitting on their thrones, talking to a group of men who were dressed in clothes which made them look like exotic birds from some faraway place. But the moment one of the guards inside the throne room noticed that the door had opened a crack, he immediately turned, frowned and shooed her away. Rizpah took fright and walked quickly back to her apartments to lay on her bed and think.

There was a tiny commotion at the banqueting hall end of the throne room which distracted King Ahab's attention for a moment. He looked up to see what was happening. A guard on the far door had closed it quickly against some intruder who had no right of admission.

The King immediately grew annoyed. Didn't people realise that this delegation from Damascus was bringing him intelligence about the southward journey of the great King Sarkin-Ashurbanishpul of Assyria who, along with his army, had already crossed the city limits of Pethor and was heading towards Aleppo? It was obvious that the man had war on his mind. This was the third time in as many years that Ahab, and his father Omri before him in the last year of the old King's life, had news of the southward movement of the Assyrian. It seemed that, each year, the King of Assyria made threatening moves to go to war against the southern kingdoms, but no war eventuated. Yet this year, it seemed as though it would be different.

In his last year, Omri had sent an army of a thousand charioteers to the northern border of Israel with Phoenicia. The King of Phoenicia knew, of course, that it was a show of strength for the spies who would report the movement to their Assyrian master. To prove that his southward movement would result in disaster, Ethbaal, King of Phoenicia, had moved his entire army northwards to the banks of the Orontes River. Confronted with such determination, and knowing of the onset of the flooding of the Nile and the prospect of sudden torrential rains, the King of Assyria had withdrawn from his southward flight and had turned, instead, to the region of Bit Adani which he had conquered in a bloody massacre. There he remained to regroup and reconsider his future conquests.

But now, it appeared, he was again on the move. For two days, Ahab had been listening to the demands of various delegations to his court; to the ambassadors from Damascus, from Tyre in Phoenicia, from Judah and Edom, all of whom feared that if Phoenicia and Israel were to fall, there would be nothing to prevent the Assyrian empire absorbing their lands with the ease of bread absorbing oil.

Bombarded by information of numbers and troop movements and by the ambassadors' fear-mongering, Ahab put up his hand, and said, 'What sort of a man is this Sarkin-Ashurbanishpul? Tell me of the man, not of his conquests.'

The Ambassador from Damascus was surprised at the question. One did not need to know the mind of a king to fear the size of his army.

'He is a fearsome and mighty monarch, Highness. He is cruel and ruthless. But the people also sing of the way in which he celebrates his victories by banquets bigger than anything which has before been known. They even sing of a certain banquet for seventy thousand men which he paid for out of his treasury when he put down a revolt of the tribespeople in the hill country to the north of Assyria. They say that his guests feasting in celebration numbered the same as those that he killed, flogged and enslaved.'

Ahab felt Jezebel grab his hand in concern. He turned and reassured her with a kind smile.

'And if I send my army to join those of Damascus and Syria and Phoenicia, how many will we number?'

'How many stars are there in heaven, Highness?' the ambassador asked. It was the standard reply. The numbers promised rarely matched the numbers which kings said that they were going to send. Experience had taught each monarch that when he sent the main part of his army, another neighbouring country, seeing the land denuded of defence, would attack in the hope that the departing army would be wiped out and then they would conquer the neighbouring land without a fight. No king could allow that to happen, and so rarely did more than half of an army travel to fight in a war.

But this time, things looked and sounded different. Not since the time of Ashur-Dan had such a fearsome king come out of Assyria. King Ashur-Dan was known throughout the region. He was as famous as King Solomon and King David. He was reputed to have been one of the most cruel and efficient military leaders of his day, and people still shuddered when they recounted his exploits. Yes, Ahab knew all about Ashur-Dan II of Assyria. He was a King of whom legends were made, stories told. His kingdom had been plagued by the Arameans for years, weakening the defences of the Assyrians and killing the people. But when an army was sent against the Arameans, they disappeared into the mountains and the deserts of Mesopotamia, and couldn't be found.

The Arameans tested Ashur-Dan's resolve. And they found to their cost that he was more resolved than any previous king. When they attacked a border village, King Ashur-Dan was prepared. He had deployed his army in secret places, and the moment word reached his border commanders of the incursion of a raiding party, an elite group of the Assyrian army raced to the village before the Arameans had a chance to escape. They tortured a hundred men, until they had confessions of where the Aramean strongholds were in the mountains. Then, they forced the Aramean warriors to lead them to the villages. And there they enacted the most terrible slaughter, killing ten Arameans for every Assyrian who had died. The women were taken into captivity and were made the playthings of even the most hideous and ugly Assyrian who begged in the streets; the children were hung from baskets in the marketplaces of the cities of Assyria until they cried no more from hunger and thirst, but died horrible deaths. Yes, he was a mighty King.

And now another had arisen. Sarkin-Ashurbanishpul was merciless when he conquered a city or a country. The ambassadors had told Ahab of something which at first mystified, and then terrified him. It was this that he wanted to clarify before he committed his chariots and his army.

'Ambassador, yesterday, you told me of the reports from your spies on the border of Mesopotamia who had witnessed the battle fought in Haran.'

'Yes, Majesty.'

'Tell me again about the aftermath of the battle. How cruel was Sarkin-Ashurbanishpul to those he had defeated?'

The ambassador cleared his throat. It wasn't unusual to have to recount the details of a spy's report for others in the court, but rarely did a king demand to hear the details a second time. 'Sire, the King of Assyria was clever and cunning in his cruelty. His enemies who had fought against him in Haran suffered the agonies of defeat. Some were impaled, some were flayed alive so that the corpse was nothing more than blood and bones; others were beheaded in vast numbers. They were lined up in the market square and teams of men with swords walked down the rows, hacking off heads cleanly and quickly. As the headless body fell, so the townspeople of Haran, especially the wives and children, were ordered to pick up the trunk of the fallen soldier, remove it, and then a new victim was escorted in by his family who were forced to assist in his execution.

'But the King's skill goes far deeper than that, for he realises that by killing men, he makes them into heroes. So he destroys the country by collecting half of the remaining men, women and children, and deporting them to other parts of the Assyrian empire. And in their place, he moves people from his capital cities to repopulate the devastated and captured town. This makes the captured people into a divided people, submissive and slave like. They cannot plot and scheme together because they now live in different towns and villages; and of course they are treated like slaves or enemies wherever they go. Yes, King Ahab, His Majesty Sarkin-Ashurbanishpul is ...'

Ahab interrupted. 'Tell me now of the way in which he wages war.'

The ambassador immediately knew that Ahab wanted to hear about the horsemen. 'He has troops on horseback who fight with weapons such as bows and arrows and spears. These soldiers on horseback carry shields. They ride swiftly at the opposing army and ...'

'How do these men fight from the back of a horse?' asked the Queen Jezebel. For two days the ambassador had been talking with the King, while occasionally the Queen had interrupted. His King in Damascus would be most interested in the fact that a woman, even a Queen, was sharing the throne with King Ahab, and was asking questions in meetings of state. Such a thing had never before occurred, except in that incestuous and evil nation of Egypt where the sisters of ancient pharaohs – sisters who were also wives – were said to have ruled with the same authority.

Out of contempt for being addressed by a woman, even a Queen, the ambassador continued to face the King when he gave his answer, 'They sit on stiff blankets which prevent them from slipping off the horses' flanks. The blankets are tied underneath the animal with ropes.'

The Queen persisted, irritated by the ambassador's rudeness, 'Yes, but how can they defeat two or three men who ride against them in a chariot? I don't understand.'

He was forced to turn his head and address her. 'Highness, the chariot is drawn by two horses. This gives it speed, but not manoeuvrability. It cannot stop quickly nor turn with any amount of ease. Against soldiers on foot, it is a fearsome weapon, and has been responsible for the deaths of many soldiers in wars. In olden days, especially in use by the once mighty Hittites, the chariot was a terrible weapon on which the Hittite nation grew to power. But the weapons of the Hittites were bronze and it was only a small army which could be mounted for the tin which makes bronze is very scarce.

'Today, great Queen, our strong weapons are made of plentiful iron, our armies are far larger because more men can be armed with swords and spears and arrows, and this means that with a vast host for an army, who don't rely on chariots, the ground on which the men fight can be better chosen. The King of Assyria knows this, and when his army fights another army, he chooses ground in which he takes a high position on a hillside. The other army with its chariots can't climb the hills, and so he sends his men on horseback to attack. And my spies have seen the results of this attack. The chariots and the charioteers are like dying cattle in a drought. They stand there useless, as the swift-moving horses thunder in and out of range, firing arrows at will. The spearmen and archers in the chariots fight back, but by the time they have loaded a second arrow or let fly their second spear, the horsemen have disappeared from range.'

The ambassador fell silent, realising that the entire court was holding onto his every word. He looked at Ahab, whose face had turned white. Even the olive-skinned Jezebel looked terrified.

Rizpah knew that something was seriously wrong when she saw the look on Jezebel's face as she returned from the throne room. It was a look of thunder, dark and menacing. She knew well enough to keep out of the young woman's way. But she didn't have the chance because, moments after entering her private apartments, one of Jezebel's servants came running to find her. Thus commanded, Rizpah hurried to the apartments. As was the habit of the court, the moment she entered the presence of the Queen she fell prostrate full length on the floor, until the Queen allowed her to stand. And there she waited, listening for the Queen's kindly invitation for her to abase herself no longer, but to sit with Jezebel and talk about Israel.

But this time, there was no gentle invitation for her to stand. Instead, her Queen's voice was hard and uncompromising.

'Rizpah,' said Jezebel to the Israelite woman on the floor. Her tone was different from any she had previously heard from the lips of this woman. 'Your husband, Elijah. You say you don't know where he is. I know you're lying. Get word to him by whatever means. Give him this message. Tell him that Israel is at war with Assyria. Say to him that he must cease his preachings against the House of Ahab, and against me.

'Tell him that he must leave my husband Ahab alone. The moment is very grave. We are in great danger. If your husband stirs up revolt and revolution in the heads and the hearts of the people, then my husband will be overthrown, and you and your children will be the first to die.

'For the sake of Yahweh, whom you say you love, and for Yahweh's country, get word to Elijah that he must not write any more scrolls to the priests telling them to curse and fight against Ahab. The House of Ahab must be supported by all the people. Go now, and remember what your husband must be told. Your life and those of your children are forfeit if one more word against my husband or me is uttered by the priests.'

Rizpah, terrified and paralysed from fear, didn't move until one of the servants picked her up under her armpits and helped her walk away from the Queen's chamber.

Elijah hadn't known freedom like it since he was a boy running up and down the hills of Gilead. That was the last time he remembered being truly happy. Not even when he was playing with his two children, or at the celebration of a holy feast day, eating wonderful fruit underneath a tree in the middle of a crop field, was he this happy; because the voice of the Lord God was always in his mind, telling him to do this, and commanding him to do that. Had his father known from his birth that Elijah would be the vessel of God's will? When his mother was singing him songs as she washed him in the river, did she know? Or was the voice of God for him, and him alone? But surely his father, who knew everything, must know this ... for surely that was why he'd called his son Elijah which meant 'Yahweh is my God'.

God had been with him since the time when he was turning from boy into man. He remembered so clearly back to those days of happiness when he was a boy. He particularly remembered the very first time God had spoken to him. He was with other boys from the village and they had just come from the house of the teacher. Instead of going straight home, they decided to go out into the orchards and see if any ripe fruit had fallen on the ground. The law said that if the fruit had fallen the length of a man's body from the trunk of the tree, then it belonged to whomsoever picked it up. If it had fallen within the shade of the tree, then it belonged to the farmer, provided the skin hadn't been broken by the fall, or eaten by insects, in which case it must lay there and be returned to the earth.

The four of them had scoured the orchard looking for recently fallen fruit. It was a hot day – that he could remember clearly – and he wanted a drink, but the river was too far from the orchard, and so he searched and searched for a ripe and juicy orange or grapes from a vineyard or pomegranates to satisfy his thirst. And then, in an orchard, he spied one; a big fruit, whose skin was still dark orange and which he hoped didn't have any white scars to prevent him eating it.

The other boys he was with hadn't seen it, and Elijah raced quickly over to the tree to lay down on the ground, and ensure that he wasn't breaking the law, hoping that it had fallen far enough from the tree. Even though he wasn't as big as a man, the law didn't mind him using his own body as a measure. He placed his feet on the trunk of the fruit tree, and lay down, praying that the orange would not be close to his head. It wasn't. It was almost out of reach of his hands. He could pick it up and eat it … share it with his friends. But then someone called out, 'Pick up this fruit, Elijah, as one day you will pick up the fallen of Israel.'

He remembered standing suddenly in shock and looking around to see who had spoken to him. But apart from his friends, searching in other parts of the orchard, there was nobody near him. He was terrified.

He had heard the voice as clearly as if his father was speaking next to him. Yet he was alone.

Elijah decided not to say anything. Instead, subdued, he tore the skin from the orange and ate several juicy segments, brushing away some ants which had crawled onto his skin while he was lying on the ground. He called out to his friends, who came running over and then divided up the remaining segments between all of them. He asked his friends whether or not they'd heard the voice, and they said that they hadn't. And they looked at him strangely, so he said nothing else about it.

He heard no more of the strange voice for many years afterwards. Indeed, he forgot all about the injunction. Not until he had finished his first day as a farmer, assisting his father with the sowing of the next season's crops, did he hear the voice again. He had left the village teacher, who admitted reluctantly that there was little more that he could teach the boy, and joined his father the following day in the field they owned. With his son to assist him, Elijah's father returned to the house to mend some implements while his son continued to sow the rest of the field. And it was there that God spoke again to Elijah. The young man had come to the end of the last row, and was preparing to return to the house to assist his father with sharpening the blades and strengthening the plough, when the voice said to him, 'As you once picked up the fallen fruit so long ago, now you sow the seeds of growth for my people, Israel.'

At first Elijah was frightened, and fell to his knees, hiding his face in one of the furrows in the ground. But the voice continued inside his head, 'Why do you hide from me, Elijah? Do you not know who I am?'

Elijah told the voice that he didn't know.

'I am that I am,' the voice said.

Elijah didn't understand, and told the voice that he was confused.

'I am He that is He!'

Still not understanding, Elijah had asked, 'Who is that?'

And the voice had said, 'As I told my servant Moses when he asked me what he should tell the Israelite people, so I tell you that I am who I am.'

It was all the voice said, for the moment the words entered his mind, a great flash of light erupted in Elijah's tightly closed eyes. He heard the voices of angels singing in his ears. He heard a great rushing of water, like the tide of the sea going out. And Elijah realised that, just as God had spoken to Moses, so God was now speaking to him, through him.

That had been twenty years ago, and God had not abandoned him since. Not even when, in fear of his life and the remorseless pursuit of Jezebel and Ahab, he had realised that the only place they would never look for him would be in Jezebel's homeland. And so he had crossed the border where he had first met Jezebel two years earlier, and walked in trepidation into the land of Ba'al and Asherah and El.

For that first year, living under a different name, he had wandered the roads of Phoenicia, staying for a month in this village and a month in that, sometimes by the sea, sometimes within walking distance of the cities of Sidon and Tyre, sometimes in the hills to the east. He took jobs from local villagers in return for food and lodging. And at night, when he had rested and revived himself, he wrote letters to the priests of Yahweh in Samaria and Jerusalem and

Ashkelon and Gibeon, and gave them instructions about what to do and what to say to counter the assaults on the one true faith which Ba'al and Asherah were making upon the people of God. He told them how best to undermine the kingship of Ahab and the lustful and immoral ways of Jezebel. And from time to time, a messenger would be sent to him to inform him of what was going on.

What wasn't told to Elijah was that his wife and children were incarcerated in the palace, for this wasn't known to the priests, and the occasional and infrequent letters which Elijah sent to his home in Tishbe naturally went unanswered, for even if she had received them, Rizpah wouldn't have known where her husband was located so she could not send her own messages.

During the second year of his stay in the land, travellers into Phoenicia told him horrifying tales of how the evil Jezebel had now built a temple to Ba'al as well as to Asherah in Samaria; and her evil had spread southwards over the border between Israel and Judah and now the people of the Holy Land of Judah were turning their backs on Yahweh and were beginning to worship the Phoenician gods. There was even rumour that Prince Jehoshaphat, son and presumptive successor of King Asa of Judah, had an idol of Asherah in his private bedchamber and was conducting immoral orgies night after night in the very palace of Jerusalem, the palace built by Solomon.

His letters were carried by carefully selected travellers or passengers on caravans who were travelling south. He would study a caravan as it stopped at a village well to refresh itself, or would travel to one of the caravanserai in the east of the country. There might be forty or fifty people with the caravan. But Elijah was only interested in one. Whomsoever stepped off a camel or a donkey and immediately knelt down to give thanks and pay homage to God without taking out an idol, he who turned towards Jerusalem to pay silent worship to Yahweh, he who mumbled the prayers of gratitude that Yahweh had seen the traveller safely to this place, that was the man in whom Elijah showed interest.

He would engage the man in conversation, ask him where he had been, ask him where he was going. That answer was invariably Jerusalem. Sometimes it was a town or village north or south, but always one within walking distance to the temple. But Elijah didn't give over the letter yet. Oh no! For Jezebel's spies were clever and used to the ways of mankind. No, Elijah would bid the man God's speed and appear to walk away. But he would continue to observe the man from a distance. And when Elijah was certain the man didn't realise that anybody was looking, the prophet would watch once again for the sign of devotion to the Lord. For if the traveller said prayers and blessings to Yahweh before eating his meal – prayed to Yahweh without thought of being noticed – then Elijah could be absolutely certain that the man was no spy, that he was a man of God. And it was then that the Almighty told Elijah he should approach the man and beg him to carry his letter to one of the priests in the temple.

And every day that he was in Phoenicia, Elijah had felt an exultation, a freedom. He felt as though a great and terrible weight had been lifted from his shoulders. For although Almighty God spoke to him every day and warned him of the dangers of looking at the asherahs and straying close to the groves where Ba'al was worshipped throughout the Phoenician countryside, Almighty God didn't command him to convert the people. He didn't have to frighten them, or warn them of the dangers of their ways, or threaten them with dire consequences unless they turned from the paths of worshipping false idols. These were a lost people, unable to live in the blessed light of the Almighty; and so there was no point in his ascending the plinth of a building, or standing on a precipice and screaming his anger at the people below. Instead, Elijah could pray to the Almighty in his own mind, and pity those around him who would suffer an eternity for their false and wicked ways.

And that was the way it had been since he had left the land of Israel, and travelled into the territory of the enemy disguised as an ordinary man. For week after week, he had lived as a simple man, working, eating, sleeping. And it was a wonderful life. He hadn't realised how difficult his life had been as a preacher of the word of God, until he lived the simple life.

And then the anger erupted into the air; then talk of a coming war with Assyria was everywhere. Men who walked now ran; children disappeared from the roads; women carried bags of grain on their shoulders to store against a coming siege. Elijah hadn't before seen preparations for a battle; yet it felt as though the very air itself was charged with consternation and fear.

Suddenly the roads were filled with mighty chariots and war wagons and horsemen carrying urgent messages, and soldiers at home in their villages were shaken awake in the middle of the night and told to report to the capital. And overnight as the news of the gathering armies spread from one end of Phoenicia to the other, from the sea to the mountains, everyone changed from being content with life to being sullen and morose and confused and frightened.

It was the children who were most obviously affected; their noisy ways and innocent laughter disappeared from the landscape the moment they were told by anxious parents to stay inside their homes and not to wander; men made sure that crops were quickly harvested and fruit trees denuded against the incursion of an invading army; grapes which still had weeks to ripen were plucked off vines and squeezed to make wine to prevent the invaders from having supplies; cattle and sheep and goats were rounded up and kept tethered close to the homes of their owners; grain and other crops were taken on the command of village elders from private homes and placed into communal storehouses which were filled against invasion or siege of the country; pots of water were filled and buried underground against the salting and poisoning of wells; elderly men and women, always the first to be slaughtered because they held no value as slaves, were sent to live with relatives high in the mountains, out of the path of the forces of the Assyrians; and the simplicity of Elijah's life in Phoenicia came to a sudden and abrupt end.

He surveyed the changed earth from his position high on a mountain whose view took in the distant city of Tyre and the sea beyond. He looked at the orchards and the vineyards and the fields, and thought he could discern an emptiness which had not been there when the earth was bursting with plenty.

It was then that he decided to return to Israel when the army of Ahab had left the country to fight the Assyrians. When the country was at its weakest, Elijah would use the absence of the King to attack Queen Jezebel in a direct confrontation and make the people rise up against her. He had to warn the people of the danger they were in from Assyria while ever the Phoenician idol worshipper was sitting with Ahab on the throne.

Without a second thought, he stood, and began the long journey south to the land of God and his wife Rizpah and his family. Unlike every Phoenician and Israelite, who watched in trepidation as their armies marched northward to repel the might of Assyria, Elijah found that he was walking southwards and smiling.

Jezebel was a different woman. The openness and understanding she had shown to Rizpah evaporated like water left in the sun and was replaced by sullenness. To the rest of those around her, she was cold and aloof. Austere. Ungiving of herself and ungenerous to those who had travelled from Phoenicia with her. She felt alone, abandoned, the sunshine of the early days of her reign was darkened by the cloud which was gathering in the north. The King of Assyria was casting his shadow over the entire landscape; even the messages she received from her father the King Ethbaal were curt and devoid of the personal phrases which she had come to love.

Where once there had been the occasional warm greeting, sometimes even a genuine pleasure at sharing their company, now there was a solid barrier between Jezebel and Rizpah, as though a wall had been erected. Where they had once openly exchanged views about their different gods, now there was demand and immediate answer. And where once Jezebel had relied on Rizpah's advice on how to deal with the Israelite people, suddenly the Queen's ear was captive of other mouths.

'Reports have come to me of your husband Elijah crossing the border between Phoenicia and Israel two nights ago. He preached in the city of Ak-Kah. Despite my instructions, the watch officer didn't arrest him and bring him before me. For that, the officer will be flayed and stoned to death. When Elijah had preached, he was feted in the homes of the priests of Yahweh, and given food and drink for his journey south. These priests will be punished by banishment.

'Tell me, Rizpah, and tell me honestly for fear of your life, did you know of this? Did you know your husband was returning to Israel? Did you know he had been in my country of Phoenicia?'

She didn't allow the older woman to answer, but continued, 'In spite of my commands that you tell me where your husband is, did you disobey me and send word to warn him? Tell me the truth, or you and your children will suffer a fate worse than you could possibly imagine.'

The past week had been horrific for her, days and nights of loneliness and fear and hideous uncertainty. And suddenly like a dam bursting, Rizpah could hold back the tears no longer, and began to sob. She put her hands to her face, and cried out aloud, 'No! I have no idea where Elijah is. Why are you persecuting me like this? Why do you hate me so much? Please, great Queen, help me. I'm a woman alone! I have no friends, no husband. Please help me. I'm so frightened.'

The Queen assumed that this was a confession, and summoned her guard to force the woman to her feet, and drag her before the royal throne. Held in a vicious grip by the men, her hair suddenly pulled so that she was forced to face the Queen, her accuser, Rizpah stopped crying out of fear that at any moment her throat would be cut, and she would die. Then who would protect her children?

'Tell me now,' said Jezebel, her voice cold and heartless, 'do you know where Elijah is? Are you in communication with him? Have you received letters? What are his plans? Will he still preach against me and call me "whore" and "false queen"? Israel is beset by enemies and by the threat of war! Ahab cannot allow his kingdom to be weakened by the words of your husband.'

Barely able to speak, Rizpah sobbed, 'I don't know where he is. I haven't heard from my husband in nearly four years. I didn't know that he was alive until you just told me he was in Ak-Kah. Please believe me, Queen. I swear by the God Yahweh that I don't know the answers to your questions. Please believe me. Help me, Jezebel.'

She continued to sob. The Queen looked at her in contempt. She couldn't abide weakness in anyone. All her life, she had been taught to be in command of herself if she was to command others as monarch. Now this woman, old enough to be her mother, was at her feet sobbing.

A wave of bitterness swept over the young Queen. She had taken this woman in as a friend when she'd first arrived in Israel, when the woman's husband Elijah had screamed abuse at the royal majesty. She'd tended her illness, and shown the hand of friendship; where once her father Ethbaal would have had her tortured and put to death, Jezebel had been kindness and friendship itself. Yes, she'd been forced to threaten Rizpah from time to time, but she'd never had any intention of carrying out the threats. Surely Rizpah knew that. When Rizpah had been brought from her village to the palace as hostage against Elijah's return, hadn't the Queen shown the woman a generosity which would normally have been accorded to a royal friend?

Yet here she lay, at the feet of the most powerful woman in the land, sobbing and wailing and gnashing her teeth like a wife in childbirth. Jezebel's bitterness at Rizpah's rejection of her hand of friendship suddenly turned to disgust.

'Take her away. Throw her into a dungeon. Feed her stale bread and salt. Refuse her water. Do the same with her children. And when she is able to confess to the whereabouts of her husband, the false prophet of Yahweh, bring her back to me in chains and make her beg for my forgiveness.'

CHAPTER SIXTEEN

THE NORTHERN LANDS OF SYRIA

King Ahab of Israel stood on his chariot and surveyed the scene before him. Assembled on the flatlands of the valley floor below was a vast field of men and the equipment of war. The armies were in formation, and divided in parallel rows according to their nationalities. Each and every man was prepared to do battle in a war which had not yet been declared, in a battle which might never have to be fought.

Wearing their different uniforms, it was a simple task to determine the countries which the men of war represented. Just as it was a simple task for Ahab to recognise the monarchs who stood with him on the hilltop overlooking the valley where the armies had been positioned. He knew some of them by sight, but those with whom he wasn't familiar were immediately recognisable to him by the uniforms they wore – leather or silks, or cloaks.

Having contributed the second largest army to the gathering, Ahab stood behind the King of Babylonia, whose neighbouring tribute country, Bit Adani, the source of much of Babylonian wealth, had been carved out of his northwestern corner by the advance of the King of Assyria. Now Assyria was marching westwards and southwards towards the nations of Syria, Phoenicia, Israel, Judah, Philistia, and ultimately to Egypt.

Behind and to the left of Ahab stood Ethbaal, King of Phoenicia, who had sent a somewhat smaller contingent of men than the other monarchs would have liked; and behind him, in order of the size of their contribution to the massive fighting force, were the kings of Syria, Moab, Judah, Ammon and Philistia. Today these monarchs swore eternal brotherhood; yesterday, they'd spent their lives attempting to stab each other in the back.

The intention of their common enemy, King Sarkin-Ashurbanishpul of Assyria, was obvious. He was marching south in order to intimidate the southern kingdoms, to make them into client nations so that he could take over control of the King's Highway, the great crossing place between the west of the world and the east of the world, between the south of the world and the north of the world. This crossing point was the source of much of the wealth of Israel and Phoenicia; but the other kingdoms had joined in because all knew that Sarkin-Ashurbanishpul wouldn't be content with just conquering the two nations, but would eventually embrace the rest, like a bear embraces its prey.

Since time began, the King's Highway had been the prize sought by every adventurer king whose eye was on conquest and the expansion of his empire. It was both Israel's blessing and its curse. Every merchant bringing spices and silks from the east to the west had to cross the King's Highway and was forced to pay tribute and taxes. It was a vast and never-ending source of wealth which made Israel and Phoenicia rich.

And the land of the Fertile Crescent was as valuable as the trading route which straddled it, for the food which grew in the region was plentiful and good in years when there was rain; the cattle and goats and sheep were as numerous as grains of sand on the shore of the sea; and the people paid their taxes and life was good. No wonder King Sarkin-Ashurbanishpul coveted the land, as had so many kings of other nations before him. The Fertile Crescent was Yahweh's gift to His people; it was also His test of their resolve. Yes, for good reason the King of Assyria wanted to control the Fertile Crescent. Its wood was valuable for making chariots, ships, houses, and more. It was this land which the desert and landlocked nation of Assyria looked at with jealous eyes. It was here that Sarkin-Ashurbanishpul wanted to spread his kingdom, and ultimately take control of the riches of Ethiopia and the dark lands of Egypt and Africa.

And it was at this point that the great King Sarkin-Ashurbanishpul had to be stopped. For if he came beyond Aleppo and gained ground in the south, especially if he fought his way to the sea, then the kings who had joined the great defensive army and today proudly stood before their men, would take fright and return home to defend their kingdoms. And that meant that each would be defeated, one after the other, and would fall like the wooden pegs children played with.

At the nod from his King, a Babylonian trumpeter sounded a long call. His note was taken up by other trumpeters positioned down the hill. Theirs was taken up in short order by trumpeters who were gathered at the heads of each of the armies. Within moments, the vast noise of the combined army which had gathered in the flatlands on the plain below the mighty kings of eight great nations, fell into silence.

Having the largest contingent, it had been agreed by the other kings that the King of Babylonia would ride slowly forward onto the promontory above the field and speak to the assembly. And what a gathering it was. There were over thirty thousand men, eight thousand horses, three thousand chariots, two huge slingshots, ten battering rams, and bullock-drawn carts full of bows, arrows, daggers, small slingshots, stones, rocks, wood for fires, food, wines, ale and everything which an army needed for a siege or a battle.

The King cleared his throat and began to speak in as loud a voice as he could. As he began, men stationed on the hillside below him listened carefully and repeated his words, shouting to the men before them. Their words in turn were listened to and repeated by commanders at the head of each division within each army, so that by the time the King had finished a section of his address, the men who stood at the very back of the army far away and almost invisible to the monarch, were beginning to hear his words.

'We are gathered, a vast and numberless multitude, the most powerful and fearsome army to arise since the gods created the world, to end the expansion of the most evil of men. King Sarkin-Ashurbanishpul is the son of the most infamous of all monstrous unions. His mother was a she-lion and he was suckled by a goat; his father was a leprous beggar disguised as a wandering wise man, who seduced the ancient Queen, and made her heavy with child. This I tell you, men of war from many nations, is the man you have assembled here in order to fight. But that is not the reason why you are fighting.

'You all know of the reputation of the King Sarkin-Ashurbanishpul's army. They are the refuse of the earth robbers, thieves and rapists. Every one is chosen by this evil King because he has killed a child which was suckling at his mother's breast. And if we allow this spawn of the monsters of depravity to succeed in overcoming us, each and every one of your mothers and sisters and wives and daughters will suffer the unending misery of ravishment, slavery and cruelty.

'If you are men, if you are soldiers, if you love your mothers and wives and sisters and daughters, then you will die before allowing one of Sarkin-Ashurbanishpul's soldiers to win against you. When we advance beyond this plain, when we march northward to Aleppo, think of this: that we stand as an army in the sight of our gods; that we are invincible; that we are beloved in the sight of all those who live lives of plenty. Fight and you will be rewarded with peace for evermore.

'But if you draw back; if you retreat in the face of the host which confronts you; if you show signs of cowardice and weakness; or worse, if you show mercy to your enemy, the rapists and murderers before you, then be assured that the commanders of your army who stand behind you will put a dagger into you. Because any sign of weakness by you will be considered to be an offence punishable by your death. There will be no judges to judge you. You will not be brought before me or any of my brother kings. You will die the death of a coward, your body will be left on the battlefield for the vultures and the birds of prey and you will be excluded from the heavens and your rightful place as heroes to sit at the feet of the gods.

'Now go, and fight like men. Defeat your enemy. Kill him and destroy him. Cut out his heart and his tongue. Cut off his manhood and throw it to the birds to eat as carrion. Shame him with your strength and manliness and never again allow the name of Assyria to be heard in the markets and meeting places of our nations. Salt his fields and poison his drinking water and take him, his wives and children into slavery and show the world, from the Nile to the Euphrates, that our armies are the greatest armies in all of history, and we are blessed in the sight of the gods.'

A cheer rose from the men in the front rows in the plain below; it was followed like waves upon the seashore moments later by more cheers, and then further cheers as the King's message spread to the back of the army, until the entire field was shouting and cheering and all the men were slapping each other on the back.

Satisfied, the King of Babylonia wheeled his horse around and faced his brother kings who were in their royal chariots. He was higher than they, and looked down upon the others, some of whom were his friends, others enemies now joined in an uncomfortable union of peace against a common aggressor.

'Well?' he asked.

'The men are happy,' said Ahab. 'But what chance do we stand against Sarkin-Ashurbanishpul? His army numbers twice ours. Now he has incorporated the army of Bit Adani into his number, can we withstand him?'

The King of Babylonia smiled. 'Last night, coming late into my tent, one of my spies returned from Bit Adani. He tells me that he has arranged a sum of money sufficient for the army of Bit Adani to revolt against the King Sarkin-Ashurbanishpul in the thick of the battle. They will then cross the line of the skirmish and join our forces. Their numbers aren't great, but the effect will be demoralising and will devastate the Assyrian troops. When the King Sarkin-Ashurbanishpul enters upon a battle, suddenly a significant number of his men will revolt and leave the field. Imagine the way in which the resolve of his remaining army will be tested. That surely, will win us the war and rout Sarkin-Ashurbanishpul.'

There was a wave of relief from the other monarchs as the King finished telling them of his plans to win the war. But he wasn't smiling. And they realised that more was to be announced. 'Ensuring the revolt of the army of Bit Adani has cost me dearly. You will pay me for my costs. It will be arranged by my secretaries before we move north from this place,' he said.

The other kings had little choice but to agree.

Having already spent two days waiting for the armies of the eight nations to assemble on the Plain of Hamath, and four further days of journeying to reach the south of the city of Aleppo, the kings now left the leadership of their armies to their captains. The monarchs were required in the Great Council of War, and only returned during the day to inspect the preparations which had been made by each nation's individual army. Games were arranged every night in which the champions of each nation vied against each other for supremacy in horse racing, charioteering, sword fighting, accuracy with slingshots, wrestling and throwing the dagger. When the games were done, each king in turn put on a banquet for his brother kings; it was a time for nation to outdo nation in the splendour and richness of its bounty. Banquets which began as the sun descended went on throughout most of the night, and kings and courtiers soon became so exhausted that they no longer bothered to return to their tents, but slept in the banqueting arenas.

The fights and encounters between warriors were conducted to ensure that few, if any, champions died in the mock battles. These were not like the battles between slaves for the enjoyment of the monarchs, but were tests of strength and courage; and the last thing which any of the monarchs wanted was for a nation's champion to die, and for that nation to be demoralised before it went into battle. So the sword fights were brought to an end before one of the champions was seriously injured; the dagger throwing wasn't at live targets, but against trees; and the slingshots were aimed at caged birds which were allowed to escape. The higher they were allowed to fly before they were brought down, the greater the cheer from the crowd.

The Moabite slingshot champion amazed all others. His aim was unbelievable. It was as though he had the eyes of the gods. The bird would be released from its cage, and as it flew from the entrance upwards towards the clouds, Machar the Moabite would let loose one stone, then another, then another in a fluid action, almost defying the eyes of the observers who tried to see how he managed to refill the shot so quickly. Yet the bird was always felled with one of the three stones, falling to the ground at the foot of the cage in a flurry of feathers and blood, accompanied by an enormous roar of approval from the soldiers.

On the fourth night since the entire army had come together on the Plain of Hamath, Ahab found a moment when the other kings were distracted by the entertainments to talk to Basar, King of Babylonia

'What do you know of this Sarkın-Ashurbanishpul? What manner of king is he? Have you received his ambassadors? I was approached half a year ago and told to pay him tribute, but I refused. He threatened me with war, but no further word has come from him. Has he approached you?'

Basar licked his fingers clean of the goat's cheese he was eating, and drank a cup of wine. He belched and breathed deeply before answering. On the journey north, he had got to know Ahab, and liked him. He had known his father Omri very well, although each was in fear of the other. And in the beginning of his reign, he had thought that the young man was foolish and impetuous and would be the ruination of Israel; yet his marriage to Jezebel, although the idea of Omri, seemed to have worked well. The nation was rich and prospering, and seemed to be holding Judah in its thrall. Trade with Phoenicia was increasing and both countries were growing richer. And the brief years of his kingship appeared to have matured the once impetuous youth who had now become more sophisticated and sensible, and whose actions were to be admired.

Perhaps now, thought Basar, was the time to join closer with Israel; maybe even to negotiate a treaty of eternal friendship with the young King. For this treaty would lull the King into a sense of security which would give Basar the ability to go to Moab or

Edom, or maybe even Philistia, and use the treaty as a negotiating platform to stab the young man in the back, and take possession of the land. Yes, he thought, eyeing the young man, perhaps Israel was ripe for plucking ... Whatever happened in the future, now was the time to involve Israel in his plans, as he would covertly involve all the other kings until his scheme was complete.

'I tell you this, Ahab, but it must be between you and me. Sarkin-Ashurbanishpul will not fight us. We will arrive at Aleppo, and we will not find his army.'

Ahab was astounded. 'But ... then why are we here ...?'

King Basar put up his hand, and continued to speak in an undertone so that he wasn't overheard by the other monarchs, even though they were outside the banqueting tent, watching the sport.

'There was an incursion of mountain tribesmen from the east and north of Nineveh, the capital of Assyria, two months ago. Sarkin-Ashurbanishpul was in Aleppo when it happened. He was forced to take his entire army north to fight off the raid. It was the biggest yet, and my spies tell me that Sarkin-Ashurbanishpul has lost control of his mind with anger at the continual incursions he is suffering. His rage is so great that he is marching a hundred thousand men at arms into the mountains, even up to Lake Van in the north and the highlands of Media in the east. He is determined to put to death each and every one of the tribesmen, to destroy their villages. He isn't even talking about taking them as slaves, but filling the valleys of the region with dead bodies.'

Ahab was still stunned. 'Then why are we marching north?'

Basar smiled. 'Because of the threat caused by Sarkin-Ashurbanishpul, we are all in danger. Not today, not tomorrow, but next year or the year after. If word reaches Nineveh of a great army on Assyria's south, a coalition of the greatest nations of the Fertile Crescent, then he will not know what to do. Should he move only half his army south to meet us and continue the slaughter of the hill tribes? Or should he move his entire army southwards to meet our challenge, and allow the mountain tribes again to raid Nineveh and the lands of the border?'

Basar looked at his young colleague. 'It is then that we will send an emissary to King Sarkin-Ashurbanishpul. And we will suggest to this haughty monarch that for the sake of peace in his nation, and peace in the world, he signs an eternal treaty of harmony and friendship, a sharing of the lands. That he returns Bit Adani to me and pays me tribute for his capture of my lands.

'When he agrees, as surely he must, it is then that we will sue for peace ... when Sarkin-Ashurbanishpul is at his weakest and most indecisive. And this you must keep to yourself, because I don't trust our brother monarchs as far as I can see them.'

Ahab nodded. Neither did he. And neither did he trust Basar. For now he knew exactly what was happening, and why Babylonia had put together this coalition. Babylonia would sign a treaty with Assyria all right, and it was exactly what Ethbaal his father-in-law, King of Phoenicia, had whispered to him as they rode together north of Tyre; for in this evil treaty, the two Kings, of Babylonia and Assyria, would carve up the lands from the Tigris and Euphrates, all the way to the Nile of Egypt. And he knew from Hattusas that one day, Babylonia would seek a peace treaty with Israel to secure its southern borders. But Hattusas told him that the treaty would be broken within a year, and that Israel must not entertain it.

In his brief years as monarch of Israel, Ahab had learned a lot about diplomacy, and what men really meant when they spoke words of friendship. By assembling the armies of all the nations south of Aleppo, Babylonia would suddenly join with the evil Assyria and trap the armies of the nations of the Fertile Crescent like mice are trapped in the pincers of a scorpion before being stung to death. Surrounded, there would be great destruction and all the nations would be humbled before the might of Assyria to the north and Babylonia to the east. Then Assyria would demand, and would be given, suzerainty rights over Hamath, Aram, Damascus, Tyre and Sidon; and Babylonia would take Israel and Judah and all the lands to the south and east.

Ahab now realised that Ethbaal of Phoenicia had been right all along. That he and all the other kings had been brought north, not as part of a conquering army, but to become captives of the Babylonians, held by the silken threads of friendship until the two great armies would attack the lesser kings, and Babylonia and Assyria would control most of the world. It was an audacious plan.

Maybe even before they saw Assyria's army, the Babylonian King would take each of the other kings captive; threatening them with death in order to make their armies lay down their weapons. Maybe he was planning to attack each of their armies at night when they were drunk and asleep. Who could determine what was in the mind of such a cunning opponent?

Whatever this King was plotting, one thing was certain· Ahab had to warn his captains and withdraw his army and their supplies and weapons before dawn; he had to return to Israel. And he had to recount this conversation to Ethbaal. He felt like a fly, caught in the web of a fiendish spider.

The Israelite army had bedded down for the night, when the fight began. It was a squabble at first, but then a brawl. Four Israelite soldiers, drunk from too much wine, accidentally wandered into the camp of the Philistines. At first, there was good-natured banter, the Philistines telling the Israelites to go home and sleep it off. But then one of the Israelite soldiers had said something which one of the Philistines found offensive, and the two men stood, facing each other in menace.

Unwilling to back down, they fought. The Israelites shouted for help from their campmates across the way. And then there was a melee. Dozens and dozens of men grabbed swords and daggers and shields and crossed the boundaries which separated the camps. Suddenly the night was filled with the sound of battle, of metal swords against shields, of flesh being punctured and men screaming in agony.

The leader of the Israelite army, a young and handsome man named Jehu, was roused from his sleep by his commander. 'Sir,' shouted the older man, 'Captain Jehu, there's trouble ...'

Jehu jumped to his feet, thinking that the army was being attacked by the Assyrians. But in the light from the campfires, he saw instantly what was happening. Fifty or more Israelite soldiers had crossed the boundary between the two camps and were involved in the murderous attack. In the few moments that Jehu watched, he saw that more and more Philistines were standing and emerging from their tents to join in. If he didn't put an end to it immediately, it would spread like a plague, and engulf not only the two nations, but the entirety of the assembly. He turned to his commander, and shouted, 'Get me a chariot. Immediately.'

Within moments, one of the charioteers had ridden through the tents and was at his side.

'Quickly, ride down to the middle of the battle,' Captain Jehu ordered as he ascended the chariot.

The man did as he was told. By riding into the thick of the battle, Jehu drove a wedge into the mass of fighting men.

Suddenly there was uncertainty. Where there had been anger and violence, men from both nations looked around to see which of their colleagues was close to them.

Then Jehu shouted, 'Enough! Put down your weapons.'

It didn't happen immediately. Some who stopped fighting were targets for those who ignored the order; but soon the fighting stopped, and all the men from both armies looked at the Israelite captain to see what he would do next.

Through the assembly from the other side, a delegation from Philistia arrived, led by the captain of the Philistine army. The two leaders knew, and disliked, each other.

The Philistine shouted at Jehu, 'Your men are to blame. They came into our camp intent on mischief. My men defended themselves against your aggression.'

Jehu looked at the other commander. 'Your eyes are sharp. You see what cannot be seen, and know what cannot be known. Or you're a fool and a liar. Tell me, which is it?'

The insult was a challenge between the two men. The rest of the army began to draw back. This was no longer a battle between nations, but between men. Jehu dismounted from his chariot. The leader of the Philistines looked around him for support, but none was given ... this was his fight, and his alone.

'So,' said Jehu, 'once again it is Israel against Philistia; David against Goliath; and as in the days of the ancients, David has the keenness to kill whomsoever is Philistine. But this David won't fight with a slingshot as did our brave King. I will fight with a sword and a dagger.'

He pulled a dagger from his belt, and pulled his sword from its scabbard. Jehu walked forward and faced the captain of the Philistine army.

Jehu had a fearsome reputation as a fighting man. He had killed many men in battle, and the Philistine commander knew that it was an unequal match; he knew that he would die if he fought Jehu alone. When he'd approached the melee, he hadn't expected Jehu to single him out. But neither could he draw back, for that would mean the end of his command. Jehu saw the look of fear on the Philistine's face. He knew that he'd already won the battle. To kill the man now would be to create unnecessary and damaging tensions between the armies. The Philistine captain took his sword and his dagger, and walked forward to meet his end. But without warning, Jehu said, 'Of course, we could always settle this by getting our champions to see who can drink the most.'

And there was a roar of approval from both nations, and the Philistine captain breathed a sigh of relief. The drinking champions were brought forward as the dead and injured were cleared from the field, and the tensions between Israel and Philistia were poured out.

Elijah felt the retreating Israelite army before he saw it. He was lying on the ground near the road from Ak-Kah near the northern border of Israel, when small stones and dust dislodged from an overhanging rock sheltering him from the sun. He brushed off the dust, and stood. There was no wind in the middle of the day, and he was afraid that it might be the breath of a wild stalking beast which had caused the tiny landslide.

But as he stood, he heard the war engines being pulled down the road, then he saw the cloud of dust made by horses. The prophet of the Lord Yahweh looked for somewhere to hide, but this was an exposed piece of land, and he knew he had been seen by the front riders. To have run into the distant bushes for cover would have made them ride him down and treat him as an enemy. So instead, he stood there, moving off the road to allow the army to pass him by.

The ground shook with the mighty weapons. Elijah looked at the men who were riding horses; they were Israelite soldiers, the same men he had seen riding northward towards Aleppo only two weeks previously. One of the horsemen, an imperious and arrogant looking man, glanced down at the traveller as he rode past.

'Did you win the war?' Elijah called up to the horseman.

'There was no war. We withdrew on orders of our King before we engaged the Assyrians in battle. We return home to protect our wives and children.'

No war? How could that be, he wondered. His question was answered when the rump of the army rested before the steep descent from the hills into the coastal plain of the north of Israel. The horsemen and charioteers had ridden on, protecting the war equipment, but by the time night fell, the foot soldiers struck camp on the hills near Ak Kalı and the Israelite traveller was invited to join them and share in the bounty.

Elijah looked at the way in which the men of the army came to a halt at the command of their captains, and suddenly fell to the ground in exhaustion, or struggled up the nearby hillside to gather wood and began to light fires. The provisions wagons had just trundled to a halt at the back of where the men had positioned themselves. By now the horsemen and chariots and war engines, the elite of the army who travelled separately from the ordinary foot soldiers, were well ahead on the road – they might even be approaching Samaria by now – and the bulk of the Israelite army lay across the path leading south. According to the soldier to whom Elijah spoke, a man from Megiddo called Hazakel, the forced march south had been gruelling. They had crossed the length of Phoenicia in only four days; men had fallen by the wayside in exhaustion; those who managed to keep up spent the night hours treating blisters and foot sores with ointments and unguents and lotions given to them by the doctors attached to the army. Hazakel told him that muscles in legs and calves and backs were stressed so much that the army would be incapable of fighting if suddenly called upon.

Elijah kept quiet. He didn't want to say too much,

in case his well-recognised voice alerted a captain that the hated enemy of the King was in their very camp. But as night fell, and raw food was brought to the fire which had been built for ten men to huddle around, and a spit created so that the portion of sheep meat could be cooked, along with roots of turnips and ears of corn, Elijah felt compelled to say something.

Quietly, almost as an aside, he asked the ten men who quaffed wine and were mumbling complaints about their exhaustion, 'Are you men believers in the one true God, Yahweh, the Almighty?'

Hazakel looked at him, Elijah's face seeming to glow in the last light of the sun disappearing into the great Eternal Sea, and said, 'I am. I believe in Yahweh. Always have. He's the God of Israel and Judah.'

'Me too,' said another. Most of the others around the campfire attested to their faith in Yahweh.

'Do you pray to the gods of Phoenicia which the new Queen of Israel, Jezebel, has introduced into our country? The gods Ba'al and Asherah? Are these gods also deserving of your prayers?'

Hazakel shook his head. 'I've prayed to Asherah once, but never since. And never to Ba'al.'

Thankful, Elijah said quietly, 'Then shouldn't we thank the Almighty One, Blessed be He, for delivering you safely from what could have been a conflict and your deaths, for putting a spirit of wisdom into the minds and hearts of the men of war, and for allowing you to enjoy this meal of meat and fruit from the bounty of the earth?'

They looked at each other. The only time prayers were normally said by an army was just before they entered a battle. If it was a great victory, as was the victory under the leadership of King Omri years earlier when he beat the Moabites, then prayers were also said after a battle. But nobody ever said prayers before a meal. They were always too tired and hungry. Two soldiers shrugged. Taking their lead, Hazakel said to the stranger, 'Say prayers if you will.'

And Elijah did. He thanked God the Almighty in a voice which began softly so that he wasn't overheard, but when the spirit of Yahweh descended on him, his voice rose, until he was shouting his thanks to the Lord, and praying fervently for His kindness and His goodness and His mercy. Hazakel and his colleagues bent their heads in supplication, suddenly realising that they weren't just in the presence of a traveller, a man of the road, but were before a man who was of God, perhaps in the presence of a priestly man, even though he wasn't dressed in the rich robes of those of the Temple of Samaria. Other men at nearby fires stopped talking and eating, and listened to the preacher who was invoking the names of God and Yahweh from the other fire. And so did other groups, some far distant, who, despite their fatigue, stood and walked over to listen to the priest beseeching Yahweh to descend from the heights of heaven and assist His people of Israel to return to the paths of goodness and righteousness.

It quickly dawned on the rest of the gathering crowd watching the strange and unkempt traveller that he was no ordinary man. No itinerant, no merchant or journeyman had a command of words as did this preacher. It was Hazakel who first realised that this man was more than a priest, but must be a prophet of the Almighty. And it was he who first dropped to his knees in reverence and worship of the strange man who had come out of the wilderness to share their food and to preach to them.

But it was a man at the back of the crowd, Tema the Shechemite, a man who had been in the deserts east of the River Jordan when he had joined a large throng of people who travelled throughout the day to listen to the words of Elijah, who was the first to realise who it was that they had in their encampment. And when Tema told his colleagues that the great Elijah, prophet of the Lord Yahweh, was in their presence, the word spread throughout the camp, until most of the Israelite army dropped to their knees to the surprise of the army's commander, Captain Jehu.

Jehu had ridden back from bedding down his charioteers and their horses for the night, and was intent upon ensuring that the Israelite army of foot soldiers was secure. He thought he would enter an encampment where the exhausted men were either asleep or eating and falling asleep over their food and wine. Yet what met him was the extraordinary sight of thousands of men, all on their knees before the diminutive figure of an itinerant beggar. Jehu dismounted, and walked towards his genuflecting men, where he could see the hirsute beggar. But the speaker didn't see him. Although he looked directly at him, Jehu knew that the man couldn't see him. His eyes were fixed beyond Jehu and the road above Israel; they were fixed far over the edge of the great Eternal Sea. They were fixed in the heavens above the earth.

Jehu listened to the preacher whose words had enchanted his entire army, bringing them to their knees more swiftly and surely than any great king could have done. The man was talking about the Kingdom of Heaven, and the dangers of worshipping false idols. He was making treasonous remarks about

King Ahab, his commander and ruler; and what he was saying about Queen Jezebel was enough to have him put to death.

Yet! Yet Jehu was spellbound, entrapped by the same mystery of words which entranced his men. He walked slowly from the back of the host, through their ranks, to the front where the man was preaching. And Jehu was washed clean by the warm and pure waters of his words. This man spoke of the justice of Yahweh, of the mercy which He would show to those who were loyal, of the evil of looking at clay idols as though they were the body and the spirit of a God powerful enough to create the heavens and the earth and all the creatures therein. And as Jehu listened, his life clarified before him, for although he had always been loyal to Yahweh, only now did he realise that God was God, and that all else beside was dust.

Overcome by the power of the preacher's words, Jehu fell to his knees, and then onto the ground, entranced and immobile. His men had rushed to his aid, but Jehu lay there, unmoving. Only when Elijah stepped down from the rock from which he was speaking, and placed his hand on Jehu's head did the young man move.

'Arise, Israel,' Elijah had commanded, his voice loud and powerful with the strength of Yahweh.

And Jehu slowly stood. He was a head taller than Elijah and strong of arm and shoulder. Elijah looked at the handsome face, and shouted before the assembly, 'Open your eyes, army of Israel, and see the land before you,' he turned the young man in the direction of Samaria and Jerusalem. 'See the land of Israel and beyond it, the land of Judah. One land become two. Divided because Israel has turned its face from God and now it buries its head in the perfumed breasts of the whores of the temple and the evil daughters of false idols.'

Jehu had opened his eyes, and looked below him. The sun was descending into the Eternal Sea, and its last rays were setting fire to the mountain tops, bathing the world in the glow of a rose, the blush of a woman's cheek. It was as though the Divine One had spread His mantle over the harsh white hillsides and made them luminescent and lustrous. It was then that Jehu realised Elijah spoke with the voice of God. And that his path was clear.

From that moment onwards, Jehu became bound up in the landscape of the Almighty which the preacher painted in his mind. The majesty of Ahab and Jezebel faded in comparison to the eternal majesty of the one and only Lord Yahweh. He walked to the edge of the promontory with Elijah and, again overcome, Captain Jehu fell to his knees onto the ground in front of the prophet, who he now realised had been his mortal enemy, a man whom he had sworn before the King and Queen to kill. And he shouted out, 'Hallelujah!'

And Jehu prayed to Yahweh through the mouth of Elijah.

Jezebel reacted with girlish happiness, clapping her hands and shouting praise to Asherah and Ba'al that they had saved her husband and that he was returning to her safely with his entire army intact.

The messenger wondered whether or not to complete the message. The young Queen was so excited that she seemed as though she would jump off the throne and embrace him at any moment. He looked from the Queen of Israel to Hattusas, the man standing behind her, and his eyes asked the Phoenician advisor whether to continue. Knowing that there was more to the message, Hattusas nodded his head slightly to tell the messenger to continue.

'Highness,' said the exhausted man, 'His Majesty Ahab commands you to send word to every village and town and city throughout Israel to make preparations for a coming battle with Assyria which is likely to be fought on our holy soil. Your father Ethbaal King of Phoenicia has sent this same message to the governors of his provinces. I am commanded to tell you that storage silos are to be filled with grains and produce, and that you are to write an edict under the name of King Ahab that no house in Israel is to store any food other than bread and oils, but all other foods must be surrendered to the storehouses for the common good, under pain of death.'

The Queen's jubilation suddenly dampened. 'His Majesty Ahab is expecting war? But he is returning from a war.'

Hattusas bent down and whispered into her ear, 'Listen carefully, Jezebel. It is as I feared. A war which is over only days after the army has left our nation cannot be a victory ... not against so mighty a foe as Assyria.'

The messenger overheard what the old advisor had said, and agreed. He explained the conundrum, Jezebel listening carefully. Her girlish happiness turned to consider the grave responsibilities of kingship. When he'd finished explaining about the treachery of King Basar of Babylonia, Hattusas called the King's secretary, and dictated an edict to be read by proclamation to the governors of every village and town and city throughout the land. A mood of sombre reflection settled on the throne room. Jezebel stood and retired to her private apartments. There, she was met by her maidservant.

'Send word to the prison. Rizpah and her children are to be released and sent to me.'

Before the sun began to set, Rizpah was admitted to the Queen's private bedchamber. She looked much older and more haggard than when she had been abducted from her home and forced to travel to Samaria. Imperiously, Jezebel said, 'Kneel before your Queen.'

Rizpah fell to her knees.

'You've been in prison now for three weeks; still your husband preaches against me. There are now reports that he is preaching to the army. I am told that for most of this time he has been in my own home country of Phoenicia, hiding in disguise like some accursed spy. What do you know of this?'

Rizpah knew that she was about to die, as were her children. Soon all this evil would be over, and they would enjoy the eternal sunshine and love of Yahweh. So she said bitterly, 'How can I know anything of this? You've had me imprisoned for all this time. We've eaten stale bread, and the salt has made us unbearably thirsty; yet your guards have given us only a cup of water a day. My children are ill and have lice and skin eruptions.'

At another time, she would have burst into tears, but now she was in a state of fury. Death, soon to be her companion, had taken her tears from her and left her full of hate. Jezebel began to speak, but Rizpah interrupted. 'No wonder my husband screams about your evil. You *are* evil, Jezebel. You've done terrible things to me and my children, and we haven't once raised our voices against you. When you first brought us here at the point of a sword, you let my children swim, you fed us and you were so gentle. Yet now you're evil and horrible.'

She was going to say much more, knowing that the Queen would have her killed and then her suffering would be over, but the Queen appeared to draw back from her and a look of distress appeared in her eyes. Rizpah closed her mouth and remained silent; there was nothing more she could say; this wasn't the reaction she'd expected, for looking into the eyes of the young woman, Rizpah saw there something which she least expected … she saw a look of wretchedness in the Queen's face, a feeling of shock, of incomprehension, of bewilderment.

'I'm not evil,' said the young woman in a voice which Rizpah had to strain to hear.

Rizpah looked at the Queen and, slowly, her anger and hatred began to dissolve. The long and awful days in prison were present in her mind, but she had to deal with the now, and the problems which confronted her. And then she saw that beyond the confidence which queenship had given Jezebel, beyond the poise, the young woman's self-possession started to evaporate. Before her, Rizpah saw a grown-up child, a little girl being told off by her mother for being naughty and mean. And most surprising, Rizpah saw Jezebel suddenly flush with embarrassment.

Rizpah had been out of prison for a week when the Queen's mood returned to the way it had been when she'd first been brought from Tishbe. Then she'd been a Queen – firm and fearless – but welcoming and even friendly to her children. Yet during the time in which the conflict had erupted with Assyria, Jezebel had suddenly become hard and cruel, and, latterly, confused and at times bewildered.

During the week, Rizpah had been kept confined in a palace apartment with her children, but their food had been good, and she and the children had been visited by a doctor who applied natrium and a balm made from the acacia tree to their scalps and skin to get rid of the lice and the sores they'd developed in the cells.

Occasionally, Jezebel had sent a toy to the apartment for the children to play with. Rizpah recognised them for what they were – peace offerings. She was bemused. Jezebel was Queen of Israel; Rizpah had shouted at this Queen and should by rights have died on the spot, skewered on the end of a sword. Yet she and her children were alive and being treated with increasing respect by the guards and the Queen's other servants.

Rizpah had seen the look which came over Jezebel's face before. She'd seen it on the face of a wife in Tishbe who had looked at a traveller in a way which wasn't appropriate to a married woman, and the mother of the wife had berated her in front of the whole village. This neighbour had stood there in the hostile sun, looked upon by her friends and fellow villagers, and even though she was a mother of seven children, had looked like an embarrassed girl. Now Rizpah had done this same thing to her Queen; she hadn't realised that queens were capable of this sort of embarrassment, but it made her

409

realise that even young queens were also young women.

When the servant opened the door of Rizpah's apartment and commanded her presence before the Queen, she was no longer afraid. She knew that she wasn't going to die. She had been given a new lease of life, and was encouraged by the change in her circumstances. But the moment she entered the Queen's private apartments, Rizpah knew it was bad news. She was frightened again, not for herself, but for her Queen, and remained silent.

'I have had further word from my husband. He is now certain that there will be a war; that the King of Assyria is following him with a great army, a multitude, and no one will be safe. My husband, the King, is already close to Samaria and returns from the battlefield without having fought and defeated King Sarkin-Ashurbanishpul. I don't know why there was no battle, for his letters are confusing; but he has given orders for Israel to be defended against Assyria. My father the King is also defending Phoenicia.'

Jezebel looked at Rizpah, a woman who had once been her captive, the wife of a man who was her mortal enemy and who told lies about her throughout the length and breadth of the country. Yet she had grown to respect this straight-talking guileless woman, Rizpah. She would be a comfort and a companion in the days ahead; she would be the sensible one to whom Jezebel listened, unlike the voices of the other courtiers who said silly things and flattered her unnecessarily. As she listened to Hattusas and gained comfort from his wisdom, so she would have Rizpah near to her and draw from her a sense of proportion, of reassurance and calm in what would be turbulent times.

'Rizpah, when there is a war, the most dangerous place to be is in the capital of the country. Although we have strong walls and will prepare for a siege, even a short siege produces illness and plagues and hunger and anger amongst the people. You have been honest with me while you have been here. You said I was cruel and evil. Well, I'm not. Because I realise that you have no idea where Elijah is, even though I hate your husband, I cannot hate you. You have my permission to send your children back to their home beyond the Jordan River. In your village, there is less chance of the army of the Assyrians passing through, and they will be safer.'

Rizpah looked at her young Queen. 'And me, Majesty?'

Jezebel shook her head. 'No, you will stay with me and tend to my needs.'

Rizpah looked sad. The Queen examined the face of the older woman. Older? How much older? Ten years, fifteen maybe? Younger than some of the half-sisters and half-brothers with whom she had shared life in the palaces in Sidon and Tyre. And hadn't most of her sisters and brothers, the children of Ethbaal's many wives, proven themselves to be her enemies, jealous of the love her father the King showed her; jealous of her emerging beauty and the favouritism she was shown by her father; jealous that, while they sat in the dining hall and banqueted with ambassadors and kings from other countries, it was always Jezebel whom their father Ethbaal asked to sing and dance to the assembly; angry that she was allowed full reign of the palace while they were confined to their mothers' apartments; and didn't they attempt to sabotage her relationship with her father the King whenever they had an opportunity? Had it not been for the determination of her own mother, the King's favourite wife, for Jezebel to prosper in the court, she might have been crushed by her brothers and sisters and their envy as easily as a cockroach in a royal kitchen.

Rizpah was like no brother or sister she had ever known. From the very first moment she had known this woman, she had been searingly honest with her. Like a mother, yet unlike her own mother, for Jezebel's mother had been absent for most of the time she was growing, preferring instead to leave her nurturing to wet nurses and servants and Egyptian teachers while she ensured the downfall and elimination of the King's other wives. But Rizpah was different. This crude, untutored and totally unsophisticated Israelite woman, wife of her enemy, showed Jezebel the honesty and openness which she had always sought and which her own mother had never shown her. Even when Jezebel had released her and her children from imprisonment, Rizpah had shown few signs of anger and resentment, but instead exhibited an almost overwhelming sense of joy at being freed, at being alive and seeing her children flourish, revelling in their safety and saying how grateful she was that she and her children were unharmed.

Jezebel said, 'I would like to go out by my pool and swim. Now that Ahab is returning, I will need to refresh myself.'

The Queen seemed able to put the anguish of the coming war beyond her; from her shock of hearing that Israel was about to go to war with Assyria she was suddenly uplifted. She looked across the room at

Rizpah and asked, 'Why not bring your children to the pool and they can join me; before they return to the desert land where you live, they can swim in the refreshing water. I'm sure they would enjoy that, and I'd like to have their company. I feel a need to be among happy and young voices like I was when I was a child in my own palace.'

The Queen often swam in the water at the base of the palace walls. But it was always a very private affair, and it was known throughout the palace that the place was reserved only for Her Majesty and His Majesty, where they retired at the end of a long day. Often howls of laughter could be heard coming from the pool when the King and Queen were bathing. And when the howls of laughter suddenly ceased, the servants would smile knowingly that the Queen was out of the water and laying on divans, pleasuring the King.

For Jezebel to invite Rizpah's children to swim with her was an unexpected and great honour. As the Queen retired to her private dressing chamber to remove her clothes and dress in a gauze wrap covered by a *jallabiyeh* for the swim, a Nubian servant was sent to bring Rizpah's children from their chamber. Rizpah stood for the long moments until she heard footsteps approaching the Queen's chamber; for she recognised those footsteps as her own children's. The slave entered the chamber, and hiding behind her were Rizpah's two children, Nehamia and Samuel. There was a look of utter terror on their faces, but Rizpah smiled in encouragement, and mouthed the words that everything was all right.

The moment they saw their mother, their faces shone with the brightness of the sun. They both screamed, 'Imma!' at the same time, and ran over to her, burying their bodies in the voluminous folds of Rizpah's linen caftan. She felt the bodies of her two children and she hugged them to herself, rubbing their heads, and shoulders and backs, whispering that everything was all right, and they had been brought here to play. She felt Nehamia crying, her body shaking within Rizpah's skirts. She remembered her daughter shaking and crying like this when she had once just managed to escape being bitten by a snake in the fields when the child was younger.

'The man came to kill us,' she said.

Rizpah bent down and whispered into her children's ears, 'No, we are safe. You are to return to your home.'

'And you're coming too?' asked her son.

Rizpah bit back tears. 'No, I am to stay with the Queen, but you will be looked after by Rebecca, and you know that you like what she cooks ...'

Jezebel walked over and collected the children from their mother.

'Come with me. What are your names? I've forgotten.'

Rizpah reminded the Queen.

'Oh yes, come down to my pool, Samuel and Nehamia. You've been cooped up in that apartment for a long time and the warmth of the sun will do you good.'

And without another word, the Queen turned and walked through the doors of her apartment and descended the side steps to the footings of the palace where the stream which ran down the hill on which Samaria was built, collected in a natural oasis before it overflowed and ran away into the channels which flowed through the marketplace far below the level of the palace. Rizpah had only once been permitted to go down to the pool. It was when the queen had left her bronze mirror there and ordered Rizpah to go down and collect it. She was amazed by the luxury of the oasis within the walls. The pool was a deep crevice, cool and blue in the brilliant light of the overhead sun. Around it were placed divans, shaded by palm trees which seemed to grow out of the very rock itself. Steps had been carved into the rock surrounding the pool so that their Majesties could enter and leave the pool easily. Rizpah remembered wondering, *'Could there possibly be more luxury in life than this?'*

And now she and her still-worried children followed the Queen down the marble steps outside the apartment walls. Rizpah continued to comfort her children, but Nehamia seemed reassured that her brother Samuel, who still had two years before his entry into the manhood of the community of the people of Israel, seemed to have lost his fear of what could happen to them, and was suddenly excited by the prospect before him.

The pool was on the bottom level of the palace, and even before they reached its level, they could hear the music of the water trickling down the stream before it plunged from the height of a man into the oasis within the walls. Jezebel arrived at the bottom of the steps first, and walked over to one of the divans which was within the sight of the sun. Shortly afterwards, one of her Nubian slaves, a tall man with the blackest of skins, arrived and walked over to her. Without being asked, and seeming to know instinctively what to do, he removed the blue silken *jallabiyeh* and the gauze wrap from Her Majesty's shoulders. Both garments fell to the floor, and were picked up by the slave.

Jezebel turned, and greeted the others as they arrived down at the level of the pool. Wide-eyed in astonishment and horror, Rizpah saw that the Queen was suddenly naked. Instinctively, she covered the eyes of her two children and hid their faces in her caftan. Showing no modesty whatsoever, making no attempt to cover her nakedness, the Queen walked in front of her slaves and came over to Rizpah and tried to extract the two children from the folds of Rizpah's dress.

Angry, Rizpah said, 'Have you no shame, Jezebel? Don't you know you're naked?'

Too surprised to be angry, the Queen said, 'Of course I'm naked. Shame? Why should I feel shame?'

'But you're naked. You are without clothes. In front of my children! You expose that which no man should see other than your husband.'

Jezebel burst out laughing. She was always amazed at how prudish and withdrawn Israelite women were. In the palace she was surrounded by her own courtiers from Phoenicia and they found no shame in their bodies. And her slaves were either naked or wore the briefest of loincloths.

She knew she should discipline Rizpah for her intemperate words before her slaves, but the news of her husband's return – even though there could soon be a war – had made her happy and she didn't intend to have her swim spoiled by having to order Rizpah to be flogged.

'Silly woman,' said Jezebel. 'You're just as foolish as the other Israelites who hate themselves and all of the world around them. Come, give me your children.' And she forced them away from their mother's hands, uncovering their eyes, and allowing them to stare straight into her pouting breasts. 'Is that so bad?' she asked Samuel.

The boy said nothing. He just stared at the Queen's small dark nipples, now erect from the sudden warmth of the sun on her body.

'Well?' she asked, turning her head to Nehamia. 'Is it so bad to be naked and warmed by the sun?'

The young girl also stared at Jezebel's breasts, the first woman's breasts she had ever seen, except for a surreptitious glance at her mother's breasts one day when she had awoken late in the evening, and had seen her mother and her father fighting in bed, and been frightened by her mother's moaning and her father's hands over her mother's mouth telling her to keep quiet or she would wake the children. Then her mother's breasts had been exposed when she'd risen after their fight and gone outside to get a cup of water from the water jug.

Jezebel put her hands on the children's heads, and pulled them gently away from their mother; but Rizpah couldn't allow her children to be in the company of nakedness and lasciviousness, for what would her husband Elijah say when she told him? Only when an Israelite woman was an adulteress was she seen naked by others other than her husband; then, she would be stripped bare of all her clothes by her husband in a public humiliation of her crimes; her husband would be the first of the rest of her village to stone her to death.

Rizpah knew of the shame of being naked in front of others. She tried to restrain her children from going with the Queen, but at a look from Jezebel, a servant held back Rizpah from any attempt to interfere with what the Queen was doing.

The servant, a friend of Rizpah's, whispered in her ear, 'Jezebel will have you flayed if you resist. Allow your children to have fun, and you will all end the day laughing. Trust me, Rizpah, no harm will come to your beloved children.'

Jezebel led Samuel and Nehamia across the outer edge of the pool to where the divans were placed. And there, to Rizpah's horror, she encouraged them to remove their rough and stained tunics, which dropped to the ground. All three were now naked, her two children and the Queen. Rizpah felt faint. It was all so wrong. It contravened the very word of Almighty God; for didn't He command all Israelite people to be modest and that nakedness in public was a sin; and weren't the sons of Noah blessed in the eyes of the Lord God Yahweh because they had covered up their father's nakedness and walked backwards from his drunken form and out of his tent? And now Rizpah's own children were naked before the court of Israel, and she was held back by her own fear of being flogged.

She looked at what was happening to her children. They didn't seem as horrified as she. Indeed, the sun on their bodies warmed them, and made them happy, for Samuel was not trying to cover his manly parts and Nehamia wasn't trying to hide her budding breasts, but both were following Jezebel to the pool. Still restrained from leaping forward to remove her children from this nest of iniquity, Rizpah saw her children slide into the cool blue water. Try as she might, she couldn't prevent her feelings of horror at seeing the nakedness in front of her.

Nehamia screamed at the coldness of the pool. Rizpah felt her body stiffen as she heard Elijah's voice in her head. '*Woman, take my children from this place of harlotry and iniquity ...'* Samuel, her son, disappeared into the cold water, his head completely submerged, only to reappear a moment later like an apple fallen into a stream; he too yelled with shock and delight at the icy freshness of the mountain stream.

The servant released her grip on Rizpah's arms. Jezebel walked forward and descended the steps, immersing her body and joining the children. She, however, was far more sedate, and swam away from them, to luxuriate in the movement of the stream of water before it overflowed from the pool and went cascading down into the river which ran into the city and its marketplace, where people used it for drinking water and to refresh their tired feet and hands.

The Queen lay floating, gently moving her hands and her arms as her body seemed to hover at the surface of the water. Rizpah felt a gorge rising in her throat. She felt dizzy from the immorality in front of her. Nakedness was forbidden in the eyes of God. She tried to remember whether the sons of Noah suffered or were blessed by seeing their father's nakedness. And now it was happening to her children. And her own eyes were sullied before the nakedness of the Queen of Israel. She cried out loud to Yahweh, turned, and ran up the steps back into the palace.

CHAPTER SEVENTEEN

Captain Jehu was a captive in the thrall of Elijah from the moment he heard the holy man beginning his prayers. Since he had entered the camp and listened from the periphery, then walked slowly forward as though approaching a light, he was like a silvery fish caught in a net, slowly being hauled in towards the man on the shore. From that moment onwards, he hadn't been away from the holy man's company. The time he spent with Elijah was like the opening of his eyes, as though a flash of lightning had suddenly illuminated a dark landscape, and for the first time he could see shapes and sights he'd always suspected were there, but were invisible to his eyes. And dangers! In the vivid light of the vision Elijah painted for him of his home of Israel, Jehu saw in stark clarity the dangers of what was happening to the nation.

They travelled together from the northern border of Phoenicia, slowly trundling down the southward road in an ox-cart. Elijah denounced the House of Omri with every turn of the wheels, Jehu listening, sometimes interjecting, but mainly learning.

'How can a young woman be this evil?' he asked.

Elijah told him.

'Why can't Yahweh simply overthrow the other gods?' he asked.

Elijah explained again, more demonstrably this time.

'Is there no possibility that Israelites could worship Asherah and Ba'al in their homes, but Yahweh in the temple?' he asked.

Elijah explained why the Israelites were the chosen people, and what that responsibility meant.

By the time they were deeply into the territory of Israel, Jehu was fully aware that he must convince Ahab to force his Queen to put aside her worship of the Phoenician gods. For like some revelation from Yahweh of which Elijah spoke, Captain Jehu realised that he'd been so busy in the training of the expanded army of Israelite soldiers, that he'd allowed matters concerning the court to pass him by; he'd shown no interest in them or allowed them to involve his thoughts. He was a soldier, and not given to matters which concerned kingship; yet listening to this holy man, he acknowledged how negligent he'd been.

Jehu felt ashamed that he'd failed his God, his family who worshipped Yahweh, his countrymen who should all be worshipping Yahweh, and most especially, himself – Yahweh's servant, the man whom Yahweh had saved in battles with the Moabites, and who had been spared in the battle which was no battle against the Assyrians. But most especially, he was the man whom Yahweh had spared to return safely to his home from foreign nations and put Israel to rights. He owed much to Yahweh.

'Elijah,' he said to the older man. 'I now understand that it is time for me to repay my debt to

Yahweh. I've been so busy building a strong Israelite body that I've stood by and allowed its heart to be eaten by a Phoenician worm. While I was helping to save Israel from its neighbours, I've been too busy to heal the rift which has split the land Yahweh has given to us into two. I shall make myself the instrument which heals the breach.'

Elijah shouted his thanks to the Lord. Soldiers nearby looked around in shock.

Jehu felt sick to his stomach for the way in which he'd neglected the affairs of the state. When the young soldier had left for the war, leading King Ahab's army to fight the Assyrians, he had known of the young Queen's worship of Ba'al and of Asherah; but he had chosen to ignore what was happening in Israel. For Jehu, it had been the business of the priests in the temple. If Israelites wanted to worship other gods, then let them, provided they didn't try to prevent Jehu from worshipping Yahweh. But Elijah had proven to him how wrong he'd been.

All his thoughts had radically changed and in abasement before God, he had fallen on his face, prostrating himself before the Lord's prophet. Now that he was travelling with him, Jehu was confirmed in his belief that Elijah was a great man who saw with open eyes, a man who spoke with God's voice, a man who seemed to have the light of Yahweh in his eyes. It was as though Jehu was able to see clearly for the first time, even though his eyes were open on the road ahead.

When he'd prostrated himself at the prophet's feet, Elijah's words had washed over him and somehow through him, and Jehu understood the purpose with which he had been put on this earth. It was to use his skills as a soldier and defend Yahweh against the assault of false gods, even those in Israel itself. And in the week since he'd genuflected before the Almighty's prophet, he had been thinking and planning and scheming, using the skills he'd learned as a soldier and tactician, plotting to convince his King to put aside the desires and imprecations of his young wife, and cleanse the temple of the abominations.

He and Elijah had travelled together in the ox-cart in the lee of their army. Their journey had taken them down the southern road from the border between Phoenicia and Israel, and Jehu had spent the week resting his army for the coming war to be fought on Israelite soil against the Assyrians and the Babylonians. He'd been training them, building up their morale for the trying days ahead, as well as imbuing them with a love of Yahweh. To his horror, many of the soldiers admitted that they prayed privately to the Phoenician gods El or Haldi or Ba'al or Asherah or even Kothar, while professing in public to pray only to Yahweh. He determined to institute a series of punishments for anyone found with the idol of a foreign god in his possession, but when he consulted with his other commanders, they advised against it.

'Sir,' one of the older captains, Jeremiah, told him, 'these are simple and honest men. And when they go into battle, they have to feel the protection of their gods. If it's Yahweh, then so be it, but if they fight better knowing that some other god is looking after them, then by forbidding them these gods you will reduce their strength and your actions will weaken our army.'

Jehu listened to the reasoning, and accepted it. But in order to appease Elijah, he gave instructions that a pit be dug, which he called the Abraham Pit after the patriarch who had smashed the idols of his father, Terah. And into this pit he invited all soldiers who wanted to show their solidarity with Yahweh to throw in their idols to other gods. Some did, others didn't, and many of the men weren't happy, but Elijah preached again to them, and explained the power of Yahweh over the mere clay figurines they'd just cast aside. This encouraged more of the soldiers to throw away their idols, but even so Elijah wasn't happy, and told Jehu that he would demand the soldiers be loyal to Yahweh. Jehu explained to Elijah the reasoning of his captains, but the prophet ranted about the strength of the nation being weakened. And so the army divided into two, and an uneasy truce existed between those of Yahweh, and those of Yahweh and other idols. As the journey progressed, the anxiety of the men deprived of their idols began to subside; every morning and every night, Elijah talked to the army about the love of Yahweh, and the great things He would do for the Israelite nation.

He travelled with Jehu, who asked Elijah about his men and their worship of false idols. It wasn't an easy journey, and it was made more difficult by the mention of the false gods, for Elijah couldn't listen to their names without anger and occasional imprecations. Even the ox-cart seemed to discomfort him. At first, the prophet had not been comfortable with this mode of transport, preferring to walk, as he had done all his life, but the captain persuaded him. And as they rode, he asked Elijah what he should do to turn his men's hearts back to the worship of

Yahweh. But instead of answering his question, Elijah asked one of his own.

'Are you not worried that you will be reported by one of your idol-worshipping men for travelling with one such as me, one who is hated and excoriated by the Queen, one whose life she is dedicated to ending? Isn't your life endangered by talking to me so openly?'

Jehu pondered carefully what Elijah said before answering. 'What's better? To be accused of treason by the Queen and stoned to death, or to turn my eyes from Almighty God and suffer for evermore the eternal torment of allowing my nation to remain a people which worships false idols? If I turn my face from Yahweh then the light of the divine within my body will be extinguished for ever and I will be lost to the sight of God. Didn't our Father Moses curse his people Israel for building an altar for a golden calf in the desert and kneeling down before this false idol on their return from Egypt? And don't our storytellers and priests tell us that the people were condemned by Yahweh to spend the rest of their lives wandering the endless desert, unable to enter the Holy Land of God?'

Elijah was impressed that this young man knew the history of his people so well. And he told him so. 'Jehu, you are a young and good man. I tell you this: I have travelled throughout the length and breadth of Israel and it shocks me how little our people know of their origins and what they owe to the Almighty One.'

Jehu flicked his whip, and one of the laggardly oxen moved forward slightly.

Elijah continued, 'Most Israelites know nothing of the struggle which their forefathers suffered. They rarely go to the temple where they would learn of these things from the priests, who would relate the holy words to them. Oh, the men of Israel can recite some of the legends and they know the names of Abraham, Isaac and Jacob; and some even know of the exodus from the famine of Israel when the people were forced to go to Egypt. But do they know what happened in Egypt before God chose His people from all others? No, not a thing!'

Jehu was about to argue, but Elijah spoke on, 'Do they know of the enslavement of the children of God before the evil Pharaoh and his taskmasters who forced them under the pain of the whip to build the treasure cities of Pithom and Ramses? Do they know of the struggle of the great Moses the Lawgiver to bring the multitudes of the children of Israel through the desert? And what do they know of the struggle which Moses endured for forty years to fulfil God's commandment?'

He spat on the ground in contempt.

Jehu said, 'But they must be taught ...'

'Of course they must be taught. They must be forced to go to the temple and listen to my words. If these simple soldiers of Israel knew that God prevented those of our forefathers above military age who had left Egypt from entering the Holy Land because they had turned their faces from the Lord and had sinned by bowing their knees before false idols and gods, do you think that they'd continue to worship anybody else? These men are putting their lives in jeopardy.'

Suddenly a thought came over Jehu, a prospect so overwhelming that Elijah looked across at the young man in surprise at his reaction.

'You are Moses,' Jehu said in a quiet voice. 'God

has sent you to lead the people back from the Egypt of false gods and prophets to the purity of Yahweh's Israel. Jezebel is our Pharaoh, our taskmaster; she is the Nile which prevents us from reaching our Promised Land.'

Elijah stared into the distance as the words of the remarkable young man washed over him, like the waters of the Nile flooded the plains of Egypt. Could this young man be right? Could Elijah have indeed been sent by Yahweh to be another Moses? In only a few hundred years the children of Israel were again forgetting the lessons their forefathers had learned so painfully. Could not Elijah be sent by Yahweh to be another Moses come to judgement, suffering the same torments as his noble predecessor all those years before? Was he not the voice of God, crying out in the wilderness for the people to be true to Yahweh?

The wagon trundled onwards, both men sitting in silence.

The following morning after prayers, they began their journey again.

'What will you do when you return to Samaria?' asked Jehu. 'Will you leave the army at the base of the mountain and escape into the countryside?'

Elijah burst out laughing. 'Fool that you are! Don't you realise that Yahweh has sent you to me to be my Aaron? You are my strength and my hope. Till now, I've been a voice, crying alone in the dark night of loneliness. Now I have your strong right arm. No, Jehu, I won't evade my responsibilities any more. I know now what Yahweh expects of me. What I shall do is to preach the word of the Lord to the people of Israel in a voice so loud that it will shut out the whimpering and simpering of the Phoenician whore.

I'll tell them that they must overthrow the evil Jezebel and Ahab in order for God to visit the land of Israel and fend off the attacks of King Sarkin-Ashurbanishpul. I will preach in every village and every town, tell the people that the nation of Israel will be crushed by the iron heel of the Assyrians unless the House of Omri is removed from the throne.

'For in my darkest moment along the road, returning into the black maw which is Israel, God has sent me a captain, an arrow called Jehu which will strike right at the heart of the kingdom. When I first saw you, dark-haired, dark-skinned and handsome standing before me, listening intently as I preached the word of the Lord to the army of Israel, I knew that you were sent by the Lord.

'All others who listened to me were wailing and gnashing their teeth as I denounced the men of Israel for their sins. But you, Jehu, stood there and I could see that you were transfixed by my words, transformed as the light of God Almighty descended on you. And when you fell headlong onto the ground in front of me, as though in a faint, I knew that Yahweh had entered your heart and that you were mine.'

Jehu remembered it well. Never before had he been so overcome with remorse and joy at the same time. He had seen his King's enemy, Elijah, a man whom he had promised on oath he would kill on sight, and yet when he saw him and listened to his words, he realised that this was the mouth of God.

So he had broken his blood oath to Ahab and Jezebel, and now he was returning with the King's army and the King's enemy to Samaria. His job as a captain was to prepare his men for the onslaught of the Assyrians and the treacherous Babylonians. But he also had another mission, a higher mission from Yahweh Himself, to cleanse the temple and purge it of idols; of Asherah and of her incestuous consort and son, Ba'al.

He would seek an audience with Ahab. He would stand at the head of the army and tell his King that the army wanted Israel purged of idols and false gods so that Yahweh would revisit the land, and the Assyrians would be turned back on their heels. And this is what he said to the prophet, his voice cracked and harsh from his fear of being in the presence of Yahweh.

When Elijah heard these words, it seemed as though he would jump out of his skin with excitement. He shouted and cheered and thanked God in heaven. 'And if the King refuses then you will draw your sword and slay him, because you have the army behind you, and God will be strengthening your outstretched arm,' he said. 'Then you will wrest the kingship, and I will be guided by Yahweh to find a man to crown who will become King in place of the House of Omri; and Israel will be saved.'

But Jehu was horrified and drew back as though defiled by the thought. He brought the ox-cart to rest, and turned to Elijah.

'No! No, I cannot do that. That is beyond treason. That's regicide! I cannot raise a sword against my King. I have already committed treason by not killing you and allowing you to preach to my men, but I cannot kill my King. I will persuade Ahab that it is the will of the people.'

Elijah grew angry. 'Persuade? This man can't be persuaded. Jehu, his wife has closed his ears to reason. This she-demon has infested his brain, like worms infest an apple fallen on the ground. He has not listened to my voice. He will not listen to yours. Stupid man, Jehu, you cannot talk to Ahab. You must strike him dead. In the name of the Lord.'

'I cannot, Elijah. I have taken a blood oath and sworn my loyalty to him and his successors. I have sworn in the name of Yahweh. You can't expect me to forgo my oath. For what is the value of an oath if I can break it?'

'Yahweh will allow you to break your oath. You swore it to Him. It is His to receive and His to return. It is for the noblest of reasons. For Yahweh Himself.'

'But Yahweh above all must know that once an oath is given in blood, it can never, ever, be repealed. It is death to break a blood oath.'

'Stupid man!' screamed Elijah, his mouth twisted in fury. 'Fool of a man! You must kill Ahab and Jezebel. I command you!'

Slowly, silently, Jehu faced Elijah and shook his head. 'God will strike him dead. God will be the sword. I cannot ... *will* not be.'

Struck dumb with the unanswerable logic, Elijah remained silent, fulminating in his anger at the stupidity of the young captain of the army. And the two men continued in silence until the ox-cart and the rest of the army camped for the night.

During the following day, Elijah remained morose, but by the time they were three days' wagon ride from Samaria, Elijah had come to terms with the fact that the quick and simple act of slaying the King would not take place. He had also come to see that his safety was suddenly secure, for did not the King's very own leader of the army ride with him? How then could Jezebel or even Ahab himself threaten Elijah's existence? Now, perhaps, the prophet of God

Almighty could continue with his ministry, could resume spreading the word of the Lord Yahweh throughout Israel; and maybe he could determine a way, through Jehu, of rejoining one land with another to make one complete nation out of two halves. Yes, Elijah now realised that he must use Jehu for other purposes than to kill the King and the Queen. For that would only do half the job. The entire progeny of the House of Omri, Ahab's wives and mother and sisters and brothers and his young sons, must be totally and completely destroyed. There must be an end to the House of Ahab, son of Omri and of the accursed idol worshippers.

The banquet was planned for his homecoming. It was a meal of cock birds, roasted and formed into the shape of a battle shield. Ptarmigans, lark, cattle egrets, flamingo, and laughing doves formed concentric wheels from the outside to the inner part of the massive dish which needed ten strong men to carry it into the middle of the banqueting hall. And in the centre of the gigantic shield of birds would be an effigy of the King of Assyria kneeling before King Ahab whose foot would be crushing the Assyrian's head, the image of the two Kings sculptured from a mixture of Egyptian and Philistine gums, flavoured with dyes and other colourings and crushed nuts, all concocted into a paste of fermented goat's milk and allowed to stand overnight to solidify.

But the banquet was delayed for some time. Indeed, guests who had been invited to celebrate the return of the conquering Ahab wondered what was happening and demanded answers of the seneschal. His only comment was a wry smile, and an apology, telling the assembly that they all were waiting on His Majesty's pleasure. Only the seneschal knew what was really going on, and he couldn't say for fear of his life. For King Ahab was not attending to official matters, but was with the Queen, and from past experience, his time with Jezebel precluded all other activities; never had the seneschal seen a man more smitten, nor a woman more guileful.

The King had galloped to Samaria ahead of his army which was still some days behind, near to the border of Phoenicia. He was accompanied by six of his captains as well as his secretaries, his advisors, ten priests and priestesses of Ba'al and Asherah, and two priests of Yahweh. His entry into Samaria was greeted by a huge multitude of the townspeople who erupted onto the streets the moment the trumpeters on the Tyrean Gate announced his arrival. As he rode beneath the gate they cheered loudly with every step of his horse.

Ahab took their greeting in his stride, smiling and waving like a genuine hero returning victorious from a war. But in his heart, he felt like a man defeated. For along with Ethbaal, his father-in-law, King of Phoenicia, he had left the collected assembly of armies and retreated to protect his homeland from the certain advance of the King of Assyria and the traitorous Basar, King of Babylonia. And no doubt, in some short time, this arrogant Assyrian and the treacherous King of Babylonia would thunder to the door of Israel with their war machines and their battering rams and their chariots, and slowly defeat one town after another until they lay siege to Samaria itself.

In time, Ahab would have to make up a story to explain to the people of Israel that his return wasn't in victory, but in preparation for almost certain defeat. He would tell the people by proclamation that Israel must prepare itself for war; and in defeat, slavery. But in the meantime, he rode through the streets of the capital enjoying the acclamation he was receiving.

In truth, he had rushed home to be with Jezebel. It was the first time in their four years of marriage that they had been separated, and he was overwhelmed with anxiety to be with her, to smell her perfumes, to touch her young and slender body, to thrill to the way in which she understood and ministered to all of his needs.

When the King of Israel bounded into his palace, he expected Jezebel to be waiting with a retinue of sycophants who would sing his praises; but to his surprise and disappointment, she was not there. He felt suddenly hurt and angry, demanding to know where his Queen was. His chamberlain stepped forward and whispered in his ear, 'Majesty, the Queen Jezebel is in her bedchamber, waiting for you.'

And so Ahab rushed away from the startled sycophants and their prepared speeches of acclamation, and ran down the corridors of his palace until he reached his wife's private apartments. He flung open the door, expecting to see her in bed, waiting for him, as once she had been when he returned from a visit to the King of Edom. But again she had done something which took him totally by surprise. When he threw open the doors, her room was in almost total darkness, the windows having been draped against the sunlight by heavy dark cloths. He smelled a perfume in the air, unlike any he had previously smelled. It was the smell of sex, the perfume which rose from a woman's body when her desire was at its strongest. He stepped inside the room and heard the door closing. He called out softly, 'Jezebel?' but all he heard was the door closing behind him, impelled by unseen hands.

He was in the dark, enshrouded by the silence. Instead of the touch of his wife, he felt the touch of silk threads brushing against his face, as though he had entered a room of cobwebs; and then the singing began. Gentle wafting voices accompanied by a harp. The room was too dark for him to see who was singing, but they were the voices of angels.

Two hands gently reached down and grasped his wrists; then, he felt his arms being tied together behind his back by silken ropes. He smiled and allowed the games to continue. For weeks, his life had been lived under threat. Every glance carried with it a threatening meaning, every loud noise the prospect of attack. But here, there was an intense excitement, not of danger to his person, but of sex. Although he had no idea what was about to happen, he knew that his wondrous wife Jezebel had been planning something special all the time he was away; she'd intimated as much when he had left. He recalled what she'd said to him as she'd kissed him goodbye: '*Return victorious and safe, husband, and I'll show you paradise in your very own bedchamber.*'

So this was the entrance to paradise. The hands which bound him now placed a mask over his eyes. Again, the mask felt as though it was made of the softest eastern silk; as if a thousand silkworms had spent the time while he was away on campaign specially spinning their magic for him. Now blinded and bound, he was led to his wife's bed, and gently laid on top of the skins. He felt hands ... the soft and gentle hands of many women, unbuckling the hasps which held the leather and bronze of his breastplate, untying the knots which fastened his forearm bands, the greaves on his legs, the metal skirt, and the undergarments. Gently they were coaxed from his body until he was naked.

Then the silk ropes which held his arms bound were released, and they were raised, to be tied to each of the two posts which supported the top of her bed. Having secured his arms, the hidden hands now secured his legs, tying them to the bottom of the bedposts.

The King of Israel was now as spread-eagled as were the men he punished for cowardice, tethered to pegs with arms and legs splayed on the ground, tied down on top of an ant hill until their flesh was stripped from them, piece by tiny agonising piece. But it was no ant hill he was lying on. And when he felt warm perfumed flannels washing his body – his legs, his arms, his face – and his hair combed and his scalp massaged by the strong and expert fingers of a barber, he knew that he was beyond the gates and into the realm of paradise.

In an agony of desire, his voice hoarse from lust, his body rock hard with desire, he called out, 'Jezebel!' And in the enveloping darkness, as though far distant yet near, her dreamy and sultry voice replied, 'Not yet, my love. My King. Not yet; you're not ready for me yet. For much has to be done in the homage of Israel for its returning hero. The way has to be prepared for the moment when you enter into my body. The rod of the hero has to be hard and solid if it is to support the weight of the body of its most loyal subject.'

Then he felt warm towels drying his body: his fingers, his arms, his shoulders, his chest, the area of his manhood, his legs, his feet and his toes. And when his body was scrubbed and wiped of the month's dirt of the road, he was then massaged by many pairs of willing hands; again, they knew every part of his body, from his fingers down to his toes. But it was the woman who massaged his manhood, his hugely erect penis, which gave him the most bliss and caused him to moan and groan into the darkness of his pleasure. She used her fingers and her mouth to massage life back into all those parts of his body which were the least used during the month he'd been away from the palace.

He thought they'd finished. When the aromatic and sweetened oils had been rubbed and massaged into his tired body, and his rough skin scraped off him with a dulled blade, he assumed they would take off his mask, and leave the chamber so he could be alone with his wife; but he was wrong. Instead, he felt the lips of four, perhaps six women, kissing and sucking his flesh; their tongues gliding over every part of his body, warming, wetting and titillating every crevice. And when a slave placed the King's massive member again in her mouth, and began licking and sucking it, he cried out in ecstasy, fearful that he wouldn't be able to restrain himself any longer.

'Jezebel,' he shouted, 'how much longer can you stay separate from me? Take off these binds, this mask, and let me see my wife.'

He heard her laugh. 'Even now, Majesty, you are not ready to plough the field of my love.' She knew that he had returned in defeat – the messenger had told her so – and she was determined that he would know that in her eyes, he was a conquering hero, a complete man.

He became angry. 'How long do I have to bear these tortures of heaven? I demand ... I command ... you to come to me. Be gone with these women. It's you I want.'

'Not yet!' she said firmly. 'Because there's one final pleasure I want to give you before I become the scabbard for your sword.'

Suddenly the blindfold was removed. The room was in partial darkness, for now some candles had been lit, illuminating her bedchamber. His eyes slowly adjusted, and he could clearly make out six naked women, all of them he recognised as priestesses of Asherah. He looked around for Jezebel. She was sitting on a chair which had been suspended from the ceiling by ropes. She too was naked. Her legs were dangling in the air over the edge of the seat, spread wide open in front of him. And licking the womanhood between her legs was her black Ethiopian slave, a woman taller and stronger than a man, more bodyguard than servant. The slave's head was deeply buried in Jezebel's thighs, licking her bush of hair like a cat licks itself.

Ahab had never seen such a thing. Not in all his life had he seen two women in the act which God Almighty reserved as the province of man and woman. Yet here she was, within touching distance, his Queen's eyes closed in abandon, her lips parted in ecstasy, her head back as though she was about to drift away from this world and into the heavens.

And as Ahab stared wide-eyed in amazement at his wife coupling with another woman, one of the priestesses mounted the King and placed his manhood deep within her. She rode him several times as a horseman rides a mount, yet his eyes were not on the priestess, but were looking all the while at Jezebel. Ahab made three deep thrusts, and then the fountain erupted from him; he fell back onto the bed, shouting in rapture, screaming like a baby. And as he screamed, the Ethiopian drove her tongue deep within Jezebel's crevice and the Queen of Israel grasped the black woman's head and drove her face hard against her, and screamed in unison with her husband; each joined one with the other, together but apart.

Four men were snoring loudly close to the throne, partly because of the wine they had drunk, partly because their mouths were still full of food when they had fallen into their drunken stupors. Others were apologising to the King and Queen for their inability to stay awake. And still others were fighting the desire to run from the table to be sick, knowing the insult which this would be to the royal family. Everyone at the table wondered how Ahab and his Jezebel could remain for so long, looking so composed, talking to everyone, being in a near-constant state of euphoria, not appearing to suffer any effects from the orgy of food and wine.

The palace had spent the past two whole days since the King's return, in continuous feasting and entertainment. Achean poets, Egyptian conjurers, Phoenician storytellers, Ethiopian dancers, acrobats from the ancient valleys of the Edomites, men who walked on fire, women who wove patterns in the air with long ribbons and a host of others, had been performing throughout the past two days and nights.

Guests continually excused themselves and retired to antechambers to catch a few moments of sleep, only to return trying to look refreshed and willing to participate in more revelries for that, and following days.

Nobody heard the commotion outside of the palace gates. Nobody realised that Captain Jehu had returned with the bulk of the Israelite army, who were unpacking their carts, and greeting their overjoyed and greatly relieved wives and children. And nobody heard him climb the palace steps and enter the banqueting hall.

But Ahab saw him, standing surrounded by an aura of light in the doorway. Something impinged itself on Ahab's brain; he had seen this before; he was in a banquet and a figure had entered the banqueting hall, and his life from that moment on had changed. But the tiredness and the wine prevented him from working out what the memory was.

When he looked at his young army captain, King Ahab also saw another figure standing in Jehu's shadow, someone whose body shape he had also seen before; not a man standing with the straight bearing and strength of a soldier, nor a man puffed up with the self-importance of a priest, nor a man who appeared dressed in the fineries of a foreign ambassador. No! The man standing behind Jehu was a traveller, a desert wanderer. And an awful feeling of dread suddenly came over Ahab. For although he couldn't see the man clearly, he knew with every fibre of his being that he was staring at the man who cursed him before Yahweh. He was looking at the dark and forbidding form of Elijah. And then the memory of where he'd seen this all before flooded back into his mind ... his father had stood before Elijah in this same room. And it had led to Omri's death. Would the same now happen to Ahab? Sweat appeared on his brow, and he began to tremble with fear.

Captain Jehu walked into the centre of the feasting arena. Elijah stayed at the entrance to the room, waiting for his moment to enter.

'Majesty,' the young man shouted. The entire banqueting hall came to a sudden hush. 'Your army has returned victorious. And I am informed by despatch riders that Sarkin-Ashurbanishpul and his army have had to ride to the east where the mountain people have mounted an attack upon his lands and have inflicted damage upon his towns and villages. The King of Babylonia has returned to his lands, and is now the enemy of all those who surrounded him once in friendship; his name will be cursed for evermore.'

The stupor which had confused King Ahab's mind during the sex and feasting and drinking suddenly cleared.

'What?' he said hoarsely, trying to focus on the importance of the words.

Standing firm in the centre of the room, everyone's eyes on him, the young commander of the king's army, said loudly, 'The Assyrian lion has slunk back to his den. As he and Babylonia were marching towards Phoenicia and Israel intent upon attack, a sudden and momentous thing happened.

'Assyrian troops were attacked by a huge army from the northern mountains of his country, his army is split and too weak to march southwards; he has retreated to his country to lick his wounds. The

Babylonian lioness, abandoned by her mate, has retreated to protect her cubs. Israel and all the lands from Phoenicia to Egypt are now safe of the menace from the north. Hail to Yahweh for giving us this victory.'

Ahab stood and nearly jumped over the table to embrace his commander. He was reprieved; the war would not be fought. Now he had time to create new alliances and form a bulwark against the aggressors from the north.

It took the rest of the people in the room some time to realise that their lives were no longer in danger. And Ahab realised that this was not the moment of his death, and breathed a huge sigh of relief. Jezebel looked at his pallid face in surprise. Captain Jehu walked closer to where the King and Queen were seated on their dais. 'And now that our enemies are defeated beyond our borders, it is time to defeat the enemy who lies within.'

Ahab's moment of relief ended then, for he immediately knew what Jehu meant, although the young man's meaning was lost on Jezebel and those around them.

The King stood, and shouted out for all to hear, 'Captain Jehu. You are the leader of my army. On your young shoulders, I have placed the safety of all Israel. And I have been rewarded for my decision by your bravery and wisdom. Now I shall reward you. Go now and rest; tomorrow, we will discuss the reward which your country will give you for your loyalty and your service ...'

But before he finished, Elijah walked forward, and yelled, 'Hear O Israel, how the corruption spreads. Ahab tries to make the worm of corruption burrow into the strongest branch of the tree of the people. But the branch will not bend. The fruit will not turn rotten and fall to your command. Before you, Israel, stands the Tree of Wisdom!'

Jezebel looked in shock at the prophet. How had he come to the palace? How dare her mortal enemy be in the same room? But he continued to walk forward, ignoring her growing fury. The guards looked on, unsure of what to do against this unarmed man of the roads, but whom they recognised as an enemy of their King and Queen. As though in a prearranged pincer movement, a contingent of soldiers who had entered the banqueting hall with Captain Jehu also walked forward with Elijah, a clear indication to the palace guards not to risk touching the prophet, or they would be hacked to death.

Jezebel also immediately recognised their movement for what it was, an assault on the monarchy. Her face was suddenly a mask of fury. Elijah saw the look of hatred in her eyes, and shouted, 'Don't think that you are safe in your beds, Ahab and Jezebel, just because Sarkin-Ashurbanishpul and his armies have been defeated and Assyria no longer threatens. Don't think that your cities are safe because Babylonia has returned to his palaces ...'

Jezebel stood, and pointed to Elijah. 'Arrest him. Kill him,' she shouted to the Palace Guard.

Her guards reluctantly unsheathed their swords, as did the larger contingent of army troops who accompanied Elijah. There would be a bloodbath. Men and women began to scream as the guards moved forward across the floor to obey their Queen and confront her sworn enemy.

Captain Jehu had anticipated her reaction. He

turned, and said to the captain of the Palace Guard, 'Anyone who lifts his hand against Elijah, the prophet of Yahweh, is committing blasphemy and will die at Yahweh's hands. Bolts of lightning will fall from the sky and reduce to ashes the man who lays the first blow. To touch Elijah is to defile the name of God.'

The Palace Guard stopped in their tracks. Jezebel looked at them in horror. They were obeying a young captain, instead of their Queen. 'Attack him! Now!' she screamed.

But the captain of the Palace Guard looked to Ahab for orders. Jezebel turned and stared at her husband in astonishment, waiting for him to protect her against her enemy.

'Wait!' he said. 'Let there be no bloodshed in the palace after such a momentous announcement.'

Jezebel glared at her husband. 'What! Are you like your father, too weak to confront this … this …' Lost for words, she continued to point at Elijah.

'You, my captain!' said the King. 'How could you have brought this enemy of Israel into our palace?'

'Majesty, Elijah isn't the enemy of our country. The priests and priestesses of Ba'al and Asherah are our enemies. The groves where the men and women of Israel commit sins of immorality and adultery are what is weakening us. Only when the temple is cleansed of these false gods will Israel truly be able to defend itself against the onslaught of Sarkin-Ashurbanishpul and those like him.'

Jezebel had had enough. If Ahab, and her Palace Guard, and the captain of the army were against her, then she herself would take a dagger and kill this evil man. She was about to stride forward, but Elijah, knowing what she was doing, suddenly pointed his staff towards the chief priest and priestess of the alien gods, who were standing shocked by the sudden turn of events, and yelled to the man, 'You! Priest! Is your god, Ba'al, a strong god?'

The chief priest of Ba'al shouted back, 'Yes. Ba'al is the strongest of all the gods. He is the Lord and Creator of the World, the God of Heaven and Earth.'

He pointed to the woman, and shouted, 'And you, Priestess, with your painted lips and painted cheeks, your wanton ways and your immoralities ... Is your Goddess Asherah a strong goddess?'

Furious that she had been described in this way, the priestess said, 'She is the strongest of all the goddesses. She commands the morning. She is the voice of the stars, the music of the heavens.'

'Enough with this,' hissed Jezebel. 'Is nobody brave enough to kill my enemy?'

She walked around the table, taking a dagger from the belt of the nearest soldier; her rage was overcoming her. But knowing her intention, Elijah lifted his staff again, and pointed it directly at her breast.

'Stop! In the name of Yahweh, I command you not to come near me.'

Outraged beyond reason, Jezebel screamed, 'Nobody commands me to do anything. I am the Queen!'

'Does Ba'al command you, Jezebel? Do you obey Asherah's commands?'

She stood still, unsure of what to do next. A smile creased Elijah's deeply etched and weather-beaten face. He nodded gravely. He had won. Even Jezebel was loath to move against him when he invoked her gods and goddesses against her.

And as though ignoring a miscreant child, he turned his attention back to Jezebel's priests and priestesses. His voice changed from that of command to that of somebody toying with the assembly, like an actor before the court. 'I'm so pleased that your god and goddess are so strong. For if what you say is true, then surely Yahweh will bow before these greater gods.'

Now everyone in the hall was holding their breath at this extraordinary scene. Exultant, Elijah exhorted, 'Surely if Ba'al and Asherah and all the other gods from Phoenicia and Philistia and Egypt and Babylonia are all so powerful, then Yahweh should bow in obeisance to them. Surely Yahweh should kneel down and kiss their feet.'

The priest of Ba'al shouted in acclamation, 'Of course He will. Old fool of the desert, our gods are ten … a hundred times … more powerful than your god, Yahweh.'

But Jezebel knew that there was more to this than met the eye. She stole a surreptitious glance at Ahab. He looked exhausted, but his mind was analysing every event which was taking place. He, too, knew that something momentous was about to happen, and she could see the fear in his eyes.

Jezebel was certain that this devil Elijah was leading them into a trap. It was like looking at a deadly snake, carefully weaving his charms and binding the company tight with his spells. But a snake could suddenly strike you dead.

Her priestess now joined the priest in proclaiming the superiority of Asherah.

'My goddess is the greatest goddess alive. Before her all gods and goddesses kneel in envy. Yahweh will kneel before my goddess and will kiss her feet. My Goddess Asherah is the earth mother and gives fruit to the trees and life to newborn animals in the spring. My goddess will marry Yahweh and make Him and all Israel happy. My goddess is …'

'Then your goddess is very powerful if she wishes to be the wife of Yahweh and she freely gives all the things you've told us about,' said Elijah. 'And your God Ba'al is just as powerful if he is all you say,' he continued, looking at the priest of Ba'al.

Elijah turned his back on the King and Queen, having no fear of being stabbed, for the company of men who stood beside him would ensure his safety. To the audience in the hall, he said, 'Men and women of Israel. You are gathered here to celebrate Israel's victory over Sarkin-Ashurbanishpul. This was a great victory. But how many of our husbands and sons died in the battle?' He waited for an answer. 'What …? None …? But how can that be? Is our great and mighty King capable of fighting a war without casualties?'

Ahab looked at the assembly, and could see their questioning, their discomfort. Nobody except he and Jezebel knew where Elijah was leading with these questions.

'But wait … perhaps one of the Phoenician gods protected the army. Maybe Ba'al decided to spread the might of his wings over the army of Israel … after all, how often has Ba'al come to our aid in the past? Was he there when Abraham broke his father's idols? Was he there when Moses confronted the evil Pharaoh? Was this Phoenician god there when the children of Israel were saved from the Egyptian army and crossed the Sea of Reeds to safety? Did Ba'al or Asherah guide the children of Israel through the wilderness with a column of smoke during the day, and a pillar of fire at night? And did Ba'al and Asherah appear before Moses on the top of Mount Sinai and give us the laws by which we live?'

Jezebel looked at the people in the hall, and was shocked to see their faces; it was as though they were waking up to the dawn of a new day. As though suddenly the light of reason was in their eyes. She was losing her battle, and she hadn't yet struck a blow.

Elijah continued, 'According to your great Queen, Jezebel, her Phoenician gods are stronger than Yahweh …'

Elijah stopped talking, leaving his thought unfinished. People waited for his next words, but the room lapsed into an uncomfortable silence as he stood there, staring at the ceiling, staring at nothingness. He was still for too long. People held their breath, waiting for him to move.

And then suddenly, to the surprise of everyone in the room, shocking women and making them scream, surprising the guards who immediately reached for their swords, Elijah threw his hands into the air, and roared, 'Aaaaggghhhh!' He clutched his head as though in the sudden grip of a severe headache, and fell to the floor, writhing like a man with the falling sickness, his legs kicking, his arms flailing, his body contorting in circles as though he was in the thrall of a whirlpool. And all the while that he writhed on the floor, his voice was deep, not of this world, calling, 'Yes, Yahweh, yes Almighty One, yes Elohim …'

Ahab's face went white in shock. His mind wouldn't focus, couldn't understand what was going on. And just as suddenly as the fit had begun, it ended. Elijah stopped moving. He lay on the ground, his arms and legs outstretched as though they were pegged into the ground, like the punishment meted out to cowards on a battlefield.

Nobody moved. Nobody breathed. Everybody in the banqueting hall just stared at the bedraggled traveller lying on the floor, his body heaving in the exertion of the seizure, his breathing rapid and fitful. Not even Jehu moved. He just looked at the prophet in horror, wondering whether to go over and help him. How could he touch a man in whom Yahweh was present? But it didn't look as though Yahweh was in the room. For Elijah's face was twisted in pain, as though a demon had entered his soul, as though he was demented.

Slowly, silently, Elijah stood, pulling himself up painfully with his wooden staff. Eyes almost closed, his face still distorted from the fit, he lifted his staff and pointed it towards the priest and priestess. In a voice deep with eternity, forged in the depths of the unknowable, words came out of Elijah's mouth which were not his words, but those of a superior being.

'I am He who is He. I am what I am. I am Yahweh. I am the Lord of Israel. I am the God who brought my children Israel from the land of Egypt, from the House of Bondage. There is no God before me. I am who I am. My servant Elijah is my voice as my servant Moses was my voice to the evil Pharaoh in Egypt; and as my servant Moses smote the Egyptian army, so now I empower Elijah to smite the false gods and goddesses of Phoenicia.

'For I shall not enter the palace of Ahab, nor the homes of Israel, while they are sullied and made unclean by the presence of false gods and idols. My servant Abraham destroyed the idols of his father

448

Terah and of his people, and walked in My path. Now My home is again made foul and pestilential by the Lord of the Flies and those who make idols and befoul my temple. I, Yahweh, God of Heaven and Earth, command you to put aside your false gods and banish them from this place, now and for evermore. I, Yahweh, am the true God. There is one God in heaven. I am a jealous God. There shall be none before Me. And there shall be none after Me.'

Everyone in the room shrank back against the sign of Yahweh, everyone except Jezebel. Men and women knew they were in the presence of the one God, and fell to their knees, shielding their eyes. Those with the presence of mind removed their shoes. But not Jezebel. For she knew about trances and spirits entering the heads of people. She had often pretended to do it herself when she wanted her way with her father and his court. She had writhed and moaned and frightened her family and convinced her father that she was full of the spirit of Asherah. And her father had given her what she wanted.

So surprising everyone who had been struck dumb and senseless by Elijah's pretence, Jezebel suddenly shouted out, 'Welcome Yahweh, it's so good to have you in our presence. I've often wondered whether you'd show yourself. We've missed you. My goddess, Asherah, has been waiting for you to come to her because she is a beautiful and warm and welcoming goddess. Follow me into the bedchamber, Yahweh, and I'll show you how you can find paradise on earth. Now is the time, Yahweh, for you to take a wife. Now you will make love to the Goddess Asherah and the earth and all Israel will be fruitful and will multiply.'

449

Elijah, his face seemingly screwed up into even more violent distortions, turned his gaze from the priest and priestess, and looked through darkly hooded eyes at Jezebel.

'Foul and evil and wanton woman,' he yelled, his voice suddenly raised to the level of a scream. 'You, who befoul the throne of Israel with your wicked ways. You, who sully the throne on which once sat David and Saul and Solomon. Death will be your reward for your adventures. You and your foul breed. Your sons will all be put to the sword. Your daughters will be sold as whores. Your body will be broken and the dogs will lick your blood.'

Coming out of his trance, Ahab drew his sword, shouting, 'No one visits a curse on the Queen of Israel and lives ...'

But before he could move, Elijah, once again with the deep voice of Yahweh, shouted at him, 'Ahab. Silence. Bow down before me. I am who I am. It was I who put you on the throne. And it is I who will remove you. Dust you were, and dust you will be. I am the Lord your God. Strike my prophet Elijah, and you strike me. And the wages of blasphemy are death.'

The room descended into silence. No one was willing to move. It was as though this was a battlefield, and each army was unclear as to tactics. And then slowly, Elijah did what he had been planning since he had joined Jehu on the journey south to Samaria.

His face contorted with hatred, and facing the royal table, he said, 'Priest of the God Ba'al. I am Yahweh, God of the Heavens and the Earth. I tell you that you serve a false god. If he is a true god, let him fight against me. If I am true, then I will win. If your god is true, then I will leave Israel forever. I,

Yahweh, challenge Ba'al and all the idols of all the nations. I challenge them at the altar of sacrifice. Bring all your priests and priestesses to an altar on a high place. Put there a newly killed ox. Put the ox on wood so that the fire will consume the ox. But do not put flame to the wood. Instead, let Ba'al be your flame. Let Ba'al send down a bolt of lightning and light the wood which will consume the ox. For that will prove that Ba'al is as powerful a god as is Yahweh. And if the ox which is a burnt offering to Ba'al is consumed, then Yahweh will leave Israel for ever, and His people will be Ba'al's people.

'But if no lightning is sent by Ba'al, it will prove that Ba'al and all others are false gods and have no power. Then I shall prove My power before all of Israel. For I will command My servant Elijah to build an altar nearby. And he will be alone, without priests and priestesses to help him. For My prophet on earth is My voice and needs none other. Elijah will build an altar with twelve stones for each of the twelve tribes that I brought out of the land of Egypt. And My prophet Elijah will place wood beneath the ox, and he will place no fire to the wood. For I shall send a bolt of lightning which will light the wood and consume the ox. And when the flesh of the ox is consumed as a burnt offering to Yahweh, then all Israel will know that Yahweh is God. Then all Israel will see that Yahweh is the one true God, and Ba'al and all others are false and evil idols. And all Israel will rise up in anger and destroy the groves of immorality in which the false Goddess Asherah forces My people to commit acts of hideous indecency, and I will rid the temple of the idols which are an offence to My eyes; and all Israel will rise up in anger and will kill the false priests and priestesses of Ba'al and Asherah. They shall be stoned to death, each and every one. And those who have come from Phoenicia will flee the land and return to the pestilential nests from whence they came. For I am a merciless God. I am slow to anger, but I am roused to rage at the way Israel has turned its eyes against Me. Yahweh your God, has spoken.'

The women in the room screamed in panic as Elijah fell again on the floor, as though in a dead faint.

CHAPTER EIGHTEEN

The word was sent out by despatch riders to those towns and cities within seven days' walk of the capital of Israel. Yet somehow the word spread and people from places much further away – Judah, Moab, Phoenicia, and even Edom – heard about the great challenge, and immediately left their fields and workshops and homes in order to journey to Samaria to be there on time. Journeying was difficult at the best of times, but people made a special effort to be there; and those who sold rooms in their homes for travellers were suddenly enriched.

A delegation of priests from the temple of Yahweh in Jerusalem told their King that it was their sacred duty to observe the undoubted victory of their one God against Ba'al as well as the combined might of the idols of other lands.

There were rumours which ran throughout the nation of Israel that some people had even travelled from beyond the Mountains of Moab, where gods were worshipped whose names were hard to pronounce, whose powers were reputed to be terrible, and whose faces were reputed to kill if seen by mortal man. But whether they were faithful to Yahweh or whether they had been secretly or openly worshipping the gods of Phoenicia or of other nations, people came from all around in order to vindicate their faith and trust in whichever was the god to whom they prayed. For Elijah had said that during this day of challenge, one of the gods or goddesses would be so roused in anger at the audacity of the contest, that he, or she, would hurl down a lightning bolt and consume the animal sacrifice.

Not since the days of the patriarchs Abraham, Isaac and Jacob, not since the return of the children of Israel and Moses to the Promised Land, nor the time of the judges had Yahweh shown Himself. And since the time of Solomon, Yahweh had only made His presence known through His voice to those who worshipped Him. Despite the fact that the people of Israel prayed and begged and beseeched Him to help them in their times of need, Yahweh had rarely returned to them and revealed His presence as a burning bush, or any other manifestation, as He had revealed Himself so many years ago to the Fathers of the religion and to Moses the Lawgiver, who had led the children of Israel out of the land of Egypt.

It was a month since the challenge, and today, they began to arrive in their thousands. Elijah was protected from harm by the priests of the temple, as well as a squadron of men posted to him day and night on the orders of Captain Jehu. He ate, walked and slept in company, always wary that the priests and priestesses – or more likely Ahab or Jezebel – would try to have him murdered.

And on the appointed day at the Mountain of Carmel, a distant walk from the city of Samaria people stood in their preferred places like grass in a field. Once the word had gone out, people began to arrive in Israel, seeking places to sleep and to eat after their journey. And for each of the days which led up to the confrontation between Yahweh and the other gods, people appeared from every direction and clogged the roads of the country.

The talk on everyone's lips was whether or not Yahweh would reveal Himself. It was assumed that neither Ba'al nor Asherah, nor indeed El, nor any of the other gods of the Phoenicians would obey the commands of their priests. These gods had only ever revealed themselves to each other, never to people. And the only way in which they manifested themselves was through those elements of nature which they controlled: the sea, the wind, the sun, the moon, the harvest, trees, rocks, and the earth itself. So the very thought that the gods of Phoenicia would respond to the pleadings of their priests was dismissed. The real question was whether Yahweh would appear. And as they walked closer, the followers of Yahweh were trying to remember when He had last appeared as anything other than a voice.

Jezebel was thrilled that so many people had come to her kingdom. This was the moment she had been looking forward to since the challenge. She had spent much time in her chambers with her priests, planning ways to make the wood burn and consume the ox, without enabling the people to see the tricks her priests would be playing. Naturally, they would somehow try to use the desert fire-water, but the danger was that many people knew of it ... Most Israelites had seen Jezebel use it before the city walls when she first entered Israel. And she had often used it as an entertainment during banquets, much to the delight of the crowd.

She kept it a secret – nobody knew what it was, or where it came from – but most knew the effects. And that was her problem, because everybody would assume if the wood suddenly caught fire, that Jezebel and her priests had used trickery. And that would give the day to Elijah. As she and her priests discussed ways of igniting the wood without being seen, reality descended upon her.

'We could place the fire-water underneath the skin of the ox, and then as you dance around the beast, you could bring a flame out of your robes and set it alight,' she said.

The chief priest of Ba'al shook his head. 'No, great Queen. The Israelite Elijah would immediately see what was happening and would scream our deceit to the world.'

'If we soaked the wood in the fire-water the previous day …'

The chief priest interrupted, 'Again, Majesty, Elijah would smell it …'

And so they talked over the issues and decided to pray to their gods for help. Ahab was just as circumspect about the future as was his wife.

Yet they and the priests were the only ones who were anxious. The merchants were doing a roaring trade, people buying almost everything which they had to sell; innkeepers and those who allowed strangers into their houses for payment were turning people away from their doors. Men who sold idols were working throughout the day and night to manufacture them; deliveries of clay and paints were like a never-ending caravan, one unloading and leaving while another arrived with a fresh load. The most popular idols purchased were of the god El and of Asherah herself. For some reason, a reason to which Jezebel paid particular attention, people were confusing the Phoenician god El with the Israelite's Yahweh, also known as Elohim. And the sellers of idols were now making double their income by selling the god El alongside his mate and partner, Asherah, for the double protection of purchasers.

When it had all started, when Elijah had first appeared with Captain Jehu at the palace, Jezebel's first instinct was to have him killed. It would have been quick and efficient, and there was good reason: word had gone out to the entire country for years past that Elijah was to be killed on sight. Of course, the moment his head was brought before her, the trouble would just be beginning. There would be a revolt from the people, from the temple, and seeing the weaknesses of the country, a border incursion from east and south, perhaps even Babylonia looking with interest despite its recent humiliation. But mainly, there would have been trouble with the King of Judah who would have ridden north and camped on the border with his legions, threatening to depose the monarchy of Ahab.

But in the end, it would probably have been no more than angry words. In the current climate of threats from the north, and now a growing threat from Egypt, no war between Judah and Israel would have resulted from the execution of the prophet, and his death would have been forgotten by the new moon. The people's revolt would have been put down, other nations' anger would have been quieted, and the temple would have been given a fortune in blood money.

But when Elijah appeared before the banquet and fell to the floor and spoke with the voice of Yahweh, Jezebel knew that she could do nothing against him. She was furious, resentful, hurt and offended that her husband had done so little to defend her from Elijah's – or was it Yahweh's? – statements. But the following day she regained her calmness, and began the process of planning to bring him down before all of Israel.

Jezebel continued to consult with the chief priest and priestess of the gods, and in the end was forced to accept their assurances that there would be a conflagration the like of which had never been seen before. 'The entire mountainside will be struck by lightning, great Queen,' said the priest. 'The entails tell us that our gods will show their power so that all Israel will kneel down before their majesty. The ox will be devoured, and I am confident, supremely confident, that the fire of Ba'al and Asherah will even consume Elijah's ox and Elijah himself. How dare this mere traveller, this desert dweller, this man who smells of the fields and carries the dirt of the ground upon his clothes, challenge the might of the very gods themselves?' he asked rhetorically.

And Jezebel was forced to believe him, because she could see no other way.

On the day of the trial between Yahweh and the Phoenician gods, the sun seemed to curse both opposing camps. Men, women and children who crowded on the base of the hill in the early morning were beginning to erect sunshades and sit beneath them in the still and enervating air, which drained them of energy and made movement uncomfortable.

But not Elijah. Even in the blistering sun, with the

loud buzzing of insects in the air, he amazed the growing crowd by running around the top of the hill like a man possessed. Perspiration was pouring from his brow; his robes were soaked; yet he seemed to notice no discomfort. He ran around the hilltop as excited as a child about to celebrate his birthday.

At times he laughed, shouted, stood still on the spot as though he were a tree, his arms outstretched, his mouth open as if he was standing in a storm, drinking blessed rain; then he would shout out in an unintelligible language and begin to run again, gesticulating at the priests on the opposite side of the hill, making rude noises and crude gestures, ignoring the consternation and ridicule of the Israelite families who were watching his every move.

Those at the bottom of the hill saw two clearly defined groups who were preparing for a visitation from their gods. On the right of the hill, overlooking the distant city of Samaria, were eight hundred priests and priestesses of the Phoenician gods. They were dressed in spotless white robes and on their heads wore garlands of flowers. The priestesses' robes were draped so that in each case, their left breast was exposed, a sign both of modesty and a oneness with nature. The robes of the priests were fringed with the designs and colours of the god they worshipped, red fringes for Ba'al, yellow for El, and green for the priests of Asherah. In the middle of the encampment which the Phoenician priests had erected were three wooden poles, symbols of Asherah so that she would recognise the obeisance of her people and come to earth in visible form.

On the other side, the left side of the hill, overlooking the distant Eternal Sea, was the solitary figure of Elijah, a man who seemed to be struck by the malice of the sun. The prophet of Yahweh wore no special robes, just the tunic he dressed in when he travelled the length and breadth of Israel and Judah and slept in the ditches and addressed multitudes of Israelites loyal to Yahweh. His hair was matted with dirt, his skin dyed dark from the strength of the sun and the earth of the field and his arms and legs were caked with rivulets of sweat which poured down his limbs as the sun grew hotter and hotter.

The people of Israel watched him in fascination and horror. At times, he jumped up and down on the spot, at other times, he ran to the invisible midway line of demarcation between his space and that of the Phoenicians, and shouted and gesticulated and made rude noises with his tongue, noises like the sound of the foul air expelled from the bottom after a meal of lentils and ale.

At first the Israelites found Elijah's antics to be amusing, but the amusement soon passed, and those in the camps below who were loyal to Yahweh were worried that this man, this prophet, this chosen one who spoke with the voice of Yahweh was playing the role of a fool. Their concern was increased when the Phoenicians no longer were amused by Elijah's antics, but instead ignored him.

And then the King and Queen of Israel arrived. He on horseback, lumbering slowly beside the chair on which Jezebel was transported by eight large, jet-black Ethiopian slaves. When they came to the foot of the hill, Ahab dismounted and walked to the side which Elijah had staked as his own; Jezebel walked over to the side of her priests and priestesses.

The people who looked carefully at her saw that while she smiled, her eyes revealed her troubled spirit. She was uneasy with the entire proceedings, and her concerns showed in her face. Her eyes darted from her priests and priestesses, to Elijah, then back again. This wasn't the confident woman who had stood before the citizenry of Ak-Kah and the other towns she'd visited on her progress into the land of Yahweh, and laid claim to the sovereignty of Israel by dance and magic; this was a woman struggling to hold on to power.

And if she was uneasy, then her mood began to descend on the people who had come to see the contest. In the years that Jezebel had ruled in Israel, she'd enabled the people to worship the idol gods publicly; what had always been a private and illicit pleasure for so many, had become manifest and acceptable. But now that Yahweh was challenging Ba'al and Asherah, so too were the actions of the Israelite people being challenged. If Yahweh won, it would be more than the Phoenician gods losing ... it would mean that the Israelite people had sinned, and in their sinning, they'd exposed themselves to the everlasting punishment of God; just as the Israelite people had been punished when they made the golden calf in the desert of Sinai, and had been punished by Yahweh from entering the Promised Land.

In the Queen's face was the image of their future ... and many people hoped and prayed that the Phoenician gods would win the day for then, too, their salvation would be assured.

Jezebel's husband, King Ahab, turned and shouted to the gathered multitude, 'People of Israel. People who have come from neighbouring countries. You will today witness a battle between the gods. Before you, lay two perfect beasts, oxen which have just been slaughtered. Both beasts have perfect skins and suffer no disease. They are fit offerings for the gods whom their priests represent. I now command the priests of Ba'al and Asherah and El to build their altars and to call upon their gods to light the flames. If their gods listen to their pleas then this will be proof of the existence and power of their gods, and a complete rebuttal of Elijah's claim that their gods do not exist. But if the ox is not consumed by fire, then Elijah will build his altar and call upon Yahweh to consume the ox of God. If this happens, then Yahweh will be God and all others will be false. That is my command.'

He turned to look up to where the priests and priestesses were standing and shouted, 'Let the building of the altar, and the god-offering, begin ...'

Jezebel bit her lip as her husband's words disappeared into the distance. In the month during which the challenge had been made known far and wide, she and her priests had thought through numerous ideas and ways of igniting the wood. Yet even though the origin of the desert fire-water was unknown in Israel, its effects had been seen by many people, and Jezebel knew with certainty that if she or her priests were to use it as a device, the people would rise up and challenge her gods. And so she was forced to believe Hamdael, her increasingly desperate chief priest of Ba'al, that the gods would not let them down on such an important occasion.

And so, sweating in the burning sun, Hamdael turned to his brother priests and priestesses, and whispered urgently, 'Begin to build the altar.' The male acolytes carried the large blocks of stone and

462

placed one on top of the other until an altar had been constructed. Priestesses carried kindling, then larger logs of wood, and arranged them so that, when the gods sent their lightning, the pile would ignite and the conflagration would enable the offering to be burnt and prove the existence and vitality of Ba'al and El and Asherah.

As they worked and sweated in the mid-morning sun, the distant voice of Elijah on the other side of the hill could be heard laughing in derision, shouting, 'Come on, hurry up with those stones, or your gods will fall asleep ... Is that the biggest pyre you can build? Let's see just a little puff of smoke to prove that somebody is awake in your gods' heaven ... Just something to show that there really is an El, and a Ba'al ... Or maybe he's gone on a journey and he's visiting Assyria or Babylonia ...'

Hamdael's anger grew the more that Elijah taunted them. In the end, he turned and exploded, 'Silence, you gibbering fool! Be quiet!'

But it merely served to inflame Elijah's mocking. 'Oh dear, if you want silence, it must mean that your gods are asleep. Shall I call on the host of Israel, those of us faithful to Yahweh, to shout a great shout and wake your gods up?' And he turned to the laughing crowd and screamed, 'Come on, Israel, let's all shout to wake up the great Phoenician gods ...'

But after a while only a handful of people continued to laugh, because what the prophet of Yahweh was doing soon wasn't seen as funny. For Elijah's success would be their loss. And that frightened many people.

Furious, Jezebel alighted from her chair and stormed up the hillside to Hamdael. Her face was a mask of frenzy. 'Do something. Now! Force this fool to eat his words. Call on Asherah to send lightning and ignite the ox. Do it now, Hamdael, before all Israel is drowned in his laughter.'

Hamdael looked at his Queen. 'Let me use the fire-water to start the fire, Jezebel. I can do it in such a way that nobody will see.'

But from the corner of her eye, she saw that Captain Jehu had followed her up the hillside and was watching intently for any sign of trickery.

She glared at her priest. 'Of course you can't, fool. The whole of Israel is watching. If you're seen to be using tricks, then the people will be so angry they'll send you back to Phoenicia, or they'll kill us all. Your job is to humiliate this jackal, to toss him into the air like chaff; make him eat the dirt on which he sleeps. Make him look stupid and imbecilic in front of all Israel. Do this for the gods who protect us and love us. I know in my very bones that Asherah has prevented us from using the fire-water. That means that she'll protect me, that she won't let me be ridiculed in front of this gathering. Do it!' Jezebel hissed. Then she retreated back to her chair, giving Captain Jehu a contemptuous look.

From a distance, Ahab watched the exchange. Earlier in the day, he'd met with the priests and priestesses to discuss what tactics they would use, and was surprised when he was told that they wouldn't be using the fire-water from the deserts of Moab in order to ignite the kindling. It worried him, but they explained their conclusions. And now he realised that they were right, for when he saw Captain Jehu standing so close to their activities and observing every action of the priests, Ahab knew that

Jehu and his men would immediately spot the deceit and report their actions to the people.

The King of Israel was distracted from his concerns by a sudden roar which erupted from the crowd. The Phoenician priests and priestesses had begun their chanting. The women began to dance around the altar, raising and lowering their hands and arms rhythmically and in tune to a harp and cymbals which were played by acolytes. The priestesses began their customary sycophancy and obeisance, beseeching the god to which they owed allegiance, while the priests looked on in support.

Hamdael looked at Jezebel, wondering whether to use the fire-water without her permission, but decided against it when he saw her face; it was transfixed in fury at the antics of Elijah, and she was earnestly praying for the intervention of the gods. He knew there was no point in doing what he knew in his heart had to be done. He just prayed to Ba'al for the day to finish as quickly as possible. And the one thing of which he was absolutely certain was that Yahweh would be as silent as were his own gods.

The people of Israel and its surrounding neighbours looked at the dancing in fascination. Most looked up into the cloudless sky, praying at any moment that a flash of lightning would descend and strike the wood; others stared at the naked breasts and rhythmic undulations of the priestesses' hips and strained forward for a better look.

But the devotions of the priests and priestesses were rudely interrupted by Elijah who began a constant wailing of his own, both to match, and at the same time to ridicule, the homage of the priests. Jezebel looked at what he was doing, and the fury, which was suppressed in her body, erupted into an outburst of great anger. Unlike the sycophancy of the priests, Elijah's mocking, leering, contemptuous and derisive behaviour was dividing the crowds. Some worshippers of Yahweh laughed and joined in the derision; but most who had pledged their bodies to Asherah and the love-giving priestesses, were frightened of their future.

The people's gaze shifted from the sincere and harmonious wailing and ululations of the holy men and women, to the caterwauling and unharmonious cacophony of the prophet of Yahweh, who danced around in a circle, alone, on his side of the hill, raising and lowering his arms in mockery of the priestesses. But the laughter was contagious, and soon the crowd was chortling with every ridiculing movement of the prophet.

How dare they laugh at Elijah's antics, the Queen thought, her outrage rising in tempo to his ridicule. How dare they look at him, rather than gaze in awe at the reverence of her priests! Jezebel's anger with her people exploded. She bounded off her chair, nearly upsetting it, and ran halfway up the hill. There, she turned and looked at a section of the crowd who realised that they shouldn't have been laughing and immediately became quiet under her stern stare.

But it didn't mollify her. She screamed at them, 'Are you fools that you laugh at the antics of this idiot? Are you little children amused at the games of a man who lives in the dirt? This is a man who sleeps on the side of a road; who lives in the desert; who takes carrion for his food; who lies to you about hearing the voice of Yahweh, and cheats and makes fun of the very gods themselves. This is a man who has been hiding from my vengeance since the day I first arrived in your country. This is a man who screamed insults at your future Queen when she was riding from Phoenicia to marry your Prince Ahab. Yet you laugh at this man. You allow him to ridicule my gods ... *our* gods. Haven't I brought you joy and pleasure in Asherah? Hasn't Israel been more prosperous and peaceful since Ba'al came down from Phoenicia with me? Don't the gods whom we worship in my country of Phoenicia now look after you as well? Yet you join with this dimwit, this idiot, in ridiculing the very gods who have been protecting you. You are the fools! You, the men and women of Israel. You are madmen and imbeciles and idiots like Elijah. I should have you all put to death for the insults you do to my gods ...'

She turned, and walked across to her astounded husband. In the background, high on the hill, the priests and priestesses of the Phoenician gods were continuing to invoke lightning from the sky, but Jezebel could see on their faces a look of growing desperation; there was no response to their pleas, yet they were doing everything as they knew it should be done.

As Jezebel drew close to Ahab, he whispered to her, 'Are you mad? You know the dangers of what's happening. Whatever occurs, we must applaud the success of the winning god, whether it's yours, or Israel's. How could you be so stupid as to castigate our people? How could you insult them? What's going to happen when things go wrong? When lightning doesn't set fire to Ba'al's offering? We both know that the gods won't send lightning, don't we?

We've been praying for an end to this drought, and the gods haven't heard ...'

'Neither has Yahweh,' she said.

'I know. But you haven't taken the precaution you should. You haven't soaked the wood in the desert water which makes the fire. And why? Because in your heart, you're still expecting the lightning to strike, aren't you? Well, now you'll have to pay the price for your faith in the gods.'

She hissed at him, 'My gods will win!'

He saw tears beginning to well up in her eyes; and he saw a woman ... a girl ... whom he'd never before met. Here was an insecure girl, a young woman beset by anxiety: gone was the commanding Jezebel; gone the Jezebel who entranced him in his bedchamber; gone the Jezebel who had thrilled the people of Israel with her dances and her fire-water; gone the woman who had made the people of Israel sing with the songs of the body ... she was gone. And in her place was a young girl, a daughter, insecure and putting on the brave face of confidence to mask her fears.

Ahab wanted to put his arms around his wife, and protect her. But since their marriage, she'd embarked on a path which would inevitably lead to a challenge such as this. If only he hadn't been so consumed by lust and love and been like dough in her hands; if only he'd been more like his father and looked at her with the eyes of experience and reality! And so the path was set, and they were treading towards its inevitable conclusion; well, at least Ahab was confident that, despite all his nonsense and cavorting, Elijah would have no hope of invoking the wrath of Yahweh, that no lightning would strike Elijah's ox.

But the interruption to the Phoenician priests

continued unabated. Jezebel's outburst merely spurred Elijah on to even greater sarcasm. It was as though he had suddenly discovered something at which he'd never known he was talented and was exhibiting his skills in public for the first time, rising in confidence and stature as the moments rolled past. He jumped up and down on the invisible dividing line between his holy ground and theirs. He pointed and jeered. He called out, 'Where's your fire, gods and goddesses? Surely it isn't so hot today that you don't need some extra fire? What about a small bit of lightning? Just a single streak to light up the sky. That's all. Just a bit of lightning to prove you're there. Or are you still asleep? Shall I tell the people of Israel to keep quiet so that we don't disturb you?'

And at his sarcasm, despite the danger from the fury of the Queen, many of the men and women who stood closest to Elijah laughed out loud, in open defiance of the Phoenicians. Other Israelites, praying for a sign from their new gods, looked disconsolate and forlorn. And frightened!

And so the priests and priestesses continued their dancing and pleadings as the sun arched above their heads from the Mountains of Moab towards the Eternal Sea. And as they waited and waited for something to happen on the side of the Phoenicians, the people of Israel sat down under their sunshades and continued to wait; some went to sleep in the hot and still air; others wandered away, vowing to return if anything of interest suddenly happened; still others walked to the nearby brook to bathe their feet, wash their hot faces and hands, and drink to refresh themselves. Children, who had been playing games until well past the middle of the day, were now querulous and wanted to go home. Men and women who had been praying publicly to Asherah and Ba'al during the past four years, talked about how to bring themselves back into the ambit of Yahweh.

All the while, Jezebel sat in her chair under the shade of the cloth with increasing despondency, staring at the glistening skin of her priestesses, watching their chests heave in their exertion, still dancing around the altar, still trying to invoke their gods to send down lightning. But the more they danced, the more impatience and frustration and intensity they put into their devotions, the less the sky looked as though it would open up and send down the lightning for which they were praying so fervently. And all the while in the background, Elijah's mocking laughter and invective continued unabated.

And then Elijah suddenly changed. He noticed that people were beginning to drift away, bored by the spectacle. Now was the time for him to unleash his fury. Suddenly he fell down onto the ground and screamed at the top of his rasping voice, 'You have failed, you harlots and whoremasters of Ba'al and Asherah and the other rank and stinking and pestilential gods of other lands. You have had long enough. Your gods are false. You are false. The judgement of the Lord Yahweh be upon you. I curse you and condemn you and now you will see the full power and majesty of the one true God.'

The moment he spoke the lethargy which had come upon the people disappeared. They looked at the changed behaviour of the prophet of Yahweh, and their attention was riveted. Suddenly he stood up from his position on the ground. It was a different man who appeared before them now. No longer a gibbering idiot; this was a man of God; this was the Elijah which they had feared whenever he arrived in a city; this was the man who threatened them and their land with damnation unless they repented and turned their eyes only to Yahweh. Moments earlier, Elijah had been like a child's puppet, a maniac dancing and shouting. Now he arose from the ground and stood stock-still like a rock, pointing an accusing finger at the Phoenicians, finding them guilty of failing to invoke a miracle.

Jezebel sat in horror at the change which suddenly came over him. This, she knew, was a very dangerous enemy. Only moments ago, her chief priest, Hamdael, had been assuring her that the signs were positive, that he was certain the gods would soon respond to their pleadings. Yet now Elijah had motivated the crowds to gather and turn their attention away from the gods of Phoenicia and to turn to the altar which he had started to build for Yahweh.

Like a master of the ceremonies of the court, Elijah turned to the crowd, and shouted in a holy and sententious voice, 'The Lord God commanded me to gather twelve large stones, each one representing the twelve tribes of Israel, the children of our father Jacob. These I shall place together in harmony and concord as an altar. On these, I shall place my wood, and on my wood I shall place the ox, which the Lord God of Heaven, Yahweh, will consume and eat and in His goodness, He will smile upon the people who worship Him. Then the Phoenicians, who have stolen your hearts, prostituted your bodies and forced your eyes to turn away from the Eternal One, will see the might and majesty of Yahweh, and they will be afraid. And we people of Israel will pour scorn on their heads, we will stone them until every abomination in the sight of the Lord is dead.'

Elijah turned and walked towards the large rocks which he had placed in a pile in the early morning. He struggled to lift one stone after another, but even though his robes were torn in the effort, even though his skin sweated in the heat of the afternoon sun and his skin was scratched red raw from the roughness of the stones, he would allow no one to help him. Those who approached were told to remove themselves from the place, because, said Elijah, it was a holy place like Mount Sinai, and God would soon be at the place. Only Elijah, His chosen prophet, the mouth which said His words, could tread upon the ground.

The priests and priestesses of Phoenicia watched his efforts. They sat and lay on the ground panting, exhausted from their dancing, finally conceding that their gods and goddesses had not heeded their pleas. They were glad of the rest, but apprehensive of what would happen. They looked at each other, shaking their heads in sorrow at their failure. Their chief priest, Hamdael, looked in shame and regret towards Jezebel, but she was transfixed by the activities of Elijah.

When the stones had been arranged as an altar, Elijah gathered up bundles of wood. He appeared to be arranging them carefully in a particular pattern. Hamdael and the other priests looked at what he was doing, trying to discern if there was a secret to the arrangement of the stones or the wood which might give them a clue as to where they might have gone wrong. But the prophet of Yahweh deliberately kept his back to them and all the people gathered, and all they could do was try to work out if there were cryptic symbols in the arrangement.

What nobody saw, not Jehu whose eyes had concentrated on Jezebel, not Jezebel, nor Ahab, nor Hamdael, nor any of the crowd, was Elijah removing a small stone jar hidden inside one of the bundles of wood which he placed on the altar of stones. Elijah took out the stopper, and the pungent aroma of the desert fire liquid which he'd clandestinely obtained the previous month from a merchant sworn to secrecy, arose and invaded his nose, insulting his sense of smell. With hands weaving in and out of the wood, and speaking in loud and unintelligible imprecations, Elijah spilled the fire-water from the desert all over the kindling, masking what he was doing in the same way as the Egyptian magicians masked their trickery.

When enough of the kindling wood was drenched in the fire-water, he picked up the young ox, which, though small, still weighed almost more than he could carry. With a struggle, he managed to hoist the carcass up onto the wood. From a secret compartment sewn into his tunic, hidden from everybody, Elijah removed a piece of clear, polished mica which was fine and sufficiently transparent to focus the rays of the sun. He balanced it in a niche which he'd previously carved in a stone that he had placed on top of the altar. Now all was set.

He stepped away from the altar so that he couldn't be accused of trickery. When he was close to the people at the bottom of the hill, he began to shout prayers to Yahweh, and, unlike the Phoenicians, didn't dance and sing and play, but stayed where he was, his back turned to the people. And he prayed earnestly that the mica which he'd surreptitiously positioned so that the light from the sun shone through it, would concentrate its beams into a fine point of brilliance which he focused onto the area of wood soaked in the desert fire-water.

He turned, and faced the people, his back towards the still and silent altar on top of the hill in the distance.

'Israel,' he shouted, 'say after me, "Yahweh is God".'

And as one, the entire audience shouted back, 'Yahweh is God.'

'Say again,' he screamed, ' "Yahweh is the true God of Israel".'

And they did! They all shouted and yelled, 'Yahweh is the true God of Israel.'

'Shout that all the other gods are false!'

But instead of a shout, there was a gasp. For a thin wisp of smoke suddenly appeared high on the hill, from deep within the pile of kindling wood. And the wisp grew in volume and density just moments prior to the wood bursting into flame with a roar which made the entire host of Israel gasp and reel back in awe and wonder. Elijah instantly threw himself to the ground, and shouted, 'Here O Israel, is the power of Yahweh. Here is the strength of your God. By my faith and love of Yahweh, I have begged Him in prayer to come to earth as a burning bush, like the bush which burnt for our father Moses, and showed him the way to release the children of Israel from their slavery in Egypt. Now I too will be the mouth of God, and I will release you, Israel, from the slavery of the false gods which this whore and harlot Queen has forced you to worship. Hear, O Israel, the Lord your God, the Lord is One. Death to the false idols of Phoenicia!'

The people of Israel at the bottom of the hill, and

in fields around the hill, fell to their knees in amazement. Jezebel's eyes stared in astonishment, then fury at the insults which he had heaped upon her. And then suddenly the truth dawned on her with the force of an arrow flying towards a target. At that moment, Jezebel realised that the false and lying prophet Elijah had used the same device that she herself could, would, should, have used to ignite her pyre and make a burnt offering to her gods. But it was too late. She could say, and do, nothing. For to denounce him, to unveil his trickery, would be to denounce herself and her priests for the tricks they, themselves, had played on the people of Israel. And who would believe her now.

Jezebel was trapped both by his deceit and by her own faith in Asherah. She had done so much for this people Israel. She had built buildings, given money to the poor, increased the rations from the King's granary, and made all Israel smile. Yet this old and evil man, this Elijah, was about to bring her and her priests down through trickery.

Ahab was speechless. His jaw sagged open as he looked at the ox on Elijah's altar, its flesh beginning to bubble and singe, its skin curling, mimicking life as its legs moved when its sinews contracted. It looked as though it was full of the spirit of the Lord. And the whole area became suffused with the divine smell of burning ox flesh. The people shouted and clapped and whistled. Some knelt down and prayed, others kissed their neighbours or sang prayers. Some Israelites who had renounced Yahweh turned and ran from the field of their defeat. But nobody's eyes were any longer on the priests and priestesses of the gods of Phoenicia.

Not, that is, until Elijah stood from his abasement, turned towards them, pointed, and screamed, 'Kill them! Kill the false priests of the false gods. Stone them. Pick up rocks and stones and destroy them. I have made a covenant with Yahweh that He would come to earth and show Himself at the altar if we, His people, would cleanse His land of the filth and perversions and lies and falsehoods and prostitution of these false gods. Now, people of Israel, now is the time to excise these evil men and women, to pluck them from your breasts and cast them into the pits of the damned for the lepers that they are.'

Elijah was the first to pick up a rock and hurl it at Hamdael. It missed and rolled harmlessly down the hill, but it galvanised the others in the crowd to stoop down and pick up the many rocks and stones which littered the hillside. They began to shout abuse and curse and throw rocks at the priests and priestesses. Terrified, the eight hundred men and women in white robes who had tended to their gods began to run. But they were surrounded by Israelites, some of whom were furious that the gods they had been seduced into worshipping were shown to be powerless and false; some who had remained faithful to Yahweh and were now intent upon wreaking vengeance upon idolators who had prostituted the sanctity of their Holy Land.

In horror, Jezebel watched as her hundreds of priests and priestesses ran in utter terror this way and that. They screamed as the rocks began to rain down on them, priestesses dropped to their knees, shouting out the name of Asherah and El; priests tried to gather them up and protect them but as the rocks hit their arms and legs and tore at their flesh, they too began to drop onto the ground. For there was no escape. The crowd of Israelites made a solid wall, a barricade against escape. And Jezebel suddenly realised that she, too, was in grave danger. She looked at Ahab, her eyes searching for help, but he was transfixed by the burning altar, by the sudden appearance of Yahweh; by the way in which Elijah was standing there, looking at him in contempt, a look which said that the King had no future.

Ahab stared at his nemesis. He had no eyes for his wife, Jezebel.

She turned to the captain of her guard, and commanded, 'Do something!'

But he forced her onto her chair, and it was picked up by her slaves and carried away.

'Stop!' she commanded.

But her guards didn't obey, their duty was to the safety of their Queen.

'Stop immediately. I must save my …'

Her words were drowned out by the anger of the people as they were forced to part ways for her to leave. Despite her protests, she was hurriedly escorted from the hill, leaving her husband and priests and priestesses to the judgement of the Israelite people.

Encouraged by an increasingly hysterical Elijah who saw victory almost within his grasp, the crowd searched for more and more rocks and hurled them with greater fury at the priests and priestesses. Once-white robes were now stained with blood. One priestess yelped and clutched her head, falling to the ground beneath the feet of others trying to escape, causing them to fall over her. The screaming and begging of the priests and priestesses increased in desperation, but it only seemed to incite the Israelites to higher and higher levels of anger and violence.

And throughout the melee, as the rocks and stones flew towards the hapless and whimpering priests and priestesses, the aroma of Yahweh could be smelled throughout His domain. The burnt offering, the ox which had been placed upon His altar, was burning and singeing, and the fats and juices were running into the wood causing the flames to leap even higher into the air, as though trying to reach the very heavens themselves. Dense smoke rose from Yahweh's altar and seduced the hungry crowd to an extreme level of fury with the Phoenician gods, who had made so many promises to them, which had turned out to be so false, so empty.

Now some distance from the danger of what was happening to her priests and priestesses, Jezebel called the captain of her guard to come to her side. She shouted to him, 'Go back, and put a stop to this immediately. Arrest and kill the Israelites who throw stones at my priests. I command you. Cut them down with swords; kill them with your bows and arrows ...'

'Lady,' interrupted the captain, '... if I send my soldiers against this crowd, they'll be massacred.'

'I don't care,' she shouted. 'We must save the lives of my ...'

'No! You will return to the palace!' said a commanding voice.

Jezebel turned in anger and saw her husband Ahab standing there. He had descended the hill and was standing on the other side of her chair. She got off her chair, and faced him in hurt and outrage.

'I can't allow my priests and priestesses to be slaughtered by this mob. They're my friends. I brought them to this land. Look ...' she said, crying out as another priestess was hit on the head by a rock and fell down, screaming in pain.

'There's nothing we can do,' shouted Ahab over the noise of the Israelites, now wild with blood lust.

'If you won't, I will,' she screamed, and turned to run up the hill. As she ran through the crowd, something within her told her that because of the good things she'd done for the Israelites they would listen to her appeal to stop throwing stones if she intervened. She would ascend the hill to be with her friends, she would put up her arms, protect them, command the Israelites to stop throwing stones. She would tell them that everything would be all right, that there was a simple explanation; she would tell them about the fire-water from the desert, and ...

A burly soldier threw himself at her, and knocked her to the ground. Winded, she struggled for breath. 'I'm sorry, Highness, but King Ahab ordered me to ...' And he picked her up as though she was a child's toy, and carried her back down the hill to her furious husband.

'You will return to the palace immediately. You will remain in your chambers until I call for you. You are meddling with forces which you cannot possibly understand. You've done enough damage to the House of Omri, my father. Now go!'

The look on his face told Jezebel that he could not be argued with. She had never, ever, seen him so furious. And she knew why. For both he as King and she as Queen had been made fools of by Yahweh. Elijah now had more power than either of them. Ahab's kingship was under dire threat. Elijah's victory, Elijah's trickery, could lead to their overthrow.

Ahab obviously realised the implications of the immediate danger to him and his reign. He looked up the hill at the fury of the multitudes and their attacks on the priests and priestesses and realised that nothing must be done to stop it. He saw Jezebel's face, hating him for doing nothing to protect her friends, but he said to the captain of the guard, 'You will do nothing. The people are taking revenge. This is as it was promised by Elijah before Yahweh and before the people of Israel. This is how it will be.'

Wide-eyed, like a trapped fawn, Jezebel stared at the husband she didn't recognise.

He continued, 'They invoked the gods. The gods didn't answer. They must die. And they will die by the hand of Israel. That is my command.'

In despair, Jezebel looked up the hill one last time to where her priests and priestesses were falling like leaves in a gale. Some were trying to defend themselves against the rain of rocks; others were lying still, or their bodies were twitching; still others showed hideous red stains on their robes, blood pouring from gaping wounds in their heads and arms and legs and bodies.

Jezebel couldn't watch any longer as those men and women she viewed as her true friends in this merciless and godforsaken land were ploughed into the ground by a crowd which seemed to be increasing in its fury as their enemies fell. She shouted an order to her guards to return to the city where she ruled. The crowd turned and looked at her and her husband, below them at the base of the hill, seeing that they were running away from their humiliation. In their faces, she could see their ridicule and contempt. There was no love for her. Only loathing. And as she retreated from the battleground, leaving defeat where there should have been her victory, she smelled the success of Elijah.

The rich aroma of Yahweh's victory stayed with Jezebel as she retreated, and was in her nostrils long after she was no longer able to hear the screaming and the pleasure of her people, her Israel.

It was seven days before Jezebel came out of her apartments and again showed herself in the corridors of her palace; seven days before she obeyed the command of her husband Ahab to appear before him; seven days of silence in which the young woman felt alone, abandoned, like a child once again, pacing the floor of her bedchamber as she once waited in fear and trepidation in her father's palace for one of his wives to determine her fate.

And for seven days she plotted her revenge against her mortal enemy, Elijah, the man who had ruined her marriage, her priesthood, her growing warmth with her people Israel, and her happiness. Elijah had outsmarted her. He had used the same trickery in lighting the altar pyre as she should have used, but neither she nor her chief priest, the now-deceased Hamdael, could find a way.

And because she had been unable to think of a way of lighting the pyre, Jezebel had been forced to put her faith in the gods. They'd never before let her down. Why, then, had they failed her so miserably during her time of need, during the trial which would have proven their strength?

Elijah had been cleverer than she, for he had refused to trust in Yahweh. In the end, both of them were let down by their gods. Her own gods didn't appear on earth, and Yahweh certainly hadn't sent a bolt of lightning to ignite the pyre. Or had He? For she had seen no flame from the sky, yet suddenly the pyre had burst into light. Maybe Yahweh had come to earth ... but how could Jezebel believe that Yahweh was stronger or more willing to help His people than Ba'al and El and Asherah were to help her?

It had taken her seven days to calm down, but now was the time for her to re-establish her hold on her kingdom. Now was the time to take Hattusas' advice; for the people hated her and she was told that they were ridiculing her in the marketplaces. They had transferred their allegiance to Yahweh and away from Ba'al and Asherah. The temple was crowded, the priests of Yahweh were crowing. Those asherahs which she'd built were either abandoned, or had been destroyed by villagers led by some screaming maniac who denounced the goddess of Phoenicia.

Hattusas warned her of the precariousness of her position; and she listened to him. Determined, Jezebel walked down the corridor with its rough-hewn cream plaster and its featureless emptiness – Oh! How today she missed the vivid reds and blues and yellows and greens of the murals of her father's palaces in Sidon and Tyre – and ordered the guards to throw open the doors of the throne room. There she saw Ahab in counsel with his advisors. In the past, she had taken an active interest in the counsels when Ahab was dealing with the situations which confronted his country. But now she simply didn't care what happened to his horrible little land. It could burn to ash in the hot sun as far as she was concerned. But of one thing she was certain. She would wrest back control from Ahab and his counsellors, and then she would run things; and Elijah would be the first to feel her wrath and would be punished for the death of her priests and priestesses.

Ahab looked up from a large map he was studying. He frowned when she approached. With a calculated coldness and authority in his voice, he said, 'I'm in conference. I will talk with you later.' It was as though he were conversing with one of his servants.

Jezebel shrugged, and walked over to the cushions which had been placed near to the pool in the centre of the room. She removed her sandals, and dangled her feet in the water.

'Jezebel, I said I'll attend to you later.'

She paid Ahab no attention. But she heard him dismiss his counsellors and walk over to her. 'How dare you ignore my commands for a week, and then disturb me when I'm in the middle of border problems with the Arameans. In my father's day you would have been sent to the dungeons ...'

'You're not your father. You're weak and stupid. How dare you allow Elijah to slaughter so many of my priests and priestesses.'

'I allowed no such thing. I had no say ...'

'You could have stopped him. You have an army. He's one man ...' she screamed.

'How could I possibly stop him? My army would have refused to move against a man who invokes Yahweh to do his bidding. To have gone against him would have caused a revolt. I can't be seen to go against the word, or the deeds, of the Lord. I would have been slaughtered along with the priests if I'd raised a hand to stop him – if not by the army, then by the people. You saw their mood.'

'Well if you're too weak, then I, at least, intend to stand up to this man.'

Ahab remained silent, waiting for Jezebel to explain her meaning.

'I intend to put an end to Elijah's mischief for ever. If you, my husband, are too stupid to kill him, the man who insults your Queen and wife, then I shall.'

'Touch him, and I'll have you thrown into a dungeon. I can't protect you if you raise a hand against Elijah; not now. He's travelling around the land ordering this and that … he has ten times the power of a chief priest, and today he has more power than the King. The people are forced to listen to him; some even love him because he cleansed the temple of foreign gods; they're calling him a second Moses, and me a Pharaoh. Understand, Jezebel, that I can't move against him. He's …'

'I don't expect you to defeat him … or even to stop him. I'll do that. I'll put an end to his posturing …'

'And how do you intend to do that …?'

Jezebel smiled. 'Simple. I'm going to send a messenger to where he's staying. I've sent out word to find him. He might be in some village, or with the chief priest of the temple. But wherever he is, he'll receive my message. It'll be a simple message. He will be told that by the time the sun goes down today, I, a Phoenician, a woman he hates, will have him killed. I could just send a servant to the temple and have him killed, but I want him to anticipate his death; I want him to know that it's me who will be killing him, so that when the dagger strikes and slices into his heart, the last thing on his mind will be Jezebel. I've waited long enough for you to avenge the insult done to me. Now I will act.'

Ahab drew back in horror. 'Are you mad? Have you no understanding of the danger my kingship is in? Kill Elijah and we'll both die at the hands of the Israelite people. They'll never permit it. If they don't rise up in revolt, then I'll have a war on my hands with Judah. Elijah is a hero of Yahweh in all the lands. King Asa will march north. He's the protector of … Elijah is a prophet of Yahweh …' He struggled for words.

'Of course I can kill him. I'll put an end to him. And if some of the people rise up against me, then I'll command my army to put them down; I'll ask my father Ethbaal to send me troops. It'll be quite simple,' she said, sounding almost ingenuous.

Ahab looked at her in amazement. Then Jezebel stood, water dripping from her feet and the hem of her garment where it had trailed in the pool. She turned on Ahab. He was taken aback by her mood. She was calm, but determined. He thought that she had come to him in a state of contrition and apology; how wrong he was. Hands firmly on hips, she said, 'There are many in Israel who love me, and who love the life I gave them; many who are sad to see my asherahs destroyed, many who would not be upset to see him killed.

'For the past seven days, those of my priests and priestesses who managed to stay alive have been in hiding throughout the country, terrified of coming out into the light in case some crazed Israelite kills them. Those asherahs which weren't destroyed are lying empty. There are no prostitutes to amuse the people any more. Where once there were hundreds and thousands of Israelite men and women every day going to my asherahs to pray with my priests and priestesses and enjoy the benefits which Asherah conferred on them, now they go home to their husbands and wives and have to face that misery. How long do you think the people will be happy worshipping a cold and thankless god like Yahweh?'

'What?' Ahab said in amazement. 'Do you think that the entire family of Israel relies for its happiness on having sex with your priestesses? Have you forgotten that we're the chosen people? For hundreds of years, we haven't needed sacred prostitutes or anybody to improve the happiness of our people. Yet in the space of less than five years, you've ...'

'We ...' she said angrily. 'We introduced our people to the joys of Ba'al and Asherah. We did, Ahab. You, as much as me, enjoyed their many gifts. Don't talk to me about the benefits which Yahweh can offer Israel. Where were the smiles on people's faces when I first became their Queen? Before this challenge, people flocked to my asherahs. Now ...'

Ahab tried to argue, but Jezebel held up her hand to silence him. 'I will command Elijah's wife, Rizpah, to attend me. It is she who will deliver the message.'

She turned to walk away from Ahab, but then she stopped. She remained standing for some time, and Ahab didn't understand what was wrong. Even after four years of marriage, he still couldn't understand her. Slowly she turned. There was a smile on her face which he'd only ever seen a few times in the past, and that was when she was playing the role of a Queen, when she was in council and using her womanly seductions and guile to get her own way.

'Ahab, my King. Yahweh has won a great victory. The people must know of our feelings. We must be as one with our people. We must show that we welcome the victory.'

He looked at her in astonishment. But instead of

explaining, she said to the captain of the Palace Guard, 'Send messengers out to the people of Samaria; order them to gather in the marketplace at noon. Tell them that their King and the Queen will make an announcement about the victory of Yahweh.' And she turned and left.

The crowd was enormous; there were heads as far as the eye could see. Everyone had come, intensely curious to see Jezebel for the first time after the stunning defeat of her gods, wondering what she and Ahab would say. And they weren't disappointed. She emerged, regal and haughty, onto the palace balcony followed by Ahab. Some in the crowd booed, others laughed, but most wanted to listen. And most intensely curious of all was Ahab, who had no idea how the people would react to what his wife was about to say.

To the surprise of the people, it was Jezebel rather than Ahab who stepped forward, and held up her hands for silence. 'Men and women of Israel. A week ago, the prophet Elijah won a great and magnificent victory for Yahweh over the gods of Phoenicia. We, your King and Queen, congratulate him. This proves that Yahweh is indeed a powerful god. It proves that Yahweh is a god who loves to show His strength. Who loves His people Israel so much that He has banished from your land the gods whom you once loved and who brought so many of you such happiness. And in banishing these gods of Phoenicia which I brought with me, Yahweh is saying that He, and He alone, is the one and only God. To prove this, He encouraged you, the people of Israel to kill my many priests and priestesses.

'Well, men and women of Israel! Yahweh is now the one and only God. And it is for Him and Him alone to ensure the peace and happiness of every one of you. For that is what we expect of God, isn't it? He will make it rain. He will make the crops grow. He will cure diseases in our fathers and mothers and children. He will no longer allow cattle to die and lambs to be born weak and sickly. He will make the rivers of Israel flow strong and powerful, even when the sun is shining.

'Yahweh has proven that He is the strongest of all the gods. Very well, then from this moment onwards, let Yahweh look after all of us. Go back to your homes, men and women of Israel. Thanks to Yahweh, all of you will now be rich and healthy and never hungry nor thirsty. From this moment onwards, I order that the colonies of lepers be closed and that lepers will walk amongst us, for Yahweh will cure all diseases; I order that no grain is to be released from the royal granaries, nor oil from the royal storehouses, and given to the poor, because from now onwards, there will be no poor; Yahweh will cure all poverty. Do not look any longer to your King and Queen to feed you and love you and protect you, for Yahweh will do all those things. No, don't look towards your royal family any longer, people of Israel. Look to your priests for comfort, for Yahweh has told your King and Queen that He and He alone understands the welfare of His people.

'Go to the temple and demand of the priests of Yahweh that they feed you, clothe you, heal you, cure you. Go to the temple, and tell the priests to pray to Yahweh to cure the lepers who will now be walking amongst you ... and most of all, men and women of

Israel, demand of the priests of Yahweh that their one and only God gives you the same love and devotion and happiness as you enjoyed when Asherah and Ba'al were the gods who protected you.

'And if, in the coming weeks and months, you find that your life is as mean and hard and unbearable as it was before Yahweh showed Himself to be the only God for Israel, then think about the joy you experienced when other gods shared your land …'

And she turned, and went back into the palace, leaving the people to disperse, thinking about what she said. And then the horror dawned on them – lepers would be walking amongst them …

Jezebel left her Lord and Master, and King and husband alone with his people, in a way which no Israelite Queen had ever done before. It was left to the King to dismiss the crowd. She returned to her apartments to make the arrangements for Rizpah to act as the dagger which would strike at Elijah's black heart.

As the crowd dispersed, Ahab didn't move … he remained rooted to the spot, alone on the balcony, with the world changing moment by moment around him. Would her guile work? Would the people now make demands of the temple which the priests couldn't possibly match? What would happen when the lepers left their isolated valleys and walked amongst the people? What would be the future?

He'd witnessed, and failed to prevent, the destruction of the foreign gods. Despite knowing about Elijah's deception, for the last week King Ahab believed firmly and totally that Yahweh alone would rule the land; that he would have to share his kingdom with the priests of the temple who for the past seven days had been strutting around the city like lions. But Jezebel's speech, simple yet duplicitous, might change things ... might make the people ponder the victory and wonder whether or not they were the winners.

Should he try to stop this wonderful and terrible woman? Should he allow her to continue along the path she was taking and put an end once and for all to the interference of priests to the running of Israel? Should he follow her advice and welcome in the armies of Phoenicia, and gain from their strength? There was so much he wanted to do. And in so many ways, Elijah was the barrier which stopped him doing it. If Elijah were put to death, things would be ... but he forced his mind to stop thinking these things. To kill Elijah now, after a victory which was being hailed from north to south and east to west, would be madness.

Ahab's mind was aflame with the problems he was facing – problems with the King of Judah who wanted the Temple in Samaria to be cleansed of the worship of foreign gods; problems with the kings of countries on Israel's borders who saw the victory of Yahweh as weakening Ahab's kingship; problems with the priests of Yahweh and many of the leading people of Samaria who were clamouring to benefit from Yahweh's sudden appearance the week before on the mount of Carmel; and now problems with his wife.

Would the problems of kingship never end? When he was growing up in the house of Omri his father, he had so admired the way in which his father commanded, and people obeyed. But now, he realised, it was all an illusion. Kingship was all about treading the course which would do the least harm and damage. And power? The more powerful he was, the less power he held. Like the love of a woman, it was all vanity.

CHAPTER NINETEEN

It was the most terrifying moment of her life. She had known terror many times since Jezebel first came to the throne, but not terror like this ... for there was a finality about this young woman's words which was the sentence of death. On previous occasions her fear had been greater than the import of Jezebel's words, but now the young Queen's words were without subterfuge, without feeling. Cold, hard and calculating.

Since that first day when she'd been dragged from her cousin's home to meet with her new Queen, Rizpah had been prey to many different feelings. At moments in her peculiar relationship with Jezebel she had felt partly in awe of the power which this woman held. But while she'd been forced to play the part of mother, of sister, of best friend, she'd always been a loyal subject of Israel. Loyal, but never subservient, for whenever Jezebel had asked a question, Rizpah had answered honestly and without guile, even if she knew that the answer would anger the young Queen. And it was her searing honesty which enabled Jezebel to trust her.

Jezebel had shown Rizpah an extraordinary amount

of leeway; other servants in the palace were amazed that she hadn't immediately killed the wife and children of her hated enemy, Elijah. Yet for reasons which Rizpah assumed were to do with some undefinable bond which had grown between the two women, Jezebel more often treated her as a loyal subject, even a confidante and friend, than as part of the enemy.

Yet Jezebel was a woman of many shades and often a remark one day would be treated differently from the same remark the next. Rizpah had once asked Hattusas why the Queen was so different to her from one day to the next. The old counsellor had smiled and replied that few could fathom the mind of a king, and fewer still the mind of a king who was a woman. Rizpah hadn't understood his words then, and as time went on, the logic of what was happening to her seemed more and more remote. She felt like a child's plaything, picked up in one moment of exuberance, put down the next and ignored for weeks on end.

As Rizpah stood in her Queen's apartments, waiting for Jezebel to make an appearance, she didn't know which role she was expected to play. Her heart was pounding because of the uncertainty of what lay ahead. She had been sent without further word to a small chamber close to the Queen's private apartments in the palace. She'd been left alone all morning, and now, in the middle of the afternoon, she was dragged into Jezebel's rooms.

Suddenly the door to the inner chamber was thrown open and Rizpah was ushered into Queen Jezebel's chamber where the young woman was in her bath, having her back scrubbed by a huge black-skinned woman, a new slave whom Rizpah hadn't seen before. Jezebel's body was turned away from her, and the black-skinned woman continued to rub oils and perfumed salves into Jezebel's back and shoulders and neck, the only sound in the room being the gentle splash of water, like the noises from the shore of a river. Rizpah had rarely seen a naked woman before, and only ever in this palace. Now she was seeing two, the tall black-skinned woman and Jezebel.

At some unseen sign, the black-skinned slave stopped what she was doing, and fetched a linen shroud which she draped around Jezebel's shoulders. Jezebel stepped from the small pool and walked across to a chair, where she sat. Rizpah felt a shock as she could clearly see Jezebel's body through the wet linen.

Two other servants approached the Queen and began rubbing oils and perfumes into her still-wet body. Jezebel seemed to feel no embarrassment about her nakedness, and looked at Rizpah with eyes which told the older woman nothing. Now Rizpah felt a deep and terrifying concern: this was a new Jezebel ... a Jezebel who was neither friend nor foe, but one who was completely without compassion.

The young Queen continued to look at her in silence. Nobody had seen the Queen for the seven days after Elijah had ridiculed the gods of Phoenicia; then she had suddenly appeared on the balcony and challenged the priests again, causing not anger among the people, but fear; now, suddenly, the wife of the prophet had been called to the Queen's presence, and Rizpah was stunned by the indifference in her face. It was as though she didn't know her ... as though they had never met.

And Rizpah, desperate to look away from the

glistening skin of the naked young woman, to take her eyes off her nemesis, knew with absolute certainty that she must not flinch, must not allow her eyes to be anywhere but looking into the eyes of her Queen.

Slowly, in a calculated voice of grave ill-humour, Jezebel said, 'You are aware that last week your husband Elijah murdered almost eight hundred of my priests and priestesses. He has caused me great pain. He has insulted my gods and goddesses. It is my desire that he be put to death.'

Jezebel waited for the reaction, but Rizpah surprised her; for Jezebel had threatened her husband with death before. So Rizpah waited for the rest of the Queen's decision, which she knew would be coming ...

'I know that he now lives with the priests in the great Temple of Samaria; that he gloats and postures and struts like a cock bird before his new bride, Israel. I want you to tell him that his Queen, Jezebel of Israel, commands him to be here. When he arrives, I shall force him to bow down and kiss my idol Asherah. I shall then put him to death, knowing that he has turned his face from Yahweh. Yes, he will die. But not immediately. Not quickly, but slowly, like he forced my priests and priestesses to die slowly and painfully, broken by the rocks which your people threw at them, breaking their arms and legs and making them die a painful death in the boiling sun, the blood and life draining from their shattered bodies.'

Ashen, Rizpah stared at Jezebel. She shook her head, stunned by the awful finality of the words. 'I will not turn my husband from Yahweh!'

'Then you will die.'

Rizpah remained silent.

'And your children also will die.'

Again the older woman refused to speak. By now, she knew Jezebel well enough to know that her words carried more than their apparent meaning.

'Aren't you afraid of what I'm saying?' the Queen asked.

Rizpah shook her head. 'Since you became Queen, I have been a dead woman. From time to time, you have shown me friendship and warmth and helped me, but there was always something more that you wanted from me than I was able to give you. If my time has now come, then I will accept my death … and that of my family.'

Jezebel frowned. She rose from the chair letting the linen shroud fall to the ground. She was naked, her body firm and lithe and glistening with oils. It was as though she hadn't heard Rizpah's refusal, the signing of her own death warrant; as though no matter what Rizpah said, the Queen had another, truer, course which she was following. 'But death is so unnecessary,' she said conspiratorially, 'especially when, between women such as us, there's often another way.'

Rizpah hardly dared to breathe. What did this strange and alien woman want from her? 'What way?' she whispered.

'Go to your Elijah and tell him that his Queen wishes him to be dead. That his Queen hates him and detests him and wants him alive no more. And when he is in a state of terror, then tell him that his Queen rules only over Israel, but that she has no spies that can kill him in Egypt. Tell him that the only path of safety is for him to leave this land, to go as far away as possible, and never to return. He disobeyed me once, and came back. Then he was protected by Captain Jehu. I was powerless to kill him then. But this time I will be obeyed. This time, if I fail to kill him and he escapes and never comes back to plague my land and kingdom again, then my wrath will be satisfied.'

Again Rizpah tried to read the meaning behind the words. Did the Queen want to kill her husband or not? She asked the question.

'Yes. But if I do kill him, then it will be like stabbing myself to death. The trickery he engaged in at the altar seems to have shown the people that Yahweh is stronger than my gods. But soon the people will come to understand that Yahweh can provide them with less than the gods of Phoenicia, and they will call for the return of the ways I brought with me. But Elijah is the obstacle to their return. My revenge is that he will never come back to Israel. I've spoken to my husband, and he agrees that this is the best way.'

'I ... I don't understand ... What trickery ...?'

Jezebel smiled. 'Ask your husband.'

'You want me to tell my husband to leave Israel and never come back?'

'Yes. In that way, he lives, the kingdom will survive, and he will no longer bother me ... and I will continue to rule Israel with Ahab. In a year or two, I'll begin to build my asherahs again, and things will be as they were.'

The Queen continued to speak in a low voice, meant only for Rizpah. 'Understand this, Rizpah, I am killing your husband by saving his life. But should he ever return, then my fury will overcome any powerlessness my position might suffer and he

497

will die a painful death. Tell him that for him to live, he must go south to the land of Egypt or Ethiopia or east of the Mountains of Moab where the sun rises in the mornings, or the distant valleys of India where the rivers are said to be like seas, and where the people's skin is the colour of pitch. Tell him that if I learn he is still in Israel tomorrow, then he will surely die.'

Rizpah nodded, and turned. She intended to run from the room of this woman who held the power of Yahweh in her hands – the power of life and death. But she was barely able to move. She was rooted to the spot like a tree, her head feeling as though it was underwater, heavy and inconstant. The words which Jezebel spoke were swimming in the air between them. Rizpah understood, but didn't comprehend. She was commanded to tell her husband that he was about to die ... that there was no reprieve ... yet now this Queen was giving him a way out, a reprieve, because Rizpah was commanded to tell him to remove himself to Egypt and never to return. But she and her children had never been further than the boundaries of their land ... and even then their travelling had been a discomfort, the children misbehaving and anxious to get back to their village and their friends. And now she would have to uproot her family and transport them to Egypt. Or India. She had heard of India but had no idea where it was.

But she knew all about Egypt. That was where the ancestors of the Israelite people had been held in captivity. Egypt. Her mind played with the word as though it could define itself through repetition. There were strange gods in Egypt; gods much more frightening and menacing than the Phoenician gods which Jezebel had brought with her, gods whose heads were strange and beastlike, gods which ate people.

Yes, Rizpah had heard of Egypt. She'd been told once that there was a large and prosperous community of Jews loyal to Yahweh in some island in the middle of the River Nile, but this was small comfort for her ... and Elijah would be in a terrible state, separated from Judah and Israel and the temples and Yahweh Himself ... and surrounded by beastlike gods.

Her musings were ended by Jezebel asking, 'Where are you going?'

Rizpah realised that she had walked to the door without doing the usual obeisance which was demanded of subjects.

'I'm going to my husband Elijah in the temple and I'm going to tell him what you said, great Queen. Then I shall return to the house of my cousin and gather my children and together we will travel to Egypt as you have commanded.'

Jezebel shook her head. 'No! You're not to go to Elijah on your own. You'll go with one of my guards. Then you will gather your lambs, and you and your children will return here to the palace and become my servants. You will stay here until you die. And Elijah will know that if ever he returns to Israel, if ever he sets foot in Judah or Israel or anywhere within a week's ride of Samaria, I will have you and your children put to death immediately.'

Jezebel turned to her bodyguard and said, 'Accompany Rizpah to the temple. If Elijah's there, then make sure that she gives this message to him. If he's not there, give the message to the chief priest, and tell him to make sure that it gets to Elijah. Then bring Rizpah back here to me.' Jezebel turned to her Ethiopian woman servant. 'Go to the house where Rizpah's children are staying in Samaria. Collect her children. Bring them to me.'

Jezebel turned to the horrified Rizpah 'Don't look so surprised. Do you really think that after what he's done, I'd allow your husband to escape without suffering? For the rest of his life, I want him to understand what it is to be lonely. I came to this barren and dry country, and I was lonely for my people and the comfort of my family. Well, Rizpah, now your husband will be lonely for his wife and children for the rest of his life. I think that's a far crueller fate than a sudden death ...'

Rizpah burst into tears. She was terrified now for herself. She and her children were suddenly slaves. Where just this morning she'd been the respected wife of the prophet of Yahweh, where people had smiled at her and told her how wonderful her husband was ... now she was a servant at best, a slave at worst. It had happened before, and now it was happening again. She was beside herself with fear for her own and her children's future.

Jezebel was mystified by Rizpah's reaction. She hadn't been thinking about her actions as an assault on Rizpah or her children, just on Elijah.

'Why are you crying, Rizpah? You will live in a palace. You won't have to live in your little village, and I'll have you as a companion. Anyway, I want you to understand my Goddess Asherah. In time, you'll come to love her as I do. And because your husband is away from you for the rest of your life, you'll really get to enjoy the advantages of having Asherah as your own goddess.'

The young woman smiled. The horror of the situation overcame the older woman who fainted on the floor. Jezebel looked down at her. She was surprised. Rizpah seemed to faint very often.

The man she looked at was not the man she had married. That man, all those years ago, had been indecisive, vague, lost in the uncertainties of life. But the Elijah before her was a man driven by certainty, by the absoluteness of wisdom.

'So this devil woman thinks that she can still my voice by killing me!'

'Husband, she will kill you unless you flee this country.'

He paused and considered for a long moment, his lips moving as though he was in conversation. He was whispering words such as '*Yes … yes, I understand, yes, Lord …*' but they were barely audible.

Elijah turned to his wife, again with the look of one who is in command. 'And her guards will assault the temple and kill me if I remain in Israel beyond tonight?'

Rizpah nodded. 'Once before, husband, you left this country because of Jezebel. Now is the time to leave again to save yourself. And your children, because if you are still here by tomorrow, then for certain, we will all die.'

Again his lips moved and he turned his face from her. Was it Yahweh to whom he was speaking? He was talking, but not talking … and she was becoming frightened. Her safety, and the lives of her children, depended on his leaving the land. But would the strangeness overcome him again and make him distant from his duties?

'I will leave. But I will be back. And when I return, I will be accompanied by all the hosts of heaven, by the Lord Himself and all the ministering beings who will burn the heart of Israel until she is no more. Don't worry, Rizpah, you will be safe until my return. You will be hostages for the Lord. And when I return, you will be free to return to your home in Tishbe because the kingdom of Ahab will be no more.'

He turned, and began to arrange his meagre things. There was so little for him to take. Some food which was left over from his last meal, some clothes, parchments on which he had scrawled his writings ... Rizpah realised that there was almost nothing which would remind him of his family.

'Shall I cut a lock of my hair for you to wear so that you think of me while you're away?' she asked.

He turned absently, and nodded. Then he continued with his preparations. Rizpah looked for a knife, but there wasn't one in his chamber. She would do it later.

'I must go!' he said. 'The evil queen of the night has given me no time to prepare for my journey. I shall go to Egypt where there are many Hebrews who live on islands in the Nile. There, I will gather support and plan my triumphal return.'

He crossed the room, and kissed her on the cheek. 'Rizpah, you are a good woman. Look after our children until I am back. Tell them to walk true and straight in the ways of the Lord Yahweh and nothing bad will ever happen to them. Tell them to remember their father.'

Silently they looked at each other. How could this strange and distant man be her husband, a man who listened to another and not his wife? Indeed, she no longer viewed him as her husband. It was all so strange, so distant, as though to him, she were no more than a face in the crowd.

And then she asked him the question which had plagued her mind since Jezebel had first mentioned it. 'Husband, at the altar when you were praying to Yahweh to light the wood … what happened?'

He hefted the sack of his possessions onto his back and looked at the exit to his chamber. 'What do you mean?' he asked.

She repeated the question.

'The Lord Yahweh sent down a bolt of lightning and lit the wood. He showed that He is Almighty and all-powerful and …'

'Was there lightning?'

He rounded on her, and asked her directly, 'Are you presuming to question the ways of the Lord?'

'I am questioning your ways,' she said gently, not wishing to infuriate her husband and stir up the demons which were in his mind.

'Questioning me …?'

'I want to know how the fire was lit.'

'It was Yahweh …'

'It was you. How did you do it?'

He pondered for a moment, and then a smile came over his face. In a whisper, he told her, 'I did it as I will do it throughout the land of Israel to prove that Yahweh is the one and only God. I used the same fire-water from the desert that Jezebel used when she first entered our Holy Land, when she danced like a lascivious whore before the children of Israel. I countered her tricks and beat her. And Rizpah, I will do it again and again until I have driven her and her brood out. The Lord has shown me the way. He sent a merchant who sold me the desert water. I fight fire with fire. And in this way, we will win an eternal victory.'

His face was shining with the joy of his triumph. He kissed her again, and turned, leaving the chamber. But Rizpah didn't move. A chasm had opened up in front of her, and she was teetering on the edge.

How long is a journey when the sun no longer makes its circuit across the sky but stays for ever at its burning zenith, draining the life out of anything which moves on the earth below? How much distance has been travelled when all that is visible is the endless ribbon of road which winds its way along the curve of the seashore, sometimes lost, covered by the sand dunes which have blown in from the desert and which have obscured the path, a path trodden by travellers and wanderers and merchants since time began and which narrows into the distance and disappears with the junction of the land and the sky?

How agonising is the journey to Egypt, a journey which cost Father Moses his life while wandering this desert for forty years, and from which few of the Israelites whom he brought forth from the land of Egypt with a strong right hand and an outstretched arm, survived? Most perished in the desert, just as Elijah now realised he too would perish.

While he had been travelling on the coastal road from Gaza towards Egypt he had done well. He had eaten and drunk in the many fishing villages which hugged the shore like infants clutching at their mothers' breasts. He had gained strength from telling the villagers about the wonders of Yahweh and had been given sustenance to enable him to carry on until the next village. And he was passed by many caravans travelling from the riches of Egypt who would then travel along the King's Highway to trade their wares with merchants in the lands of the north. He was confident that he could arrive in Egypt without too much exhaustion and ill health.

Indeed, he had his entry into Egypt planned. He would petition the Pharaoh to mount an attack on the King and Queen of Israel, and then Elijah would install Jehu as King and all would be well.

But as he trudged westward towards Egypt, Yahweh had shown him a sign. It was a pillar of smoke ... far distant, but impossible to ignore. It rose into the firmament like a column of stone, grey and menacing, and omnipresent. No matter how often he looked, it was always there, far to the south, beckoning him to follow. Sometimes it was faint, sometimes it seemed as though it would envelop him in its awesome size.

He pointed it out to other travellers bound to or from Egypt, but their eyes were blinded to the truth and they couldn't see it. Only he. For it was a sign from Yahweh, and it was intended only to be seen by those whose eyes could see the truth, and by those in whom the faith was strong. He knew that the pillar could be seen from the land of Israel and that Jezebel and her husband Ahab would be shaking in fear as it rose above their heads and into the firmament, because it was the wrath of the Lord God of Hosts and it pointed straight into their black and evil hearts.

When he was four days' walk past Gaza, but still in the land of the Philistines, he came to a road which travelled directly south. He asked the leader of a caravan, 'Where does this road lead?'

The man looked down from his blankets perched high on a camel, and then looked back down the road to the south. 'That road leads to death.'

'If I travel that road, where will I arrive?' Elijah asked.

'At the end of the world.'

He retained his patience. 'Is there a place at the end of the road?'

The merchant, his skin like leather from spending a lifetime on top of a camel in the hot desert sun, shrugged, and said laconically, 'This is the peninsula between the Sea of Aqaba and the Sea of Reeds. There is nothing but sand and rocks and misery. Not even the people who live in the desert remain long in this peninsula, but cross it as quickly as possible to get from Egypt to the land of Midian.'

'Are there no towns, no roads?' Elijah asked, his excitement increasing as he realised where he was.

'Some roads. One crosses from east to west, from Suez in Egypt to Ezion-Geber at the head of the Gulf of Aqaba. This one,' he said, spitting at the same time as his camel growled, 'travels from the sea to the mountains at the tip of the peninsula, and then on to El-Tur, though why any living man or woman would want to visit El-Tur is beyond me. A week's journey for twenty houses and all they do is catch fish in the Sea of Reeds.'

Elijah could hardly contain his exuberance. This was the purpose of the sign from Yahweh, of the column of smoke which had enabled the children of Israel to find their way from the taskmasters of Egypt to the land of milk and honey. This was the sign from the Almighty One, Blessed be He. Elijah tried to remain calm and asked the weather-beaten merchant, 'And in these mountains at the tip of the peninsula … is there one called Sinai?'

The camel master looked at him suspiciously. Softly, he said, 'Some call the mountain Sinai. Some call it Jebel Musa, others call it the Mount of Horeb. It is of no interest to me. Why do you ask?'

'Because my forefather Moses, the great prophet, received the word of the Lord God from there, and I have been shown a sign by Yahweh, my God, that I must follow in Moses' footsteps.'

The merchant looked at him in amazement. 'You are going to walk into that wilderness!' he said, pointing southwards, into the desert.

Elijah nodded.

'Without camels, without enough food and water to sustain you, on foot, in the heat of summer?'

Again, Elijah nodded. The merchant shrugged his shoulders. He met many madmen and madwomen along the roads. Here was another one.

'Then you will die,' he said matter-of-factly.

'My God will sustain me.'

The merchant remained silent. Then he hawked another globule of phlegm and spat it onto the ground. It wasn't his job to dissuade a madman from his purpose. The gods put madmen on this earth to ensure that sane people like him knew that they were sane. If he wanted to kill himself, so be it. He kicked the camel's flanks, and the beast growled and snorted and lumbered on, leaving Elijah behind, looking at the train of camels which passed him by, totally indifferent to the fact that they were leaving a man alone in the desert.

When the last had gone by, and the stench of the camels was replaced by the hot dry purity of the desert winds, Elijah took one last long look at the vast stretch of the Eternal Sea, cool and inviting. He fancied that from his position on the road, high above the dunes and seashore, he could see the curve of the bay as it stretched northward to Canaan and Israel and Phoenicia, and westward towards Egypt.

Then he turned and faced directly south where the small track, dusty at the beginning, but becoming sand-covered as it disappeared into the distant hills, beckoned him forward. And at the end of the track, like a beacon which lit his way on a dark night, was the column of smoke. And this, he knew, was Yahweh's finger, showing him the path he must take.

He had already trodden in Moses' footsteps. When he had first escaped the wrath of Jezebel and Ahab in those early days when she was just Queen, he had hidden in the desert land east of the River Jordan, Yahweh had looked after him, just as Yahweh had looked after Moses and the children of Israel in the desert. Later, Yahweh had sent Elijah a widow who fed him just as Yahweh had sent Moses food, manna in the desert, with which to feed the children of Israel. In return for the widow's kindness, Elijah had been able to cure her son of snakebite, his hand guided by instructions from God. He had been a Moses, living in the desert and fed by the word of Yahweh who directed the hand of the widow. Now again, Elijah was walking in the footsteps of his Father Moses. Again, where Moses had triumphed and led his people, Elijah was being given the same task and set the same tests.

He walked away from the sea and down deep into the desert, stepping with the gait of a boy, refreshed in his body, vigorous in his mind. For he knew with absolute certainty that Yahweh was with him, and that when he was hungry Yahweh would feed him; when he was thirsty, Yahweh would provide him with a cool and refreshing drink. And when he had finished walking, he would know that he was in the holy place which Yahweh had chosen to hand to Moses the law by which every Israelite man, woman and child throughout the world must ultimately live.

Rizpah looked sad. She had been sad for many days. Jezebel had ordered her slaves to provide her with distractions, with entertainments. But when she saw that this wasn't alleviating her sadness, in exasperation, she had commanded Rizpah to smile and not to mope around the palace; but Jezebel knew that the smile was false and that the happiness disappeared the moment her back was turned.

'What's wrong with you?' she suddenly shouted.

Rizpah looked at her in shock; then cast her eyes down as though she was a naughty child caught in the act of something of which her parents would disapprove. She said nothing.

'I don't expect you to be joyous now that you're a widow, but I command you not to look sad. It depresses me. I want to be surrounded by people who smile. Anyway, surely this palace is better than the home in which you lived in Tishbe. The captain of my guard described it to me. It sounds horrible and small and mean. Isn't this better?' she said, pointing to the high ceilings and the stone walls.

'And your children are learning from tutors. I've seen to that. They eat well, they sleep in a clean room with the delicious smells of the kitchens. They can leave the palace whenever they want ... What's wrong with all of that? Why aren't you happy?'

Rizpah continued to look at the young woman. She was so beautiful, so dark-skinned and radiant, her eyes luscious, her black hair shining, her clothes like a rainbow; her proud neck and young strong shoulders bared without embarrassment. There was so much in Jezebel that Rizpah admired ... and so much which she found repulsive. She was like a beautiful desert snake, breathtakingly gorgeous but with deadly fangs for the unwary. She could be hideously cruel while smiling and offering friendship. At the same time as she was ensuring Rizpah's comfort in the palace, she had separated her and her children from Elijah, and called Rizpah a widow. And she was intent on destroying Rizpah's husband because he was a prophet of Yahweh.

Yet at times she looked after Rizpah's interests as though she were a daughter. It was all too much. The years of horror, of tension, of not knowing where her husband was, of whether, despite what Jezebel had promised, he hadn't been allowed to leave the country but had been secretly killed and was now lying alone, unfound, buried in some unconsecrated shallow ditch.

Rizpah's eyes filled with tears; her mouth quivered; she tried to hold them back, but she began sobbing. It was the second time that Rizpah had cried in front of Jezebel, who had been taught from an early age that crying betrayed the mind and it was better not to display emotions, for then people wouldn't know what you were planning.

But Jezebel felt some sympathy for the older

woman. She walked over to her and led her to a divan and sat her down. 'What's wrong? Is it because you miss Elijah? He's an evil man. You should never have married him in the first place. You know what he says about me. He hates me. Nobody should hate his Queen. That's why he has to die if ever he returns to this country. Can't you understand that? I thought you were intelligent.'

Rizpah shook her head, trying not to sob. 'But you're trying to kill my husband. The father of my children.'

'No I'm not,' said Jezebel. 'That's why I've exiled him. At first I wanted to kill him. When he murdered my priests and priestesses, I wanted him put to death. I'd have killed him myself if I'd had the chance. But Hattusas spoke to me and convinced me that it was more dangerous for me to have him killed, than to banish him for ever from the land and into some faraway place where he'll be forgotten. It was Hattusas who suggested that you and your children should remain here as hostages so that Elijah would never return.

'That was why I decided to do what I did. Hattusas is very wise. And he was right. Elijah will never return, knowing that if he does, I'll kill you and your children.'

Jezebel put her arms around Rizpah. 'You understand that, don't you? I have to keep you here, or your monster of a husband will return. Then my reign as Queen might as well be over. How will I ever bring the people back to the worship of Ba'al and Asherah if I'm no longer Queen? All Israel will suffer, just because of your husband.'

Rizpah nodded, and controlled her tears. The logic was simple to follow, but encased within it was a flaw, and Rizpah was too tired and upset to work out where the flaw lay. If only her husband Elijah were here ... he'd understand and be able to respond. But while her mind tried to understand the implications of what Jezebel was saying, her heart was in turmoil. This woman was keeping her in a silken prison, she was the mortal enemy of her husband ... yet ... yet she had her arms around her, she appeared to love her as a daughter loves a mother, she seemed only to want her to be happy. Rizpah didn't understand.

And then things became a lot worse and more complex. Jezebel beamed a sudden and mysterious smile.

'I have a wonderful idea. I know you haven't enjoyed the love and joy and happiness which Asherah brings to the world because your husband Elijah forbade you to, but he is no longer able to command you. You are a widow. So now I command you. I want you to experience for yourself the beauty and wonders of Asherah. I want you to come with me, and together, we'll pray to Asherah for understanding. And when you do, you'll see the reasons why I, and my husband, love Asherah so much.'

Jezebel grasped Rizpah by the hand, and led the confused woman out of the room. But she held back, saying, 'No! Stop! You know I'm forbidden to worship an idol ...'

'She's not an idol,' said Jezebel. 'She's a goddess.'

'But Elijah would forbid me to ...'

'Elijah isn't here,' said the Queen angrily. 'You're a widow!'

They knew for days that a man was walking alone through the desert. They had known since their lookouts first alerted them. Out of curiosity, they gathered on the mountain tops and in the passes looking down on the valleys through which he would pass. They watched him wandering along the road, sometimes running, sometimes falling down. He weaved like a rabbit between the dunes and over the rocky surfaces. Sometimes he would fall into a deep gully and appear dead. He would remain rigid, and they would creep down into the gully and feel his skin which was clammy and cool, but showed signs of life. And so, being desert people, they left him water and food and then crept away; for they were afraid of this strange man who shouted out to his God and appeared to know the nature of the heavens and the earth.

When Elijah awoke from his sleep, or from the many falls he suffered, he would find that Yahweh had protected him yet again. He would find a gourd full of cool and pure water, and he would find bread and olives. And he would eat and feel refreshed. Then, before he trod the path which would take him towards Sinai and closer towards being Moses, he would shout his thanks to Yahweh and fall to his knees and pull at his hair and rend what remained of his clothes as his obeisance to his Lord and Master.

Then he would stumble on, throwing off the icy coldness of the night as the sun climbed in the sky and heated the air until it was suffocating and it burned his skin and hair and made his eyes feel as though they were on fire. But still he continued to run and walk and stumble and fall, ever southwards until Yahweh would ensure that he reached the holy mountain where Moses, his Father, received the tablets of the Lord.

The desert people would watch him, and whisper questions to each other about what he was doing, why he was alone and where he was going. And they would ensure that when he fell or sat and went to sleep from exhaustion, they gave him sufficient water and food to keep him alive. For it was commanded by their gods that no man was to be left without water and food alone in the desert, unless he was your enemy.

The chief of their tribe had made the decision not to make themselves known to him. There were too many madmen who wandered the desert. If they made themselves known to everyone, then the mad disease might spread through the tribe. Better to fulfil the traditions of their tribe, the commandments of their forefathers and the injunctions of their gods, and offer hospitality to wanderers, than take such a risk.

For four days, the tribe wandered south, following the madman in his journey. Many of the tribe wanted to go to him, to put him out of his misery, and to bring him to them so that at night he could have the warmth of a fire and the comfort of company; but there was something about the man which made the chief of the tribe hesitate. This was no ordinary man, he thought. This was a man possessed, and the last thing he wanted was for the madness to infect those who obeyed him.

As it was, they were travelling that way in order to drive their goats and camels to pastures which were found along the shores of the Sea of Reeds at El-Tur. And on the fourth day, as luck would have it, the madman stumbled upon another tribe of desert wanderers who were camped in a valley at the foot of the mountain range which included the high mountain known as Jebel Musa. Satisfied that their responsibilities for ministering to him were now at an end and the madman was safe in the arms of one of their rival tribes, the desert people headed eastwards towards the sea.

Far below them in the valleys of the convoluted ground, Elijah staggered into the encampment of a tribe of desert wanderers. They stood when he rounded a rocky outcrop and came into full sight. The children ran like desert rats to hide from the spectre of the man who was shouting to himself, pointing to the heavens and both laughing and crying at the same time. Women also ran to the safety of their tents; the men of the camp stood, and took out knives to protect themselves in case there were more who followed. But, as he approached the camp, it became obvious that he was alone.

'Yahweh again protects His worthless servant,' Elijah screamed as he came to the periphery of the camp where the animals were tethered, causing the goats to bleat, the donkeys to heehaw and the camels to growl and belch. Elijah walked unsteadily towards the stone hearth, now cold but still containing ashes and scraps of meat from the previous evening's meal.

The chief of the tribe, Abd Masood ibn Kefr, stepped forward to greet the unexpected stranger.

'I bid you welcome to my humble camp. Are you alone?'

'I walk with Yahweh.'

'Where is Yahweh?' ibn Kefr asked, looking behind Elijah for the approach of any others.

'Yahweh is my God.'

'Even a man who walks with his God still needs food and drink. Come, sit and share of our hearth.'

The chief snapped his fingers, and moments later a woman emerged from her tent bearing an ornate silver tray, intricately carved with swirls and patterns of the sea. On the tray were meats and pastes and olives and dishes containing red and yellow and white spices. Another woman also emerged carrying gourds and pot cups. She poured a small amount of blood-red wine from the gourd, and from another gourd poured a yellow-white liquid which Elijah recognised as goat's milk. The woman bowed in respect of a traveller of the desert, and handed the concoction of wine and milk over to him. He took the proffered cup and drank deeply. The mixture tasted strange, somewhat acidic like a lemon's juice. But it immediately refreshed him, and he smiled as he offered the cup to the woman, the gesture in which he was asking for more.

Ibn Kefr reached for Elijah's arm, and led him over to where the men had been resting. They sat, as did all the other men of the tribe, and watched Elijah eat the cheeses and dip the slices of bread into the pots containing the spices. He ate in silence for a long time, his hunger being satisfied only when the woman brought out more olives and bread.

A woman, dressed as the others in a large black burnous covering everything of her body but her face as a way of protecting her from the sun, approached Elijah and gave him a bowl of water with which to wash his hands and face. Knowing something of the ways of the desert people, he recognised that this was an overwhelming act of generosity, because water in the desert was only ever given to honoured guests.

When he had finished, he looked around at the men, who waited patiently for him to end his refreshments. Ancient custom told them that the first thing a traveller had to do was to refresh himself ... then they could talk. But the first word had to be his.

'I thank you for the wonderful meal. May Yahweh enter your hearts and enable you to prosper and always find water at the end of your journey.'

The men all smiled and nodded. These were the right words for the traveller to say. They waited for their chief, Abd Masood ibn Kefr to speak.

'May I be permitted to know the name of the man who has just honoured us with his presence at our miserable table?'

'My name is Elijah. I am a prophet of the Lord Yahweh, the God of Israel and the people of Judah. And your table groaned with the generosity of a wealthy man,' he said, remembering their customs from when he'd travelled through the Negev Desert of Judah.

Abd Masood ibn Kefr nodded. This man was obviously from a city, and from his accent and manner, he was from one of the Hebrew cities of Judah or Israel. But even if he was a Hebrew, Abd Masood ibn Kefr was still impressed by this man's knowledge of the desert and its customs, even if he had arrived at the campsite undressed and without food, water or animals. 'I perceive that you are here to climb the mountain which the people of Israel call Sinai.'

Elijah looked in astonishment. 'You know of this mountain?'

Abd Masood ibn Kefr smiled as he explained, 'Every year, some man will enter our lands and will ask directions to the mountain called Sinai. Today we call this mountain in our language Jebel Musa after the man you call Moses who we call Musa. I am told that your god gave this man Musa something on the top of the mountain, but beyond that nobody will tell me.'

And so Elijah spent a long while explaining the origins of his religion, telling the men (and women and children who were hiding in the tents, but listening carefully through the door flaps) about how Abraham had been called by Yahweh to sacrifice his son and to smash idols, but at the last minute God had stayed his hand, and Isaac had gone on to become one of the great men and founders of the Israelite religion; and the people had followed their Father Jacob, who became Israel, to Egypt many years earlier to escape a terrible drought. But the faces of all the people had only turned to God through the stature of the Father Moses, who was the greatest prophet and the giver of the law and the word of the Lord. Elijah told Abd Masood ibn Kefr and the men of the tribe that the word had been inscribed in stone tablets, which were now in the Temple of Jerusalem, and the stone had been inscribed by the very finger of the Lord Yahweh.

He talked late into the night, and the men listened, as did the women. He told them about the fight between King Solomon and Makeda the Queen of Sheba and of the illicit son Menelik whom Solomon disinherited; and Elijah told them of the quarrel between Judah and Israel and how the twelve tribes which had come from Egypt had now split into two countries, ten tribes going to Israel in the north and two tribes remaining faithful to the Temple of Jerusalem in the land of Judah in the south.

By the time that the stars made the air very cold and the camels were growling just before they lay down and slept for the night, Elijah asked, 'How far am I from this Mountain of Sinai?'

Abd Masood ibn Kefr smiled. 'You are here. This is the Mount Horeb which you call Sinai and which for generations we have called Jebel Musa.'

Astonished, Elijah looked around him. 'Here?' Elijah looked into the dark night sky. From where he sat, deep in the valley, he gazed upwards to the summit of the nearby mountain. Now he knew where he was. He should have realised it without being told, because there was an aura of light which came from the mountain, as though the entire edifice was burning from within.

'Mount Sinai?' he asked.

Abd Masood ibn Kefr and the other men nodded. But their amusement turned to shock when Elijah jumped up, kicked away his sandals as though they were alight, and screamed at them, 'Remove your shoes and cover your heads! You are on holy ground. You are in the presence of the Almighty ...'

Jezebel had assured her that she would feel different in the presence of Asherah, but nonetheless, Rizpah was nervous as she walked towards one of the residences of the goddess. She'd seen the booths in fields, on the sides of hills, and a large one had been built on top of Mount Carmel. She hadn't seen this one because it was too far north for her to travel, but she'd been told that it was very large and that terrible things took place in it – unnatural acts between the women priestesses and the men of Israel. And she'd also heard it whispered that some of the priests of Asherah liked to pleasure the women of Israel. Many of the asherahs had been destroyed since her husband's victory over the Phoenician gods, but some had been repaired in the past few weeks, and again, some men and women of Israel were tentatively visiting them for prayers and whatever else they did in those foul places.

Of course, as the wife of the prophet of Yahweh, it was incumbent upon Rizpah never to set foot in one of these asherahs; but now it appeared she had no choice. She knew that these were the places where the fertility of women was determined according to those who believed in the goddess; and it was also said by her devotees that the fertility extended beyond women into the very fields themselves, and the animals who walked in the fields; for they believed that if the Goddess Asherah smiled upon her worshippers, she would make barren women fertile, make the fields heavy with crops, and make sheep and goats and cattle produce offspring for the wealth of the following year.

And now she, Rizpah, was being led into a place which was forbidden to her by the word of her husband Elijah, and by the God whom she followed devoutly. The young Queen Jezebel, as keen as a spring lamb, was leading her by the arm to make her enter. And although Rizpah continued to object and strain against the strength of the young woman's encouragement, and to say in bitter complaint that to enter into the asherah was wrong for her, that a woman of Yahweh was forbidden to enter the house of a foreign god, Jezebel would have none of it.

At first she made light of Rizpah's objections, but when the woman continued to complain, Jezebel began to lose patience. The young Phoenician couldn't understand why the Israelite woman was objecting so strongly. Didn't she understand that the visit to the asherah was going to unburden her, that it would unleash those spirits of happiness which were caught up inside her miserable body? Why didn't she understand that to be without the comforts of a man for so long made any woman unhappy and dispirited, and that being made love to by one of the experienced priests would be a miraculous way for Rizpah to regain those feelings of joy and youth which she so badly lacked.

Couldn't she comprehend that it was for her benefit that Jezebel was taking her to the most highly prized priest and priestess in all of Israel? A man who was endowed with such wonders between his legs that he could make stone gasp, and a woman who knew every aspect of lovemaking that there was, and who knew how to soothe her way into a new life.

Why couldn't this straight-backed Israelite accept and understand?

He was close to exhaustion by the time he reached the top of the mountain. When he was a child, he learned how Moses the Lawgiver had been twice to Sinai – the first time when he was a simple shepherd for his father-in-law Jethro after he had escaped from the evil Pharaoh of Egypt. Then, the Lord God Yahweh had appeared before him as a burning bush and told him to return to Egypt, and there to lead the children of Israel out of the House of Bondage where they were worked to death as slaves; and the second time was when Moses was leading the children of Israel out of Egypt towards the land of Israel, and he climbed up the Mountain of Sinai to receive the word of the Lord. It was on this occasion that he had left his people Israel in the valley far below, climbed up to the top of Mount Sinai, and there looked into the face of the Lord which was smoke and fire. It was Yahweh the Almighty Lord in the smoke and it was seen by all of Israel just as Elijah had seen the flames and smoke the previous night from the valley down below.

But what he hadn't learned as a child was how high the mountain was, nor how rocky and difficult the climb, nor how exhausting. How could Moses have spent so many days on a mountain which had no water, no food, and little shelter? But this was what had been done in the past, and Elijah was walking in the footsteps of Moses and was going to return to Israel and lead his people out of the bondage and slavery to the false gods of the Phoenician whore and lead them into the Promised Land of the worship of Yahweh.

His hands were cut, his knees bleeding, his feet aching and shredded from the sharp stones and rocks which littered the way to the top ... not that there was a way. Here was no road, no pathway, no signpost to assure him that the route he had chosen was the right one. Here was only scree and boulders and fields of pebbles, and when he had ascended to the top of a particularly difficult climb, his foot would rest on a rock, and it would dislodge and he would slide a long way down, cut and bruised and bleeding, the rocks falling from the sky and hurting him badly. But this was where Moses had climbed, and both Moses and he were the servants of God, and Yahweh would provide.

One thing he knew with absolute certainty was that he would survive his encounter with the mountain, because Yahweh had a purpose for him ... to lead the people as Moses had led them. And so he would be safe and would survive every difficulty.

Eventually, Elijah arrived at the entry way to the summit of the mountain. Dust and smoke and fire seemed to rise from its very peak. Despite the blood which poured from his wounds, despite the bruises and the torn clothes, Elijah straightened himself, and bowed before the majesty of God.

'Lord, your servant Elijah has arrived.'

In the vastness of the wilderness, the only voice which could be heard was that of the wind. Elijah looked up at the peak, wondering whether or not to climb further upwards, to the very home of the Lord Himself.

'Lord,' he said diffidently, 'Elijah has come ...'

And then God spoke to him. It was a voice which nobody else could have heard. For it was a voice which sounded inside Elijah's brain. Was this how Moses heard Yahweh? And the children of Israel who were terrified by the thunder from the Holy Mountain?

The voice said, 'Elijah, why are you here?'

Silently, without moving his lips nor opening his mouth, Elijah said, 'Lord, I am here because I alone am the only man who still worships you in the land of Israel.'

'You are my Moses. As I gave the law to him upon this very mountain, so I pass on his mantle to you. As Moses was my servant, so you too will be my servant. As he parted the Sea of Reeds with his staff, so you will part the River Jordan with your staff. As he defeated the House of the Pharaoh of Egypt, so you will defeat the House of the King Omri of Israel, and Ahab and Jezebel and all her descendants shall be destroyed. And dogs shall lick her blood. I am the

Lord your God, I am He who brought you and all of Israel before you out of the House of the Pharaoh of Egypt and out of the House of Bondage. I am who I am. I am He who is He. Mine is an outstretched hand and a mighty arm. Go back to the land of the Israel and anoint Jehu as the rightful King of Israel, and take for yourself a servant who will follow you when you are dead. Go now, and do not turn your face towards me again.'

Elijah fell onto the stony ground in a dead faint.

Rizpah refused to kneel before the wooden staff which was planted firmly in the ground. And she refused to remove her cloak.

Jezebel became angry, and said, 'You silly woman. It's only a pole. A wooden pole. It isn't the goddess herself, just the symbol of her which we worship, just as we worship idols which aren't the god or goddess, but only the objects which remind us of them. You kneel before a tree when you have a meal in a wood, don't you?'

'That's different. I am forbidden to worship any other gods before Yahweh.'

'But it's not like you're worshipping Asherah. All you're going to do is to enjoy yourself with her priest and priestess. Relieve the loneliness of being without a husband. Know what it means to have a joyous god who is your companion. It can't be so difficult to kneel, can it?'

Reluctantly, Rizpah agreed to sit on the ground, but told Jezebel frankly that she wasn't happy. 'My husband would object, would be furious, if he saw me inside this place. He says it's an abomination in the eyes of the Lord.'

'Your husband, Rizpah, is away from this country for ever, you'll never see him again. Think of him as being dead. It'll be easier that way. And when you do, understand that unless you want to lead a very boring life, a life without the pleasures of the body, you might as well enjoy yourself here. I've brought you to this asherah because it's far from the palace, nobody will see you and you can enjoy yourself fully without being talked about behind your back.'

But Rizpah still objected. 'This isn't permitted to us. We are not allowed ...'

'Look,' said the young Queen in exasperation, 'when an Israelite husband dies, if the widow has no children, then she has to marry the husband's brother, doesn't she? It's the ancient law. My husband Ahab calls it the Levirate law. It's good and it's sensible. In that way, she still stays a woman, can be comforted by a man's touch, she isn't left to live alone in a house where she might be attacked or raped, she isn't shunned by other women in case they think she's trying to seduce their husbands, and she has someone to look after her when she gets old and can no longer make food or wash clothes. That's all I'm saying. Until I can actually divorce you from Elijah, and get you married to someone younger who'll play with your body like it was a harp, and make you scream with happiness, then this is the best thing I can do ...'

As she said it, a priest and priestess walked into the asherah. Both bowed low to Jezebel, who smiled at them. As they entered, Jezebel stood and dragged Rizpah up with her. Both the priest and priestess were young and very attractive, and smelled of flowers of the fields. They wore long white robes, the priestess's robe falling below her left breast, exposing it. The sight no longer shocked Rizpah, for she had seen more naked men and women since she'd spent time in the palace than in all her previous life.

'Welcome friends,' said the priest. 'You're here to enjoy the benefits which my Goddess Asherah shares with the people. Which one of you two worshippers and believers wishes to enjoy the endowment of Ba'al and Asherah with me?'

The priestess beamed a welcome and walked over to Jezebel, kissing her fondly on the lips; Rizpah's eyes widened in shock, but what surprised her even more than the priestess' brazen sin was that Jezebel seemed to respond favourably, indeed to smile and enjoy the exchange rather than withdraw in disgust at the touch of another woman.

Then the priestess looked over towards Rizpah, and held out her hand in a gesture of welcome. From within her pristine robe, she withdrew a circle of intertwined flowers. She handed them over to Rizpah.

'This wreath of flowers was created especially for you by our priestess in chief. She asks that you accept it in the name of Asherah with our love and our hope for your future happiness. It represents the fullness of life. Look carefully at the wreath, Rizpah. You will see that it is life itself. It begins and ends at the same point; as we die and our bodies return to the earth and the dust which we become, so we are reborn at the same moment. Our body goes into the earth but our essence goes up towards Asherah and she makes the decision as to where we will be reborn to begin our lives anew. The flowers from which the wreath are made will soon die, but only this morning they were alive and bursting with sap.

These flowers show the potency and strength which we have over all things which are alive today; but they also show the fragility of life and demonstrate that unless we worship Asherah and her consort and son Ba'al, then our lives are as fragile in their hands as these flowers of the field are in our hands.'

Rizpah took the flowers, and the priestess helped her put them on her head as though they were a crown. Jezebel walked over to them and joined them in holding hands. The three women moved closer to each other, their legs touching, their bodies touching.

But Rizpah was afraid, and didn't enjoy the warmth of the other two women. Instead, she moved away from the group.

'Rizpah, why are you afraid?' asked the priestess.

'I'm not afraid.'

She smiled, and said, 'Yes, you are. Your body was shaking with fear. Some women shake with the tension which intercourse with a priest or priestess will soon relieve, but you're shaking through fear. Are you afraid of Jezebel?'

'Yes.'

'That is very natural. This Queen has the power of life and death over you. Yet she holds your hand and touches you as a true and loyal friend.' The priestess looked closely into her face. 'Are you afraid of me?'

'No.'

'Are you afraid of yourself?'

'I don't understand,' she said softly. Her mouth was becoming dry. She sounded hoarse.

'Are there sensations in your body which you've never felt before? Is there a warmth in your womanhood which feels wonderful, but which makes your mind guilty?'

She remained silent. It was as eloquent an answer as the priestess could expect.

'Rizpah, come back here. Join Jezebel and me. We won't harm you. We're your friends.'

But the older woman refused to move. The priestess went over to her, and drew her two paces back to where the Queen was standing. They both put their arms around her shoulders.

'Rizpah, remove my robe,' said the priestess softly.

She felt her heartbeat increase, her breathing become shallow. 'I don't want to. It's a sin in the eyes of the Lord.'

'Is it a sin to help another woman undress?'

'I mustn't see another person naked. It's a sin in the eyes of the Lord.'

The priestess put her finger to Rizpah's lips. 'Is the Lord here? This is Asherah's domain. You are out of the sight of your Lord.'

'My Lord is everywhere,' she said. But her words were unconvincing.

Softly, Jezebel said, 'Rizpah, remove her robe.'

Rizpah knew that she had to obey, or Jezebel would force her. With unsteady hands, she undid the tie at the priestess' throat. Then she pushed the cloth gently so that it slipped over the priestess' shoulders and fell to the ground. The woman stood there naked, unashamed. She had perfect breasts, the sort of breasts of which Rizpah was so proud before she had children. She couldn't stop her eyes wandering below her breasts to the triangle of hair between her legs. It had been somehow shaved as though she was a man.

It was small and neat and carefully trimmed to look like a rose. It appeared to have been tended to with great care, as though the priestess used a knife to sculpt and cultivate that which was wild on other women. Rizpah had never seen such a thing. Yet it looked far more beautiful than the bush of black and curly hair she sported between her legs. She couldn't take her eyes off it.

After what seemed like an eternity, Jezebel said softly to the priest who had been looking on with patience for the moment he should become part of the group, 'My servant Rizpah would like to be entered by Ba'al and Asherah.'

'Good,' said the priest. He moved across to where Rizpah was standing and stroked her hair.

She objected, and brushed his hand away. The priest looked quizzically at Jezebel, who nodded for him to continue what he was doing. So he tugged at Rizpah's cloak, and tried to remove it, but the woman clutched it tightly to her throat. Then the priest stood closer to Rizpah, and weaved his groin in a circular motion close to Rizpah's womanhood. The older woman began to move away, but Jezebel said, 'Stay Rizpah, and enjoy what Asherah has to give to us.'

Rizpah turned to her Queen, about to tell her that she could no longer stay in this den of snakes, that she had to leave for her modesty as a woman of Israel. But as she was about to say it, the priest slipped off his tunic, and exposed his large, engorged penis. It stood there, huge and ennobled, close to Rizpah's rigid body.

Rizpah's eyes widened at the size and stature of it. Then she fainted dead on the floor. It was the second time she had fainted in two days. Jezebel looked at her prostrate form in frustration and amazement, wondering when she should try to rouse Rizpah so that her servant could be conscious in order to enjoy the full fruits of the gods Ba'al and Asherah and have her body filled with their bounty.

CHAPTER TWENTY

She walked with an unsteady gait. As she left the asherah, Rizpah occasionally was forced to stop and support herself against a wall for fear that her legs would buckle and she would fall. The young Queen was concerned. She had not expected this reaction. She'd thought that a door would open into the very core of Rizpah's existence and she would be transformed by the experience.

But Rizpah was embarrassed by her giddiness. She saw something very different in the eyes of Jezebel; she saw a look of victory. Rizpah knew her body well enough to know that she only had one course of action open to her, and that was to commit suicide … for although killing oneself was a crime against the Lord, it was less of a crime than the knowledge that her body had been defiled, that in her faint, she had been entered by a priest of another religion, that she had given herself, willingly or unwillingly, to a man other than her husband.

Rather than wait for the priests of Yahweh to find out what had happened, and throw her from the turrets of the city to her death, Rizpah determined that it would be easier to slit her wrists and allow her life to drain away. For there was more than her guilt and giddiness. There was something worse, much worse; if she truly admitted it, she had awoken from her faint feeling distant ... removed.

She remembered Jezebel asking her how she felt; she, the Queen, had asked her whether she wanted the priest inside her. Had she responded? She tried to recall. What had she said? Was it something like ... perhaps it was ... could it have been 'Yes'? ... Through a haze of uncertainty, she remembered that without her objection he had lain on top of her, and suddenly he was inside her, and her reaction had shocked her. Rather than feeling dirty and defiled, her body was suffused with feelings she'd never known before. She'd looked up with misty eyes into the face of the priest, and felt his body sliding into and out of hers, and her body had wanted more; at first – when she was still affected by her faint – she felt disconnected from the reality of what was happening, but when she felt her body glowing and responding and opening, she had abandoned herself as wife and mother and Israelite woman, and she had enjoyed herself.

She walked trembling, her mind reeling with the past and the future. It was all becoming clearer and clearer to her now. When she first became truly aware that he was riding her body as though she were a horse, she felt as though her head were in a whirlwind. The priest saw her eyes staring at him in sudden shock. He had looked at Jezebel to see what he should do. He withdrew at Jezebel's command, and the Queen gave Rizpah water to drink to refresh her.

It was then, when she said she felt recovered, that the priest had continued his work on her body. When he had laid her head down again and kissed her and smoothed back her hair and whispered silly things in her ear, things about her breasts and her hair and her legs, Rizpah's mind, still dazed from fainting, was awakened by the way he touched her breasts; suddenly her body was ablaze like a fire, twisting like a desert wind. At one moment, she wanted to scream like a mad woman, saying 'Yes' and 'Yes' again. This man who didn't know her was saying things and doing things to her breasts and her intimate parts which, even in her most private moments, she'd only ever dreamed about. As he lay with her, his body hot and rigid, hers arching with feelings she'd never before felt, she wanted him more badly, more desperately than any other man she'd ever known.

But then the other part of her heart began to caution her. It was then that she wanted to scream and shout and object; but she was silent, as though her heart was separated from her mind, and her mind was divided from her body. One part of Rizpah told her to throw the man off and leave the accursed place. Another part told her she had to stay, for there were feelings in her body which she'd never before experienced and which her heart told her to explore to the full, just as when she'd been a little girl she'd always been eager to explore new places around her home, or secretly watch men undress and wash themselves in the river.

But these feelings she had experienced were of warmth, of joy, of overwhelming passion, the sort of passion which she had always expected she'd one day enjoy with Elijah, but which never came. And those early feelings within her had disappeared rapidly as the Lord Yahweh became more of a lover for Elijah than she, his wife. He had wandered from her, telling her that the highest ideal was to love the Lord, and not obey the desires of her body.

And all of these feelings suddenly rushed back into her mind as the priest of a foreign god, a man whom she didn't know, placed his mouth on hers, his tongue within her mouth, and kissed her in a way she'd always dreamed of being kissed. No man had ever kissed her on the mouth since she married Elijah and yet here she was being kissed by a man who was not her husband, and she was opening her lips, slightly at first, and then wide, parting them so that she could experience the flickering of his tongue over hers, his warm and moist lips on hers, his tongue meeting her tongue as though they were betrothed together before the sight of God.

But then things began to happen which were of this earth and which she sensed were wrong; things which she knew instinctively were against the laws of Yahweh. For as the priest of Ba'al parted her robes and kissed her stomach and as she felt his warm breath cascading over her private region and creating a desire which brought her to the point of screaming, Rizpah sensed movement beside her, and there she saw her Queen, Jezebel, laying down beside the beautiful priestess of Asherah, and she saw Jezebel's breasts exposed and the priestess touching them and kissing her nipples; and Rizpah knew that it was wrong ... but the priest was now moving his face and mouth down towards her most private area, and her mind again went blank, all she could think about were the thoughts which had been forbidden to her since she was a child.

She knew she should have objected, screamed and shouted accusations against this assault on her, but she couldn't. And when she felt the man's hand thrusting aside her gown and parting her legs, she felt a warmth and a wetness which she had never experienced before, not even in the early days of her marriage to Elijah; it was the type of feeling which her sister once described to her about the relationship she enjoyed with her own husband, but Rizpah had refused to listen, too ashamed to tell her own sister that she couldn't comprehend the physical actions which she was describing.

And when this man, this priest, put first his tongue, and then his member inside, she felt as though the very heavens themselves had opened up and she could feel the ecstasy which she had only ever heard described by Elijah when he was overcome by the Lord and he fell on the floor and his face shone with the divine radiance.

The priest of Ba'al thrust and thrust, and every thrust he made was a new experience, a new pleasure, heightening the sensation she had felt when he kissed her. Then others were kissing her on the lips, Jezebel and the priestess, but Rizpah didn't care, because she was lost in the desires of her body, and her entire being was directed only to reaching a climax she hadn't known since she was a girl lying in the field under a hot sun and fingering herself until she exploded.

And explode she did, again, now an adult, a woman, filled with the strength and vigour and potency of a man who understood the music in the body of a woman. And then it was over, too soon, too soon ...

And when it was finished, the priest had emptied himself inside her, and she had experienced the divine climax of which her sister had spoken, and which she had been denied since the day she married, it was then that she knew she must commit suicide. It was at the moment when her body was more relaxed, more at peace than she'd ever known, that she comprehended the true scale of guilt which she must suffer all the rest of her life. As the priest rose from her body, leaving her wet and sweating and panting, her lips dry and throbbing, her private parts exposed to the gaze of the priest, the priestess and Jezebel, it was then she knew that she had descended to the very depths of the hell which Elijah said was reserved for idol worshippers. She had known a man other than her husband; she had kissed two women, not as sisters but as lovers; she had performed evil deeds. Death was the cleansing agent she must seek; suicide her only salvation in the eyes of the Lord.

When they arrived back in the palace, Rizpah and Jezebel walked slowly back to the Queen's apartments. A wave of shame and grief washed over the older woman with such power that it nearly swept her off her feet. It was at that moment that the decision to commit suicide for the sin she had just suffered was confirmed and made irreversible. For the moment of shame had been overcome, and now her mind was in control of her emotions, she realised that suicide was the right choice for what had just happened, for a sin which could never ever be removed. Rizpah was glad that this had clarified in her mind.

'My Queen,' Rizpah said softly but firmly to Jezebel, 'you have committed a great sin against me. You have made me do the things which are forbidden to me and which are against my religion. You have made me into a prostitute and this is something which I can never reverse. It is the reason that I have taken the decision to end my life. I beg of you, as a woman who has shown affection and friendship for me, that you look after my children and that you do nothing to harm them. As of tonight when I have ended my life, they will have neither mother nor father. Will you have them taken to my sister, and will you promise not to act against them?'

Jezebel was stunned. This was all so sudden, so completely different from what she'd expected. Jezebel thought she had done a wonderful service for her friend now that her husband was no longer part of what was, to all intents and purposes, the life which she once led. Jezebel truly believed that introducing Rizpah into the joys of the sexual side of life, would make her into a new and better woman, one able to smile, to laugh, to know happiness, to understand the joy of sexuality and comfort which men – and women – could bring.

Jezebel stopped in the corridor, and grasped her friend by the shoulders. There was so much difference between them, such a void – their ages, their status, their sophistication, their knowledge of the ways in which the world operated, their clothes … yet Jezebel looked upon Rizpah in the same way as she looked upon her own mother or as the older sister she'd always wanted to be able to turn towards when, as a child, she was left alone by her parents and family. Her own mother had been everywhere and nowhere, always on show as the consort of a great King, yet never there for her children when they'd hurt themselves, or when they wanted to talk and enjoy themselves. Life in Phoenicia had been so lonely; life in Israel would be just as lonely without Rizpah.

'Are you mad? You would end your life, just because you've been known by one of the priests?'

'Yes.'

'But … I … Why?'

'Because. Just because. My God commands it. It is the law. I am forbidden to know a man other than my husband. Adultery is a sin punishable by stoning to death. Rape is a shame which drives women to kill themselves. It's as simple and harsh as that.'

'But I don't understand why this is rape. Rape is when a man forces himself upon a woman. But the priest didn't force himself. You let him.'

'I didn't let him. I was still dizzy from the faint when he first entered me … I didn't know what I was doing.'

'Dizzy? No! You weren't dizzy. You knew what was happening. I told you, and asked your permission, and you said yes,' said Jezebel angrily. 'You had been unconscious on the ground, and we waited for you to awaken. I gave you water to refresh you. We talked. Then, and only then, did the priest begin to kiss your stomach and your womanhood. And you wanted him, Rizpah. You wanted him by the noises you were making! You lay and made the noises of a woman who is enjoying herself. I was there. I heard you. You moaned and …'

'Stop! When I was in a faint, he entered me without my permission. This is rape.'

'That's a lie!' shouted Jezebel. The Queen was suddenly overcome by fury. For she knew that Rizpah wasn't violated while she was in a faint. Jezebel would never have allowed the priest those liberties if Rizpah wasn't aware of what was happening. How could she say those things?

She looked at Rizpah, but the Israelite's face was of stone. And the words she had spoken were said so harshly that Jezebel was unsure of what to say. Nobody had spoken to her in this way since she was a child in her father's palace. Jezebel stood back in shock.

But the Queen's reaction didn't stop Rizpah. 'You have done this to me, Jezebel. You have killed me. You and your foreign ways. My husband is right about you. You've introduced baseness and evil into the land of Israel. God's land. By what right do you …?'

'How dare you!' shouted Jezebel, suddenly infuriated that another Elijah had come into her palace. She stepped away from the other woman as though she was a leper. 'How dare you speak to your Queen in that way. Kneel down, woman, and kiss my feet. I am Jezebel, Queen of Israel and Princess of Phoenicia. Do homage and penance to me, or I'll put you to death!'

Rizpah looked at her Queen. All she saw was a young girl, a girl of no morals who, through her actions, would bring down the nation which Rizpah loved. And here she was, threatening her with death!

'How can you kill a woman who's already dead?' Rizpah asked softly, and without kneeling, walked calmly away from the astonished Queen, back to her own apartments, waiting for the executioner's sword.

The air smelled stale and gritty. Her skin felt aged. Her clothes seemed to hang off her as though they were rags. She knew that she was about to die, yet she had to remove herself from the palace, even if only for a morning; to see the fields and hillsides of Israel, the rivers in the bottom of the valleys, the eagles wheeling in the air high above the city … then she would return to the palace and say goodbye to her children. Then she would feel the cold of the executioner's sword. Or would Jezebel insist on the Hebrew punishment and have her flung off a precipice and then stoned?

When she had left the Queen, for once totally unconcerned about her own safety, she had gone straight to the kitchens to see her children. But when she saw their innocent faces light up as she entered the rooms, she was overcome with an inconsolable grief, and had to run out.

Now she was walking through the streets of Samaria, tears in her eyes, intent only on seeing as much as she could in as short a time as was left to her.

'Rizpah?' called a voice from the other side of the square.

She looked, and saw a familiar face, a man she had travelled with when she had journeyed alone from the River Jordan to Samaria. It was Absalom. He walked towards her to ensure that it truly was Rizpah.

'Rizpah, I've looked for you often. How are you?'

She smiled, but he saw that there were tears in her eyes, grief in her face.

'What's wrong?'

He walked over to her, and grasped her arm.

'I …'

She couldn't talk.

'Come,' he said, 'let's walk beyond the city. If we go down towards the area of the metalworkers we can see the distant hills. Come with me, Rizpah, and tell me what's upsetting you.'

Without saying anything further, she went with him. They left the city by the Damascus Gate and trod the stony path around the rocks on which the city was built. Slowly the air became purer, more perfumed … the sort of perfume she smelled in the spring in Tishbe when the wheat and barley was first flowering and the bees were flitting from flower to flower; it was the time she enjoyed most, especially walking through the orchards and being overcome by the erotic aromas of the orange and apple and lemon trees.

And she began to cry at the thought that she would never sense these wonders of the Lord again. Absalom sat her down, and together they looked out over the distant hills of Mount Carmel.

'You seem to have the weight of all Israel on your shoulders,' he said.

Drying her eyes, she looked at him, and said, 'No, but I am about to die …'

And she explained to him what the Queen and the priest of Ba'al had done to her body.

The old man listened for a long time as she unburdened herself. Softly, he asked, 'When was the last time you and your husband Elijah were together as man and woman?'

'Many years ago,' she told him. 'His work is more important than the needs of our bodies, he tells me.'

Absalom nodded. 'He's a prophet of Yahweh, isn't he?'

'Of course.'

'And are you?'

Rizpah looked at him in surprise. 'Of course not.'

'So,' said Absalom, 'he's commanded by Yahweh not to waste his time in the enjoyments of the flesh, and he passes this commandment on to you as his wife … yes!'

'Yes.'

'And to his children? Would he forbid his children to do the Lord's bidding and be fruitful and multiply?'

'Of course not.'

'Then why must you obey the commands given to your husband, but which Yahweh has not commanded you?'

'I'm Elijah's wife. I can't look upon another man.'

'But what about the demands of your body?'

'I must control those demands,' she said.

He listened, and remained silent. Then quietly, he told her, 'Do you remember I told you that I had been a sailor, and had sailed to lands which you could only dream about ... that I've seen things which you would never believe ...'

Rizpah told him she remembered well.

'In these lands, the people do things which would horrify you ... yet for them, they are normal. In the land at the very end of the Eternal Sea, where the two edges of the earth nearly touch, there is a huge rock. Beyond this rock live a people whose skin is less dark than ours, yet whose women enjoy the flesh of their men ... and other women's men. They do so without shame.

'When I landed there to trade in cloth, as an honoured merchant, I was given my own house on the shore of the sea. In the middle of the night two women brought me food and drink. Of course, I was much younger and better looking then, without lines on my face and with my teeth still in my mouth. These women served me, and then lay with me all night, enjoying themselves and me at the same time ...'

Rizpah looked at him in shock. She had heard of these things in the palace of the Phoenician Queen of

Israel, but didn't think they happened to ordinary men.

'Well, in the morning, when I awoke, the women had gone, and there were their husbands, sitting outside my door, talking. I thought they were after money for the services of their wives, or they were going to assault me for the sins I'd committed. But Rizpah, they asked me if I had enjoyed myself. I told them it was the most wonderful night I'd ever spent. Then they thanked me, and we drank and ate together, and went away happy.'

Rizpah didn't understand the purpose of the story, and told him so.

'People throughout the rest of the world have very different thoughts about the role of a man's and woman's body. They think differently about sex. They enjoy their bodies, they don't feel guilty, and they don't allow priests to tell them what's right and what's wrong.

'Yes, I know that Yahweh told the children of Israel that they must only enjoy the bodies of their spouses, and turn their backs on all others. But only Yahweh seems to be saying that ...'

'But Yahweh is the one true God,' she responded.

Absalom thought for a moment. 'Yes, that's what He tells us, isn't it ...'

It was half a day before someone entered her apartments. She had been sitting on the divan, thinking about her children, smiling at the antics she remembered, crying that she hadn't even been able to bid them farewell and give them advice for their future lives. But when Rizpah looked up, she was surprised that it was the Queen herself who was entering the rooms; since returning from her walk with Absalom, she'd been waiting and anticipating the arrival of the captain of the guard and the executioner.

The young Queen was wearing different robes to those she had worn earlier. These were made from a green material, which looked as though she was wearing grass; the Queen's clothes were so colourful ... they must be very expensive, Rizpah thought.

Out of deference for the status of the young woman, Rizpah stood.

'I've come to understand you. At first, I was going to have you put to death. Nobody talks to the Queen of Israel and the Princess of the royal court of Phoenicia in that way. But I like you, and I want to learn to comprehend why you are behaving in this way. I don't understand. Early this morning you were writhing on the floor of the asherah and my priest was making love to you. You were shouting in happiness. You were saying that he was wonderful. You told him how much you were enjoying it. You said you had never known a feeling like it. You told my priest that he was the man you'd always dreamed of, that his penis was like the trunk of a cedar tree. You cried when you reached your climax.

'Yet now you want to kill yourself. I've opened your eyes to a life you never knew when you lived beneath the body of Elijah, your husband. But now you tell me that you have no lasting joy from what I've done for you. When I was little more than a child and my parents first introduced me into the wonders of a man's penis, I couldn't wait to have it inside me again. But you don't want it to happen again. No! Worse. You're so ashamed that you call it rape and you want to kill yourself.

'Sex with a man or a woman isn't like the summer rains, which sometimes come and sometimes don't and you can't rely on them, no matter how hard you pray to the gods, as sometimes they don't hear and then there's a drought and people die. No, sex isn't like that at all. It's always there … it's a gift from the gods. It's their way of smiling down on us. Even when a man or a woman is hungry or tired or sick, they can always desire. Their private parts still respond to rubbing and to massage and to perfumes and oils and such things. They're always able to be used, ready when you want them. I can prove it to you. Tomorrow I can have ten men waiting outside the doors of your apartments, each one happy to make you scream again like you were screaming on the floor of the asherah this morning.'

Rizpah looked at the Queen in horror. 'No!'

'But why?' she asked earnestly.

'You wouldn't understand, Jezebel.'

'Yes, I would. I want to understand you. Rizpah, I have few friends left in this horrible country because of your husband. He's killed the people I loved, the friends and advisors who were with me, by my side. There are only a few priests and priestesses left in Israel, and my father refuses to send more because he says that the madmen of Israel will just kill the new ones. Of course I'd understand you. Just tell me what was so horrible this morning.'

She looked at the older woman, dressed in the black of a widow. Rizpah sat down again on her divan and stared up at her.

Jezebel asked, 'Why can't you tell me what I did wrong, Rizpah?'

Softly, Rizpah said, 'I have been defiled.'

But as she said it, she thought of Absalom, and realised that she was lying even to herself ... she was obeying the dictates of her husband, and ignoring the demands of her own body.

Jezebel could see that there was little sincerity in what she said. 'You've enjoyed yourself. You had a moment when you reached the pleasure which the gods and goddesses experience every moment of their lives. You are a privileged woman. Why say you're defiled?'

'Because my God forbids men and women who are married to experience others. A man and a woman have to be virgins when they marry.'

'Yours is a very harsh God, Rizpah. He needs a wife very badly. My gods and goddesses have sex often. How many times during the year does your God have sex?'

Rizpah remained silent. She could still hear the words of Absalom.

Jezebel smiled. 'He doesn't, does He? He just sits there in His heavens and looks down and when He sees men and women enjoying themselves, He feels jealous and angry, and He wants them to stop.'

'No,' said Rizpah shaking her head in defiance. 'No, that's not true. Yahweh loves people. He loves to see them happy and enjoying themselves. He loves it when a man and a woman enjoy their married life together.'

'And did you and Elijah enjoy a full married life together? Did you lay on the banks of a river, naked under the sun, and make love until you screamed? Did you climb a hill so you could see for ever, and then fondle his manhood until he was taller and stronger than the mountain, and beg him to fill you up? Did you ...?'

'No!' Rizpah shouted. Again, the Queen was surprised by her vehemence.

'No, I thought not. That's why you're so angry with me and my priest. Because for once, you knew what it was like to be a woman. For once, you experienced joy and satisfaction and the true meaning of sex between a man and a woman. And you're angry ... but not really with me. You're angry with your husband. Your anger is against Elijah, because all these years he could have been doing these things to you, and he didn't. Because since the day you married, he could have been kissing you and fondling you, but instead, he was making love to his God.'

Rizpah looked away, staring at the floor. And then, suddenly, an idea arose in Jezebel's head. She withdrew into her own thoughts until the idea clarified ... and then it became as clear as the water of a brook. 'Or is it Yahweh you're really angry with? Is it the God you pray to? It's not me, is it? It's Yahweh against whom you're screaming. Is it Yahweh who has let you down so badly that you now can't bear to live with yourself, Yahweh who prevented you all these years from knowing what it was like to be a woman? Your priests say that Yahweh instructed you to go forth and multiply, but He never told you that you had to enjoy yourselves in doing it, did He? Well, Asherah wants us to enjoy coupling; she encourages us to set our bodies alight, for then we are approaching what it means to be a god ...'

Rizpah looked up at the Queen and felt tears welling up in her eyes. Had this young woman sent spies out to overhear her conversation this morning with Absalom? If not, how was it this young woman knew so much of her inner secrets, those which she didn't dare admit even to herself? How did she understand what Rizpah didn't? It was what she had been thinking since she screamed out aloud as the priest made her climax, as she'd grasped his buttocks, wanting him to fill her more and more ... but when he'd finished and she realised the full enormity of what had happened, she was then too terrified to admit these feelings, even to herself.

Jezebel was right. It wasn't she who should feel shame. It wasn't Rizpah who was wrong in what she'd done. It wasn't her fault that suddenly her body had been set alight. No, it was the fault and failing of Elijah. For now she realised that there was another part of her life and her body which had been closed off to her through and because of her marriage; and because of Yahweh. How could a God whom her husband said was so loving and compassionate be so cruel as to deny Rizpah's body so long of so much that she desired?

'Well?' asked Jezebel.

Rizpah didn't understand.

'Do I have to explain everything to you?' said Jezebel.

'What are you saying?'

Jezebel sighed. It was all so simple in her mind, yet Rizpah was making it so complicated.

'For all of you women of Israel, I'm going to make Yahweh into a softer and more accepting god. I'm going to weaken the power of the priests by bringing Asherah back into the life of the land as co-equal and co-regent.'

Rizpah began to speak, and then found she couldn't say anything.

'What do you think of the idea? It's so simple. I've been looking for a way to do it ever since I came from Phoenicia. And now the time is right. Your husband showed that Yahweh is the God of gods ... very well, but the people have demanded that Asherah be brought back. They love her, and want her to protect them.

'The priests of Yahweh hate this, and again are fomenting things against me; so now is the time to strike. Now is the time for Asherah to rule. I will marry Yahweh to Asherah, and ...'

'But Yahweh can't marry.'

'Why not?' asked the Queen.

'Because it's blasphemy. Elijah said that Yahweh is the one true God, and ...'

'Then it can't hurt if we marry Him, can it? If He's the one true God, then He'll smile at what we're doing. If He's not the one true God, then I'll marry him to Asherah anyway, and He'll be happy for evermore, and He'll allow His people to be happy and to enjoy their bodies ...'

Seeing the dilemma in Rizpah's eyes, Jezebel continued, 'Ba'al and Asherah are married, and they're mother and son. Many gods marry in order to fertilise the land – to make it fruitful and to make it multiply. And your god, Yahweh, desperately needs a woman. I'll bet the reason He's so stern and angry and has priests who never smile and laugh is because He hasn't had sex since He was born. I'll bet that He's ...'

'Stop, Majesty!' shouted Rizpah, but this time not in fury, only in self-righteousness. 'This is my God of whom you speak. The Lord of heaven and earth, God of my fathers. The God who gave the law to

549

Moses, the law by which we live. And Moses gave it to us. "*I am who I am. I am He. I am the Lord your God who brought you out of the land of Egypt, out of the House of Bondage.*" You can't speak of my God like this. He's my ... my ... God.'

'Yes, a god who makes women as cold and dry as a desert in winter. A god who fails to shower the land with water to enrich the crops because its men and women aren't enjoying themselves and spilling their seed on the ground to fertilise it. You have a harsh and distant god, Rizpah. No wonder this is a harsh and distant land.'

'But your gods are no better, Jezebel. They also don't send the rain. Yours leave women barren so their husbands can cast them out into the desert; yours make innocent children into orphans; yours ...'

'All the more reason, then, to make the gods happy. We'll marry Yahweh to Asherah and then everything will be well ...'

A gentle breeze stirred the window coverings, as though the Lord in heaven was listening outside and had suddenly decided to enter the room.

After a few moments, Jezebel asked, 'Well, will you join me?'

'Will I help you to marry my God Yahweh to your gods?'

'Not my gods, no! ... To do what I wanted to do when I first became Queen of Israel. To marry Yahweh to my Goddess Asherah. She's such a gentle and loving goddess. She will make Him a good wife. She's not weak like the other goddesses from other countries. She's strong and determined and powerful, but gentle and considerate and loving. She'll make Yahweh a good consort. Then He'll rule in heaven with Asherah, and there'll be prosperity for Israel and everything will be all right. And we'll make idols of Yahweh and Asherah and have them smiling and we'll give Him a huge penis and we'll instruct the idol-makers to fashion Asherah to have open legs so that all who worship them will be encouraged to make love and make the land fertile again.'

'My husband will return to Israel if this happens, and you and your family will be overthrown. He'll call this blasphemy and he'll curse you even more.'

'Your husband is dead in my eyes, and should be for you. As far as I'm concerned, he is like a ghost who walks in my memory. The quicker you forget about seeing him again, the easier it will be for you and your children.'

'Will my husband ever be able to return to Israel?'

'No!' the young woman said emphatically.

Ahab was amazed by his wife's political astuteness. He'd even called her brilliant in front of his Council of Advisors; even Hattusas, older and less active than when he'd travelled with the young and inexperienced Princess from Phoenicia, was astonished by how easily the Israelite people had changed.

After the defeat of Ba'al and Asherah and the other Phoenician gods, Hattusas had watched in fear as people rose up and accepted the strength and power of Yahweh. He had been on the verge of demanding an army be sent from Phoenicia after the massacre; but Jezebel told him to wait. And, just a week later, the young woman had again challenged the might of Yahweh ... but this time not in a way which He could win. Now that this Israelite god,

Yahweh, was all-powerful, she had told the people and the priests, let him cure the ills of the world.

And when the people saw that they were still poor and still sick, and the drought continued to plague the land, and lepers walked the streets and highways, panic gripped them, they began to look in doubt at their own priests, to ask why Yahweh didn't make them happy.

Then, somehow, she had managed to force Elijah out of his stronghold in the temple, where he was holding court as though he were the very king himself. After his victory, he had demanded absolute loyalty and obedience of the people, commanding them to bring food and tithes to the priests; and he had ordered a revolt against Ahab and Jezebel. But little had come of it because Ahab had stationed a garrison of soldiers around the palace, and it would have been a bloodbath. And now this ... Hattusas watched the beginnings of the ceremony and pondered the words of praise about Jezebel that he would use in his report to her father, Ethbaal, King of Phoenicia.

The King of Israel looked resplendent in his purple robes, fashioned on the colour of the sky in the dawning hours. The dye had come from the lands to the north of Phoenicia, a land where the water of the sea was turquoise.

He had chosen to wear this particular robe because he felt that it was befitting to the occasion. Ahab had been dressed carefully by his manservant, a gift from Jezebel, and now he was dressing more in the style of the Phoenician court than of the court of the Israelites. More colour, more style, more dignity. Although the men of the House of Omri were warrior princes who owed more to the country than to the city, Ahab realised that his was the authority of government, and as such he had to impress the people. He remembered with embarrassment how he'd been dressed when he'd first ridden out to meet the entourage which Jezebel had led in her entry into Israel. He'd been a wild and crudely dressed soldier, stinking of the sweat of horse, and filthy from days spent on the road.

Now, as he and Jezebel joined hands and walked from the steps of their palace across the public marketplace to the steps which led up to the courtyard of the temple, Ahab felt every bit a King. And many of his people responded. He was surprised. He knew that the captain and soldiers of the Palace Guard had been out since early morning ordering people to line the streets and to attend the wedding ceremony, but he was surprised, not only by the numbers, but by the feeling in the crowd.

He'd assumed that there would be great and dangerous hostility from the many who had hailed the victory of Yahweh. But the voices of Yahweh's supporters had been muted since Jezebel's challenge. And more and more of the people had begun to question the priests of the one true God. Ahab had checked with his spies inside the temple and was told that donations were significantly less this month than last, that the priests had not been given as much food by supplicants, and the paucity of the donations of money had surprised even them. Also, the disappearance of Elijah had diminished much of the passion which people expected on coming to the temple.

He and his Council of Advisors had added to the people's disquiet with Yahweh's victory, by reminding the priests that responsibility for feeding the poor had been put with the temple authorities. It took only three days of inactivity for the starving to demonstrate and demand that the palace open its granaries. And that had diminished the power of the priests even more.

And now this: another strike against the meddlesome priests, another assault on their assumption of kingly power. He could barely restrain himself from laughing out loud as he walked beside his beautiful and brilliant young wife. Yes, he thought. She truly is my wife and my soulmate.

Jezebel felt the strength and pride in her husband's step. Where once he'd objected and was concerned about her plans to marry Yahweh to Asherah, now he was fully and totally in favour. She looked at the crowds, and even she, who, since the massacre, had come to hate the people of Israel more than any other people, began to see the beginning of a change in their hearts. Some, of course, looked at her with hatred; others in bemusement; still others were crying and wearing sackcloth and ashes on their foreheads, symbolising mourning for the death of Israel. But many had come because, since the challenge, Yahweh had let them down.

Once again, the asherahs were slowly starting to be visited, money was beginning to trickle like a rivulet into the hands of her priesthood; and best, and most blessed of all, the priests of Yahweh were angry that they had enjoyed the love of the people for so short a time. But Jezebel had known that eventually the people would want to come back to her gods, for they provided so much more in the way of entertainment than the God of the Temple of Samaria.

Yet much of the return to Ba'al and Asherah was because of Jezebel's simple but brilliant idea of marrying Yahweh to the Phoenician goddess. Yes, it was so simple, so direct, but so devastatingly clever, it had caught the priests of Israel completely off their guard. When they heard about it, they postured, jumped up and down, threatened, shouted, prayed ... but many of the people of the countryside warmed to the idea, especially when Jezebel announced that for the entire week, there would be free grain and the oil of olives distributed from the royal storehouses throughout the land. Of course, some in Israel talked of revolt and the curse of Yahweh and of blasphemy. But their thin voices were drowned out by the desire of the people to see Yahweh happy, married, and more forgiving.

Those who vehemently objected to the marriage between Yahweh and Asherah had been dealt with. One, a man named Eli who owned vineyards and who was a servant of the Lord, openly cried in the marketplace and gathered around him a large group of people. He wore ashes on his forehead and in his hair, and painstakingly, he explained that he had been born a poor man, and all his fortune had come from his devotion to Yahweh. He begged the people to rise up against the abomination which Ahab and Jezebel were about to perform. At first the people listened and began to rejoice in what he was saying, but then the guards came from the palace. The crowd was dispersed and when Eli returned to his vineyards, he found his house burned to the ground, his crop destroyed and his fields salted.

Others who objected were beaten by the King's guards until the people were aware of the reality of opposition to the King and Queen's plans. Some had their lands confiscated to the crown for treason, and were expelled from the country to beyond the mountains of the east ... that stopped much of the protest; but the priests in the temple, fanatical followers of the law of Moses, wouldn't be threatened and kept up their preaching and exhortations and wailing. And there was trouble from some of the older families of Samaria who still travelled every year to Jerusalem to worship in the great temple on top of the hill, many of whom were supporters of the House of Omri. But when Ahab promised them new concessions in trade, their objections were mentioned less often. Soon, opposition only came from the priests. Those who still objected whispered their agony, or discussed aloud, but only in the temple.

It was a hot day, one of the hottest of the spring. And it constantly reminded Ahab that unless spring rains fell soon, the crops wouldn't grow and ripen and summer would be spent hungry. And if summer made the people go hungry, then starvation would follow in winter and there would be much anger and discontent throughout the land.

He and Jezebel had worked out that there was enough grain and oil stored in the storehouses to feed the people for a week, but after that the stockpiles would be exhausted, and they would have to purchase these stocks from a neighbouring country. But it was a reasonable price to pay to ensure that the people were happy, that the priests of Yahweh were kept in their place, and that the Israelites loved their King and Queen.

But if the rains didn't come soon, and the crops failed, then rebellion would be in the air. And it would come from Captain Jehu, who was constantly a source of problems, and these days always had to be warned and put in his place; although silent since the expulsion of Elijah, he was known to be a follower of the hideous prophet, and although they had had no contact for an entire year, Ahab's spies told him that the young captain had followed the journeys of Elijah with interest. One day soon, Ahab might have to put Jehu to death.

As the sun beat down, Ahab and Jezebel walked the distance from their palace to the temple. In the far corner of the marketplace through which they walked, hidden by the heads of the crowd, Ahab detected some commotion.

Alert to possible assassination attempts by a fanatical follower of Yahweh, the head of the Palace Guard walked forward, commanding five of his men to follow. The crowd parted, and Ahab saw who it was.

Jehu, captain of the king's army, and a man who had caused him more problems than any other soldier during the past year, was advancing towards him with a small company of men ... not enough to assault him and his wife, but sufficient to worry his protectors.

The King stopped. Jezebel looked at her husband in surprise.

'You delay entry into the temple for Jehu. Why, Ahab?'

'Because he carries the army. He's loved and respected. I must wait for him.'

Jezebel whispered, 'If you'd killed him long ago when I told you to, you wouldn't have these problems.'

'And if I'd done that,' Ahab whispered back, 'I'd have had an army mutiny on my hands.'

The King held out his hands in welcome. 'Jehu! Brave and glorious commander of the armies of Israel. I greet you as a brother.'

'Majesty,' the young man called out theatrically, 'I greet you as a King and father to your nation.'

Jezebel froze in her steps. She looked at Jehu, wondering whether he would continue with the greeting. Her worst fears were realised. Before Ahab could respond, Jehu continued, 'You are a worthy successor to Omri, your father, and the other kings of Israel. And you are a leader of Israel as was Moses and Aaron and Jacob and Isaac. And dare I say, Majesty, that you also walk in the footsteps of our forefather Abraham.'

The crowd fell into silence as they sensed the tension between Jehu and Ahab. A response was called for; Jezebel prayed to Asherah that her husband would know what to say.

'Jehu,' Ahab began, 'I bless you for coming. There is no more loyal subject in all of Israel than the young captain of my army who defeated the hosts of Assyria and Babylonia. And there is no more loyal servant of Yahweh than Jehu.'

Ahab turned to the crowd and raised his voice to a louder pitch so all could hear his words. 'Captain Jehu has compared me to Abraham and Isaac and Jacob. These are our forefathers, and I am flattered by the comparison. But what pleases me most is his comparison of me with Moses, who gave us the law and who brought the children of Israel out of the Land of Bondage which is Egypt.

'But as Jehu will be the first to acknowledge, Egypt is now our friend. We trade with her. Our ships sail to her shores, our merchants take our goods and sell them in her cities. Times change, and Egypt is no longer the enemy she once was.'

He turned back to Jehu, his voice still loud. 'And just as times change between nations, where once bitter enemies are now friends, so times change in our faith. Which is why my Queen, Jezebel, and I are performing this ceremony ... and why you, Jehu, and the representatives of your army, have come to join us. Now, let us proceed to the temple ...'

And he immediately walked forward past Jehu. The ranks of the crowd closed behind them, and Jehu and the men he'd brought with him were swallowed up.

Jezebel squeezed her husband's arm. 'Wonderful,' she said.

'I've only shut him up for the moment. Tomorrow he'll have more to say. He will be dealt with. I'll send him to a border post and he'll be killed by a surprise attack from Moab. I'll grieve for him for thirty days. Then all Israel will see how I love my young and heroic captain.'

Inside the temple, the glare and heat of the outside was gone. Within, it was cool and mysterious, the scent of perfumes and burning spices adding to the occult sense of otherness. They stood beneath the huge stone architrave in the entrance until their eyes adjusted to the gloom. Within, the enormous space was lit by hundreds of candles and the dark of the upper levels of the building was cut by shafts of light from the vertical slits in the roof.

The temple was already full of priests and acolytes as well as wealthy members of the merchant families of Samaria who had paid the King heavily for the privilege of witnessing the marriage of the two gods.

And for the first time, to Ahab's surprise, the priests of Yahweh stood with those of Ba'al and El and the priestesses of Asherah. He had assumed that those loyal to Yahweh would have refused to be present, but it appeared that they had changed their minds.

All the priests looked resplendent in their robes. Those of Phoenicia wore blinding white robes which picked up the light from the ceiling, and made them look as though they, themselves, were alight. Beside the Phoenician priests and priestesses, the priests of Yahweh were dressed in robes of green and red and yellow stripes. The chief priest, Hazarmaveth, stood in the middle of the central aisle, wearing his mantle, the *ephod* and the breastplate containing the objects of divination. The breastplate was made of golden and linen threads which had been died purple and scarlet and blue in intricate and beautiful whorls, between which were the precious stones which represented the twelve tribes of Israel. Even from this distance, Ahab could see the topaz and the sardius, the emerald and the sapphire, the diamond and the jacinth.

But as he and Jezebel began to walk down the steps of the vestibule into the main room of prayer, Hazarmaveth, chief priest of Yahweh in Samaria held up his hand.

'Be warned, vain King,' Hazarmaveth shouted. 'You are embarking on a stony road and leading your people Israel into a desert. Foolish man! You were anointed by Yahweh, and now you spit in His face. How long do you think Yahweh will allow this blasphemy to continue? How long ...?'

The murmur in the prayer room came to an immediate halt as people looked in astonishment. But instead of Ahab stepping forward, it was Jezebel who walked slowly and deliberately down the aisle until she was within touching distance of the surprised priest, and whispered so that only the two of them could hear, 'Listen to me carefully, Priest. I know how Elijah lit the wood of his altar; I know the encouragement which he gave Yahweh in setting the fire. Do you understand what I'm saying? I know of the desert fire-water. Stand out of my way now, or I'll tell the people of Israel all that I know. If I do, then how long will your god last? Now go, before I end your rule …'

They stood looking at each other, an unbridgeable gulf of hatred between them, until Hazarmaveth stepped backwards, turned to his priests, and said, 'The priests and all those loyal to Yahweh will leave the Temple of the one true God and avoid seeing this blasphemy.'

All the priests of Yahweh left, and several people in the audience also walked away. It was a poor demonstration, not one which mattered. Their point had been made. Their opposition was at an end.

This was the beginning of a new future for Israel, and everybody welcomed the events which were about to take place in the temple. Jezebel had planned the ceremony down to the last detail. At a nod from her, the chief priest of Ba'al walked forward, and sprinkled rose-water at the feet of the King and Queen. He led them to the dais which had been set up at the end of the prayer room and they sat in their two chairs.

Then the singing began, a gentle ululating murmur from the priestesses which rose and fell like the sibilation of waves on the shore of the sea. The priests then joined in, and the audience of Israelites, unused to such noises, listened in utter fascination. More rose-water was sprinkled and as the perfume evaporated in the heat of the prayer room, the atmosphere became increasingly heady and erotic.

Then a priestess approached the King and Queen, kneeling before them. She shouted out, 'You are Yahweh and Asherah. You are our King and Queen, our god and goddess. I give to you the nuptial bread which will join you as husband and wife.'

She handed up two silver platters which contained warm bread in which was embedded raisins and pieces of fruit and honey. Ahab and Jezebel tore off bits of the bread and fed each other.

Twenty priests of Ba'al, imported with the generosity of King Ethbaal of Phoenicia especially for the ceremony, lined up before the Queen; and twenty priestesses lined up before the King. As each was presented, the priests said, 'I pledge my life to Asherah and to support and love you with all my heart and soul and might until I die.' The priestesses who came before Ahab said, 'I pledge my life to Yahweh and promise to serve you with my body and my heart until I die.'

Corn and flour and freshly caught river fish, as well as rare fish caught the previous morning from the sea, and other things of the land and of the water as befits offerings to the gods, were then brought down the aisle and laid at the feet of the King and Queen, who were performing the roles of the gods.

When the congratulations and offerings were ended, Yahweh turned to his Asherah and said, 'Queen of the Skies, I promise my undying love and affection. I am Yahweh and I give to you a golden mirror.'

Ahab stood, and handed Jezebel a highly-burnished bronze facing so that the goddess could see in her reflection the face which would please her master Yahweh.

As Jezebel took it, she herself stood, and said to her husband, 'I am Asherah, and you are my lover and master and god, Yahweh. To you I give this of myself.'

And Jezebel handed to Ahab a terracotta figurine of Asherah standing on a pillar. It was an idol with large breasts cradling a baby. This was the model of the idol which Jezebel recently approved and which all the idol-makers and potters throughout Israel would now be copying and making as a household deity of Asherah for people to purchase and use in their homes.

Yahweh received the idol. 'Know this, wife and goddess. When I am in other parts of Israel and away from you, I will always have this to remind me of the beauty and fertility of my wife.'

They sat again on their seats in the temple, and the chief priest of Ba'al and the chief priestess of Asherah came forward and placed golden crowns on their heads. The crowns were then removed, and placed on the other's head.

The audience shouted their cheers as the wedding ceremony was finalised. It was the moment for the musicians to play their tunes.

Ahab and Jezebel, still portraying the roles of Yahweh and Asherah, rose from their thrones and went behind the curtain to the Holy of Holies where the chief priest sacrificed spotless and pure animals as blood offerings. The curtain was drawn, and for the first time all day, they were completely alone.

He whispered, 'I don't know if I can do it. Not here. Not where they sacrifice animals and light the holy lights on the most sacred days. This is where Yahweh appears before the chief priest ...'

She pushed him playfully. 'You have to. If you don't, then the ceremony isn't complete, and the gods aren't married. Then there'll never be happiness in the land. Here, let me help you,' she said, and went over towards him.

It wasn't long before her ministering fingers made him forget where he was.

Silence descended on the temple, and the only sound was the moaning of two gods behind the curtain of the Holy Place. And as the moaning and groaning and laughter grew louder and louder, and the congregation became more and more influenced by the perfume and the spices and the heat of the prayer room, bodies began to rub against bodies, and hands strayed to where they could do the greatest pleasure, and a priest and a priestess who had been looking at each other longingly disappeared out of the side door of the temple.

And then a man's cry was heard from behind the curtain, and the cry of the man was joined by the cry of a woman. And the congregation breathed deeply, for they knew that all was well.

When they emerged from the Holy of Holies, Ahab shouted out, 'The marriage is consecrated. Yahweh has done His duty ...'

The audience cheered wildly.

Jezebel held up her hands for silence, turning to the Israelite audience. 'Go out and tell the whole of the land of Israel ... tell all the people that Yahweh will be happy from now on. He will no longer be a stern and angry god. He has a wife and a companion. Now rain will fall, crops will ripen, and Israel's enemies will know once and for ever that Israel could never be defeated, because the Lord of Hosts has taken to Himself a wife and is happy and will allow nothing to affect His chosen people. Tell all the people that everything will now be well ...'

And again the priests and priestesses and all the congregation cheered wildly. All except the chief priest of Israel, who was watching from his secret place high in the roof. He shook his head in horror and muttered to himself, 'All is lost. This is the worst of all blasphemies.'

As they crossed the square after walking out of the temple, Ahab glanced surreptitiously across to his beautiful wife, and a sadness came over him. In all the years since he'd married her she'd matured into an even more beautiful woman than the handsome and alluring girl he'd raced across the hills to meet when she entered Israel. This woman, whose ways with her body never ceased to amaze and excite him, had won and lost the hearts of Israel. And now she was trying to win the hearts of the people yet again. He couldn't help but admire her for her courage.

What would he have been if he hadn't married her? She had an amazing ability to perceive danger where he could only see opportunity; she could win over the biggest army without even firing an arrow; she could make the same people love her one day and hate her the next; she had taken the kingdom of Israel in her grasp and shaped it in a way which his father, Omri, could never have done with all his building of cities and temples. Yes, she was an amazing and an astounding woman.

But still he felt sad. For she was playing a very dangerous game. He had tried to warn her, but her enthusiasm and guile had won him over, just as she was determined again to win over the hearts of her people and to instil the love of Asherah in the same way as the love of Yahweh.

Ahab didn't have the heart to tell her that if she failed this time, the priests of Yahweh would have won for ever, and she would spend the rest of her life as a figure of hatred, almost certainly confined to the palace, unable to venture outside for fear that she would be stoned by the people. Such hatred was not unusual. It had happened to the land in the south, when King Asa of Judah had been forced to imprison his very own grandmother Maacah because she worshipped Asherah. But then, she must know this. She was so clever and perceptive ... she must know that if she lost this time, she would lose for ever.

Of course, Ahab would never, ever imprison Jezebel, but if things did not go well after the marriage of Yahweh to Asherah, if the drought continued or there was a war on the borders, or swarms of locust suddenly appeared from Egypt, then the people's love could turn into the people's resentment and hatred very quickly.

They journeyed hand in hand through the marketplace and smiled at people whom they knew from the city. Some were the wives of courtiers, some were the families of potters or bakers or butchers or candlemakers or weavers who sold their wares to the palace. There was a pleasant smell in the air, which Ahab realised was the smell of herbs being burnt in braziers on top of buildings, a thoughtful and clever effect which Jezebel knew would excite the admiration of the crowd.

And so they arrived at the steps of the palace courtyard. Normally, Ahab and Jezebel would be greeted by trumpeters, cymbalists and drummers, who, at an appropriate moment, would part to make an aisle in their midst for them to enter their home.

But this time, their way was blocked by two people who had hastened from the temple to the palace. Dressed in the blinding white robes of nuptial purity, as though they themselves were about to marry, were the chief priest of Ba'al and the chief priestess of Asherah. Both beamed smiles at the worshippers.

'May Ba'al and El and Yahweh and Asherah and all the other gods and goddesses in heaven bless this meeting and the union you have just enacted. May all the gods and goddesses smile upon Israel and Phoenicia and make their lands rich and bountiful and plentiful,' said the priestess.

And Yahweh and Asherah ascended the steps of the palace. Following them from the temple were other dignitaries who were going to join them in the nuptial feast. And in the fourth row of the procession, behind the important courtiers and ambassadors of other countries, wearing a yellow robe and roses in her hair, Rizpah walked in the warmth of the sun. She smiled as she saw her King and Queen ascend the steps to the palace. She clutched the heads of her two children, in whose hair the Queen of Israel herself had placed flowers. Both looked up at her and smiled radiantly. They were so happy.

She gazed at the crowd. It was a huge gathering, many were there because of their curiosity, many because they genuinely believed that this was a seminal moment in the history of Israel. Since the time of their Father, Abraham, Yahweh had always insisted that He was the one true God; a stern and uncompromising God. Well, now that He had been given a wife, perhaps He wouldn't be so unyielding and hardhearted. Rizpah sensed that this was a mood flowing like honey through the crowd.

There were faces which she recognised, men and women who smiled at her. She was well known now as part of the palace retinue, often seen in the company of Jezebel, and she was well liked. Rizpah would often go down to the areas where the potters and the metalworkers plied their trades, and talk to them. Her children were fascinated with the way in which these people made pots and jewellery and other wondrous things which were made for the palace of Jezebel and Ahab and the other courtiers. Coming from such a small town as Tishbe where no such trade was carried on, both Rizpah and her children really enjoyed this aspect of a large city such as Samaria.

In the crowd, Rizpah saw a face which she recognised above all others. It was Absalom, the man she'd met when she'd first come to Samaria on her own. He smiled and nodded; she returned his greeting. His advice had been good. Why not worship Asherah? Why not do as he suggested and enjoy these times?

How quickly what should have been anathema had become a part of her love. And all because of Elijah. All because he had used that trick with the desert fire-water. He had admitted his trickery to her just before he fled. He'd even boasted that he'd beaten Jezebel at her own game. He didn't realise that his admission had shocked her and damaged her faith in Yahweh and in him. He was so blinded by his own righteousness that he didn't understand her tears. And so he'd left her ... and she had left Yahweh.

Rizpah was amazed by the swiftness with which she'd come to love Asherah. Only months ago, she had been ravished, and contemplated suicide; then Jezebel had opened her heart and her mind to the joys of the body, and now she loved Asherah with all her heart. Rizpah saw clearly for the first time in her life. She saw that Yahweh was a good God, but a stern and uncompromising God. But she hated the priests of Yahweh for their trickery; they were evil priests, and now she realised that Elijah was the most evil of them all.

How could Yahweh possibly control the heavens and the earth on His own, without help from other gods? Jezebel was right – it was a silly proposition which the priests of Yahweh had told the people to obey.

And so over the months since her ravishment in the asherah, Rizpah had come to follow the path of the Phoenician goddess, and her body had never been happier. At times, she ached to return to the asherah and the priest and priestess who made her body and her mind dance with feelings and passions she had only felt as a young girl, alone in the fields on a warm summer's day.

But in the distant part of her mind, a voice whispered into her ear, and Rizpah wondered what her husband Elijah was doing now; and more importantly, she wondered what he would say if he knew that she had found such happiness with the worship of Asherah and Ba'al, and that her body felt like that of a young girl.

She was being silly, because she knew exactly what he would say. He would scream and rant and rave and threaten her and curse the ground on which she walked and run around in circles in that strange way of his, and tear his hair and terrify the children and make her cower at his madness.

Odd that she should have thought of him at this moment, for he had been a long way from her thoughts for many months. And what did his reaction matter? Why was she concerned at how he viewed her blasphemy? For no matter what Elijah might do or say, Rizpah had spent the past many months knowing feelings which had been denied to her throughout all her life as a worshipper of Yahweh. And those feelings were far, far more holy for her than the worship of a stern God.

And Elijah would never find out, because he was banned from the nation. As far as she was concerned, he was dead. Yes, she was glad to have been chosen to be in the procession of the wedding of Yahweh and Asherah. Maybe with this union, the whole of Israel could experience the feelings to which her body had been thrilling for the past months. Then everybody would be happy and all would be well.

CHAPTER TWENTY-ONE

Elijah's first sight of Elisha's village was a surprise. For he had passed this way before many times; yet it was unfamiliar to him. Like his own home in Tishbe, Elijah could look down into the beautiful and fertile valley, and see that the young man, Elisha, and his family lived simply as befitted any farmers.

Of course, had he wanted, Elijah could have lived like a king, as did many of the priests of Yahweh in Samaria. People were always wanting to give him money for his prophecies, for his blessings, to cure them of their illnesses, to make them rich, to ensure their crops grew ... but he always refused this way of easing his life, for he was the servant of the Lord, and the Lord Yahweh demanded much of those who worshipped Him. And never once did he claim miraculous abilities for himself. If he was able to make a child live again by breathing Yahweh's breath into his body, then it was the cure which Yahweh had decreed; Elijah was merely the agency by which Yahweh made His presence known.

Yes, the life of ease wasn't for him. Yahweh had chosen a lonely and rocky path for His servant, and Elijah was willing and happy to follow it. An easy life might be right for the priests of the temple, but not for a true prophet of the Lord. And so Elijah lived a simple and godly existence – poor, struggling, and often without money to purchase oil for the lamps or for cooking, but his wonderful wife Rizpah didn't complain, and neither did his children whom, he'd prayed, would follow in his footsteps. But that was until he saw the face of the Lord when he set foot on the holy Mount Sinai. Elijah now realised that it wasn't his children who would follow him, but another. For Yahweh had spoken to him and him alone, and it was not for his children to follow his path … no, Yahweh had ordained that he must find a young man whom he'd once met, and order him to follow Elijah's footsteps in the path of the Almighty One.

Whenever he thought of his wife and children, he felt bitter tears welling up inside of him. Elijah desperately missed Rizpah and the children. He prayed for them every night, knowing that the Lord Yahweh would protect them, and not allow them to be harmed by the evil of that woman, the Queen of Israel. And as he drew closer and closer to the city of Samaria, after years of being away in the deserts and wandering throughout the lands preaching the word of the Lord, thoughts of Rizpah seemed to invade his mind more and more. These days, he even dreamed of those early days of their marriage, when her smile had excited him and her touch had made him breathless.

But those thoughts were unworthy, both of her and of him. Yes, now that he was back in the land of Israel with all its abominations, all these thoughts must be banished. As he approached the home of Elisha, he forced himself to put thoughts of family, and the ease and comfort they provided him, out of his mind.

What most surprised Elijah was not so much the house of Elisha, but that he had passed this way many times before, most recently on his way to Phoenicia, and yet he hadn't noticed the beauty of the valley, nor the richness of the land so close to the River Jordan. His mind was always so occupied with thoughts of the Lord that he'd never allowed himself to appreciate the true beauty of the Lord's handiwork. And when he'd last passed this way, he'd been escaping the wrath of Ahab and Jezebel and his mind had been on survival. But even so, it was such a peaceful and verdant valley that he should, by rights, have noticed the beauty which Yahweh had placed on the earth.

He stood on the hill overlooking the elegant valley and enjoyed the simple pleasure of the sun on his face and the gentle winds blowing from the far distant ocean. There was the smell of salt in the air, an air very different to the sulphurous summit of Sinai which had burned his nostrils and scorched his hair as he had stood barefoot and terrified in the presence of the Holy One, Blessed be He.

The view that Elijah enjoyed of the valley was made more peaceful by the sheep grazing on the hillsides beneath him. How green and pleasant was the land of Yahweh!

But why, of all the young men whom Yahweh could have selected, had He guided Elijah's mind to settle upon Elisha? And why a man whose family lived in so remote a place from Jerusalem? Elijah had only met him once, when the young man, son of Shaphat who had lived for generations in the village of Abel-Meholah, 'the meadow of dancing', close to the city of Beth Shean, visited the Temple of Yahweh in Samaria. The two men had talked at length about the appalling idolatry into which Israel was sinking through the onslaught of Jezebel, the fiend from Phoenicia, and Elisha had impressed the older man with his passion and zeal for Yahweh.

Indeed, so impressed was Elijah with the young Elisha, that he had enquired about him from other priests. Little was known, but in time Elijah was told that Elisha was of the tribe of Issachar, and lived in the town where the Wadi el Maleh emerged into the valley of the River Jordan. People said that it was a rich meadowland, moist and luxuriant. Yet the young man was just a farmer, and didn't appear to have been touched by the hand of the Lord. And so, like the thousands of young men in whom Yahweh's spirit burned fiercely, and who knew of the ancient laws and ways of the Israelite peoples, Elijah had given the farmer his blessing, and the young man had disappeared into the crowd. Elijah forgot about him until the Lord Yahweh had commanded His prophet to go to the village of Abel-Meholah and to anoint Elisha as his successor.

And even as he'd journeyed northwards for many dark days and nights from the shores where the Gulf of Aqaba met the Sea of Reeds he had not yet managed to understand Yahweh's instructions. Why Elisha? There were so many young priests in the temple who had the vision and the passion to take up the mantle of Elijah and carry the battle with him to the very doorstep of the palace of the accursed House of Omri, yet now Yahweh's prophet must put his trust and faith into the hands of a farmer. He shook his head. Strange were the ways of the Lord.

Still, the Lord God of Hosts had given Elijah instructions that this young and crude man, Elisha, was to follow in his footsteps, and God's word cannot be ignored. He rested a few more moments before starting down the hill to the collection of houses which comprised Abel-Meholah, and where he knew that Elisha lived with his father and mother and two sisters and a brother. Through the village ran a brook, dividing the homes one from another. A small bridge made of wood had been constructed across the brook, and Elijah could see that in other parts of the river stepping stones had been placed so that neighbour could visit neighbour at will.

And then he remembered that he had, indeed, seen the valley before … he'd once glanced down at the village in the valley as he'd walked the high road above the Valley of Jezreel, which meant 'God Sows', on his way north from Samaria to the upper reaches of the land of Israel to pray to those who lived closest to the cursed idolators of Phoenicia. Indeed, he'd stayed for over a week with a man and wife who lived in the Plain of Esdraelon between Mount Gilboa and the Hill of Moreh because they had offered him shelter when the weather had turned horrible and the gales and rain had made the land into a bog and there was always the danger of the road sliding into the valley floor.

This was the road he preferred, the higher road, because the other road, which ran through the Valley of Jezreel, was the most popular road from Egypt to the lands of the north and there were always caravans and traders there to rob him or to disturb his peace. This road was the more difficult secondary road which ran north from Jerusalem through Shechem and Samaria to Megiddo. It then made its way toward the coast at Ak-Kah, then northward along the coast to the cursed Phoenician ports at Tyre and Sidon. But he'd only ever once taken the road to Phoenicia, and that was both his undoing and his salvation, for even though he had been far from Judah and Israel, in Phoenicia he had met Jehu, whom the Lord had told him would be crowned king and bring an end to the House of Omri for ever.

Elijah looked north and envisaged the beautiful Mountain of Carmel whose shoulders and valleys he knew so well and which had been the scene of his triumph over the Phoenician gods, so long ago now. He ached to be there, to walk over the verdant land and to commune with the Almighty who had helped him vanquish his enemies. But now he didn't have that luxury; now he had to descend into the valley, seek out Elisha and inform him of the honour which the Lord had bestowed upon him.

He half walked, half ran down the mountainside, only spying the track which he should have taken as he was close to the brook. He hopped over boulders and jumped over convolutions in the land. People who worked in fields or housewives grinding wheat or meal outside their houses looked up in surprise at the noises and movement which disturbed their peace. At first they thought it was a boy hopping down the hill, but as he drew closer they realised that it was a man of forty or more years.

One of the young men in the fields beside the brook, watering the ground where cotton grew, looked up and thought he recognised the man racing down the hillside towards the village; but he couldn't place him. He stood up straight, and watched as the nimble figure navigated his way over boulders and around hillocks.

Eventually the traveller, because that was undoubtedly what he was from his filthy locks of hair and his stained and torn cloak, reached the houses. The man spoke to a woman who was washing garments in the brook. She stood and pointed in Elisha's direction; the traveller crossed the brook by the stones in the water and walked quickly towards him.

'Elisha. Greetings in the name of the Lord of Hosts, Yahweh.'

'Greetings,' said the startled young man. His father Shaphat walked towards the traveller, fearing that his son might be in trouble. There were eight strong men in calling distance within three fields' distance who could easily deal with this stranger if he made trouble.

'Elisha, put on your cloak and come with me. We have much work to do.'

Elisha looked at him in surprise. 'I know you. You're Elijah, the prophet of the Lord Yahweh,' he said.

Elijah said, 'Yes. Of course I am. We've spoken in the Temple in Samaria. Come, quickly. We have little time to lose if we are to defeat the cursed Jezebel and her evil followers.'

Elijah turned around and began to walk back up the hill, but Elisha stared in shock.

'Where … What …?'

Both men looked at each other in consternation. The void in their understanding was bridged by the arrival of Elisha's father Shaphat who had left his northern field to see what the stranger wanted.

'Who are you, sir? What do you want with my son?'

'I am Elijah, prophet of Yahweh, God of Israel. Praise the Lord and sing His name for ever. Your son is coming with me as my servant and my follower. He is to wear the Mantle of the Lord on my death.'

'What ...?' said the father.

Exasperated, Elijah responded angrily. 'What's the matter with the people of this valley? You say "*where*" and "*what*" and then you say nothing more. Didn't you understand what I just told you? I said that a great honour, the greatest possible, has been bestowed upon your son. Now time is pressing. The fangs of that snake in Samaria, Jezebel, are biting deeper and deeper into the body of Israel. We must be away.'

The older man scratched his head, wiping his brow in the hot sun. 'You want my son to lay down his tools and follow you ...?'

'Yes! Of course! I just told you, didn't I?' said Elijah in frustration. 'Hasn't the sun yet dawned on your land, or is the dew blinding your eyes? Your son is now a prophet of the Lord Yahweh. He is honoured above all men. You should bow down to him and respect him.'

'But he's helping prepare for the harvest ...'

Elijah looked at the father in incomprehension. 'He will harvest more than just crops when he follows in my footsteps. His name will be sung throughout all of Israel. He will harvest the people as Yahweh's crops ...'

'But he's not even married ...' said Elisha's father.

The gulf of comprehension between the three men grew wider. Elijah shook his head. 'Married? What has marriage to do with it? Elisha won't be thinking of women and marriage and family. These things are for ordinary men like you. Elisha is a chosen one of God. Can't you understand that?'

The father turned to his son. 'Elisha, go into the house and tell your mother that we have a visitor who has come and will require food and rest.' The young man walked away.

'I have no time for food and rest. Don't you understand that ...?'

But Shaphat raised his hand and looked sternly at Elijah. 'Listen to me, prophet of God. I know who you are. I was on the Mount of Carmel when you called down the fire of the Lord to the altar and offered Him a sacrifice. And I was there when you encouraged the people of Israel into a frenzy and they slaughtered hundreds of priests and priestesses. Much was right with what you did in the name of the Lord. But I watched the massacre, and I wondered if God wanted that to happen. The worship of these idols is against the word of the Lord, but does that allow us to slay so many, especially women? It was murder, and the Lord our God said that murder is a sin and ...'

Elijah screamed, 'Don't dare to question my authority in the name of the Lord!'

At a distance, Elisha turned in shock at the way in which the silence of the valley was suddenly rent by anger. He watched Elijah draw close to his father and threaten him. Should he run back and defend ...? Whom? His father, or the man of God?

'"*I am the Lord your God. You shall have no other gods but me* ..." This is the word of the Lord, Shaphat. "*No other gods but me!*" Which means that we must destroy all gods and all those who serve false gods and all those who worship false gods. That is Israel's role.

Not to be the subservient follower, but the destroyer of all those who try to turn our heads, and force us to follow to kneel before idols. Woe unto him or her who turns us from the footsteps of our Father Abraham. Woe unto him or her who does not bow before Yahweh.

'And the Almighty has chosen your son, Elisha, to be that destroyer. Stand against me, Shaphat, and death will be your reward. Believe me when I say that if I leave this valley without Elisha a great curse will come upon your land, and death shall visit you and your family. Your ground will be as a field of salt and your stream will turn into brackish water. You and your family will grow poor and starve and the worst diseases of leprosy and plague will fall on you from the sky.

'For this is what it means to turn your back on God. And just as I have killed the priests and priestesses of the foreign gods, so I will call upon the Lord God of Hosts to smite you and end your days of happiness. Now, Shaphat, prepare Elisha your son to follow me.'

Shaphat looked in horror into the eyes of Elijah. But all he saw there was the infinity of night.

She drew back in fear, thinking the man in the cloak was about to attack her. He looked like a traveller, a man of the streets who slept rough and ate and washed only occasionally when the opportunity arose. She would have called the guards, but there were people around, and when she looked more closely she realised that although he was a traveller, he was also a young man, little more than a boy, and that his manner wasn't really threatening. The problem was that he'd startled her while she was deep in thought.

'Rizpah,' the young man hissed from across the marketplace. Rizpah had just emerged from the temple of Yahweh after attending another service of consummation of the marriage between Yahweh and Asherah. In her pocket she carried an idol which was fresh from the potter showing both gods in happy abandon; it was a present for Jezebel.

'Rizpah,' the young man continued to hiss.

She crossed the square and approached him. 'Yes?'

'Is it you? I asked a trader and he said that you are Rizpah, wife of Elijah the prophet of the Lord Yahweh. Are you the woman Rizpah?'

Her blood turned cold at the mention of the name Elijah. It was a name which hadn't been on her tongue in months. It was strange to hear the name again. She looked at the young boy. There was an innocence in his face which inclined her to trust him. He threw the hood of his cloak back, revealing his face. And it was then that she felt a shock race through her body … he was the very image of Elijah when she first married him. Indeed, it could have been the Elijah himself of fifteen years ago standing there before her, the Elijah who had held her hand in the meadow and the orchard, who had lain in the long grass with her and kissed her tenderly on the lips.

Rizpah's eyes opened wide in shock. In a hoarse voice, she whispered, 'I'm Rizpah.'

'I was told you'd be wearing dark robes. Yet you're wearing robes which are the blue of a summer sky.'

'Yes?' she said. His voice wasn't Elijah's voice. She forced herself back to reality and wondered whether this youth was both a traveller and a madman. 'Who are you? What do you want with me?'

'I'm Elisha. Tell me whether you are Rizpah who is the wife of Elijah?'

Again the name; again the shock. For months and months, his name had been forbidden to be used in public. The only time she ever heard the name of her husband the prophet of Yahweh used was when it was whispered by one of her children, asking if she knew whether he would return.

'What do you want with me?'

'Are you the wife of Elijah?' he insisted.

She remained silent. The young man smiled. 'You are. I can tell by your eyes. He said to me that your eyes reveal the thoughts which are in your mind. You are Rizpah, wife of Elijah of the village of Tishbe.'

'He said to you ...? You've spoken to him?'

'Just this morning.'

'Where? In Tishbe?' But it couldn't be, for Tishbe was almost seven days' travel ...

'No,' the young man smiled, 'not in Tishbe, but here in Samaria.'

Rizpah nearly fainted, and held onto the wooden beams of the building that were beside her. She felt herself drawing back from this boy, Elisha, in utter shock. Her husband was here, in the city. And this young man had mentioned the name of Tishbe. Thoughts of her home flooded her mind like a river bursting its banks in the summer rain. Images of it invaded her eyes, but they were distant images, and she couldn't focus properly or even remember clearly what it looked like after living in the luxury of the palace; her children had tutors, she had her own servant, they had more than they ever dreamed possible; not once in the past years had she washed linen or made candles or ground flour; everything was done for her. All that was expected of her was to be a companion to Jezebel and to follow in her footsteps when she walked in public procession towards and from the temple.

But now she was again thinking of Tishbe and Elijah and she was so confused …

The young man was becoming anxious at her silence. 'You are Rizpah, the wife of Elijah, aren't you?'

Softly, she replied, 'Yes.'

'Come with me. I have wonderful news.'

He turned and disappeared down the Street of the Lamp Makers, where there was noise and the smell of smoke from braziers. She followed him slowly and unsteadily down the narrow street where shafts of bright sunlight cut sharp outlines into the dusty air. He waited for her until they emerged into one of the smaller streets of Samaria, the Street of the Skin Makers, where goat and sheepskins were scraped and washed and prepared for making into coats. Her nose wrinkled at the assault of the stench. But she overcame her nausea as he hurried along the street and they emerged into a covered bazaar where men and women who sat cross-legged on blankets sold lamps and dishes and pots.

He was half walking, half running, and she was too shocked to keep pace with him and his enthusiasm. She felt as though a great stone weight had been hung from her neck. 'Wait,' she called out, but he didn't hear her. She maintained her pace. She turned a corner, and suddenly came face to face with him. He stood in an archway, the entry to a house. She had no idea where she was.

'Come,' he said, his eagerness not taking into account the fact that the shock she had felt when she first met him was now making her feel ill … close to fainting.

'This is the home of Abimelech, a friend of Yahweh,' he said, the words almost bursting out of his body.

They climbed the narrow steep stone steps to one level, but instead of entering the rooms, continued upwards in a narrowing stairway to a second level which opened up into a light cool room looking over the roofs of houses below. An old man wearing the striped robes of a desert dweller, his wife and three other women met them. But instead of introducing himself, he ushered them urgently through the room and onto the balcony, a place which was hidden from the view of surrounding houses by trestles adorned with flowers and vines.

Panting and excited, the young man turned. He was sweating from the heat and the rapid journey. He again withdrew the hood of his cloak, and she saw his face more clearly now. He was dark-skinned and had jet-black hair; no, on closer inspection, he wasn't a young Elijah, but his eyes were burning with that same mixture of love and hate, fear and anger.

Elisha smiled. He said quietly, 'My name is Elisha, son of Shaphat. I am the servant of the servant of Yahweh. Your husband Elijah has returned from the wilderness of Sinai where he spoke directly with God. He has come back, Rizpah. He is near, just beyond the city walls. He told me to collect you and your children from the clutches of the evil Jezebel and her husband Ahab and to take you from imprisonment into the freedom of Tishbe while he finishes his work of destroying the House of Omri and brings the walls of Samaria crashing down onto the dogs of idolatry. He waits close by, in the wooded valley beyond, waiting for you to come to him.'

Hoarsely she acknowledged, 'My husband is returned!' It was neither statement nor question ... more a prediction of the rocky path which suddenly lay before her.

'Close by!' said Elisha with almost overwhelming enthusiasm. 'A walk of not more than a thousand paces. He hides in the valley below the walls of the city, where the waters meet.'

'He's here?' She kept repeating it so that she understood the awful finality of the words.

'Yes, woman. Your husband is close by. Elijah is near. Isn't it wonderful! He's come to take you and your precious children away from this den of iniquity, from this place outside of the sight of the Lord. He's going to slay the evil idols in the temple, just like our Father Abraham slew them in the time of his migration from Ur in Chaldea to Holy Jerusalem.'

The eagerness in Elisha's face was beyond her comprehension. His eyes seemed to glow with a divine radiance. It was as though the thoughts and actions were too big for his body, and would burst out of him into the surrounding air.

Suddenly a wave of overwhelming guilt swept through Rizpah's mind. She felt as though she had been caught in the act of adultery ... and she had been. For her regular prayers with a priest of Asherah had become the most welcome part of her week. Did she not open her body to his touch, his feel, his manhood? And did she not welcome the way in which he kissed her and made her body thrill to his fingers as they reached down from her throat to her breasts, to her womanhood? Didn't this priest, for whom she ached as a kind and gentle lover, know more about her body in the short time since they'd been introduced, than she had learned in an entire lifetime? And hadn't he opened her up as though she was a dormant bud, bursting out of the grasp of the cold winter soil and flowering to the warmth of a joyous spring day?

But that wasn't all. For aside from the orgasmic experiences she was having nearly every day as a new and enthusiastic acolyte of Asherah, didn't she also enjoy every moment of her life in the palace? She sat at the left hand of Jezebel when they banqueted; she played games with Jezebel; she occasionally enjoyed the company of Ahab who was a strong King in his dealings with his ministers and advisors and a great builder of cities, but weak and deeply in love like a boy whenever he was with Jezebel.

And Rizpah and her children enjoyed the freedom of the palace and the city, and the benefits which the city could bestow on a person – meat always available from the streets of the butchers; candles there to purchase whenever they were needed; never had she been forced to wash her own or the children's clothes ... so much in her life added to her pleasure and her leisure.

But now all that life was over; for Yahweh had returned and had opened her eyes; and Yahweh was a stern God and He would punish her for the sins she had committed. Elijah would never tolerate any reason for her walking in the darkness – not her loneliness, nor her isolation, nor her fear – no, he would never accept or understand her corruption.

Now Rizpah would have to return to an unyielding God and an uncompromising husband and the condemnation he would rain down on her for her actions. And he would call her 'whore' and 'idolatress' and 'harlot' and he would take her out into the fields and strip her naked and condemn her with the righteousness of his zeal. And her neighbours would come out of their houses as Elijah cursed her; they would pick up stones from the field and throw them at her and she would run naked into the forest and try to hide. And her children would scream in fear and they would be restrained by neighbours who would tell them that their mother was dead in the eyes of the Lord.

And if that didn't happen, if she lied and kept silent about what had gone on in the palace for these past months, then what would happen? Would Jezebel, furious that Rizpah had returned to the hated Elijah, tell all Israel what she had done? No, not Jezebel, for in the time that the two women had been intimate friends, Rizpah had come to know Jezebel as a kind, generous ... wild and irresponsible, certainly ... but loving young woman. And indeed, Rizpah loved Jezebel as the younger sister she'd always wanted, open and honest and physical and loving.

What should she do? Should she return to the cold home of her marriage and the empty love of her husband, the barrenness of their lives and the dryness of their bed, always thinking of the hot and passionate lovemaking she'd enjoyed in the asherah and palace instead of the reality of her husband who snored, cold and immobile beside her? Should she move away from the seductive pleasures of the palace and back into her former home with its damp and cold earth floors in winter and its suffocating heat in summer, with the dust and the flies and other insects which made her and her children's lives miserable. Would she have to wash clothes again, attend to the cooking and wait alone, without the help and comfort of a man, for the weeks and months that Elijah was away from Tishbe praying or saving souls or trying to bring the Lord Yahweh closer to His people Israel …

But no, it was more … far more than all these transitory pleasures. For in her time with Jezebel, she had learned what a hard and uncompromising God Israel had chosen to govern her. Because the worship of Asherah had given Rizpah a freedom which she had never enjoyed under Yahweh. As a lover and worshipper of Asherah, Rizpah and other women weren't condemned for being women – they weren't made to feel evil and guilty for enjoying their own bodies – and they were never made to feel self-loathing when they somehow failed to live up to the demands imposed upon them by their goddess. Yet the priests of Yahweh did all these things.

Should she go back to the worship of Yahweh? How could she? Was she thrilled that her husband had returned? Was a criminal thrilled to be thrown into prison? Was a leper thrilled to say goodbye to the world and walk down into a lepers' valley? Her mind was in turmoil.

'Does my husband want to see me now?' she asked Elisha.

But Elisha didn't understand. 'Of course! He wants you and your children to escape with me and return to Tishbe. There you will be safe while he and I and Captain Jehu and others loyal to Yahweh sweep out this nest of vipers with our outstretched hands. For Yahweh is with us and the Lord will give us strength and courage.'

'But you and he will be killed. The army …'

Elisha smiled knowingly. 'Rizpah, the army of Israel is the army of God. Yahweh will direct them to follow us and will make their eyes open and their hearts change. These are men who have defended Israel in the past against the enemies of Yahweh; and when they see that Israel isn't under attack from forces beyond her borders, but from forces of evil within, then they will rally behind Captain Jehu and victory will be ours. Then the cursed House of Omri, father of the evil Ahab, will be ended for ever.'

He looked up into the sky, and shouted out, 'Yahweh is the Lord. Praise be to Yahweh, God in heaven and on earth.'

Rizpah began to back away from him. He reminded her so much of Elijah; that zeal, the fanaticism, the inability to listen to her voice of moderation, the supreme knowledge that he above all others was right. And this was only the half of it; for when Elijah had returned to their home from one of his ministries, or when there were times of crisis in the land and he raged about things which she didn't properly understand, then he was lost to her and she was never certain that his mind would ever return. These were moments when she feared him and worried about what he might do to her and her children; sometimes his rages and shoutings terrified the family, and they would all run into a field and hide until he calmed down. Once they had hidden in a neighbour's house for a week, the whole village listening to Elijah scream and shout and run around the fields wearing just a loincloth.

And now Rizpah saw that Elijah's acolyte, Elisha, was suffering from the same diseases of the mind, a madness of the spirit, demons in his head which made him terrifying.

Softly she said, 'I will not go with you.'

He didn't hear, or if he did, he didn't understand. 'When?'

'I will not go with you,' she repeated more loudly.

'What?' He looked at her as though she was making a joke or beginning to tell a fable as men around a campfire tell stories to each other.

'I am staying here. My children need me.'

And understanding dawned. 'Of course! Yes, but your children must come with us. Return to your prison in the palace and gather your children. Don't worry, Rizpah, they will be safe because the day of the Lord draws close. Today, tomorrow, Israel will be freed from the yoke of idolatry.' He looked at her and smiled. He was so young, so innocent, Rizpah thought. He walked over to her. 'You are a good and caring mother. Now go and gather your sheep, and return with the lambs. I will be waiting to escort you to your husband and freedom.'

But she stepped back from him.

'No!' she said more vehemently. 'They will not go with you.'

'What?'

'My children remain here, but I must see Elijah. Now!'

Again Elisha smiled. He was completely misunderstanding her. 'Of course you'll see your husband, but first gather your flock; then you can all experience the joy of reuniting with Elijah.'

'Fool!' she shouted. 'My children remain here. I want to see Elijah now.'

Elisha sprang back, as though a snake had bitten him. 'Woman,' he said, 'gather your children.'

'My children are safe here. I must see Elijah. There is much danger in what you're planning. He must be warned.' Her manner told him not to argue any further. Anyway, he reasoned, she could always return to the palace after she had met Elijah.

They left Samaria in silence. She walked fifty paces in front of him because she was afraid that the guards on the gate might recognise her and she didn't want to be seen in the company of a man such as Elisha. They walked down the hill, and then turned south along a track in the direction of distant Jerusalem. The day was already boiling hot, and people who made early morning journeys up the hill into Samaria to sell their wares were already long absent from the roads. In the distance, some shepherds were driving their goats to lower pastures near to the river.

They descended further and further until they began to enter the area where the cedar trees grew in the valley. As they entered the forest, the air became cooler, the light increasingly indistinct, the insects in the air thicker. It was a relief from the intensity of heat in the upper world of Samaria ... yet she felt no great relief. Instead her heart was beating wildly, her mouth was dry, her mind reeling. It felt as though she were about to enter into another prayer session for

Asherah with the priest; yet this wasn't pleasure she was feeling, but an overwhelming sense of dread, a deep and morbid fear of meeting Elijah again and telling him of her decision.

And when he looked into her eyes, he would know instantly that she had become an adulteress; because her eyes were younger, clearer, and happier than he'd ever seen them. Indeed, her eyes were the eyes of a young girl, the eyes which had been so admired by the young men of surrounding villages before her parents had betrothed her to Elijah. And there was no way she could disguise the feelings which showed in her eyes.

She stopped beside a large and gnarled cedar tree. Her legs wouldn't carry her any further. She put her hand against the ancient bark, and felt that her body was rooted to the ground, just like the cedar tree. Elisha looked behind him, and returned to her. 'Not much longer now, Rizpah. Just to the end of the valley, and then we climb to the caves. Elijah is waiting for you.'

She began to weep. 'I can't go on. How can I look my husband in the eyes? He will know immediately that I have sinned before the Lord, and that I would sin again tomorrow if I could. Now that I must face my husband, I know that he will hate me for what I've become, so how will he ever understand that I can never return to what I was? I'm so unhappy,' she wailed. 'Why did he have to return?'

But Elisha wasn't listening. Instead, he told her, 'How can you be blamed for living in the house of iniquity when you were forced to? If a knife is held to a man's throat, then the actions he commits as a result are not his fault. The Lord sees into your heart, Rizpah, and He sees a good and honest woman of Israel. Walk on with me. Salvation is soon at hand.'

And she followed him.

He saw her before she saw him. He was high up in the mouth of a cave, hidden from any wanderers in the depths of the dark shadows. When he saw that there were only two travellers, he could restrain his impatience no longer.

'Rizpah!' he shouted out, startling her. His voice carried across the whole valley and reverberated off the rocks and hillside, as though there were many Elijahs all around calling to her, accusing her.

'Wife. I am returned. Elijah your husband is returned. Where are the children? There is much to do,' he shouted, jumping over rocks and running through the foliage to reach the path they were treading. As he ran he shouted, 'We must call Captain Jehu to meet us beyond the walls in the morning. Before dawn so that we catch them by surprise. Just like I caught their priests and priestesses by surprise when I made fools of them at the altar I built to Yahweh. Where are the children? Elisha, did you see anything of what I told you to look for in Samaria? The army, what of their disposition? Are they in force? Are they loyal to Yahweh? Rizpah, where are the children? Elisha, have you arranged for those loyal to Yahweh to meet in the marketplace upon my command. This cannot be done by the followers of Jehu alone; the entire population who are still loyal to Yahweh must rise up ...'

He bounded down the steep hillside, and with a final jump from a rock ledge, reached their path and stood in front of them, barring their way. Rizpah looked at him for the first time in over five years, and was shocked by the change which had occurred in her husband. He was older, but by far more than the five years they had been separated ... this man looked many years older than when she'd last seen him. And he carried in his eyes a look which she'd never seen before, not even in the days when he was overtaken by Yahweh and his mind was taken from her.

He was a stranger, this bedraggled man who stood before her. She barely recognised him. His eyes, always eccentric and far distant, now were almost absent. They looked, but they did not see. He hadn't even noticed the way in which her hair was plaited with flowers, or the light blueness of her robes, or the way in which paint had been applied to her nails, or the red of her cheeks and lips. He just stared through her.

But that wasn't what shocked her so much. For in front of Rizpah was her husband, yet he was like a man in the throes of death, here but not here. His clothes were torn and tattered, his hair falling out in places where it had once grown sturdy; his skin was darker than she'd ever seen it before, dry and flaking. He looked ill, yet his manner was that of a youthful boy, enthusiastic and full of life, and his body was moving and twitching in the way of children before they play some game. He almost jumped up and down on the path.

'What was the disposition of the city, Elisha? People? Were there many people in the streets? And the temple? Was the hideous idol still there to the blasphemous Asherah? ... I can hardly bring myself to speak her name.'

Even Elisha was taken aback by the confusion of his mind. 'Elijah, I have brought your wife to see you. Here is Rizpah.'

But Elijah demanded answers to questions about Samaria, and repeated them. 'Elijah, there are many people in the streets; and I wasn't there long enough to see who was loyal to Yahweh, and who had gone across to the worship of the other gods. I was there to do your bidding; I went to bring Rizpah and your children to safety before you smite the ungodly of Samaria like Yahweh smote the godless of Sodom and Gomorrah.'

A peace suddenly seemed to descend on Elijah. His eyes focussed on Rizpah. He smiled, and held out his hand. She lifted her own into his. His skin was as rough as the bark of the cedar she'd touched; would he recognise the difference in her hands? Now they were so smooth and oiled; before they'd been so rough and crude.

But he didn't notice. Instead, he led her along the path to where there was a natural seat in the rock ledge. He invited her to sit down. 'How have the years been to you, Rizpah, my wife?' he asked. 'You seem well.' He looked at her hair and the flowers, then at her robe. 'They have forced you to become like them, an abomination in the eyes of the Lord. Don't worry, for our enemies will pay with their lives. As I smote their eight hundred priests and priestesses, so I will smite the King and Queen, all their offspring and all who have bent their knees to the worship of the gods of Phoenicia. All Samaria will cry out for their sins. Children will be orphans, wives will be widows, husbands will curse the day their wives entered these groves of foul iniquity and evil and gave themselves like whores to the priests of Ba'al.'

Rizpah listened in increasing horror. But if her disposition was becoming increasingly distressed and isolated, Elijah didn't seem to notice it. 'The Lord Yahweh will unleash a torrent of fire upon the capital of Israel and cleanse the evil; and then He will unleash a torrent of rain which will wash away the sins and the iniquities. And the rain will continue for forty days and forty nights and will cleanse the land of Israel; good men and women who have been true servants of the Lord will emerge unscathed from their hiding places and they will rejoice in the name of the Lord and there will be dancing and singing and feasting. For the day of the Lord will have come, and then Israel and Judah will be reunited as one land, one nation, one people. They will be a mighty people as the Lord of Hosts has foretold, as He said to me, Rizpah, on the holy Mountain of Sinai. And I am his vessel. I am he who will rise up and smite the enemies of the Lord Yahweh.'

She remained silent. But Elijah was not on the seat, nor in the wood, nor in Israel, he was somewhere else, travelling in the infinity of his mind.

Softly she asked, 'Elijah, would you punish me, your wife?'

He said nothing, but looked at her. He didn't hear what she said.

'Husband. Would you punish your Rizpah?'

She sensed that Elisha was looking at her in consternation.

Louder, she said, 'Would you punish your wife, Elijah, if you found that I had been one of those who you condemn? For I have been unfaithful to Yahweh.

Since you have been gone, and of my own choice, I have been a worshipper of Ba'al and Asherah. I have been into the temple and have knelt down before the false gods.'

Elisha intervened, 'You were forced by the evil …'

'No!' she shouted at him. He jumped back in shock. 'No, I wasn't forced. I did things of my own will. I decided. I did. Me, Elijah,' she said, looking at her husband. 'It was me, Rizpah, who went into the asherahs and lay with the priests and gave my body over to them.

'And I tell you that you're wrong. You are so very wrong, Elijah. For these are not evil gods, and neither are the people who worship them evil. And neither are their priests and priestesses evil. I was at the ceremony in which Yahweh was married to Asherah. Understand this, Elijah. Yahweh your God has taken a wife. She is Asherah. She is gentle and good and understanding and brings me great comfort. She is responsible for the fertility of the ground and for the making of children between a man and his wife, and for the spring lambs and goats and calves in the fields. Hers is the abundance of heaven. And since she became wife and consort to Yahweh, we have never been happier. The people are happy. The children smile. There has been summer rain and the streams are full. The crops have been gathered. Widows and orphans have food in their stomachs and wood for fires at night. In the year since Yahweh and Asherah were wed, there hasn't been a single case of leprosy in Samaria. And nowhere has there been reported locust flying in from the sky to eat our future.

'Do you understand what I'm saying, Elijah? Yahweh is married. He has taken a wife. Yahweh is happy. He doesn't want death and destruction any more. He wants love and peace and for people to enjoy themselves.'

She looked carefully at Elijah to judge his reaction, but his view was still beyond the forest, into the vastness of elsewhere. Rizpah looked at Elisha. He was staring at her, his eyes wide in shock, his mouth open but silent. She looked again at her husband, though the man she saw wasn't her husband but a stranger, a man who hadn't heard a word she said.

Rizpah stood, and silently walked back up the path, leaving the two men staring at her receding form. But they saw very different things.

CHAPTER TWENTY-TWO

Jezebel was shocked by the condition of her servant and friend, Rizpah. She had left the palace that morning to serve Asherah as one of her acolytes in the temple and to supervise the new moon ceremony of the consummation between Yahweh and Asherah, but she returned looking like an old and frightened woman.

She had returned to the palace with one of the new idols for the union of Yahweh and Asherah, for which Jezebel had created a special niche in the wall of her bedchamber upon which the idol would stand and supervise the lovemaking between herself and Ahab. It had special significance because it was the first of a new batch that the young Queen had commissioned showing Yahweh and Asherah married and together, the first joint idols that she had ever seen. Not even the idol-makers or potters had thought to put two gods together in the same idol, yet Jezebel knew that the joined idols would be very popular with travellers and the citizens of Samaria and would mean additional income for the potters and that would mean additional taxes for the coffers of Israel. Special moulds had had to be made, and

Jezebel was anxious to see what they looked like, and which colours the idol-makers had selected for their painting.

Yet Rizpah stood still, in the middle of the afternoon, long after she should have returned to the palace from the temple; her hair was a mess, her robe was covered in leaves and bracken from the forest, and she was sweating and panting. Yet the silly woman would say nothing.

'But why?' asked Jezebel.

'Because I am caught between two terrible things. I must betray one or the other and I don't know where my duty lies.'

'Your duty lies with your god and goddess, your King and Queen, and your people. If there's something which you should tell me, then tell me quickly.'

Rizpah started to cry. In sobs, she said, 'To tell you betrays somebody else to whom I now accept I have a deep and abiding duty. I didn't understand it properly until I was walking back to the city from where I met him; I looked up to the city walls, and the glow of Yahweh was in the air; then the light of Yahweh shone on me and my eyes were opened. It is a duty which follows me from Tishbe, my village, and which was a part of my past ...'

And then suddenly Jezebel felt her entire body turn cold and numb. For she realised what had happened to her maidservant and friend. 'Elijah's here, isn't he?' she said quietly. Rizpah remained silent. 'I thought so. Where? Tell me Rizpah, or you'll be committing treason.'

Rizpah looked with red-rimmed eyes at her friend and Queen, 'How can I betray any remaining vows I took when I married Elijah? Even to you, whom I love as a friend and sister.'

Jezebel could feel her temper flaring, but knew that she must remain calm. Elijah could only have returned for one reason, to create more death and mischief as he'd done all those years ago. Now, truly, he would die. That she would ensure.

But why had he come back when he knew it was certain death? He wouldn't have returned unless he was leading an army or a group who could do damage to the kingdom. Yet there had been no reports of an army crossing the border! So to find out what was happening, she must gently coax the information from Rizpah, rather than try to drag it from her closed mouth.

'Did you meet with him?'

'I was forced to go to where he was. But he's changed, Majesty. He's not the man I married. He has seen Yahweh. He's been with Yahweh in the wilderness of Sinai where our Father Moses was given the law. And Yahweh has commanded Elijah to return here and cleanse the temple of the idols and the worshippers of Ba'al and Asherah and the other gods.'

Jezebel nodded. 'And do you want to go with your husband? Do you want to leave me and the palace and go back to the life you once live if this husband of yours manages to cleanse the temple?'

Rizpah shook her head vehemently. 'No! No, of course not. No, dear Jezebel, my Queen and my friend. I want to remain here. I've never been happier. My body ...' She lapsed into silence.

Jezebel fought hard to restrain her temper; but like a fawn, she knew that Rizpah would startle if her

Queen were to behave in a manner which was too aggressive. So the Queen smiled. And it became a genuine smile ... for suddenly Jezebel knew precisely how to extract Elijah's whereabouts and what he intended to do.

'My dear and true friend,' said the Queen. 'You look so hot and tired. You must have walked so far. Enough of these questions! You know that I sometimes bathe in the milk of goats. It's so warm and inviting. Would you like me to order a bath be prepared for you, so that you can lay your whole body in the soothing white warmth and relax your mind?'

It took the better part of the night, but after she had inadvertently parted with the information, the priest interrupted Jezebel and Ahab's evening meal to tell them the news.

'I know the ravine,' Ahab said. 'I used to play there when I was a boy. A party of soldiers will flush him out in no time. There is only one road in and one out. I'll surround him and crush him like a piece of stale bread.'

'No!' Jezebel said vehemently. 'No! Do that and you'll have an uprising on your hands. The army will revolt. You heard what Rizpah told the priest about your beloved Captain Jehu. If you move against Elijah, he'll rally the soldiers loyal to Yahweh and march on the palace.'

'So? What of it? There can't be more than a quarter of the army who prays only to Yahweh and to none other. Almost all the men in my command love both gods. I know that most of them have now accepted the marriage between Yahweh and Asherah.

They're the first into the temple in the morning. And those that haven't will either have to, or we'll arrest them all, purge the army and be done with it.'

She dismissed the priest with her thanks and threw him a purse of money. When he'd left the apartments, she turned to her husband and whispered, 'Dearest, I understand your desire, but there's a need for caution. Why should we risk an uprising and your unpopularity, when we can achieve everything we want without any blame coming our way? Why not end his reign of terror against us in such a way that no blame will fall on the House of Omri? And when we're told the awful news of his death, we'll be as shocked as the rest of Israel. We'll observe all the rituals of Yahweh's religion. We'll rend our clothes and wear mourning dress and put ash on our foreheads and in our hair and curse fortune ...'

Her husband looked at her incredulously. 'But how? This isn't Egypt! We kill men by axe or sword or stones. Are you thinking of poison?'

Jezebel laughed. 'No, Majesty, nothing as crude as that. Elijah's death will illuminate all Israel.' She reached over and held his hand. 'Leave it to me,' she said comfortingly.

She instructed four men in their task. None was known outside of the palace, either in the city of Samaria or in Israel in general. They had arrived during the night a week earlier, a gift from the chief priestess of Asherah in Tyre. They were not yet priests, but acolytes part-way through their training. As acolytes, they remained in the temple until they became priests. Jezebel had been forced to ask special permission of the chief priestess of Asherah in Samaria for the young men to leave the temple before their training was ended, and she had gladly given her consent. Jezebel particularly wanted these young men because they were young and eager and strong, and had accepted the challenge of living in Israel willingly if it meant that they could serve their goddess.

The men collected their equipment, and before the dawn, walked out of the Judah Gate and down the hill towards the dark forest. Unfamiliar with the terrain, they stumbled and fell over rocks which they mistook in the dark for the path, but eventually they found the correct road which led to the river valley, and then progressed southwards towards Judah and eventually Jerusalem.

They had been told by Jezebel that when the main road came to a copse of trees, it forked and a small and little-used path went to the river. A village had once been built on the banks of the river, but constant flooding meant that it was now deserted and few people ever took that path. Yet this was where Elijah was hiding with his acolyte, Elisha. This was their destination. Their mission was to kill either one or both men in the name of Asherah. But if only one, then it had to be Elijah. They were well instructed by Jezebel in how it was to be achieved. Their goal was to eliminate any enemies of the goddess and to enable her to fully enjoy her marriage to Yahweh, and to allow all Israel to live in peace.

As they entered the forest which ran down to the river, the dim light of dawn, which was slowly illuminating the hillsides around the city, was extinguished by the denseness which surrounded them. It was pitch-black inside the growth of trees.

They progressed slowly, the leader of the four telling his followers to remain silent, and do their best not to stand on any twigs or branches which might snap and give away their position. But it was a vain request, because the floor of the forest was impossible to see, and they continued on, sounding like ravenous bears on a rampage.

But inevitably the sun rose over the mountains of the east and illuminated the tall treetops, and the dim light filtered downwards so that the men could more easily see where they were walking now that their eyes were accustomed to the darkness. They spotted the black ribbon of the river, below them. Now they were feeling more confident of themselves.

Two men carried the equipment, one led the way, and the other ensured that they were not being followed. The four rested for a few moments beside the river before walking southwards along its path. By the time the sun was illuminating the middle branches of the trees, they had rounded a rockface and could clearly see in the distance the cave which was still dark and fearsome, and which, in the looming forest, looked like the mouth of a giant god.

Elisha didn't want to waken Elijah. Last night, the prophet of God had been particularly full of the Holy Spirit. He had shouted and screamed his hatreds and threatened vengeance against everybody. Since the visit of Rizpah, his wife, the previous day, Elijah's mood had changed dramatically. Now, he wasn't just threatening to bring down the House of Omri, but the whole of Israel for welcoming the cursed idols into the sacred temples and for forcing his own wife and children into prostitution.

Elisha didn't know what to do. When they had first met in the fields, when they had feasted and Elisha's mother and father had eventually understood that their son had been chosen by God, both had made the decision that his path lay in following Elijah in the way of the Lord. Elisha had willingly followed Elijah, even though in those first weeks, he'd spent much of his time in terror of the older man's shouting and ravings. But in the months that they'd been together, hiding from the soldiers, from the sight of anyone who might be a spy for Jezebel, he'd grown to understand that the older man's words were the voice of God, and he'd come to love the prophet with all his heart and soul and might.

Yes, he knew Elijah was seen by others as being touched by uncleanliness or madness or demons in his head ... but Elisha knew with utter conviction that what was in Elijah's head was the voice of God. And that the Lord's voice had to be obeyed.

But last night, for the first time, Elisha had begun to doubt his master. For when Rizpah had gone back up the hill to Samaria, and Elisha had painstakingly explained again and again to Elijah the full import of what his wife had said, the older prophet had gone berserk. He'd grabbed Elisha by the neck and nearly strangled him. Then, he'd run around the cave, banging his head against a wall until blood poured out. Then he'd lain on the floor of the cave and cried out like an animal in a hunter's trap. Elisha had run away from the prophet and hidden in the dark undergrowth, listening to the animalistic howls and screams from the dark cave mouth; but eventually silence had fallen with the night.

When he was sure that the rage had passed, Elisha

had returned to the cave and had soothed Elijah's head with cool water from the distant stream. He'd made a broth of lentils and other vegetables which he'd picked from fields around Samaria. Again he'd tried to explain to Elijah the reasons why Rizpah might have been forced to become a servant of the servants of the false idols. But it had been an impossible task, because every time the young man had tried to explain it, Elijah had railed and spat and fallen to the floor picking up handfuls of dust in his hands and rubbing them into his hair and over his face. Elisha had been terrified the whole night.

But eventually Elijah had lain on the floor, his body heaving with the exertion, and a quiet had overcome him. It was then that the Lord Yahweh appeared before him in the cave. In all his time with Elijah, Yahweh had been distant, with Elijah telling him what God said and did and wanted. But now, for the first time, Yahweh was close, speaking to Elijah. The younger man couldn't hear the words, but from Elijah's reaction, he knew that Yahweh was close by, perhaps invisible in between them.

Initially, Elisha hid his eyes from the sight of holiness, utterly terrified of what was happening. But from Elijah's reaction, it was apparent that the Lord's will was made clear. He could almost visualise the Lord's words, as though they were letters etched in stone. He heard Elijah saying, 'Yes, Lord. Yes, I will. But why must I kill her, Lord? Kill Rizpah? But the children, Lord? Follow you. Yes, Lord. Yes, now I understand ...'

And Elisha sat in the dark beside a wall of the cave as Elijah talked quietly and gently to Yahweh, his friend who was beside him in the cave.

The young man was awakened by the noises of the forest, birds and animals, beginning to stir in the early light, and wanted to collect water to make Elijah the soup he most enjoyed in the early morning – crushed bulb of fennel for taste and the leaves of chrysanthemum for bitterness to freshen his mouth, and today he would put in something which he'd found completely by accident when walking through the forest the other day, a bush of belladonna. Yes, in large quantities he knew that it was deadly, but Elisha would use it sparingly and would crush only one of the leaves and place it in a lot of liquid, because he knew of its effect. It would make Elijah's spirits rise, and he would come alive and the prophet of God would feel more happy and certain than the previous day.

Softly, he pulled back his blanket, found his sandals in the dark, and rose carefully from the cave floor. His neck and shoulders were stiff from the cold earth, but according to Elijah, it was pain and suffering which brought him closer to Yahweh, so the young man was grateful for the discomfort of his surroundings.

Picking up the large gourd outside the cave, he trod carefully down the rock until he found the pathway. It was still very early in the morning, and Elisha knew that Elijah would sleep until late. So he had plenty of time to fill the gourd with water and find other herbs which he could use for the midday meal, and save himself another journey.

They watched the dark figure clamber slowly and cautiously down the rockface and onto the path. The dark, hooded man descended below the path and disappeared into the undergrowth, obviously intent on reaching the distant river. One of the brother priests whispered to the leader, 'Is that Elijah?'

'I don't think so,' he whispered back. 'To me, that looks like an acolyte. For why would a master be carrying a water gourd? No, that must be Elisha, his servant.'

'What should we do? We were instructed to kill both.'

The leader was about to answer, but then decided not to. He could understand the need to murder Elijah, for he was a man of evil, and wanted to offend Asherah, but the leader had grave misgivings about taking the life of a boy as young as Elisha who had not yet experienced the joys of becoming a man. He'd argued with Jezebel, and she'd told him that if they could escape with just killing Elijah and leave the boy unharmed – and especially with no knowledge of who had committed the crime – then so be it. The boy leaving the cave was a gift from Ba'al and Asherah. The boy would eventually be shown the kindness and goodness of the gods, and then he would be encouraged to worship them for they had saved his life.

When Elisha was long gone, the leader turned to his three brother priests and beckoned them to follow him. It didn't take them long to climb up to the cave where Elijah and the boy had been living. Quietly, now that the light of day was beginning to brighten the gloom of the forest, they reached the ledge which formed a parapet for the large cave. The four men could smell the scent of human beings: the rocks and foliage around the cave mouth still carried in them the aroma of food from last night, and the bitter acrid stench of the fire which had been burning in the mouth of the cave to warm the inside and protect the inhabitants from the wild animals of the woods.

As they stole closer and closer, they saw that the fire had just been relit by Elisha before his departure, and the bowl of hot ashes had also ignited dry leaves and twigs he'd placed there. Soon it would set fire to the branches he'd placed on top of the leaves. It was a wonderful omen for the priests, because now they wouldn't have to scavenge around to find dry tinder or gather wood. Here, thanks to Elisha, was the fire they needed.

Using the language of signs, the leader told one of his colleagues to prepare the fuel. The man unstoppered the large and heavy bottle and crept inside the cave, where it was perpetually dark and musty. All he could hear was the rhythmic breathing of a sleeping man, occasionally punctuated by a deep, guttural snore.

The leader followed his colleague into the cave and took the bottle from him. Softly, carefully he poured the stinking liquid fire over the ground where Elijah slept. If he woke up from this, a knife was ready to kill him instantly. But Elijah remained asleep. Then the leader poured the liquid over the blankets and robes of the sleeping man. The more he poured, the more surprised he became. He now assumed that Elijah must be drugged, for surely any normal man would awaken from such an evil smell. But Elijah continued to sleep and snore as though he were an innocent boy.

When the leader had poured the contents of one bottle over the sleeping man, he indicated to another of his colleagues to hand over the second bottle which had been meant for Elisha. This, too, he poured over Elijah's clothes and sleeping blanket until they were sodden and inundated. Now, when the smell of the fire liquid began overpowering the men inside the cave, Elijah began to stir and cough from the fumes. The four men retreated immediately. The leader picked up a flaming brand from the fire, and threw it from the mouth of the cave deep inside towards where Elijah was starting to move.

Having been warned of its potency and danger, the four men immediately ran out of the direction of the flames and around the edge of the cave; they just managed to escape the huge roar and rush of fire and smoke which engulfed the very air itself. It blew out of the cave mouth and blossomed like some hideous cloud of the devils themselves into the open air. The leader looked back. As the smoke and flame roiled and cascaded in billowing waves, it reminded him of the nests of vipers he used to see in the hills near his home. He shuddered in horror. The roar was deafening, but above the noise was the sound of screaming.

The four priests ran as quickly as they could along the parapet of the cave, jumped down over the rocks onto the path, and ran for their very lives up the path and away from the hellish maw of the cave mouth. They stopped and looked back, and could see nothing but black belching filthy clouds of smoke, through which giant tongues of yellow and red flame licked greedily at the air and nearby trees.

None of the priests had appreciated the sheer power or enormous potency of the fire liquid. They'd only ever seen it used in small quantities. They fell to their knees in awe and fear.

And through the wakening forest, an increasing and horrifying noise could be heard. A noise so hideous that the four men had to close their ears. It was a demonic sound, the sound of a man begging and screaming from the very depths of despair, imploring his God for help, crying in a pain which nightmares couldn't imagine. As one, the four men on their knees began to pray to Asherah for the man's hasty and painless death.

Deep below, in the forest and beside the water's edge, Elisha heard the roar of the conflagration and the noise of thunder. He stood and ran, bounding back towards the cave where he'd spent the night with Elijah. He was much lower than the cave mouth when he first came in sight, and looked upwards to see what was happening. Panting from the exertion, his eyes at first couldn't understand the scene. In the moments since he'd left, the fire he'd lit at the cave entrance to warm Elijah had gone out of control, and looked as if it was burning the entire rockface.

His first thought was of Elijah. Was he trapped inside the cave? Had he managed to escape? He began to climb higher to reach the pathway; he would get as near as possible to the flames and carry his master out of danger ... but these were flames the likes of which he'd never before seen. These were the flames of the nether regions of hell, the flames which had destroyed Sodom and Gomorrah, the flames which his father had warned him he would suffer if ever his eyes strayed away from Yahweh and towards a young woman.

Overcome by the sudden understanding that Yahweh was present, instead of continuing his climb upwards, he fell to his knees in the thick undergrowth below the pathway, and prayed to Almighty Yahweh for protection.

It was then that he heard the screams above the roar of the flames. Opening his eyes in trepidation of the presence of his God, Elisha looked upwards to the mouth of the cave, and there he saw a sight which would glow in his eyes for the rest of his life. In the entry way was the burning figure of Elijah, cloaked in his flaming blanket, arms outstretched, shouting of his joy and love of the Lord God of Hosts, enfolded and engulfed by the Almighty Eternal One who had come to earth as a flame, as He had appeared before the children of Israel in the Desert of Sinai. Elisha's mouth gaped open as his Lord and Master, the prophet of God, stood on the rock ledge screaming in his ecstasy to God and to the heavens and the earth.

The burning man's flaming arms took off the wool blanket he was wearing and tossed it over the parapet. Like a missile from the sky, it fell blazing onto the vegetation below, and set it alight. In the dryness of the summer, the bracken instantly caught fire, and added to the flames which were still pouring out of the mouth of the cave.

The figure of Elijah in the cave mouth, dancing for the joy of coming to Yahweh, began to disappear amidst all the obscuring smoke and flame. Although he knew he should avert his eyes from the presence of the Eternal One, Elisha couldn't avoid looking. He was just able to make out Elijah taking off his robe, and throwing it towards him as though he wanted Elisha to catch the mantle. But the cloak was imbued with the spirit of the Almighty and was alive with his burning breath. It was a linen material, and was well alight, and as it left Elijah's burning hands, it was caught in the strong updraft of the fire and flames from below, and instead of falling to earth, the burning remnants were lifted heavenwards and disappeared upwards, ever upwards, beyond the rockface and the cliffs, and into the very heavens themselves.

The conflagration engulfed the whole area. Elijah was no longer visible. Nor were his screams of joy in his oneness with Yahweh to be heard. Instead Elisha listened to the voice of God Himself, which was in the roaring of the flames in the tops of the trees and the hissing of the bracken and the hysteria of the animals which began to emerge and scamper from the might of the Almighty One, Yahweh, God of Israel.

Elisha prayed to Yahweh for the blessing of carrying Elijah upwards to Him, but the flames were spreading in his direction, and he rose to escape. For even though his master Elijah was favoured by the Almighty and had been gathered to His bosom and would now sit with Moses on God's right hand, Elisha's mission was here on earth. He had been thrown the mantle of Elijah. His day had come. His path was clear.

The news spread around the city as quickly as a grassfire in summer. First one group was told and began to discuss the extraordinary event; then someone ran off to tell his wife and neighbours and other groups became involved; then a large group, seeming to sense the presence of some divine force in the air, emerged from the temple and began to ask questions. They received the answer in shocked silence.

And in the middle of the disorder which rent the peace of the mid-morning marketplace, was a young man wearing the detritus of the forest in his hair and on his clothes, robes which were singed and which smelled of the burning which was still in the air.

He was a man calling himself Elisha. He carried an air of authority with him, a stature beyond his years, his eyes aflame with the zeal of a prophet who has gazed upon the fiery face of the Lord. And he spoke like a man who must be listened to ...

The crowd, once huddled in small groups, coalesced around him until he was forced to stand on a wooden cart to be seen and heard by the multitude. At first, he was reluctant to stand, mumbling to himself, saying he was unworthy; it was as though he were waging a war within himself. But when he saw that people were listening to his words, he seemed to gain in strength, and he jumped up onto the wagon and faced the onlookers.

He shouted aloud, his voice growing in stature and confidence as Yahweh filled his soul, 'I say to you, Israel, that you must listen to my words. I am Elisha. I am the follower in the footsteps of the prophet of God, Elijah. This morning, in the valley beyond, in the woods which are between this city and Jerusalem, Elijah was taken up by God Almighty in a fiery conflagration; it was the very breath of Yahweh Himself. The Lord God of our people has visited our lands, and He commands that you listen to me. Yahweh, Almighty God, embraced His prophet Elijah in His hands. I saw this happen with my own eyes. The flames and smoke you saw when you awoke this morning was Yahweh Himself in the forest where Elijah and I have been in hiding, awaiting our chance to enter Samaria and rid the temple of its evil and unclean idols.'

His voice gained in strength as he spoke. He'd had no experience of such public speaking and although he knew that God would be guiding his every word, the multitude in front of him grew larger and larger and a certain fear began to settle on him. He shifted uncomfortably on the makeshift stage, and continued, 'But who understands the ways of the Lord? Not Elijah. Not I. The Lord God of Hosts decided this morning as I went to fill the water jug that He was going to enter the forest where we were hiding, and was going to take His Prophet to heaven to sit on His right hand beside Moses the Lawgiver.

'Now I am left to carry on the task of Elijah. I was born in Abel-Meholah, near to the city of Beth Shean. I am the son of Shaphat the farmer. Elijah took me from the fields, and I have been following in his footsteps ever since. God has touched my heart and opened my mouth and He is strong within me. I know that I am to carry on the work of my master Elijah because just before God took him up into heaven, Elijah removed his cloak and threw it down to me, a radiance in his face, his eyes shining, his body jumping for joy that he was soon to be lifted up in body and in spirit.

'Yes, people of Israel. Your prophet Elijah was dancing with a greater joy than I have ever seen. But his cloak was aflame with the breath of Yahweh and it floated up to the heavens before I could catch it. Blessed is the name of the Lord God of Hosts.'

Some in the crowd shouted, 'Blessed is His name'.

Elisha was now gaining rapidly in confidence. He shouted, pointing an accusing hand towards the windows of Ahab's palace, 'I call upon the citizens of Samaria to make good the promise which Elijah made to Yahweh. I call upon you to cleanse the city of idols and priests and priestesses of false gods. Remember, "*I alone am the Lord your God who brought you out of the land of Egypt, the House of Bondage. You shall have no other gods before me."*

'Come to the temple and throw out the idols and the idol-makers and the cursed priests. Follow the ways of the Lord Yahweh, Host of Hosts. And when this land of uncleanliness has been purified, then we will overthrow the House of Omri and rid Israel of this cursed dwelling place of evil.'

Rizpah looked out of the window of one of the upper rooms of the palace, listening in horror to the words of the man whose face she recognised, yet whose manner was strange to her. Yesterday Elisha was no more than a boy; now he stood before the assembly of Samaria speaking like a man ... like her husband Elijah had once spoken and inflamed her mind with the love of God, before he'd gone mad with the spirit of the Lord.

So now she understood what her heart had told her, but her mind had refused to believe. Now she knew that the dark and ominous stain in the sky hanging over the city of Samaria in the early morning was the smoke of her husband's death pyre, the breath of Yahweh. She'd seen it rising up from the river valley. It had drifted towards her, thin clouds of black smoke breaking away and directing menacing fingers at her as she watched helplessly from the roof of the palace. It was God's will to point the black finger of death at her. She had sinned against the Lord, and now she would die. It was foretold by God in front of everybody, the vast judgement of the Lord written in black in the sky above the city. Nor was there any need for her to wait for the day of her judgement, for she knew with absolute certainty that it was upon her; that this was the day of her death.

Her husband Elijah was dead. But somebody else would have to tell her children that their father had been taken into the hands of God, for she must go down to Elisha his follower and meet her fate. She must put on the black garb and robes of a widow and smear cold ashes on her forehead. She must rend her dress as an outward sign of her mourning; but she would not be able to return to Tishbe to tell her relations and neighbours that their blessed Elijah was no longer of this earth. That would be left to those who took in her poor orphan children.

Two days ago, her life had been light and glorious. Her body felt as it had never felt before, tingling and thrilling to the thoughts of being touched by her favourite priest. She almost ran to the devotional services, like a little girl runs to play by the river. She waited impatiently for him to enter the asherah ... She would be sitting on the floor, close to the holy pole of Asherah, and would smile demurely as he entered. Sometimes a priestess would enter as well, and she would conduct prayers to the goddess; but Rizpah couldn't wait for her prayers to end, because the priest was smiling knowingly at her, and when they were alone, he would move over to be close to her side and he would slip off her robes and kiss her breasts and rub aromatic oils into them, into her stomach and into her womanhood and she would be ready for him because she wanted him so badly. He never failed to satisfy her and she would end the session of prayers screaming out the name of Asherah as her most loyal and loving subject.

Rizpah was devoted to the Goddess Asherah in whom she could see such compassion, such gentleness. And she was particularly proud of her place as the instrument of the gods, having been part of the ceremony which had seen the angry and merciless Yahweh suddenly flower and grow gentle in His love of His bride, Asherah.

But that was all in the past. That was all another life. Perhaps everything since she'd left Tishbe was a falsehood, placed in her mind by demons. For now Yahweh had come to take His revenge on her wickedness, on her turning from Him and bowing down before idols.

Now she felt ill with grief and worry, and questioned whether the joys of her body had infected the reason of her mind; because Elisha had come unexpectedly into her life and now her husband Elijah had been taken up by Yahweh and she, Rizpah, was accused before the assembly of Israel for her sins. Yahweh was pointing His black finger at her ... and she knew with every fibre of her being that because of her, Asherah had been confined to nothing by the jealous Yahweh, that Yahweh had turned His face from His goddess bride and was now going to take His revenge.

Yes! The answer to Rizpah was obvious. Yahweh was angry with her and she was being punished for Elijah's death and for her wickedness. Yahweh had pointed His finger at her heart for turning away from Him. He had rejected the love of Asherah and wanted the children of Israel back in His bosom. There could be no other explanation for His descending to earth and taking up Elijah in a fiery embrace. None.

Yet deep inside her, despite trying, she felt no grief for the death of Elijah. Yes, he was her husband in the eyes of the ancient law, but not in her eyes, not for the last few years. In the beginning, he'd been open with her, explaining things to overcome her ignorance; he'd loved her and loved the children. But those were the early days. And as God grew stronger in him, his speeches to the people had become wilder and confusing. He'd lost control of what he was saying, breaking off in the middle of his extended sermons and staring into the distance for long periods as though there were something in the sky which only he could see.

Of course the people thought he was touched by God, and loved him for it. They flocked to his long sermons in the hot sun. But in truth, Rizpah knew that Elijah was losing his mind. She would be grateful when he went away to preach in some distant part of Israel or Judah, grateful for the peace and quiet and she would smile and laugh again. And when he would return, darkness would again descend, in the later years, it had taken her longer and longer to bring him back from where his mind had been.

And in the end, when she'd seen him the previous day, he was no longer her husband. She barely recognised him, and he didn't see her at all. She could have been Jezebel for all he knew.

So when she told him about her devotion to Asherah, the reality didn't enter his mind. She could have been talking to the stone walls of the cave. But on her way back to Samaria, Yahweh had come to her and had shown His presence. The very air was pink with His glow, and the stones of the city were alive with His majesty; she stopped and looked at the walls, and they spoke to her in her mind. They said to her that the city was a corrupt and evil place and that she herself had become corrupt and evil. Then images of Tishbe appeared in her mind's eye, and she saw the brook and the orchards and the fields and she saw her children when they were young, running and playing in the fields, and she smiled. But in her heart's heart, she knew that she would never see Tishbe again, for she had sinned.

And Almighty God must have informed Elijah's heart and his mind of her evil, because Rizpah's defection to the goddess was the last straw for him. He must have realised that if the transgressions of the people of Israel had reached into his own home, his own wife, then he must sit on the right hand of God Almighty and bring the people back to their senses.

Rizpah turned away from the window and took off the delicate blue dress which had been a present from her friend Jezebel. She stood naked in her room, and walked over to the chest where her dresses and robes were laid. At the bottom of the chest was her old robe, the one she wore all the time in Tishbe.

She lifted it out. It was her old life: dirty, withered, poor. She touched the fabric, and it was rough and crude. She put it on, and went over to the fireplace, where she poured water over the cold ashes, and daubed the wet sludge on her forehead. With her bare hands, she tore at the neck of her robe, feeling the old and thin material rip easily; like her life in Tishbe, it was so fragile. Then she left her apartments and her children, never to return.

Elisha was shouting instructions and encouragement to the crowd. Some of them responded with enthusiasm, but there were still many who shook their heads and were obviously unmoved by what he was saying. But suddenly the crowd became silent and paused; just like his dead master Elijah, Elisha was transfixed and he just stared. But he didn't stare into the sky, as did Elijah. Instead, the younger man looked at the periphery of the large crowd in the marketplace. He remained speechless as the woman, dressed in a dark robe, torn at the neck in the way of a widow, her forehead daubed with mourning ashes, walked towards him. The crowd parted to let her through. Most recognised her as Rizpah, wife of the dead prophet Elijah, friend of Jezebel and those in high places.

She walked in the aisle created as people moved aside for her, and she stood below the new prophet of God. Elisha looked down at her.

'Woman, admit your sins,' he hissed.

In the beginning her voice was soft. Only the people who stood by her could hear her words. 'I have sinned in the eyes of the Lord. I have worshipped at the foot of an idol. I have committed adultery many times. I have turned my face from the Lord.' With each admission, her words became louder and louder, listing her sins for which she, more than anyone, knew the punishment. And by her punishment, she hoped to save the people of Israel from the vengeance of the Almighty.

But most in the crowd had committed the same sins. Few there were willing to condemn her. Yes, they realised that their city had become like the cities of Sodom and Gomorrah, but they didn't care. They enjoyed their lives; they believed that God was happy with His new wife, and the land was prospering.

'Woman, your sins have brought great grief and destruction to the land of Israel. You and others who worship false gods do so in conflict with the will of Yahweh. By your actions, our greatest prophet, Elijah, has been taken from us. His mantle has passed to me. Woman, what would Elijah have sentenced you to, if he were to hear your sins?'

'Stoning,' she whispered.

'Louder!' Elisha shouted.

'Stoning,' she said, but her voice hardly carried.

'Louder!' he yelled. 'Tell the world your punishment.'

Hysterically, Rizpah suddenly threw back her head and screamed, 'I am condemned to death by stoning.'

Elisha, young and potent, nodded his head. 'Let her trial begin immediately, in the name of the Lord.'

But the crowd wanted no trial. They wanted her to be punished. A roar went up from a section of the crowd; they were men and women who had remained loyal to Yahweh, who hated what their city and country had become under Jezebel. Now, they pushed others out of the way, and grabbed Rizpah's arms and legs as she fell to the ground, screaming.

Horrified, Elisha tried to stop them, shouting: 'She must be tried!'

But it was too late.

Those who, like her, had worshipped Asherah and Ba'al, backed away, terrified that this could happen to them. Many ran back to their homes to remove idols from their walls.

The loyal followers of Yahweh dragged the screaming Rizpah to the city walls. The crowd, sensing an event, gathered as they approached, and cheered or booed according to their wishes. Fifteen men pushed and shoved and dragged Rizpah over the gravel and stones of the ground until her legs were covered with blood, the skin of her arms in tatters. She half fell, half ran down the steps which led to the Gate of Tyre. It was here that harlots and adulteresses were stoned to death in the days of Omri. Some were pushed off the wall and fell to their deaths; others who had committed great wickedness were stoned while they were standing. This was Rizpah's fate.

The crowd pushed her against the walls of the city, and picked up rocks and stones which were strewn in the path. And they began to pitch them at her, hitting her on her body, her legs, her arms, and her head. Within moments of being hit by a large rock thrown by a man whom she thought she knew, she was unconscious. Rizpah didn't feel any other of the stones that rained down on her, ending her life.

Long after the crowd had disappeared, long after the dust of the road had settled, a solitary woman in a yellow robe came to the Gate of Tyre. She was accompanied by a priest of Asherah. Together they stared at the broken and bloodied body of Rizpah. Both had tears in their eyes. Both had lost a good and loving friend.

An old man was sitting beside her, holding the hand of the dead Rizpah. He looked up as Jezebel came near.

'I am Absalom. I was a friend of Rizpah. This is a cruel day, when Yahweh could take the life of one so innocent.'

Jezebel nodded. 'Israel will pay for this ...' she said in disgust.

'Israel already has,' said Absalom, getting up and walking away sadly. 'How many among us are like Rizpah? And do we stone all those that are?'

Jezebel turned to the priest, and hissed through her clenched teeth, 'For this, I will take a mighty revenge. I will confiscate land from all who did this; I'll behead the leaders of the mob; I'll burn the temple of Yahweh and forbid His worship ... and as for this boy, this follower of Elijah, I'll have his innards cut from his body while he's still alive and they'll be spread around the marketplace, and as he dies, he'll watch the carrion birds eat his guts.'

She turned and looked at her friend Rizpah, now dead, a woman who, almost from the beginning, had been with her from the beginning of her journey in Israel. Until now. And Jezebel could hold back the tears no longer. She began to sob; to cry for the loss of her friend, her companion, the first Israelite woman to whom she had shown the true joys and beauties of Asherah. And the tears fell like rain on the parched and dusty ground.

The priest had listened to what she said, but he knew that her threats were empty. For something far more terrible had happened today than the stoning of some adulterous wife. What he realised, and what Jezebel would soon come to understand, was that Asherah had been banished from Israel for ever; that every time an Elijah was killed in this cursed and loveless country, an Elisha would rise up and condemn Jezebel and the followers of any god other than Yahweh. And there were more prophets of Yahweh in Israel than blades of grass in a field.

The priest knew that Jezebel would continue to rule, as would Ahab and their children, but without the love and comfort of Asherah. For by the stoning death of Rizpah, Israelite woman and acolyte of the gods and goddesses of Phoenicia, the prophets of Yahweh declared that no matter how many battles they lost, they would always win the war.

Elijah had murdered almost eight hundred priests and priestesses; now this ... where would it end?

Would Yahweh eventually kill all those who loved Ba'al and Asherah? How many would Yahweh have to kill to prove that He was God?

The priest shook his head in sadness for Rizpah, for Jezebel, and for himself, and led his Queen, grieving and sobbing, back to the safety of her palace.

AND SO IT ENDS ...

THE CITY OF SIDON, PHOENICIA

The sun slowly descended into the sea illuminating the very tops of the walls of Sidon. Far out to sea, fishermen on the evening tide looked back and smiled as they watched the towers of the city seeming to burn in the light of the last rays.

This evening, the city did not settle after dusk as it did on most nights. In the air itself, the erotic smells of meats, wines and perfumes were insinuating themselves into people's homes. It had been raining for much of the day, but had stopped just before sunset. As the winds freshened in the evening, scattering the clouds, curious citizens emerged from their homes expecting to revel in the freshness of the air, but instead were greeted by the sounds and aromas of a banquet, the likes of which they knew their King Abimel enjoyed every night.

But this was not in the palace; men and women looked at each other in surprise, wondering from where the seductive aromas were coming, invading the streets. The silence of the city night too was invaded with the voices of bells and trumpets, of harps and lyres and drums shimmering between buildings and beckoning the citizens of Sidon towards the source of their rhythms.

Curious, they gravitated to the outskirts of the city, to where the high walls prevented them from seeing beyond. But the music and the smells overcame their hesitation of treading where only guards and soldiers were usually permitted. Tentatively one, then two, then hundreds of people ascended the steps which led upwards to the balustrades. And as they reached the top of the walls and could see beyond the confines of the city, they stood and stared in astonishment. Soon they were joined by more and more people, until it seemed as though the entire population of Sidon was standing together, silent, awestruck, gazing at the scene below. The guards made no move to prevent the people's trespass onto their territory. They, themselves, were staring fixedly at a sight which none had seen before.

The stars appeared above the city for the first time in the three days of heavy rain and cloud. And then the real performance began. Suddenly the soft and lulling voices of the instruments erupted into loud, rhythmic melodies, some harmonious, some as fast and erotic as acts of lovemaking. The people immediately strained forward to see more than was revealed by the dim light surrounding the musicians or the feeble glow of the pits where sheep and pigs and an entire cow were roasting.

The reverberation of music filled the air as the thirty musicians gathered outside the city walls sang and cried and wailed to the demands of their passions. And as the people on the city's walls turned to each other to ask what was happening, harsh voices below demanded that the way be cleared for His Majesty, King Abimel.

The ruler of Phoenicia climbed the steps and people moved out of the way so the King could witness the event. But as with his own people, King Abimel could only watch as he neither had forewarning or understanding of the performance below the walls of his city. And as though from some unseen cue, the moment the King was positioned at the balustrade, a trench surrounding the entire encampment of entertainers burst with flame and the burning snake wound its way around the charcoal pits and the musicians, and the people gasped in amazement at what was revealed by the light.

In the middle of the encampment, previously hidden by the darkness, stood a young woman. As a life-sized idol of a goddess, she posed motionless on a platform held aloft by four wooden posts. Slowly, she lifted her head, seeing beyond the walls, beyond the eyes of King Abimel, beyond the very stars themselves. Her lips opened in silent prayer to the gods and goddesses in the heavens.

Men and women alike were breathless as they looked at her regal bearing, her painful beauty. The woman's attendants lit braziers which surrounded the platform, clearly illuminating her body; the citizens gasped at her transparent gown which shimmered in reds and blues and greens and golds, and through the light, at her naked body, clearly visible beneath. All strained forward for a closer look.

Isha-Ashtoreth, Priestess of Asherah, Consort and Connubist of El, Most Beloved and Revered Bride of the Moon and the Stars, favourite of His Majesty King Abimel of Phoenicia, slowly swayed to the rhythm of drums and harps. She danced and weaved, her eyes closed, her lips slightly apart, in her own world of sensuousness and eroticism.

Nobody knew the reason for the spectacle, but they were mesmerised by the performance. Men stood close to their wives, and put their arms around them; women moved closer to their husbands ... all were enthralled by the beautiful young woman who danced for the pleasure of the city.

The King, His Majesty Abimel, looked down and smiled. Isha-Ashtoreth was now his favourite priestess. He had known her almost every night during the three months since she had surrendered her virginity to him in the name of Asherah. She had conquered his heart, as surely as she was now conquering the city. He looked down at her dancing, and smiled.

Yes, this is right and fitting, he thought, as he came to understand why she was performing.

And from the dark recesses of the encampment below, beyond the light and hidden in the shadows of the night, Jezebel looked in pleasure at the young woman and at her brother, the King, and smiled. Since her escape from Israel some twenty years ago and since her secret seclusion within her brother the King Abimel's palace, Jezebel had dreamed of her resurrection, of again conquering Israel and driving Yahweh from the land. And now, she realised, she would not have to, the mantle had been passed on ...